I0717687

STOLEN VENGEANCE

DIANNA LOVE

Praise for
the Slye Team Black Ops Romantic Series

FATAL PROMISE

"Fatal Promise left me speechless and in awe."
~~Heathercm, Amazon

"It was a slam dunk in terms of guns, international travel, romance, killers and resolution."
~~ Goodreads

STOLEN VENGEANCE

"This is one of those books where your body tenses, you stop breathing and you just can't read fast enough."
~~ Amazon

"If you love romantic suspense, you will adore Dianna Love's latest Slye Team."
~~ IMHO reviewer

DECEPTIVE TREASURES

"This may be my favorite book in the series so far. I swear they just keep getting better and better."
~~Heather CM, Goodreads

"Complex. Ongoing series. Nonstop action. Romantic suspense."
~~ Madison Fairbanks, Amazon

KISS THE ENEMY

"A FREAKING AWESOME continuation of the Slye Team series by Dianna Freaking Love!!! She did not disappoint."
~~Goodreads

"Kiss the Enemy is a high octane thrill ride through the high stakes world."
~~ J. Cazares, Amazon

HONEYMOON TO DIE FOR

"It seems with each book this series gets better."
~~The Reading Cafe

"…constantly believable and packed with intrigue."
~~Single Title Reviews

NOWHERE SAFE

"The love story is tender, steamy, erotic, and full of electricity, and the action plot will satisfy the reader's thirst for danger."
~~IndieReads review

"Blending taut pacing with sizzling tension, a little bit of James Bond with an engaging personal drama, this is a story for suspense fans and romance readers alike."
~~Goodreads

LAST CHANCE TO RUN [prequel novel]

"I could not put this bookdown...Once again Dianna has thrilled my suspense taste buds with an extra dashof spicy romance."
~~After Hours Rendezvous

"Engrossing, thrilling and wonderfully steamy...a pitch-perfect suspense that will keep readers breathless from the first nerve-racking scene to the last shocking revelation."
~~The Romance Reviews

Dedication

This book is dedicated to June Tinker who has always supported me and shares her smile with everyone she meets.

Chapter 1

DINGO PADDOCK KEPT his head down and his shoulders stooped as he swiped a threadbare sleeve across the sweat running into his eyes. Nighttime heat turned the layers of too-large, secondhand clothes into a furnace, but he'd chosen them as camo, as well as for mobility in a fight. The layers lent him the appearance of the homeless who wore everything they owned.

Plus, the clothes concealed a Chris Reeve knife, ankle-holstered Glock 42, and a Sig Sauer 226 9mm in a shoulder holster.

Atlanta sometimes suffered a brittle cold night this late in June, but not this year. The temps had shot up over ninety earlier in the day.

Being armed to the teeth trumped comfort tonight.

Meeting a snitch wasn't out of the norm for anyone who lived in the shadows of intelligence work like Dingo, but meeting with this *particular* snitch tonight ... it shouldn't happen.

Coming out of hiding lowered this snitch's life expectancy to zero, and hinted that Dingo might have made a mistake the last time they met. Six years ago.

If he had, the fallout would be bloody.

Something was up. He'd used his electronics skills to search for any reason this snitch would return, but there was nothing.

Because there was *supposed* to be nothing–and no one left– from back then.

He took his time walking across a street that ran through the West End. At two in the morning on a Tuesday, most of the city slept. This area had once been a nice place to live, but that was years ago, long before the current transient residents and less fortunate were even born. He shuffled into a space between two ramshackle buildings that offered a false sense of safety to those sleeping beneath blankets of newspapers.

The area reeked of piss, rotted food and the despair of knowing tomorrow would be no better.

A reminder of Dingo's life back when abusive adults had called the shots.

He'd put a stop to that by the time he reached sixteen.

A fire burned in a fifty-gallon drum, and three men hovered around it out of solidarity and for the offer of light. Eight days to Independence Day, but this bunch had nothing to celebrate.

If Dingo closed his eyes, he could see seven-year-old Sabrina's joy at watching her first fireworks display. She'd been so excited until she noticed kids sitting on their dads' shoulders. He hadn't been big enough to carry her on his shoulders yet, and felt lacking as the big brother she considered him.

Stay in the present to stay alive.

One of the men at the fire made a move, shifting in Dingo's direction.

Tall guy who wore a faded flannel shirt rolled up to his elbows and pants sagging on his wiry frame. Lean muscle and prison tattoos on his forearms hinted at risk for anyone tangling with him.

A jagged scar ran south on his cheek.

That only made him ugly, not dangerous.

But the menace peering out of those black slits for eyes said he considered himself the most dangerous beast in this corner of the homeless kingdom.

And it might not be an empty boast.

He was sizing up Dingo as a potential threat in his territory.

Scar Cheek's next move would be to test for a weakness.

Dingo remembered his kind from hard times on the tough streets of Queens, New York, as a twelve-year-old piece of white trash with an Aussie accent to boot. Opening his mouth back then had flagged him as foreign scum, another step below homegrown.

Hadn't taken him long to think twice about speaking if he didn't want to spend more time fighting than eating. First rule of survival was to choose your fights wisely.

How many times had he told Josh and Sabrina that?

Food had been sparse enough for one before he met a punk named Josh and a scrawny hellcat called Sabrina.

He'd taught them that brains could outmaneuver brawn.

Those two had caught on fast. Before Dingo knew it, Sabrina had turned fourteen and promoted herself to the head of their little gang and he'd let it stand. He'd never wanted to run the show and had warned both of them not to get attached to him.

Only fools get attached to anything or anyone. That's what he'd tried to drill into their thick skulls.

Josh and Sabrina might have learned that simple lesson if Dingo hadn't up and marked them as being under his protection.

What'd that make me?

The king of fools, because at thirty-one he'd still step between either of those two and a bullet. They were the closest he'd ever come to having family. Some things *had* changed since then, but not by much. Sabrina now ran covert teams of deadly operatives, which included Dingo and Josh.

As Dingo passed by the drum with flames flickering out the top, Scar Cheek drifted further in Dingo's direction.

This guy thought fresh meat had just wandered in.

Even at twelve, Dingo had been no pushover. Since then, he'd faced off with predators far worse than Scar Cheek and walked away ... okay, limping sometimes, but he had no time to waste proving who was dominant tonight.

Not when he was down to eleven minutes to make his meeting with Bergman, the snitch who shouldn't be in Atlanta again.

Not after what went down all those years ago in California.

Bergman had left this country so fast his shadow had to run to keep up. He shouldn't be back now. And to be honest, Dingo doubted the snitch waiting on him *was* Bergman. More likely, it was someone Bergman allowed to use his identity to get a message to Dingo. But for tonight's discussion, he was Bergman.

If Bergman was truly stateside? That was bad news.

Understatement.

Bad would be holding a pellet gun against an enemy toting a

double barrel shotgun. This kind of news was more like shaking a stick at someone holding a howitzer.

Misery balled in Dingo's gut and banged against his chest.

Just thinking about Bergman reminded Dingo of all he'd lost. Biggest loss of all? Valene Eklund.

He shoved that agonizing memory back deep into its hole. This couldn't be connected to her. Dingo had cut the head off that snake and stomped it to pieces before he'd crawled out of the viper pit half alive.

Valene was safe.

She'd stay that way as long as he never went back.

Jagged pain sawed through him again. Tough shit. He had to accept losing her as the cost of keeping her out of the crosshairs of an insane criminal.

She was fine.

She had to be. He'd stayed out of her world completely for six years now, not even using his world-class skills to check on her from a distance, because ... he did that to hunt down the nastiest humans this world had ever seen.

He'd never use his abilities to snoop on those he respected and cared about, and even if he didn't have his own moral code for how he used his electronics skills, he still wouldn't snoop on Valene.

No point searching for more heartache.

Valene deserved to be happy, but that didn't mean he wanted a front row seat to her joy when it had nothing to do with him. She'd been *more* than fine when he'd seen her a month ago. When she'd turned her back on him.

There was no reason for the ball of dread churning in his belly right now, but good luck convincing his gut.

Footsteps scuffed close behind him.

Dingo sighed. Scar Cheek was not giving up.

If tonight's meeting with Bergman fell apart, the best-case scenario would be a twenty-four-hour delay before Dingo received a second cryptic message with new meet details.

Worst case? No second meeting, because Bergman hadn't made it through the night to see daylight.

From behind Dingo, Scar Cheek cleared his throat.

His next move would be to call Dingo out in three, two, one...

"Hold up, bitch."

At the same instant, Dingo heard a deep voice through the earpiece of his comm unit ask, "Want me to deal with your fan club?"

That would be Tanner Bodine, another member of Sabrina Slye's elite team, who had eyes on Dingo's six from where Tanner perched on a rooftop across the street.

Dingo whispered to Tanner, "When I turn, if I scratch my nose, pop him."

"Roger that."

Dingo tucked his chin against the rags wrapped around his neck and head as a makeshift scarf. Between that and his dark brown hair that had grown out in dense waves, no one would see his earpiece audio receiver unless they got up close and personal. Pivoting slowly, he kept his shoulders tucked to look as non-threatening as possible and lifted his hands waist high, palms out.

He didn't want to hurt any of these guys. "No worries, mate."

With all the Aussies now on commercials, these days his accent actually drew a positive reaction more often than not.

Scar Cheek crossed his arms. "Nobody passes without paying. What you got?"

"Not a thing, just like everyone else here."

"That's too bad, because I don't like your kind."

Seconds were ticking away. "Let me pass and I won't be back."

That drew a mean laugh from Scar Cheek who started forward again. "Hand over the scarf and anything in your pockets."

Fuck it.

Dingo frowned as if he was considering what Scar Cheek said and lifted his finger to his nose then started walking backwards.

Scar Face kept coming. "I'm not joking, fucker–"

Dingo heard the muted pop of Tanner's suppressed shot, but only because he knew it was coming.

Scar Cheek flinched and arched his back, twisting around, trying to see what had hit him.

Dingo backed away as Scar Cheek muttered, "What the

hell..." He jerked his attention back to Dingo and took a step forward then folded at the knees, hitting the ground face first.

The two men still hovering at the drum looked up at the sound of Scar Cheek's body slapping the hard ground. They took him in, then sized up Dingo and went back to attending the fire.

Tanner hadn't killed the guy.

He could have, but Tanner had carried a .300 Blackout Remington 700 sniper rifle. It was suppressed, so the shots were barely audible. An elastic cuff on the buttstock held five tranquilizer rounds–a special new tranq round Sabrina was testing. The tranq wound would hurt like a bad bee sting for the thirty seconds it took the drug to work, but now Scar Cheek would sleep long enough for Dingo to handle his business with Bergman.

In a few steps, Dingo reached a dark opening seventy feet from the men at the drum. It had once been a side entrance to the two-story building. A body-sized lump covered with a soiled blanket slept on the tiny landing between the doorframe and a stairway that *should* go up twenty steps.

That had surely been the plan when they built this place, but after the first two steps, the next eight were missing.

A metal handrail attached to the wall ran all the way up though.

Dingo leaned into the opening to be out of sight, then pulled on his night vision monocular that lit up the dark and changed everything into greenish-gray hues.

Leaping over the body, Dingo landed on the second step, then lunged up to grab as high as he could on the metal handrail. It gave under his weight, but not much. He didn't waste time as he pulled himself up in case the anchor bolts gave out. Swinging his booted foot onto the next metal step, he dragged his weight to a standing position and paused to check down below.

No one could see him up in this black hole even if one of the homeless got curious.

He hurried up the last steps to the top landing where busted wood hung from the doorway on his left. Bits of broken furniture lay scattered everywhere.

Muffled noises erupted halfway down the hall.

Bergman wouldn't have anyone else here. He operated alone.

Or he had at one time.

Dingo had known the snitch for five years before he left the country. The man normally waited so silently in the shadows you'd think you were alone if he was two feet away.

That second person creating noise might be a party crasher. Dingo had to keep Bergman alive or lose intel he desperately wanted. Needed. Just to be damn sure Valene was still safe.

He rushed forward carefully, watching his step so he didn't fall through the rotted floors. What little noise he made would bother him, but it was being covered by Bergman's high-pitched voice that cried out. "Stop. Stop! How many times I gotta tell you? I don't know. If I knew the name, I'd tell you."

"Then you're of no use to me old man. You should be careful who you screw over in the future, but then again ... you have no future."

"*Nooo.*" Then silence.

Shit.

Dingo pulled out his Sig and shoved the door open, banking on the element of surprise.

That might have worked if not for rusty hinges squealing like stuck pigs.

And Bergman's attacker standing just inside the door.

The dark figure spun around and kicked Dingo's gun away, then drove a knife dripping with blood at him.

Dingo sucked back to save his stomach and grabbed the guy's wrist, wrenching it. He slammed the wrist against the doorframe. The knife flew out of sight, but the guy was already swinging wild hits. His fists battered Dingo's ribs in rapid fire.

If the fucker had killed Bergman, then Dingo needed the attacker alive.

Dingo swung away and came back around in time to see a foot flying at his head. He ducked and shoved upright then rammed his shoulder into the attacker, who had four inches of height on Dingo's six-one. He'd given it all he had, knocking the guy into a wall.

The rotten structure shattered and the lack of resistance sent Dingo landing on top of his opponent with wood raining down on them.

A loud creak ripped through the air. The floor threatened to break away.

That body smash should have at least stunned Bruce Lee's evil spawn, but no. He wasn't even at a disadvantage being caught on the bottom of their tangled pile. Sharp strikes hammered Dingo's ribcage again, dammit.

He already felt like he'd been run through a blender inside out.

Tomorrow was going to suck, but not as bad as tonight if he lost this fight.

He'd never learned all those fancy martial arts moves.

Where he came from, the dirtiest fighter won.

Dingo shoved the wood off and pushed to his feet.

With a move straight out of Hollywood, the guy flipped over, landed on his feet and took off down the hallway toward a window opening that had no glass left.

You're not escaping that easily, Kung Fu.

Dingo charged after him, talking to Tanner as he did. "Get to the east end of the building. Chasing someone headed for a window on the second floor."

"Roger that."

But Tanner had to get down off the roof and across the street.

Dingo scooped up what looked like the leg of an old wooden chair that lay in pieces, and flung it for all he was worth. It whacked the crazy guy in the head with a solid thud.

That sent his perp stumbling just short of the window opening.

Dingo came barreling up, jumping over holes in the floor, and lost his footing as he reached the end of the hallway. The bastard staggered, but swung around with a wicked kick aimed at Dingo's head.

This time Dingo was ready, and knocked the leg aside and ducked.

Who hired this guy?

Mercenaries with this level of skill did not come cheap.

In the next second, the son of a bitch made a move that telegraphed his intention to go on attack again, even after taking a hit hard enough to give him a concussion.

What was it going to take to drop this maniac?

As the perp swung around, Dingo cupped a fist with his other hand and jammed an elbow into the guy's throat. He got a boot in his ribs for that and arched face first into the wall. Dammit. That shit hurt.

Fuck it. Dingo came around with a roar and body checked Kung Fu straight on, sending the bastard backwards into the window.

Make that right *through* the window.

Wood disintegrated as Kung Fu's body blasted through the opening and out of sight.

Dingo lunged to grab him, but came up with a handful of nothing. He leaned through the window, fighting to draw air in spite of his battered ribs.

When he looked down, his attacker was sprawled and not moving. "Shit, take your time Tanner. I think he's dead."

"Roger that."

"I'm going back inside to see if my contact is dead, too." Dingo hurried back to the room Kung Fu had come out of, but every breath hurt like a bitch.

Climbing out that window and down the side of this building to get out of here won't be no picnic either.

When he reached the room, his stomach flipped over.

It *was* Bergman.

The snitch's lungs were playing a familiar tune, the death rattle. Kung Fu had gutted Bergman with a quick X across his soft abdomen. Bergman was trying to whisper something.

Dingo dropped onto his knees to get close enough to hear, because they both knew calling an ambulance wouldn't save him. "Why'd you come back, Berg?"

"Had ... no ... choice."

Before Dingo could press him on that, Bergman said, "Three targets." Wheeze, rattle. "Part of ... big plan."

"Where are the targets?" Dingo asked.

"L ..." Gurgle. "They ..." Bergman's eyes rolled up.

Dingo shook him. "Stay with me. L what? Who are the targets? They what?"

Bergman gasped and wheezed, sounding wet. His eyes focused for a moment. "Initials. F.E.P. O... N. C." More wheezing. "P.G

... C. He ... found me. Want you."

Dingo's blood ran cold at the only *he* that could have sent Bergman back here, but that wasn't possible. "*Who* are you talking about?"

"Satan's ... Garden ... C–"

Bergman gave one last heave and air slipped past his lips in a whistle, then he stopped moving.

Dingo stared at him in disbelief.

Bergman had to be wrong.

Dingo had sacrificed eleven months of his life and most of his soul to destroy Satan's Garden Club. He'd killed Santori Garcia, the head of that murdering group, and made *sure* he was dead. No rising from the grave for that one to threaten Valene again.

She was safe. He refused to believe otherwise.

This intel had nothing to do with her.

Someone had to be using the Satan's Garden Club name again, because the only person still left from Garcia's crew was a nasty buggar who'd been fourth in command. That one had another eighty years in prison, plus he'd never been high enough in the ranks to have been fully in Garcia's confidence—not enough to know about Valene.

Tanner's voice cut into Dingo's thoughts. "You better get down here."

"Why? What's up?" Dingo finished searching for any information on Bergman. Wasted effort.

"Your guy's gone."

"What?" Dingo stood up.

"I did find something odd."

"Hold on. I'm coming to the window." Dingo found his Sig where it had landed in a pile of debris, then limped his way back down the hall. When he got there, the damn body *had* disappeared. "What you got, mate?"

Tanner had a golf bag slung over his shoulder–a way to stash the rifle so it wouldn't attract attention–and his monocular flipped up on his forehead since the streetlight at the corner of the building gave enough light to see the weed-infested pavement. He looked up at where Dingo stood at the open window and said, "I doubt this shiny gold coin has been here very long."

Dingo cursed. "Can you read anything on it?"

Tanner held the coin to catch the light. "S. G. C."

Satan's Garden Club's calling card. The impossible had happened. Garcia's people were back in business.

Whoever had found Bergman would come for Dingo next.

Or Valene.

Chapter 2

VALENE ARGUED, *"EVERYONE* is dying and has been since the day they were born, but that doesn't mean they gave up by first grade." She gripped the leather-covered arm of the chair where she sat in Dr. Bowen's Los Angeles office.

She needed to hold on to something to weather this new storm. Without her father to stand by her, this chair was as much of an anchor as anything else in her life right now.

Dr. Bowen's gray eyes were underlined with the soft wrinkles of a man who had recently seen fifty. His gaze implored her to join him in Logic Land. "We're talking about Ronaldo, not the rest of the world."

"I didn't come here to be reminded of how sick my dad is. I get confirmation every time I walk into the assisted living facility and see him shrinking before my eyes." She stood and leaned forward, dropping her hands flat on the desk. It was that or lunge across the wide mahogany surface to throttle the man who had been her dad's savior.

Until now.

She kept her voice calm, but determined. "I just need to know how much the treatment will cost."

Dr. Bowen's silver hair never seemed to grow, always trim and neat as if he'd just stepped out of the hair salon, because LA doctors didn't frequent barber shops. He placed his gentle fingers on top of her chilled ones and said, "I've gotten to know Ronaldo, and you, over the past seventeen months. Your father made one thing clear to me during our last meeting. When it came time to call it quits, he did not want me to drag this out–*his* words, not mine–and he did not want you sacrificing any more than you have. Your dad's health has spiraled down faster than I would have expected over the past two weeks. He doesn't want you doing this. He wants you to ... let him go."

Her throat muscles locked at the idea of being left behind once more. She couldn't face tomorrow without her dad.

She would not cry.

Crying about things out of your control is wasted tears, Hot Stuff, her dad had told her the day her mother drove away from Los Angeles, taking Valene's brother and only sibling to live with their maternal grandparents in Syracuse, New York.

Her mother had hurt her father deeply, much as Dingo had hurt Valene when he vanished seven years ago. But Dingo had never said vows and very likely never would to anyone.

Certainly not her.

Did she really need this reminder of the unbearable pain she'd suffered when he left without a word? Sure, she'd shed this room full of tears at the time. But she'd bucked up and taken her father's rule to heart once she realized keeping Dingo in her life had never been in her control.

She'd dried her eyes and pushed on at that point.

There would be no tears today either, because she was not about to give up on her dad.

Getting him into an experimental treatment plan *was* in her control.

She hoped.

Valene stood straight and crossed her arms, prepared to do battle. "It's my father's right to have a say over his medical treatment, just as it's *my* right to spend *my money* any way I choose. He was improving until four weeks ago. Before I do anything final, I'll talk to him myself and respect his wishes, but right now all I want to know is do you, or do you not, have a treatment option for my dad?"

Dr. Bowen sat back and scratched his forehead, sighing with a disgruntled rumble. "Yes, my assistant found an experimental program that has a test running for mediastinal tumors, but the tumors in your father's lungs are unlike any other mediastinal studied so far."

"I understand that it's a rare form of lung cancer."

"Yes, you do, but my point is that this is really a long shot.

They have an opening in five days, but the treatment is *so* risky and–" He lowered his hand. The sucky news to follow was written in his sad face. "Expensive. It will cost thirty-seven thousand to cover everything he'll need. This requires a ten thousand deposit by the day before the opening."

She sat down hard.

Thirty-seven thousand. As in dollars.

She had almost eight thousand in her checking account, but she needed that to keep her dad in the assisted living facility and a roof over her own head, meager as her home was these days. "Uh, okay... I'll–"

What?

Whip out a magic wand and conjure up thirty-seven thousand dollars in gold? That was as realistic as coming up with money any other way. At one time, she would have had triple that amount sitting in a stock account where she could put her hands on it quickly.

No more.

"Valene, don't. This is why I was trying to tell you what your dad wanted if we got to this point. He's seventy-eight–"

"Not for another week."

"Still. He's lived a good life."

She didn't deal well with desperation, but anger? Oh, she had plenty of practice at handling rage. "He's old and has had a good life so what? It's time to put him down? Is that it?"

"I'm not saying that, Valene."

"You *are* saying it's a bad investment." Just like when Mom decided she couldn't invest any more of her youth in a man with one arm, once he was no longer a gorgeous bauble she could dangle in front of two sisters who had married rich, but dumpy, men. It hadn't been enough that her dad had loved her mother, or that he'd been a highly respected associate professor of history at the time of the accident.

Against her mother's wishes, her dad had gone off on an archeological excavation in Europe where a former associate had arranged for her dad to have an active role. He'd spent months setting it up, but Valene's mother had criticized him the whole time, claiming his dream was nothing more than grunt work or manual labor. Yes, he'd lost his arm on that trip, but her dad had never uttered a word of regret.

He'd still been a very attractive man when her mother bailed on their marriage, but he'd lost a lot of his athletic physique over the eighteen months of healing from the accident.

A few months before getting injured, he'd taken a new teaching position, and since he wasn't tenured the new university had replaced him. Life went downhill for a while, but her dad had planted two feet and stood up, determined to raise Valene.

Dr. Bowen pulled out a hard-eyed gaze he probably held in reserve for difficult cases like her. "Do you have that kind of money?"

"I can get it." She had a new client who wanted a specific seventeenth- century artifact located. A small one. That's all the message had said besides asking her to meet the guy at a restaurant two hours from now.

Seventeenth century could be big money, especially if it was an extremely rare book. Ancient inscriptions were her first love, but the written word up through the Renaissance was her area of specialty.

On the other hand, anything that rare would not just appear out of thin air in one week.

Her expertise had grown out of a natural gift for uncovering obscure details from history, a bulldog attitude when it came to digging up information, and a tenacious drive for tracking something down when others quit. Or rather, that *had* been her reputation before she'd allowed so many contracts to slide. She'd been tough competition when she was at the top of her game and she could do it again.

She knew of only two other people who specialized in the same areas and who could be considered her equals. Artifact hunters were all over the place, but she was more of a bounty hunter when dealing with the Renaissance and mapping the journey of a specific item from person to person.

It was one thing to know the value of an object, but much more valuable to uncover the hands that had touched it. The other two comparable experts were on the US Eastern Seaboard.

Luck had fallen her way to have this client on the West Coast.

"What if your father doesn't want to do the experimental treatment, Valene?"

Her dad once told her he never would have survived the early cancer treatments without her being his advocate when all he'd wanted to do most days was curl up and sleep. Cancer could suck the drive out of a strong person. Her dad was a fighter and a survivor who trusted her to have his back. Even so, she'd never push him to do anything against his will.

Pushing back up to her feet, she felt the first wave of confidence roll through her, something she hadn't experienced in a while.

"I told you, the final decision is his. You mean well, and for that I thank you, but you don't really know my father, Dr. Bowen. I'm sure he thought if anyone had a chance at swaying me from this path it would be you, because there is no one else who would try. The few people I consider friends know my father and I are cut from the same cloth."

"Then why aren't you going along with his wishes?"

"You miss my point. Anyone familiar with both of us would have no doubt that I'd fight until my last breath to save my father and if ..." She paused to clear her throat. "*When* I have the full payment for this treatment, Dad will face that treatment the same way he's faced every battle in his life. He's still alive because he doesn't want to let go of me any more than I want to let go of him." She took a breath and let it out, allowing that cleansing to flow through her before she continued.

If her dad convinced her otherwise, then she wouldn't push.

But her father was not a man to give in this easily.

She went on. "Don't take this wrong, but you should be asking yourself why I'm fighting so hard for your patient and you aren't."

His eyebrows tucked close to the bridge of his nose. "I do care about my patients."

"I'm not saying you don't, but not everyone has a champion, so it falls to you to give them a fighting chance." She didn't want to argue. This man had been a good doctor. She'd hoped he wouldn't be like the others wanting to rubber stamp her father through the system. "Please make the arrangements to start the treatment next week. I'll be back in time with the ten grand for deposit and my father's blessing." She hoped, on both accounts.

But she believed every word she'd given Bowen. Valene and her dad had made a pact when her mom left, that neither one of them would ever give up on the other.

Years later, she realized he'd done that to convince her he would never leave Valene, but she'd taken that pact to heart and it was her turn to be his rock.

She carried her head up and shoulders back as she left, the way her father would expect. No one had to know that her legs trembled like overdone noodles hanging in the breeze. When she got to the street, she turned toward the parking deck.

She had to get at least ten thousand up front from the client she was meeting today at lunch. That would only happen if she picked up body language at their meeting that convinced her of how much he wanted the artifact. If she hit him with too large an amount of money up front he might back off, which would leave her completely empty-handed.

On the other hand, high-dollar clients would be wary of someone who charged too little.

Going into a negotiation desperate for the money screwed her ability to rely on her instincts.

Instead, she played out scenario after scenario in her mind. Not one of them would be worth a flip until she knew exactly what she was searching for and what resources she'd need.

After riding the elevator up to the third floor parking deck, she hurried to her 1965 frost-turquoise convertible T-bird. It was the third car she'd owned, and she hadn't wanted another one since. Her dad had praised her for the investment.

Her baby was the perfect ride for June along the LA coast.

If only she had time to indulge in a relaxing drive.

She slowed her steps, taking note of the white van that had pulled in next to her car. A "Gonzalez Brothers Electricians" vinyl sign was stuck across the back.

Vans weren't specifically threatening, but this one had a sliding door on the passenger side that faced her car. The self-defense classes she'd taken at nineteen had left her with a healthy dose of respect for *what if?*

What if someone hid in the van, waiting to grab an unsuspecting, vulnerable woman?

He'd get the surprise of his life when she turned out not to be quite so vulnerable. At twenty-nine, she had a few new moves to boot.

But no ninja jumped out of the van to attack her before she unlocked her door and slid behind the steering wheel, where a folded note was propped up.

Seven words raised chill bumps along her arms.

Don't look around. Just read the note.

She glanced around without moving her head and slowly reached for the paper.

Chapter 3

DINGO HELD HIS breath, counting the seconds until ...
The passenger door on his van opened and Valene climbed in. "What the hell is going on?"

"I needed to talk to you."

"Lose your phone?"

"This was better said in person."

"You scared the crap out of me with that note," she said, her hands stabbing her hair and flicking around. "If you need another favor, the answer is no." The words held enough edge to cut through the tension crowding the air. "I'm a busy person who doesn't have time for any of this, this ... whatever it is you're here for."

"I know you're busy and I just need to talk to you," he repeated gently. He couldn't get past just taking her in. How many days and long nights had he imagined being this close to her again?

But not this way. Not when he was about to turn her world upside down.

On long nights spent alone, he'd recall watching all that wild blonde hair blowing around her sweet face as she drove her muscle car along the coast highway with him riding shotgun.

She was the sexiest thing he'd ever known.

One of her smiles would be worth the punishment he'd put his body through by not sleeping since he'd found Bergman yesterday and going nonstop to get here, just to see her alive and safe. He knew every inch of the beautiful body hidden inside that black-on-black mandarin style suit.

Damn. If he didn't stop thinking about her sans the suit, he wouldn't be able to walk.

"Well?" Valene snapped. "You got what you wanted. I'm sitting here."

If he had what he wanted, she'd be in his arms and he'd be kissing the lips he missed more than he'd thought possible. That was never going to happen again, especially now when he had to open a wound that had never healed.

He asked, "Remember back when I was looking for information on a man named Giuseppe?"

Her gaze sizzled with fury. She crossed her arms. Yes, she remembered.

Shaking her head, she laughed and it came out as a dark sound. "Seven years. You disappear for *years*, then show up a month ago needing help *again*, and now you want to talk about the last time I saw you before you walked away without a word?"

No, he didn't want to bring that up again, didn't want to go back through time and relive all that agony. He wanted to block it out. Just like he'd blocked LA out of his mind the minute he realized she'd married.

But she didn't know he'd shown up a year after leaving, all set to jump back in where he left off. That door hadn't just closed, it had slammed shut.

He had no reason to feel cut up over Valene finding someone new.

She deserved someone she could have a life with, but that didn't mean he had to celebrate when she'd found that person, did it? He hadn't gone digging in her life, but he *had* kept an alert on his computer for any media that mentioned her name. Sick fuck that he was, the minute the legal notice of her divorce hit the papers, the muscles in his chest had eased with relief.

That was just wrong.

He couldn't help it. After joining Garcia's outfit by taking a bullet to gain his trust, Dingo had spent ten months with Garcia, waiting for his chance to take down the bastard and his closest circle of killers. But it had been a bloody end.

Dingo had dangled close to death for two weeks, then the minute he'd clawed his way back to the living and was physically able to travel, he'd flown to LA to surprise Valene, intending to make up for the year he'd gone missing.

He'd been the one rocked back on his heels when he found her married and happy. The only decent thing to do at that point was to turn around and leave without a word, which he'd done, never planning to contact her again ... until four weeks ago.

Big mistake.

One look in those challenging brown eyes a month ago had taken him back seven years and churned his gut into a constant want he'd never be able to satisfy.

He'd left her seven years ago, knowing she'd hate him.

No, it had been worse, because he'd hurt her by not saying a word. If he'd taken that risk, then the gamble to get inside Satan's Garden Club and stop them from touching her would have been for naught.

But he wasn't going to reach for the sympathy vote by explaining it now, even if he could share that information, which he couldn't.

He'd put that hurt look in her eyes, and it didn't matter that he'd had no choice.

"Giuseppe went missing–" Dingo started.

"So you need to find him again?" she broke in with acid dripping off her words. "Forget it. I made one exception to stop a terrorist. All your good deals are gone."

She'd been their key to a successful mission. He admitted, "We were lucky to prevent the Orion Hunters from pulling off that attack in May, but more than being lucky we had you. If not for you, we might have lost that battle, Val. You saved a lot of lives."

She glanced away. "Whatever."

He'd seen her eyes glisten. She'd never been one to preen over compliments. If anything, they made her wary. He'd like to know why, wished he'd have a chance to find out.

Instead of wishing for the impossible, he asked a question he knew the answer to, but hoped would lower the tension a notch. "Did you get the money for that last job?"

"Yes."

She'd surprised him less than one day after she'd turned her back and walked away. She'd dismissed his offer to pay her for helping them stop a crisis, but twelve hours later she'd texted him with the amount his agency owed and a bank account number for wiring it.

He'd been in the process of having a cashier's check made ready, because he'd intended to pay her no matter what.

Just receiving that request for money had given him hope that she might not hate him after all.

But Valene had a stubborn streak wider than a city block. The last thing he'd have expected was for her to send a request for the money so quickly after she'd turned it down.

What had changed in the few hours after she'd walked away from him?

You could have dug around online and found out.

He didn't have a lot of rules, but he believed that just because you *could* do something didn't mean you should. Unless it had to do with stopping a criminal or protecting someone, he respected the privacy of those people who meant something to him.

He'd bent that rule just to find her today by triangulating her phone signal then tailing her from her bank to this office complex, but as far as he was concerned, this fell under protecting someone important to him.

Valene had been more than important. More than he'd wanted to admit. But the deeper he buried those feelings, the better off she'd be without him, and he'd be without ever having to face the day that she sent him packing.

And she would send him packing. He'd never been keeper material.

But that didn't stop him from wanting to pull her into his arms. He'd like to be the person who held her when she needed someone, the man she could tell secrets like why she'd swallowed her pride and asked for the money from the last job.

What he wouldn't give for a chance to kiss those lips just one more time.

And right now, she was spearing him with a sharp look that made him wonder if he'd said that out loud.

Valene leaned forward, her tone low and rumbling with anger. "I will not sit here and be late for my meeting. Say what you have to say or I'm leaving."

His kiss fantasy disintegrated into a thousand tiny pieces. He explained, "About Giuseppe. I thought he was a distant relation of the man I was looking for back then, but I was wrong." Understatement of the century.

"Then you should have had me look for the guy you wanted, not his neighbor or cousin or whatever. That's not my fault."

"Let me get this out, Valene. Please."

She waved her hands in an exasperated you-have-the-floor motion.

"I was hoping what you found out on Giuseppe would give me a lead to find the man I was after, but Giuseppe was connected to a very dangerous group back then. If I'd had any idea that he was running guns for the man I was hunting, I'd have never asked you to do it."

"Guns. As in black market guns?"

"Among other things, yes."

She groused, "You work with some kind of agency, right? Not that you'd ever tell me who it is or what exactly you do, but I can put enough puzzle pieces together to get a decent picture. It seems to me that some alphabet agency with hotdog operators like you should be able to find a gun runner."

"We did."

She flipped her hands in the air again and let out a long growl of exasperation. "So what's the problem, 007? Still need help finding Giuseppe? *Again*? Run out of women to do your research or are they not letting you pay in trade?"

He flinched at the verbal strike. "I never treated you that way." What they did after hours had nothing to do with his job or her contract work for him. She knew that, but she'd waited seven years to rail at him and he deserved it. That didn't mean he could take it without grinding his back teeth.

Her gaze darted all over the place before it zeroed in on him again. "How am I supposed to know what was true and what was your job?"

Because you knew me, he wanted to say, but she hadn't. He'd kept her insulated from his life. Or so he'd thought. "Believe whatever you will, but I have never mixed business and pleasure. I would never show you that lack of respect."

She was holding on to her righteous anger and she had every right to it, but he saw her chin quiver before she sat up straight and put on her game face. "You're burning my daylight and I'm not on your payroll now. If you need Giuseppe–"

Dingo said, "No. Giuseppe died six years ago. I didn't come here to find anyone but you. I don't need anyone found or any information dug up. I only came to make sure you're safe."

Her face softened and she got that dewy look she used to have when he'd show up after being gone weeks–or months. They'd stare at each other for all of five seconds then shred clothes in an explosion of kissing and hot sex.

God, he missed the way she kissed.

He missed holding her when she slept.

He'd give up all his tomorrows for an hour with her in his arms, but not until he had her tucked away out of view.

When she didn't say anything, he took this calm moment to explain why he was here. "I need you to leave LA for a while. Maybe three or four weeks tops, I'm guessing. I can put you in a safe house, just–"

"No." Whatever softness had been there vanished under the return of an anger flash fire. "In fact, hell no."

Dingo leaned forward, drawing in all the calm he could. "There's a chance that some of those people from seven years ago are back."

"And how is that a problem for me? I'm not involved with any of them."

"I don't want to risk you being out in the open until I can confirm that you are definitely not on their radar."

She leveled him with a you-must-be-kidding glare. "Oh, so let me get this straight. You want me to go into hiding because of someone who *might* figure out that I gave you information on Giuseppe like ..." She dropped her hands. "Seven freaking years ago? Who is this supposed threat to me?"

This was where it got difficult. If he told her, Valene's insatiable curiosity would push her to find answers. That's why Dingo had ended up taking the gamble of his life to get inside Garcia's organization. He was not going to allow her to make that same mistake twice.

He said, "I don't know yet."

She shook her head at some thought then stared at him, counting off each point on her fingers as she spoke. "You vanish for *years* and show up again only because you need something. I do my part for mankind and the US of A, help you out then you're gone again–"

"I would have come back this time," he muttered, but she ignored him and kept going.

"–and now back once more with some wild story about how someone from forever-years ago might find out I helped you locate Giuseppe. Oh, and he's dead! Now you want me to go into hiding while you do what exactly?" She gave him a half beat then added, "No, let me answer. You won't tell me because you don't trust me with anything but your dick."

He wouldn't trust her with *that* right now. "I know how it sounds, Val, but–"

"Shut. Up. You did this once before and while I admit that spiriting me away for a weekend under the pretense that I had a stalker was charming, not this time. I'm done. This bullshit stops here."

"Valene, this isn't like that time." He might have gone a little overboard back then to get rid of some hardtail gym rat who thought he was being cool to show up on Valene's regular running route. "I'm serious about this. Just work with me–"

"No."

He knew that voice, it came with a rigid backbone that bent for nothing and no one.

Don't lose your temper with her. He'd had spectacular rows with Val in the past, but this was not one of those times he could let her blow off steam then seduce her.

Could he?

He reached out to touch her face.

She leaned away, giving his hand the same consideration someone would give a rattlesnake coiled to attack.

Nope. Seduction was not on the menu.

He said, "Just consider what I'm asking and we'll talk more later."

She pointed her finger, emphasizing her warning. "You come near me again and I'll, I'll ..."

"What?"

"Have a restraining order issued."

"You don't have enough information on me to do that." Damn, the minute those words were out he wanted them back.

She dropped her finger, hurt flowing across her face. "And that will never change, will it, Dingo?" she stated quietly, which was more painful than facing her anger.

He caught her hand and brought it to his lips, kissing the skin that he knew by scent.

Her hand trembled.

Did that mean she still felt something for him?

She pulled her hand back. "We aren't going there, so don't waste your time thinking you'll win this argument. As for going anywhere right now, I couldn't even if I wanted to because I'm helping someone who's very sick and needs me right now. But to be clear, I *don't* want to."

One of the last times they'd had a hell of an argument was after he'd found out about her digging around where she shouldn't have been, trying to get information on him.

A snitch had clued Dingo in that a woman from LA was asking about him.

That snitch also said that she was bumping around in areas that would get her fingers chopped off. And that wasn't just an expression.

Valene had expected answers from him when she'd met him at dinner that infamous night, and handed him snippets of intel about an op he'd handled in Chicago in the past.

She'd expected a floodgate of information from Dingo.

What she'd gotten was a floodgate of anger.

Research worked two ways, but she wasn't used to her research coming back to haunt her. If she'd continued sniffing around in Dingo's life, she would have gained the attention of someone deadly who would have loved to find a connection between Dingo and any woman.

A woman they could hurt over and over.

He'd lost it that night, and the argument had been ugly.

It only got worse the next day when she tried to make amends by returning to the work Dingo had originally asked her to do–finding out what she could on Giuseppe from birth to age twenty-one. Dingo had a pretty good profile on the guy from that age on, but he wanted to find someone from Giuseppe's past, maybe a close boyhood friend.

Without a word to Dingo, Valene had pulled markers in her vast network of resources to turn up everything she could find on Giuseppe and, in doing so, placed herself in Santori Garcia's crosshairs.

The head of Satan's Garden Club had noticed her.

Dingo vanished the next day, leaving her only a note not to look for him.

Based on the cold distance in Valene's gaze, she'd just replayed that time in her mind, too.

Without another word, she opened the passenger door and calmly stepped out, then climbed in her car.

He let her think she'd won this round.

She backed out and drove away.

The clock on the dash reminded him he had an hour and a half to reach the airport and board a flight that would get him back to Atlanta in time for the team meeting late tonight.

If he left now, would Valene be safe? Was he overreacting, when the new Satan's Garden Club might only be some idiot trying to build a name on someone else's street reputation?

If he missed his flight, Sabrina would make an educated guess about where he was and she'd be right.

She had rules. That's how she'd kept chaos out of her life since her days as a six-year-old little girl dropped at a children's home. Dingo knew her rules and respected them, just as he respected her as a teammate and friend. He was basically AWOL while Sabrina and the teams hunted for any information that would pinpoint the assassination targets Bergman had whispered before he died.

He wasn't egotistical enough to think they couldn't do it without him, but ... he was having a hard time doing right by everyone.

Flying to LA without cluing in Sabrina when they had an

active mission was grounds for being dismissed as an operative. He'd never put himself above any of the others.

He didn't even know for sure if Satan's Garden Club was real this time, or that they had any information on Valene, but if there was one slim chance that this involved her, he couldn't leave her to face a threat alone.

If this was about anyone other than Valene, he'd just tell Sabrina and she'd get what he had to do.

But Sabrina hated Valene. Not that they'd ever met. Sabrina's hate came from watching Dingo during the dark time after he'd walked out of Satan's Garden Club, broken.

She'd figured out why he'd taken on a suicide mission and that the reason had a name. Valene.

He'd rather cut one of his limbs off than hurt Sabrina or Josh, the closest thing he had to family. But where would that leave Valene if Satan's Garden Club was connected to the original group and came looking for her?

Chapter 4

WHY COULDN'T I have become a helicopter pilot? Valene checked her watch for the hundredth time and took advantage of a two-car gap on her right to gain ground among everyone else trying to get somewhere on LA's Interstate 5.

How could Dingo do this to her again?

He'd shown up looking like he had back when they were first together. Gone was the white-blond hair from his last visit, replaced by thick brown locks that danced along his neckline. Add that to two days of beard, hazel eyes and a mouth carved for pleasure and he was more tempting than all the magazine cover boys on the streets of LA.

Dingo was all man.

And out of his mind if he thought she was buying that story. If there was real danger, where was his team?

Like last time.

Her heart had been leaking misery for seven years, then he'd shown up again a month ago with a team of operatives looking to stop some crazy terrorist group. Dingo had only come back because he'd needed her help.

She should have cursed a blue streak in his face.

She should have kicked him in the head.

None of that had happened, because she had no brakes when it came to Dingo. Her heart had a bad habit of taking over all thought and driving her into his arms.

Her phone played *Here Comes The Money*, the ringtone she'd chosen for Charlie, the best business connection she'd made in a long time.

She snatched up the phone. "What's up, Charlie?"

"Did you change your mind about today's meeting?"

"Of course not."

"Where are you?"

How did he know she hadn't arrived at the meet point yet? "Are you at the restaurant?"

"No, but I made the reservation, not Smith. I just called to confirm that everything was set and to give them my credit card for anything you ordered. They said no one had shown yet. You've got eight minutes to make this meeting. If I've figured out one thing about you it's that you're the kind of Type-A who thinks if you arrive on time you're ten minutes late. So...where are you?"

Actually, she was down to seven minutes according to her phone, but correcting Charlie would not improve the tension in his voice.

"I'm close." She wheeled off the interstate and forced her blood pressure to come down from the ceiling as she maneuvered through a traffic light onto surface streets. "I'm five minutes away, tops."

"What happened?"

"I had car trouble." It was as good a lie as any. She'd strangle Dingo if he cost her this contract.

"This Smith guy came very highly recommended from my oldest UK contact. Uber-platinum. You told me you needed a big score. I found it. You can't let car trouble or anything else interfere."

Heat crawled up her neck at being chided.

She was *never* in this position. Everything she did was above reproach. Dingo had just undermined her reputation by using up the extra time she'd built in so that she'd only miss this meeting if she were abducted by little green aliens.

Even then, she'd make an alien wish he'd chosen more carefully.

That thought gave her an idea for shifting the topic off her time frame. "Just who *is* this guy, Charlie?"

"All I know is he's from Italy, he's here for a very short time and he's willing to pay big bucks to have whatever it is he's looking for brought to him. My guess is he represents some eccentric billionaire. I tried to find out more on him today just to have an idea of what our dollar parameters might be, but no one knows anything beyond what I've told you. I set the meeting in a public venue, but if you get a hinky feeling, just walk."

And lose the best lead she'd had in forever?

Not going to happen unless this guy acted like an axe murderer on holiday. "I'm good, Charlie. You know I can handle myself. If he's for real, I'll close this deal."

"Good, because if you can't, this Smith will move on and my contact in the UK won't be happy since he's getting half of my finder's fee."

"I hear you. I'm not going to drop the ball and I appreciate all you've done over the past month. This will be my chance to thank you."

"No worries, Val. I like working with you. Aram gets on my nerves. But my contact knows who Aram is so if we let this one off the hook, Aram will be standing by to scoop him."

"That is not going to happen." She hated being compared to Aram Pavlovsky, a five-foot-eight PITA who considered himself a Bulgarian Don Juan–she paused for an eye roll–and was her closest competition on the West Coast. Not that he was her equal when it came to Renaissance artifacts, but he was a shark at closing deals.

She'd been lucky to negotiate this arrangement with Charlie Rothschild–a new buyer in town–before Aram had gotten wind of the new arrival. Charlie brokered high-end, rare antiques, artifacts and antiquities to clients in Europe, and he was the best resource she'd had in a very long time.

He had a rep for big deals, but she hadn't seen anything significant until now.

"Are you there yet?" Charlie asked.

Another eye roll, then she said, "Hold on."

"Why?"

"I want to look in the back seat to see if you're sitting behind me. Chill, Charlie. I'm close."

"Very funny," Charlie groused. "I'm serious about Aram. I heard he's asking around for leads on seventeenth-century collectors. That can't be coincidental. Don't give him an opening again. Not on this deal."

Son of a bitch. "If Aram sticks his nose into my business right now, he'll get it chopped off with a few extra body parts just for good measure."

"That's what I want to hear. Make nice with Mr. Smith. Talk to you later."

Mr. Smith screamed of alias, but she'd run into people before who preferred to remain incognito.

Especially in LA.

She tossed the phone on the seat and hunted a parking space near the restaurant that was now in view. This was a quieter part of Santa Monica, where salt air from the ocean toned down the glitz.

Two minutes.

She'd lost a client four weeks ago when she missed an appointment, but her father had been rushed to the hospital with a severe drop in blood pressure.

Dad came home later that night, but by then Valene's client had turned to Aram.

About time she had some good luck, but she wouldn't sit back and wait on it. *"Being in the game every minute is how you make luck happen, Hot Stuff,"* her dad would say.

I'm in the damn game.

She'd close this deal for *him*, because she had no doubt about her dad considering the treatment. The day her mother had driven away, Valene had cried her eyes out, and told her dad she dreamed he was going to die and leave her.

He promised her right then that he'd never leave Valene without a fight, that he'd walk through the fires of hell if that was the price he had to pay so they could spend one more day together.

Fair enough.

She'd crawl through the fires of hell with her hands and feet bound, if only to spend one more *hour* with him.

She'd passed the restaurant entrance and was searching for a spot to park when a car pulled out of a space along the curb.

Rock star parking karma.

Definitely a positive sign.

Valene maneuvered her T-bird into the slot with a three-point parallel parking maneuver and flipped down the mirror to do a quick check.

Hair intact. Makeup not smeared.

Eyes mysteriously smoky instead of a raccoon impression. All good, right down to her freshly pressed suit.

She snatched her keys from the ignition, grabbed her purse and paid the meter before hurrying back the two blocks to the restaurant.

Rule number one: Always look the part and exude confidence.

Rule number two: Never be late.

She'd blown rule number two sixty seconds ago.

Thanks, Dingo. Not.

There'd been a time that he would have mussed her hair and tried to run her late just to piss her off so he could make it up to her later.

And he would have. All. Night. Long.

Dingo, get out of my mind!

Hadn't she wasted enough time on him?

Yes. Too much.

The last time he pulled something as crazy as today, he'd claimed he was concerned she had a stalker. She'd bought it, right down to going away somewhere secret with him for two days while someone "checked out the stalker." It turned out to be a guy Valene had given the time and place she normally ran. She'd wanted a running partner, but not someone she had to meet every day. He'd shown up twice.

She'd been so glad to have Dingo for two days all to herself, she'd let him off the hook with an ass-chewing, that he of course turned into an all-night make-up party.

The real reason she'd let him off the hook was because she realized his motivation.

Dingo had been jealous.

Would he ever admit it? No. But she'd enjoyed that moment of thinking she meant more than a fling.

What about an hour ago in the van? Had Dingo pulled those shenanigans because he'd seen her with Charlie, the only man she'd had lunch with recently?

If that were true, at least breaking into her car would make sense.

Her stupid heart did a little jig over it until she recalled the last time, when she'd told him he couldn't pull hoodwinks without staking a claim.

He'd agreed and said he'd never do it again.

That should have been her reality check. A warning flag to batten down the hatches of her heart, but it was too late by then. She'd allowed him all kinds of access, and Dingo wanted nothing permanent with a woman. He felt no responsibility when it came to her.

If that meant his little antic today had been about Charlie, then Dingo could stew all he wanted.

He'd lost his chance to have something special with her, when all it would have taken was meeting her half way.

Idiot that she was, she still missed him.

She shook off the distraction and paid attention to weaving through the flow of foot traffic going against her.

The sign for the restaurant came into view.

Searching ahead of the people in front of her, she noticed a man heading her way from the opposite direction. Men in LA dressed in everything from ragged jeans to tailored tuxedos, and drew attention just by the way they wore their clothes.

Not this man.

He topped out at just over six feet, trim build, and moved as if he could handle himself. The black suit and crisp beige shirt had the smooth lines of custom tailoring, and she'd bet from the wide shoulders that there was decent muscle hidden beneath. Nice packaging, but not her type. Obviously, her type was a rough-around-the-edges Aussie with commitment issues.

The more she studied the man coming toward the restaurant from the other direction, the more she realized the way he moved and observed everything around him reminded her of Dingo and his friend Tanner while they were on their mission last month.

Dingo? Again. Really?

Stupid man had no clue what he meant to her.

No, I'm the stupid fool for wishing he was still in my life.

She checked the strange man again and noticed his gaze bounce across people near her, then stop on her.

Hairs danced along her neck. She slowed her steps.

Where was her signature icy confidence?

She had to carve out some time for the gym this week. She needed a brutal workout that would leave her bruised and exhausted, but ready to face anything.

Not reacting like a sissy to a stranger in broad daylight.

As she approached the canopied entrance, so did he.

"Ms. Eklund?" he asked in a voice that had no accent. Like someone from the Midwest. Steely gray eyes took her in from head to toe with quick efficiency.

Good news? He was late, too.

Bad news? She didn't like the weird feelings zinging inside her. Was this a new paranoia or some crap left over from her meeting with Dingo?

She offered her hand to what she hoped would be her new client. "Mr. Smith, I presume?"

"Yes." He shook her hand briefly then opened the door, his face arranged into one of congeniality. "Shall we?"

Not a bad guy.

Her gut might have reservations, but she had trouble hearing any argument over her hemorrhaging bank account that was shouting, *"What are you afraid of, Valene?"*

Letting her dad down.

Other than that? Nothing. Not a damn thing.

Once they were seated with water served, Smith asked the waiter to give them time to talk, then he turned to Valene.

He withdrew an electronic tablet from his briefcase and placed it on the table. "I need something priceless recovered, but discretion is as important as the value of the recovery."

She was known for maintaining client confidentiality that rivaled any doctor or attorney-client privilege, but it was far better for a client to choose her rather than to sell him. She said, "You found me so I'm assuming you know my reputation."

"I do, but I would venture to say that this will be unlike any contract you've ever taken and, if you're successful, it will pay two-hundred-and-fifty thousand dollars."

Okay, he'd just uttered the magic words.

Her blood pressure spiked along with her interest, but she forced her face to remain passive, to hide any emotion. She was proud of her ability to sound calm and reserved. "What are you looking for, Mr. Smith?"

"First, I want your word *not* to share this conversation."

"You have it."

"Just so we're clear, I'll know if you do breathe a word of this. A scroll was stolen from the Vatican and brought into this country yesterday. If you take this job, you can *never* talk about the scroll *or* that it's from the Vatican."

Whoa. Her mental racing skidded to a stop. Television images of Pope Lando arriving in Virginia yesterday flashed in her mind. He'd arrived with his usual entourage, plus an additional team who were here as representatives visiting parishes not on the pope's itinerary.

A scroll stolen from *the* Vatican. Really?

She sat back, giving off body language for *not so quick there, buddy*. "Why me? There are two others with my expertise."

"Three, actually."

"What? If you're talking about Aram Pavlovsky, he is *not* in my league, or that of the other two on the East Coast."

"My people have not spoken to him. Yet."

She wished Charlie had joined her after all. Maybe she should have offered to split this deal, but it hadn't even occurred to her to ask since she'd never needed anyone before when she was negotiating.

And she hadn't expected to feel this in-over-her-head during the first minute either.

Smith had repeated, "As I said, I'll know if you breathe a word of this," with enough dark meaning the Godfather would have given points.

Frightened didn't quite cover the sick feeling in her stomach that if she continued this conversation she might be stepping off a ledge with no idea how far she'd fall.

"Having second thoughts, Ms. Eklund?"

If she was going to turn him down, now was the time to do it.

Stay and take a job that was making her instincts throw up red flags, or walk away and watch the financial hole she was standing in cave in on top of her?

Chapter 5

DINGO PACED THE walkway near the terminal where the door for his flight to Atlanta would close in twelve minutes. He diverted his attention from the flight attendant checking her watch after he'd convinced her to tell him exactly how long he had.

Why hasn't Pete called back yet?

Dingo had reached out to the one person on the West Coast that he would trust to watch Valene until Dingo could meet with Sabrina, then fly back to LA.

But Pete had not responded, which meant he was deep undercover.

Or dead.

Damn. Dingo would have a hard enough time making Sabrina see reason in person. Over the phone would be a shouting match.

If he said he was in LA, she'd go volcanic on him.

Then she'd have to cut him loose or lose the respect of everyone on her teams, and he couldn't put her in that position. He'd like to tell her he was taking that much-needed break she'd been trying to push on him, but Josh was finally going to have the wedding he'd put off time and again for the team.

Dingo wouldn't leave either one of them hanging.

He just needed a few days right now to take care of Valene.

He stood between two women he didn't want to let down.

The flight attendant announced the doors would close in three minutes.

Dingo's phone chirped. He stopped pacing, released a strained breath and snatched up his phone. "Where are you?"

At the stilted pause, he pulled the phone away to check the

monitor and groaned, then lifted the phone back to his ear in time to hear Tanner say, "Where am *I*? Sitting in Atlanta."

Dingo muttered, "Shit."

"Nice to talk to you, too. Sabrina has new intel. We think we know who at least one of the targets might be and she's ready to figure out a plan."

Pinching his nose, Dingo asked, "What'd she find out?"

"Hasn't shared the details yet. Said she wanted everyone together so we can move on this fast, but she did say that you were going to coordinate all the teams from headquarters."

"What?" Dingo snapped then lowered his voice. "She's got White Hawk or Blade, plenty of people to run the operation. The best place to put me is in the field unless we're after an electronics felon."

"Hey, I'm not arguing. Just playing messenger."

"Then tell her that's a stupid idea."

"You want to tell her?" Tanner asked.

"I'll tell her. This is bullshit. She's still pissed about what happened on the Orion Hunter mission last month–"

"You bet I am," Sabrina said in place of Tanner who must have handed off the phone in midstream of Dingo's rant. "First you and Tanner kept information from me–"

"To save your ass that was flapping in the wind with the State Department," Dingo interjected, but she didn't slow down.

"Then I find out you took Valene Eklund as your backup to Colorado. So, yeah, I'm pissed, but that isn't why I want you to coordinate this operation."

"Bullshit."

"Fine. If you want the truth, I admit that I don't want you to go tearing off to LA to protect someone who doesn't give a damn about you."

"That's my business," he snarled.

The flight attendant took that moment to announce that the doors were closing on his flight to Atlanta.

Silence rippled between Dingo and Sabrina.

He leaned his back against one of the thick structural supports and put his hand over his eyes. Screwed didn't begin to describe how sideways this conversation was headed. "Let me explain."

"Clearly what I think doesn't matter in the least to you. Nor are you concerned about three assassinations we're trying to prevent."

Dingo's voice was low and rough from exhaustion. "I'm at LAX because I was heading back to talk to you. I'm asking you to work with me on this. I have to know that whoever has started up Satan's Garden Club again isn't coming for Valene. I know you don't like her–"

"What made you think I don't like her?"

He paused, stuck for what to say, but Sabrina cleared up his confusion right away.

"Don't sugarcoat my words. I hate that bitch."

"Fine. You hate her, but I'm responsible for her being at risk, if she is."

"No. When are you going to get it through your head that she brought Garcia down on herself seven years ago? She's the one who went snooping where she shouldn't have and you're the one who took on a suicidal undercover role to protect her." Sabrina's voice shook when she added, "I almost lost you forever. Even when you came back, I thought I'd lost you. I will not forgive and forget. She's a liability to you."

It was hard to argue when Sabrina laid out the facts in cold precision, but that wasn't exactly the way it all happened. Valene had thought she was helping him. Should she die because of going the extra mile?

No. Sabrina wouldn't agree, but she was correct on one point. Dingo had been a shell of a man after barely escaping Garcia. Finding Valene married when he'd healed up enough to fly to LA had broken what glimmer of a spirit he'd had left.

"Don't do this again, Dingo," Sabrina pleaded softly. "I can't watch you go through that twice."

He hung his head. She didn't get it. This wasn't about him being some lovesick young buck.

This was life and death.

But Sabrina wouldn't spit on Valene if she were on fire. In fact, Sabrina would set the fire.

He cleared his throat and said, "I was about to board a plane. I was going to be on time for the team meeting. I would never intentionally make you look bad to the team and I had hoped to talk to you in person about this."

"But you aren't on that airplane, are you?"

"No. I was waiting to hear from my friend Pete. I'd planned to have him watch over Val while I was gone, but I haven't heard back. Doesn't matter. I hold myself just as accountable to you and the teams as everyone else in Slye and I understand about ..." He had to take a breath before saying that he understood that she'd have to cut him loose. It wasn't about the job. He could sign on with ten different groups tomorrow, but he could never replace the relationship he had with Sabrina and Josh.

That was the only thing he had to cling to in dark times.

Sabrina's voice sliced through the phone with a honed edge. "What you should understand is that we have a mission and new intel to sort out. We've received information that leads us to believe at least one of the targets is in southern California, which means I'm taking teams to the West Coast. We're wheels up in an hour. Your job is to be in LA ahead of us and set up safe house number four."

She was giving him an out and that last part had been said overly loud, probably for the benefit of Tanner and any other team members nearby.

He pushed off the support beam. "I'm on it." He took a step and stopped. "I really appreciate–"

Sabrina cut him off. "I'll expect you to have reviewed all the material forwarded to the safe house computer and have everything we need ready to go."

Hearing the sound of her moving around, he waited for her last words and that didn't take long.

The sound of a door closing meant she had to be in her office. She said, "There's no solid information that proves this Satan's Garden Club is in any way connected to the original group. What would you be telling me if the tables were turned and I went off half-cocked to protect Gage?"

He hated Gage Laughton, and she had too, at one time. "We're talking apples and oranges. Valene did nothing wrong, technically. Gage, on the other hand, was your CIA handler who let us get burned in the UK."

"I don't have proof of that in hand."

"So you're arguing on his behalf?"

"No, but I'm telling you I'm just as open-minded about Valene as you are about Gage. You want understanding? Here it is. Find your man Pete. Get Eklund out of the way and get your head into the game by the time we arrive." The call ended.

Only Sabrina could give him an impossible task and make it sound as though she was helping him out.

Chapter 6

VALENE GLANCED AROUND the restaurant where patrons were involved in their own conversations. No one was watching her and the mysterious Mr. Smith. No visible threats.

He watched her, expecting Valene to admit she was having second thoughts.

"I must move this along, Ms. Eklund," Smith said. "Now is the time to stop this meeting if you're intimidated by a project of this caliber."

Intimidated? Not in this lifetime.

She dismissed everything except locking this deal down. "I'm listening, Mr. Smith. You lost something from the Vatican that you're willing to pay a quarter of a million dollars to have returned. I can't mention to anyone, now or ever, that this is connected to the Vatican. I'm assuming someone slipped the scroll out without your security realizing it, which would point to an inside job. Does that pretty much sum it up?"

Smith nodded, but offered nothing more. He sat perfectly still, watching her.

If he expected her to fidget, he'd be disappointed.

Some people talked to fill in a conversation void. If *she* stayed quiet long enough, they'd talk even more, trying to convince her to take a contract.

Because some contracts were losers.

Dingo had once told her she could afford to pass up ten good jobs, but she couldn't afford to take one bad one.

Since her mind was determined to bring Dingo to this meeting, she tried to look at this the way he would. Dingo would start by trying to figure out more about this guy.

Valene asked, "Who are you, Mr. Smith?"

"I'm a part of the Vatican's security."

If she asked him for ID beyond Charlie's recommendation, she'd get about as much out of this guy as she'd ever gotten out of Dingo. A phony ID that was a hundred percent authentic looking and someone to verify him when she called the number he gave her, which would be the only number for him.

Valene skipped the exercise in futility and asked the question that would determine whether she was ready go for this deal. "How about being straight with me. Why did you choose me and not one of the other *two*?"

"Three," he corrected.

Did he do that just to see if he could get under my skin?

Better had tried.

He released a sigh that rumbled with impatience, but his face remained placid as a calm lake. "You're the only one with the level of expertise required who is not associated with a government operation or agency. This is Vatican business and must be kept silent. I'm sure you're aware of the pressure this pope is under to reform the financial dealings of diocese and organizations linked to the Vatican and its banking system."

"I see the news."

"I thought you were Catholic."

He got the past tense correct, as in back before life had shredded her belief. She shrugged. "Is that a requirement?"

"No. As I was saying, the pope is under pressure to make changes, but has also been under attack from those who don't want change. If we allow the media to get word that a rare artifact has been taken out of the Vatican, all of this pope's hard work will be lost in a thunder of outcry over the artifact."

"So the pope knows all about this theft?"

"I didn't say that."

Squeezing orange juice from a rock would be easier than getting a straight answer out of this guy. She'd heard about all the conflict going on between bishops, archbishops, monsignors, you name it. They were all priests, but they were also human. On occasion, one of those humans allowed the sin of lust for money to override his belief. To this pope's credit, he was shaking up the place.

She still wasn't making the connection. "You don't believe the FBI would handle this quickly and keep it quiet?"

"Does that work for you?"

Valene thought back over what she'd said, trying to determine if this was a trick question. No idea. "Does what work for me?"

"Talking a potential client out of your services."

Not particularly, but she'd survived a long time in this world by forcing her rambunctious side to take a back seat when caution should prevail. "I want to be sure this will work for both of us before I commit to anything. Why should I take a job that would tie me up and not pan out when I could be on one that would be lucrative?"

Oh, wait, she had the answer. *Because this is the only job I've been offered of this size in longer than I can remember.*

"As you mentioned earlier, I am well aware of your reputation or I would not be here. I'm also aware of your financial situation, which is difficult, bordering on dire."

To be told that by a client stunned her. "My personal business is just that. Personal. I don't know what Charlie shared with you–" For which she was going to rip Charlie a new one when they spoke later. "–but I'm not taking *any* contract unless I'm a hundred percent convinced it's legal and doable."

Smith tilted his head a bit with a look of mild admiration, which had no influence on her state of mind.

He continued, "I understand your caution. At one time, I would have collaborated with the FBI on this, but while performing investigations for His Holiness, my staff uncovered disturbing information on a rogue group of fanatics also looking for this scroll. From what we were able to discern, these people have infiltrated law enforcement in different countries and possibly even the Vatican. I can't go around asking everyone's personal beliefs or accusing law enforcement of having personnel with ulterior motives for their positions, especially when I'm a visitor in another country."

"Tell me about this scroll."

Smith pulled back physically, a tiny movement that televised he was deciding something, then he leaned forward just enough to show he was back in the conversation again. "This scroll contains visions Galileo claimed to have received and wrote in his own hand while under house arrest at the Vatican."

"Are you serious? I've never heard of that and I would have. Where has it been all these centuries?"

"In the Vatican. Each pope has inherited the responsibility of protecting items and secrets the world is often not meant to see or hear about."

She sat back, an elbow propped on one arm and her thumb tapping her jaw. This was very likely a wild goose chase. Much as she'd like to take the money, she'd ruin her reputation by accepting a job that every other person in her field would label a fool's errand, because there was no such scroll.

If it did exist, that artifact would be worth more money than ... she couldn't even put a price on it.

"You don't believe me." Mr. Smith stated that without the least bit of annoyance.

"I'm not questioning your integrity," she made clear, "but I am questioning the authenticity of this scroll."

"Convincing you of that is not one of my concerns. Only locating the artifact that was taken."

She sat forward, folding her arms on the table. "Was this scroll *ever* authenticated?"

"Yes, but I've answered enough questions. Authentication does not fall within the parameters of this contract, but I have photographs that were taken in recent years by someone who had been invited to study the scroll and tried to leave with the images. We retrieved the shots and they stayed in the Vatican until now."

She chuckled, still not believing this. "We're not talking about Galileo's *Sidereus Nuncius* of which twenty-five copies are still floating around." Even a *fake* copy of that publication had made it past world-renowned experts. "I've never even heard of the existence of this scroll. Things with that type of historical significance have names. What's the scroll called?"

"Are you accepting the contract?"

What if Galileo really had left a scroll in the Vatican?

There were plenty of artifacts that no one knew about stored beneath that mammoth structure, so Valene couldn't actually say beyond a shadow of a doubt that this scroll didn't exist.

Her gut whined a little, but Valene had no concrete reason to turn this down. "I'm in. Show me the photos." She stuck her hand in her purse and fished out her notebook.

Smith pushed buttons on his electronic tablet. When she looked at him again, he said, "First, we'll sign the nondisclosure agreement on my tablet, and I'll forward a signed copy to you immediately."

"Fine, but I also want a clause added to the final agreement that states the theft happened in Italy and that I will in no way be breaking US or international law by aiding you in the recovery."

Smith nodded and they both signed using his stylus, then Valene added one more stipulation. "I'll also need official documentation for chain of possession upon delivery, so there is no question that the scroll was returned to the pope's people."

Smith took his time, thinking.

That pause was actually a positive sign.

He finally nodded. "Upon delivery of the scroll, I'll provide a document stating that I took possession as a representative of the Vatican." Acting as if that had settled all negotiation, he quickly tapped a file on the monitor.

It opened to rows of images.

But she'd caught a glimpse of the icon for that file–an image of a fisherman in a circle–that she recognized as the emblem on the pope's ring.

That quieted down her suspicious side a little.

Multiple images of a scroll popped up in rows of five. He touched the first one that opened to a close-up of Galileo's signature.

She leaned in. Impressive, but if she was putting that scroll on auction it would still need to be verified by three more experts.

Smith continued touching images that provided close-up shots of age marks and star maps scattered through the writings.

It sure as hell looked like a Galileo document.

Whether it was or not, she'd agreed to find it. Smith and the Vatican could worry about authenticating it.

He caught her frowning. "Problem?"

She plastered a polite smile on her face and shook her head. "No. Keep the slideshow rolling."

When the presentation ended, Valene asked, "This may take a while–"

"You have five days to produce this artifact. It must accompany our entourage when we return to Italy next week."

"One. Week?"

"Five days, to be specific." Smith didn't blink. He was dead serious. "Did you think I would pay that much money for anything less than immediate results? It shouldn't be too difficult for you if your contact list is as extensive as I've been led to believe. The person who stole this will have to make a sale quickly to acquire the money he needs to disappear. Otherwise it will be quite obvious the minute he doesn't arrive in time to leave with us."

"You're sure it's a he?"

"The only women with any chance of involvement have been cleared by me. I'm looking for a man."

The reality of what she was agreeing to slammed home with crystal clarity. What if this guy who stole it was unstable? Wouldn't that be the *definition* of unstable? Someone who dared to steal a priceless artifact from the Vatican? "Are you planning on arresting this thief?"

"My first priority is the safe delivery of the scroll. After that, I assure you he will be dealt with."

"People who are afraid can be dangerous. What if I figure out who has the artifact and tell you, then you retrieve it?"

"If I thought the thief was one of my people or on one of our other security forces, that would be a valid concern, but I believe he's someone we'd never expect–someone on the massive staff–who saw an opportunity and has let greed overpower his faith. I would venture to say the thief is feeling quite confident right now since he's in the US with a scroll that he's managed to sneak out from under our noses."

Smith paused, glancing around then looking like a man carrying a burden meant for ten. He continued, "Unfortunately, we have two delegations in the states at this moment, and all members departed within a six-day window. The first one is here on official Vatican business, which has that team spread across the country. The second group is the pope's personal entourage. My staff was alcrted of the missing scroll as soon as the pope's entourage departed earlier this week. Both groups include the most highly trusted individuals, but none are someone I would consider a physical risk." He pinned her with a no-nonsense look. "Another reason I chose you was because of your self-defense skills. I was led to believe that you're well versed in Krav Maga."

"True."

That one word seemed to appease him. "In that case, take the same precautions you would with any other unfamiliar collector and you should be fine. However, I did not answer your question. If you prefer to contact me to intervene at any point, I will step in and I would allow you to keep your ten-thousand dollar retainer."

"What about the rest of the money?"

"You would not have earned it. I'm here meeting with you only because I can't get close to this thief before he disposes of the artifact, but you can."

She needed enough money right now to cover the deposit on her father's treatment, plus cash to buy help in tracking this thief down. This was an all-in or not-at-all deal.

Valene steadied her breathing and told Smith, "I'll find your artifact and return it as quickly as I can. I won't promise five days–"

He pulled the tablet back and began packing up. "Then we have nothing else to discuss, but I will hold you to the nondisclosure agreement."

Crap. "What I meant to say was that I would not promise five days unless the thief absolutely contacts someone to sell the scroll and unless he's looking for the kind of buyer who can actually afford something of that level."

"The list of buyers will be in single digits."

"Correct," Valene said. "In fact, it's going to take someone who is a multi-billionaire, and even then he or she will have to be convinced this scroll is real. That being the case, if your thief has a contact here who puts word out in the underground market, I'll know who he contacts. But to cover all those networks quickly and quietly, I'll need an additional forty thousand up front."

Smith tapped his fingers for several very long seconds, then his jaw hardened. "I find myself in a spot that is unusual, but this absolutely must happen. Agreed. However, if you do not deliver the scroll by my deadline and I find out it was sold in the US during that time, you will return all fifty thousand dollars."

That triggered her palms to start sweating. She sat back and dropped her hands out of sight where she clamped her thighs to dry them off. "Agreed."

"Very well." He tapped his tablet to bring up a document, typed quickly, then signed it and turned the tablet to Valene.

She took her time reading it and once she was satisfied she'd covered her butt the best she could, she signed with the stylus. He locked the file and sent a copy to her before turning the tablet around, tapping keys once more, then closing it inside a leather cover.

He stood, dropping a hefty tip for two glasses of water.

Guess our meeting is over.

She followed him out into the late-day sun warming the sidewalk, and shielded her eyes to look up at him. "What number do I use to reach you once I have the scroll?"

"If you need to reach me, contact Charlie, but I'll know when you have something and I'll find you."

She wanted one more thing clear. "I'll begin work as soon as I receive the fifty thousand dollar deposit." Big lie. She'd be on the phone to everyone who might be of help the minute she walked away.

"It's already in your account." Before she could question how he had that information, he told her. "Charlie supplied me with the account numbers. Anything else?"

"Yes. You have yet to give me the name of this scroll. Is it identified any specific way?"

"It's called *Profezia di Orione*." With that, Smith turned and strode off in the direction from which he'd first appeared.

Valene stared at his back in shock, as if his words had climbed out of his mouth, marched across the sidewalk, then rearranged themselves into the worse possible combination.

She stood there, trying to convince herself that *Profezia di Orione* didn't translate into Orion's Prophecy.

But it did.

That's what drove the terrorists that Valene had helped stop last month. Dingo and his people had been on the trail of Orion Hunters determined to launch an attack.

Why did she suddenly feel guilty?

Because Dingo would want to know this, but she'd just agreed to tell no one.

If she were honest with herself, she knew just as much about Dingo as she knew about this Smith guy.

Very little.

The only tidbit Dingo had shared was that Orion Hunters were part of an underground organization with splinter groups all over the world. The ones his team had been after were terrorists from North Korea.

Not Italy.

She turned toward her car and started walking.

Orion's Prophecy.

Prophecies were bandied about all the time in historical research. What was one more?

Besides, Dingo hadn't even mentioned the Orion Hunters earlier today. If they were dangerous, wouldn't he have thrown *that* in on top of the rest of his scare tactics?

She'd signed a confidentiality agreement. Enough said.

Time to get busy finding that scroll.

Valene Eklund had ignored his obvious alias of Smith, but that happened when someone was offered money they desperately needed.

He walked away from Eklund and the restaurant at a steady pace, confident that she would be unleashing her highly prized skills on finding the scroll. He keyed a button on his phone and lifted it to his ear just as the call went through.

Charlie Rothschild answered, "How'd it go, Smith?"

"The meeting was successful."

"Hot damn! So Valene *did* go for it."

"Did you have doubts?"

"Only because she's a tough nut to crack."

"Yes. She even pushed me for an extra forty up front."

Charlie laughed. "I told you she was sharp. If she wasn't in a tight spot right now we might not have pulled this off, but she'll find the scroll and fast. Like I told you, her dad is bad off and needs the money for a treatment plan. Nice job. You want to meet for a drink?"

And give Charlie a chance to ID him? "No. Call Hong Kong. Tell the boss Eklund is on board and is convinced I'm with the Vatican. Tell him I'll find the scroll before any Orion Hunters do, then I'll be in touch." He hung up the phone and slid into his sedan, dragging his tie loose while he sat there.

Now to put the next step into motion.

The next call was to a man known covertly as the General. He wasn't one, even though he worked in the Pentagon.

The General's baritone boomed on the line. "This better be secure."

"It is. Contracts are set. Everything is in place for the first hit tomorrow."

"Then do it and make sure there are no loose ends."

"Don't I always?" He thumbed the key to end the call and smiled over fattening his offshore accounts.

Chapter 7

SABRINA STEPPED OFF her company jet ahead of the team she'd brought to Los Angeles to find an assassin with three targets. Her Wednesday had started at three a.m. in Atlanta. It was just past six in the evening LA time, and this day would very likely not end until she saw three on the clock at least one more time. She adjusted the shoulder strap on the black case that held her weapons and laptop, then headed out of the hangar she'd leased, into the balmy heat surrounding John Wayne Airport.

Nick Carrera fell into step alongside her, thumbing a message on his phone while they walked to the vehicle parking lot. "Four SUVs are waiting for us."

"Let's get everyone settled in and start rotating down time. There won't be much sleep until we figure out for sure who this assassin is after."

"Agreed."

She could hear a crowd of footsteps and rolling wheels coming up behind them.

Nick glanced at the parking lot, looked back down at what he was thumbing then slowly lowered his phone and stared intently at the smattering of vehicles.

She took note of the way he'd gone on alert.

Four black SUVs were parked together, each windshield tagged with a paper sign that had one word and number printed.

MINE 1, MINE 2, MINE 3 and MINE 4.

Nick's sense of humor. He'd been assigned to handle transportation on this mission. She was just glad to have him whole and walking around after the damage he'd taken on their last mission out here. The team had been ambushed and Nick had taken a round way too close to his lung.

A fifth black SUV waited three empty spaces away, all by itself with the grill facing Sabrina. That's what had pinged Nick's radar.

Headlights blinked on, flashed to high beam then back to low beam, and remained illuminated in the dusty, early evening light.

Please say that isn't for me.

Her phone dinged.

The text read: *We need to talk.*

Why should she expect any part of this trip to be easy? She considered her options. Deal with this complication now or later?

Nick squinted at the lone vehicle. "Company?"

"Yes."

"Expected?"

"No, but I know who it is. Get the team fed and to the safe house. Leave a car with the keys in it. Text me if anything comes up before I arrive. I'll be there as soon as I can."

"Roger that." Nick turned and waited for the other team members, then started giving instructions.

She walked to the SUV that sat with its engine purring, opened the passenger door and slid onto the leather seat before turning her foul mood on Gage Laughton. "What do you want?"

He gave her a half smile that said so much more than the words other men spoke. "Cocktails?"

"No."

"Dinner."

"*No!*"

"Worth a try." He chuckled at yanking her chain as he backed the vehicle around to park at an angle that let them both observe the entire lot, but prevented anyone from seeing them together. He did it for her benefit and she tried to appreciate the gesture.

He wore black jeans and a long-sleeved T-shirt, so unlike his agency suits. His chestnut brown hair was shorter than last time, but still thick enough to run her fingers through if she lost control of her hands. That was always a possibility with this man. He didn't pull a string of suave pickup lines out of his hat or try to dazzle a woman.

He was raw power, coiled and ready to unleash on a threat faster than the snap of a whip. His face would never be seen in a magazine, not even with the combination of distinctive hazel eyes and a square chin.

He had a man's face. Rough and natural.

She still found him to be the hottest male she'd ever seen in or out-of pants. She'd never been drawn to charmers, never trusted a man who handed out compliments like business cards. Gage had been demanding, critical and adversarial. The two of them should have been a worse combination than oil and water, but all that passion had combusted one night and she thought she'd found her soul mate.

That's when she realized he *got* her.

He loved the woman she'd become.

She wasn't cut out for a normal life and he hadn't cared. She'd trusted him with her body and her heart.

Then it all went to hell three years ago when she dragged her bloodied team out of the UK where she'd risked her life, and the lives of the men she considered brothers, to extract a captured CIA agent. Len Rikker.

Someone in the agency had tossed her team to the wolves, but no one was about to own up, and Gage refused to hand over the names of everyone who had been privy to her mission.

Josh and Dingo would go ballistic knowing she was sitting here with Gage, and she wasn't up for that, not when she was already pissed at Dingo.

She had no time for guilt on this trip. "What's up, Gage? The agency having a slow week or what?"

"The agency doesn't know I'm here," he quipped, putting the SUV in park.

That sounded like the agency didn't know Gage was in LA, but she'd learned to interpret Gage talk early on when he'd first become her handler.

Her translation?

The agency didn't know Gage was *stateside* since the CIA couldn't operate on US soil.

Or so most Americans believed.

"Did you come bearing gifts?" she asked, trying to stick with casual when her insides were knotted up. As difficult as it was to keep her distance and sleep alone at night, sitting this close to him was far worse. Her body could sense him being near and complained at the open space between them.

"Sure, I brought gifts." Gage reached over the console separating them and pulled out two waters that were perspiring from being in a cooler.

She took hers and muttered, "That wasn't what I had in mind."

"That isn't your gift." Gage said, "I have information for you that the agency doesn't have. Is that worth a few minutes?"

That sent her antennae shooting up. She lowered the bottle from her lips and propped it on her lap.

Would this be the moment that he handed her the lead for finding Rikker–or whoever held Rikker's chain?

Probably not.

She took another drink of her water, refusing to say anything more than she had to in this verbal game of chess.

Gage's failure to hand over names connected to the UK mission had stood in the way of every effort he made to get back into her good graces.

Or in her bed.

She finally gave in first, only because she was too exhausted to walk an emotional tightrope. "I can't keep doing this, Gage."

"Can't we just have a moment without arguing over *that*?"

That being Rikker and the UK mission that stood between them, squeezing any chance of happiness out of the air.

The desire to give up the fight and climb over the console into his lap pounded her skull and her heart, but she owed a debt to the men who had stood by her when the CIA screwed her team. She was losing the battle of keeping Gage at bay until she could find answers.

She didn't handle emotional chaos well and when it became too much she lashed out. "I can't just forget what happened even if you can."

"Jesus, Sabrina, how can you say that? Didn't I give you a traffic cam shot of Rikker in DC? The agency doesn't have that either."

Guilt came knocking and her conscience opened the door, but

she was not conceding. Not after all she and her men had gone through to be here today.

"Names." She shoved that word at him to cut through all the crap. "I've been asking for names and I still don't have them."

He chuckled and it sounded sad. "Asking you to trust me is clearly out of the realm of possibilities, so how about a little patience while I figure things out?"

"Patience? I'm out of it. I used it up over the last three years."

"Not my fault. You could have been here helping me find answers instead of hiding from me."

She shouldn't have to defend herself to anyone, but neither would she let that comment stand. "I was taking care of my people who almost died that night. Josh should have." The fear of watching Josh barely cling to life had tortured her and Dingo. She owed Josh, Dingo, Tanner and Blade for what they went through when someone traded their lives for Rikker's.

Rikker had never come back to the CIA–at least not as far as she knew–but only the CIA had known about that mission.

That's what she'd been told.

She added, "Hiding from you was second to all that." Her head pounded. She hadn't eaten in fifteen hours and she could sleep on the hood at this point. "I can't keep doing this, Gage. We're on. We're off. It's making me crazy."

"Then stop running from me."

She flinched internally. "I don't run from anyone."

"What do you call dropping off the face of the earth without a word?" he said, power booming through his words, but not shouting. Not yet. "I hunted for you *every minute*. You could have let me know you were alive, but you were convinced that I had betrayed you," Gage's commanding voice never wavered until he said, "I would *never* have doubted you."

His voice shook.

Her heart wobbled at the sound.

She hurt now to think about Gage here alone and thinking she was dead, but back then she'd been furious with everyone in the CIA who had known about her team's mission. She'd threatened to kill any CIA agent who came near her.

The next time she'd seen Gage, she'd already set up shop in

Atlanta and he'd refused to share anything about the UK op. That refusal had doubled the thick walls around her heart.

She longed to forget all the bad history and feel what they had before, but she was made of stronger mettle than that. Had to be. "I got in this car thinking you had new information. Not to argue."

"I do have something to tell you." He sounded disheartened, but locked it away, always holding on to that unshakeable control.

"I'm only interested in information on one person."

"You, of all people, know it's never as simple as that in this business."

She brushed loose hairs off her face, needing to move. Sitting still was not helping her frame of mind. "Whatever. Are you going to share this news or is it on a need-to-know-basis and I don't need to know?"

He turned a thoughtful gaze on her and said, "Over this past year, your group has discovered more about the Orion Hunters than anyone I've been in contact with since you brought the hunters to my attention. I put two people, the only two I trust in the agency, on digging up anything they could find. They uncovered three major divisions of the hunters. The physicists your people extracted from North Korea–"

"Under orders from the State Department." Sabrina had owed the department for an issue one of her people created that couldn't be avoided, and it put her in a position where she'd had to take the North Korea contract.

"Right. Those two men came from what we've confirmed is the largest Asian division of Orion Hunters."

She didn't want to talk about the hunters so she finally said, "I thought we were talking about Rikker."

He surprised her when he said, "We are."

"Really?"

"Have I finally got your attention?"

Feeling reprimanded, she said, "Yes."

He shifted in his seat and leaned forward, covering the hand that she'd dropped to the console.

If she pulled it away, she'd look intimidated.

If she left it there, she risked turning her hand over to feel his fingers weave through hers.

Her heart got a cardio workout while she decided.

His voice lost the tense edge of a moment ago and he started explaining, "You think I'm intentionally holding back information, but I'm not. I've been uncovering information ... things that keep me up at night. You want Rikker. I get that, but I haven't told you some things until now because I think Rikker is just a thread leading to a much bigger organization of power players pulling strings."

"Who?"

"I'm not sure if the players are here, foreign or both. The Orion Hunters might sound like a bunch of fanatics to most people in this country–"

She cut in sarcastically, "That would be the ninety-nine percent who have no idea how close we came to the hunters poisoning a major aquifer that supplies a third of our water."

"Right, but the trail I've been on is becoming harder to navigate all the time. There's an obscene amount of money moving around in search of the five artifacts the Orion Hunters want ... and a bloody trail of bodies connected to them."

"We're getting off topic."

"No, we're not." He kept his hand on hers. That single touch shoved her mind off track.

If she didn't free her hand soon, she would be in danger of not taking it back. Scrambling to think, she blurted out, "Rikker. What were you going to tell me about him?"

"I believe Rikker's involved."

"How? When you and I talked in Atlanta last year–"

"You mean when you finally came out of hiding?" he interjected.

She ignored the taunt. "You originally told me Rikker had been tracking the Orion Hunters. Now you're telling me he's involved with them?"

"Possibly." He laid it out for her. "We found a dead Orion Hunter in Atlanta two days ago who fits the description of the one who killed Bergman."

She didn't bat an eyelash at Gage knowing that. He was in

the business of information and clearly had resources working stateside on this specific case. "How do you know it was an Orion Hunter?"

"He had intentional scarring on his neck that matched the Orion star configuration found on one of the people busted in the ring attempting to destroy the aquifer."

Her skin felt clammy. What had Dingo stumbled into with Bergman?

Gage squeezed her hand gently and she felt it all the way up her arm and into her chest. He asked, "Want to tell me what Dingo discussed with Bergman?"

"Not particularly."

"Information goes both ways."

This was the Gage she knew during missions, the one who could squeeze a name out of a dead body. "You're way behind in the sharing department, Laughton."

He grimaced and went on. "I'm about to share something with you that no one in the CIA knows. No one in any government agency knows, not unless they're involved, so I need you to tell me that you won't share this even with Josh and Dingo."

"Are you serious?"

"You want information? I'm bringing it, but it comes with that price."

"I promised them they could be a part of the takedown when we found Rikker."

"*I* didn't make that promise," Gage said, not giving on this. "You can't tell them until it's time to act. And you're not in any position to do that right now, but with the three of you out here, I don't want anyone muddying the water when we finally have a break. You have to keep what I tell you confidential until I give the word that it's on. Deal?"

He dangled Rikker in front of her nose and she couldn't let that pass. "Deal."

"First, Rikker was recently seen in LA."

Her blood pressure zoomed up so fast it should have blown the top off her head. "*Where?*"

"Downtown on another traffic cam, but it's not a good shot

and it was ten days ago. He may be in another country by now, but I think he's still stateside."

Now she got it. The information wasn't that Rikker was around, but why he was still here. "What's he up to?"

"I'm not sure yet, but I need you to know everything I do right now so that you don't walk into a trap. The Orion Hunter who killed Bergman was found dead with both eyes shot out. That was Rikker's MO. The agency warned him about making signature kills, but Rikker's ego had to be fed constantly. He wanted his hits known."

"That's what a serial killer does. Why would he do that?"

"Because he *is* a serial killer who's a legend in his own mind. He wanted the reputation of being the agency's deadliest asset."

Her mind tossed all this new information in on top of what she already knew and sorted pieces, shoving them into categories, drawing lines and making connections. Was Rikker with the Orion Hunters or after them for some reason?

"Why do we need to keep all this secret?"

"You can tell your people you have intel that the Orion Hunters might be involved in the hits, but don't share the tie to Rikker, because he's making mistakes and he thinks no one is catching them."

How could he ask her to let this opportunity pass? "Gage, think about it. I could put together an ace team and–"

Gage stepped over every invisible boundary she'd thrown between them when he slid his hand into her hair, crowding her personal space and pulling them together.

She could feel the tension in him when he took a breath and let it out carefully, along with his words.

"You're one of most skilled operatives I've ever known, but the deeper I dig the more terrifying this all becomes. The people connected to this are in-their-own-league powerful. There's no way to prove their connections. It's more of a gut feeling I have as I push the pieces around. I told you I only trust two people in the agency right now and they're not a part of my division. I haven't told you much before now because I feared you'd go tearing off after a lead and uncover something you wouldn't survive."

She couldn't think with him so close.

His gaze roamed over her face, tracing every inch the way a blind man reads a shape with his hands. He kept talking in that low, seductive voice that wrapped around her mind and shut the world out.

"I know who *wasn't* involved and those are the names you want. This runs deep and giving you names might have gotten innocent people killed, but more than that I care about what happens to you. And if you went after the agency personnel the way I know you, Josh and Dingo would, I'd learn about it when your bodies turned up. I'd eventually find the bastards doing all of this, but it would be for naught without you here. I'm so afraid of losing you again."

This man feared nothing, or so she'd thought.

He'd fought his way out of third-world hot spots where he should have died. She'd hated when he went dark for months, but it had been part of his job just as going on missions had been hers.

To him, she'd gone dark for two years and she'd felt justified the entire time.

Until this moment.

Her resolve splintered and ripped apart, shattering under the weight of what she'd done to Gage. She'd been so sure he had known who did this to her and the team, that she couldn't just pick up where they'd left off. But Gage had taken his time, inching his way back inside her heart, slowly piecing it back together from the devastation she'd suffered at believing he shielded those responsible for the hell she and her people had gone through.

Like grasping at leaves scattering from a tree in autumn, she tried to hold onto her righteous anger and came up empty.

Gage had brought her information on Rikker and she believed him. If she didn't reach out now, right now, she might as well walk away for good, because she couldn't keep doing this.

Seeing the pain peeking out from behind his stoic calm hurt her heart.

And shoving all the broken parts of her together every day

to do her job to protect the world and her people was getting harder.

She placed her hand on top of his.

That action alone changed everything between them.

She whispered, "I didn't disappear to hurt you."

"I know that, but..."

She finished the sentence in her mind. *But for two years I thought you were dead.*

And he'd mourned her.

She saw his grief in his eyes and felt it in her soul. She'd never stopped believing in him. She'd tried, oh how she'd tried and fought to keep her distance from him, because she owed that to her team. To Josh and Dingo.

But what about Gage? *I would never have doubted you.*

His words stomped on her defenses and forced her to stop laying all the blame at his feet. Pushed her to see him as the man she'd once believed in.

He pulled her to him and said, "For once, stop thinking so damn hard." Then he covered her mouth with his and her world spun out of control. She lost her anchor to reality, floating in space with no sense of up or down.

Just Gage everywhere she touched and tasted.

She gripped his shirt to keep him from pulling away and gave back with all her pent-up longing. Everything she felt for him exploded with that kiss. Her heart squeezed tight, pounding at the feel of his hands racing over her hair and down her shoulder to her breast.

Her body turned into a ball of fire, hungry for oxygen. One touch from him and she'd go up in flames.

Gage kept reaching for her and the world blurred until the only thing in focus was the love she still felt.

He pushed for more, kissing her throat and running his fingers over her cheek. "God, I miss you. Miss just being with you."

She should have had a crazy happy moment at hearing those words, because being without him was killing her. He'd brought her Rikker so why did she feel so torn with guilt?

Because every time Gage knocked down another wall to get

to her it felt as though she was letting Josh and Dingo down to indulge her Gage craving.

Gage's fingers went under her knit top and ... she clinched her thighs against the streak of heat that rushed through her.

"Gage, I...don't."

He dropped his head to hers, breathing hard, and moved his hand from her breast.

At that moment, she wanted to hurt everybody and everything that kept them apart.

He sounded sincerely remorseful when he said, "I didn't intend for this to happen."

She snorted.

"Don't get me wrong. I'm not sorry," he said, a smile coming through in his voice. "I really am trying to give you room, but I don't think being apart is working for either of us. You want to be with me. I want to be with you. Why can't we be together back in Atlanta? I can insert into your house with no one knowing. What would be the harm in that? Give us a chance to figure this out together."

She heard what he was saying.

He would keep their secret safe if she opened the door to him again. That was so damned tempting and her backbone was jelly soft when he was this close to her.

"Say yes." He kissed her tenderly and she heard herself murmur, "Yes."

The kiss he laid on her next was in a whole new level of hot.

Guilt kept thumping at her and she slammed her mind shut to it.

She appreciated Gage's offer not to put her on the spot by keeping his presence secret when she went home, but she couldn't do it behind Josh and Dingo's backs, which meant she'd have to tell them.

Their friendship had never been put to this kind of test and she hoped it would weather the storm coming, because she couldn't imagine life without either Josh or Dingo.

Chapter 8

DINGO SLUNG HIS arm over the empty chair next to him in the underground meeting room of Sabrina's LA safe house number four, counting minutes until this meeting was finished. Sabrina had spent the past hour locked away in her temporary office while the team settled in, but she was ready to start the show.

This war room wasn't quite the high-tech one back in Atlanta at Slye headquarters but planning a mission often had less to do with the location or equipment and everything to do with the people involved.

Tension filled every corner and surface in the room.

Sabrina stood at the head of a table that seated ten. At twenty-seven, she'd accomplished more in the dark world of black ops than many had by their mid-thirties. She'd been pretty as a street rat, but once she turned into a beautiful woman with shoulder-length black hair, honey-brown skin and exotic eyes, men started making fools of themselves. Her male agents knew better and respected her for the deadly weapon she could be.

She did not tolerate fools or anyone stupid enough to cross her, which made Dingo lucky she thought of him as a brother. He owed her his best, and generally gave it without question, but he'd let her down yesterday and had to fix that.

His mind finally caught up to what she was saying. For the benefit of the other agents present, she shared everything they'd learned from intel collected by Dingo and Tanner at the Bergman meeting and afterward.

Sitting across from him and closer to Sabrina, Tanner propped his big upper body with both elbows on the table and seemed less than engaged, but that would only fool someone unfamiliar with the cowboy. He had an easy smile and sharp eyes. Part of his skill set included the ability to talk like he'd just come in off a cattle drive while taking in everything around him, all without showing any sign of listening.

Dingo was surprised to see White Hawk sitting next to Tanner, since she tended to sit apart from any of the men, plus Sabrina had been judicious about where she sent the relatively new team member. White Hawk could be a twenty-something woman from any middle class neighborhood, with blunt-cut black hair, no makeup, long-sleeved, buttoned shirt and jeans that fit without looking like a glove.

But the high cheeks, broad forehead, and honey-brown skin proclaimed her Native American heritage in spite of green eyes.

She'd come to Slye via a Navajo friend of Sabrina's who had done a damn good job training the young woman. No one could shadow a target on foot the way White Hawk could. She had an impressive ability to fade into the background.

Nick Carrera's fidgeting pulled Dingo's attention to his immediate left where the dark Sicilian was a tough read. Nick wore fatigues with the same comfort as a custom tailored tuxedo. He had an uncanny knack for coming up with necessary intel at the strangest times and if his team got cornered, Nick would find a way out. It might involve a lot of destroyed property and pissing off the wrong people, but he had yet to fail at bringing everyone on his team home alive.

Ryder Van Dyke held his lean frame with a lethal stillness that came from being a former Army sniper. He lifted his silver-gray eyes from time to time, wrote notes and occasionally ran a hand over his brown hair, cut so short he couldn't mess it up. Lifting a finger to interrupt, he waited for Sabrina's nod to ask, "If Satan's Garden Club is behind the assassinations, do we have any idea if any of them are part of the original SGC?"

Sabrina's gaze lit on Dingo and he lifted an eyebrow.

She said, "We have no intel confirming it. At this point, we're working on the premise that it's a new group of copycats." She asked Dingo, "Have you anything different to add?"

When she got her back up she was a pain to deal with. He said, "No."

"Good. Moving on."

Damian "Blade" Singleton walked in, surprising Dingo. He hadn't thought the medic would make this trip.

That showed what Dingo knew.

If you mapped out Blade's face, it would be an intersection of Middle Eastern and African American. His eyelashes were so thick his dark brown eyes looked black, and he was always watching, studying everyone around him.

Blade said in his easy doctor voice, "I just picked up the extra medical supplies. What did I miss?"

Ryder gave a brief run down, bullet pointing what Sabrina had been going over.

Sabrina picked up from there. "The FBI has handed over the lead on this until we have something more specific."

Nick said, "They're probably glad to dump this on us with the pope traveling around the country."

"Exactly. I filled them in on the three initials Bergman supplied and they've passed me what information they have, which points at Eva Perdido as being one of the targets. Perdido's campaign manager has been in contact with FBI about threats she's received and notes from a stalker. The most recent stalker note indicated he would be at a large charity event to support her tomorrow."

"The *Save the Hollywood Pacific Theater* fundraiser?" Nick asked.

"That one." Sabrina used a remote to bring an image up on the monitor behind her and stepped to the side. "This is Perdido."

Dingo had seen her sound bites on television. She'd make a prime target since she'd pissed off a lot of people with her extremist position. She had black hair styled sharply around her Latino face, expressive eyes, and a shapely body she used to her advantage in every photo op. Not a woman who rang any of his chimes.

Maybe that's because Valene was taking up all his mental space these days.

Tanner tapped a pen on his notes. "She must be the first set of initials. F.E.P."

White Hawk said, "What does the F stand for?"

"Francine Eva Perdido," Tanner answered. "Word is that she hates her first name and doesn't allow anyone on staff to use it."

Sabrina added, "If she is the target, then the fundraiser is the next public outing where she's expected."

Ryder offered, "Assassins don't usually send advance notice of a hit."

"Agreed," Sabrina told him. "No one's putting a lot of stock into the stalker being a shooting threat, but we have nothing matching the other two initials of O.N.C. and P.G.C. so we start with what we have."

"I heard Warbucks was going to be there," Nick said. "He brings his own security. It'll be like working around the secret service."

Billionaire Jon Tinker had been nicknamed Daddy Warbucks by the press due to his philanthropic ventures and the business enterprises he created after becoming a Lieutenant Colonel and adopting three kids. None were named Annie, though.

"Sorry I'm late to the party," Josh Carrington said, breezing in. "But I'm up to speed on SGC and the initials slated for assassination."

Dingo sat up. What the hell was Josh doing here? He should be thousands of miles away in Miami with his fiancé, getting ready for a wedding in three and a half weeks.

Josh had perfectly groomed tawny hair and the look of a man suited to be heir apparent to massive family wealth, the result of an adoption gone right in his late teens, but he wore that look with the same nonchalance he did jeans and a T-shirt. And he was a man you wanted watching your back when bullets were flying. He hung up the sport coat, leaving him in a button-down shirt and slacks better suited for a multi-million dollar negotiation, which might be the case with a Carrington.

Dingo could never deal with the many trappings that were part of Josh's life, but his best friend handled it all with ease and still managed to be a deadly operative.

Without a look in Dingo's direction as Josh sat down, Sabrina said, "Thanks for coming in. We're going to be stretched thin on this one."

Josh caught Dingo staring and shrugged as if to say this was what happened when duty called and his fiancé understood.

No, that would not fly. Dingo had to talk to him later.

Sabrina continued. "I made arrangements for the charity event. The team will go undercover as part of the wait staff and additional security. I'm in discussions with event security and Tinker's. As a gubernatorial candidate for California, Perdido has her own personnel, but we believe she's one of the three targets based on intel we've received in the last twenty-four hours. She's tried to keep the stalker issue quiet–"

Dingo lifted a hand and Sabrina stiffened. "Yes?"

Good thing he was sitting on the opposite side of the table from her or he'd have gotten frostbite. "Has Perdido been informed that her life is at risk and going to a public venue is unwise?"

"Yes, but her campaign manager says she's been under threat for months and will not allow cowards to turn her into one. That's a quote."

He nodded and she arched a don't-interrupt-me-again eyebrow.

Man, was she pissed.

Josh shoved a narrowed look at Dingo that raised a feeling he hadn't experienced since being a kid in trouble.

What the hell?

Back then Sabrina would be somewhere close, radiating tension as she plotted a way to save Dingo from whatever punishment he couldn't avoid. At the same time, Josh would be sending Dingo a series of completely undecipherable facial expressions to hint at which lie was the best one to offer.

Thankfully, Josh had finally realized finger signals were far more effective than his nonexistent telepathic ability, but Sabrina still hadn't learned that she couldn't save Dingo or Josh from whatever messes they walked into with eyes wide open.

The truth was that she refused to accept that Dingo couldn't be saved from himself.

He would never have the life Josh, the crazy bastard, had ahead of him, or know what it was like with a woman who loved him the way Trish loved Josh, but that was fine.

Dingo had learned a long time ago not to want what others had, like a family and someone to call his own. He shook his head at wandering down that thought trail, and gave up guessing what was going on with Sabrina and Josh. Good or bad, he'd find out soon enough.

Who was he kidding?

He knew what to expect just as a condemned man knew when his last minutes drew near.

Dingo had missed nothing Sabrina said so far, but she lifted her voice and swung her gaze to take in everyone. "Tanner, Nick, Blade, Ryder and White Hawk will be working the Perdido event. I have one last thing to tell you that was shared with me in the strictest confidence. The body of the man who killed Bergman was found and identified as having intentional scars that may mean he was an Orion Hunter."

"Who found the body?" Dingo asked. "And how do they know it's the same man who killed Bergman?"

"I can't go into that right now."

Are you kidding me? Dingo sat back, trying to figure out where Sabrina would have gotten intel like that, because that meant someone had known about the meet and had tracked the killer who got away.

Fucking Laughton.

Dingo took a closer look at Sabrina. Her jaw was tight from clenching her teeth, a physical tell on her that meant she felt guilty.

Sabrina glared at Dingo for a brief moment.

Dingo lifted his eyebrows in reply. *Yes, I figured out who you've been talking to, Sabrina.*

She moved on with her instructions. "Tanner, would you ask your resource if this scarring is consistent with being an Orion Hunter?"

That resource would be Soo Jin, the woman Tanner had saved from North Korea, and who had helped Tanner and Dingo last month. She was also the woman no one could know was still alive, or that Tanner had her hidden away somewhere.

Tanner nodded and made a note, then asked, "Are we

dealing with the stalker at all or focusing only on a potential assassination attempt?"

"Both," Sabrina answered. "And we can't be obvious, which is why we're entering as staff and additional event security. We don't want to alert the killer to our presence. The threats to Perdido could be one in the same, but as Ryder pointed out, assassins aren't known for sending advance notice."

Nick suggested, "Sounds like the Orion Hunters might be going after Satan's Garden Club. Maybe the hunters don't like the SGC showing up in their city again. This might all be tied to a turf war."

Dingo hoped so, but he didn't like the new addition of Orion Hunters in the picture.

Sabrina wrapped up the meeting.

Before Dingo could question her leaving him to run the operation from the safe house, Sabrina turned to him and Josh. "You two, in my office in five."

She strode through the connecting door that led to her private area, a bedroom and office combo, leaving Josh and Dingo to follow.

Dingo asked Josh, "What are you doing here?"

"She called and said she needed the three of us to meet privately. I got here as soon as I could."

Dingo scratched his chin. "She say anything about being pissed at me?"

"No. Why should she? She's been pissed at you for the past month."

"I came out here to check on Valene while Sabrina thought I was catching some sleep."

"Shit."

"Yep. She covered with the team, making it sound like she sent me out early, but I was already here when she called me."

Josh slanted a stern look at him, but shook his head. "She isn't going to cut you loose."

"She should," Dingo admitted. "I buggared our deal by coming out here without telling her, but I have to find out if Satan's Garden Club has anyone in it from before. Anyone who might know about Valene." He blew out a rush of air and changed the subject. "I may not make the tux fitting."

Josh had stood and started across the room. He halted at that and swung around on Dingo. "Yes, you will, because Trish and I aren't getting married without you and Sabrina there, so don't fuck this up any more than it is."

Dingo scowled. "I'm trying to tell you that I don't want to delay your wedding."

"Do you think Trish will go ahead with it if you aren't there after she made us wait until Ryder got out of prison? I'm ready to marry her and none of you are fucking this up, especially you."

Ryder had been wrongly accused of murder and Trish refused to get married while she knew the team needed to focus on getting him out, which had turned dicey.

Ironically, Ryder ended up married to the FBI agent with the best case against him, while Josh was still not married to Trish.

Seeing Josh all hacked about waiting to get married would be funny if Dingo didn't care, but he did. He'd taken off all those years ago on Valene without a word. He couldn't do that to Josh. "I'm just letting you know that I'm not leaving LA until I'm convinced Valene is safe."

"Then get convinced soon, because your ass has to be in Miami in three weeks to get fitted."

Dingo waved Josh to get moving. Surely he could figure out if there was a real threat to Valene and still be in Miami in time for the fitting.

They walked into Sabrina's office, where she paced. The minute Josh closed the door, she rounded on Dingo. "You have got to get your head out of your ass and stop playing white knight to someone who doesn't care."

"Don't sugarcoat it, Sabrina." Dingo crossed his arms, ready to have this out. "I'm sorry for not telling you but this attitude is exactly why I didn't."

"Oh, this isn't attitude," she warned him. "This is all-out furious. There is nothing in the intelligence chatter about any of Garcia's old team getting back together. Not a word on the street. Why are you overreacting?"

Was he overreacting? "I'm being proactive. That's all."

She looked at Josh. "You can jump in and help anytime."

"Neither one of you will like what I have to say."

"Try me," Sabrina said.

Josh sat down on one of the three leather chairs grouped across the room from a corner computer desk. "You have to leave Dingo alone to make his own mistakes."

Her mouth opened and closed. "Lot of good you are."

"I tried to warn you."

"Thanks, mate," Dingo told Josh, glad to see someone got what was going on.

"Don't thank me, *mate*." Josh turned to Dingo. "She's got a valid point on the SGC. Your coming out here without telling Sabrina, or me, was bullshit. What you had with Valene is over and there's no viable threat, so this is you wanting her back. Nothing more, and you're headed down a path that might really destroy you this time."

Dingo grabbed his head with both hands. "You two need to both stay out of my business."

"Not going to happen," Sabrina snapped. "I will not stand by and watch you put yourself through that again. You two wouldn't stand by while I committed emotional suicide."

Dingo dropped his hands, glad for the new direction he could take in this warped conversation. "Oh, you mean like getting intel from Gage Laughton?"

If she'd expected that, she might have been able to cover her reaction, but her face broadcasted guilty-as-charged right before she shut it down. She'd been busted, but she held her head up defiantly. "You know I get intel from a lot of places. That doesn't change the validity."

"It does for me," Dingo corrected her.

"That's your problem."

"I'll tell you what my problem is. You expecting me to sit here and run the operation from this place when you have plenty of qualified personnel to do that and I'm of more use on the street."

"You don't get a say in how I run this op."

"And you don't get a say in how I run my life," he shoved back at her.

"You two sound like you did when we were kids," Josh noted.

Sabrina and Dingo both said, "Shut up."

Josh lifted his hands. "Never mind."

Dingo was done with this. "You can run the show any way you want, but expecting me to sit here when I can be out tracking information on SGC is stupid."

"Way to go calling her stupid," Josh muttered.

"Want to talk stupid?" Sabrina asked. "Stupid is doing the same thing over and over while expecting a different result."

Dingo caught her meaning about him seeing Valene again, but he was done discussing Valene. And he was done fighting with Sabrina. "What's it going to take to call a truce, Sabrina?"

"Did you find Pete?"

"No."

She was silent, looking at him while she considered her answer. "If I give you time right now to go convince yourself that this woman is not under threat, can you do that and come back with your head in the right position and do your part on this team?"

As in his head not up his ass? He wanted to believe he could do that, so he said, "Yes."

"Okay, here's my truce. You do that and be back here by midnight, get a decent night's sleep and be ready to roll before daylight. If not, then our only other option is to contact the FBI and tell them Eklund's in danger from a past operation. They'll put her in protective custody and keep her there until we can determine if the threat is real."

If Dingo thought Valene would go willingly into WITSEC, he'd have suggested that first thing yesterday. He'd hoped she would consider taking a few days to stay out of sight in a safe place he chose, but she'd said she was caring for someone sick. Convincing her to hand that responsibility over to someone else would be much tougher than taking her away from work. She was loyal as the day was long. If Dingo called the FBI in to take Valene into protective custody and away from someone depending on her, she'd want blood.

Shit. This was not what he wanted, but this was also an

argument he couldn't win. "If I say I don't want anyone to interfere, you'll still do what you want."

"Before you get pissed at me–"

"Too late," he muttered, drawing a sharp look before Sabrina continued.

"I'm being generous when I want to have *you* in lock down. I know you'll go to her no matter what I say. When you do, ask her about her friend Charlie."

Josh said, "Sabrina!"

"Don't Sabrina me. Dingo needs to know."

Dingo's gaze bounced from Josh to Sabrina. "Know what?"

"That Valene may not be as innocent as you think. She's doing business with a man whose background of being an international antiquities broker doesn't pan out."

"You've been investigating Valene?" Dingo asked, unable to keep the disappointment out of his voice.

"You're sure as hell not objective about her or you'd have found out. You'd be thinking like an operative and not with your dick."

"Who's Charlie?" Dingo asked.

"I'll let you figure that one out for yourself, but here's a tip. With the exception of our generous payment for services rendered four weeks ago, Valene hasn't deposited over a thousand dollars in her checking account at one time in the past year. Yet a fifty thousand dollar deposit just hit her account today."

"So now she can't earn a living?" Dingo snapped. If he was not objective, a fair accusation, then Sabrina was prejudiced against Valene, an equally fair assessment. Sabrina would love nothing better than to find something on Valene that would send Valene far away from Dingo.

"It was from an offshore bank. Who pays for anything legal through offshore banks, Dingo?"

That did surprise him, but while most people moving money to offshore accounts were either dodging taxes or dealing in nefarious ventures, that still did not mean that Valene had committed any crime. In fact, he'd be shocked if some of the high rollers she'd dealt with years ago didn't hide money offshore.

Hell, Slye had numerous offshore accounts they could pull from in emergencies if they were out of the country, not to mention money stashed in foreign banks for quick access when they were on ops, but mentioning that would get him nowhere.

Sabrina was worse than a bulldog with a meaty bone. She kept gnawing at him. "That should raise red flags on her if you'd take off your blinders. But I'm willing to hear a reasonable explanation if you can produce one."

Dingo swung his gaze to Josh who said, "Sorry, Dingo, but what Sabrina said is true."

"You both went behind my back to dig around on Valene? How would you feel if I took it on myself to go snooping into your fiancé's business, or her brother's, without saying a word to you first?" Then he turned on Sabrina. "What about Gage? We've never pulled out all the stops to go after him and drag his ass to a locked-down location and get some answers? You're even collaborating with the bastard."

Josh looked remorseful and ready to explain, but Sabrina pounced and swung the whole thing back on Dingo. "Really? What I do in the best interest of my teams is not up for discussion. You fly out here without a word to let us know where you were. We're in a business where bodies disappear when people die, and *still* you feel justified in being angry at me for watching your back? If you were even a little objective you'd see her in a different light. If you're so sure she's at risk from SGC, then why hasn't anyone gotten to her yet?"

Dingo couldn't answer that. He'd been too thankful every minute that no one had harmed Valene to look at all this any other way. Sabrina was right about one thing. If she wanted him to believe Valene was guilty of something criminal, then he wasn't the least-bit open minded.

But having a handful of suspicious details rammed in his face made it hard to ignore what Sabrina had said.

He had to accept her challenge and force Sabrina to stop making Valene out to be someone bad. He couldn't do that without information.

It sickened him to treat Valene the way he'd treat a perp and have to dig around for dirt on her. That meant tossing her in with the rest of the garbage rotting in his soul. Being with Valene in the past had been like stepping out of all this filth and blood and into somewhere full of light and life.

Before he flipped the switch in his head that would turn her into just one more name and set of details, before he destroyed what she meant to him, he had to get out of here and clear his head.

He stood there, fighting to keep from letting words out that could never be unheard. He told Sabrina, "The truce stands until five in the morning. Don't call me. Don't come near me. In the meantime, stay out of my business and Valene's life, and just for the record," he said, pointing at himself. "This isn't anger. This is bone-deep disappointment in the two people I trusted most."

He walked out of the silent room, unsure what his next move was, because Sabrina had succeeded at something he'd have never thought possible, or he wouldn't have taken a bullet seven years ago to gain Garcia's attention.

Sabrina had succeeded at shaking his faith in Valene.

Chapter 9

VALENE WALKED UP the third-floor flight of creaking, wooden steps to her apartment and tried to come to terms with facing yet another part of her past.

Like Dingo wasn't enough for one day,

Noise across the hall from her door sounded as though her neighbors were listening to the baseball game, a regular Wednesday night event in the lives of normal people.

Normal was boring.

She'd keep telling herself that and ignore the fact that she was exhausted but her day wasn't done. Not when she had yet to receive one positive reply from all the calls she'd made.

It wasn't as though she had an endless supply of resources. With enough time, she could locate new ones to make up for the one she'd been avoiding, but Smith's deadline loomed heavier by the minute.

There'd been no word on the artifact from any of her best sources. She was going to have to suck it up and ask for help from the one person who could absolutely help her.

He also happened to be the one person she absolutely wanted to avoid.

In truth, he didn't want to see her either. Her ex-husband, Henri Roche, met all her resource qualifications of being discreet, of being local, and of being well connected in the high-end antiques community.

But the number one reason she needed him? He had an in-house expert on Galileo who would know if someone was shopping this specific scroll.

She was damn good in her field, but her ego could admit that Henri's expert knew more about Galileo.

Plus Henri needed the money.

But would that be enough to convince him to work with her when they weren't even on speaking terms?

She'd gone to her next-best source, whose expert was a couple of steps down from Henri's, but Aram had already locked that source up for some special project.

Please tell me Aram is not involved with the scroll.

The key stuck in her tarnished door lock. Again. She jiggled it, cursed it, beat on it and finally the lock gave in to her threats.

With the sun clocking out for another day, her apartment was barely navigable through the swath of shadows. She preferred that over bright lights shining across a home that reminded her of how much she'd lost in recent years. She'd never been able to call this place shabby chic because the few pieces of furniture she owned now were just crap.

Can't dress up crap by changing the name.

She headed toward the kitchen, but stopped in her tracks. A light filtered from the opening.

That hadn't been on this morning.

She didn't leave *any* lights on. She was as miserly spending money for her own benefit as a retiree on a tight pension. Every dollar she saved was one more dollar she could use to keep her dad in decent care.

Stepping back out of the doorway to pull her Walther .380 from her purse, she did a quick sweep of the space around her and slipped silently toward the kitchen. *I'm going to feel like an idiot sneaking up on an empty room.*

When she peeked around the corner, no one was there.

Thunking her forehead with her gun hand, she placed the weapon back into her purse and yawned. Maybe she *had* left the stove vent light on. Her front door had been locked and even *she* couldn't get in the place with a key some days. She tossed her purse on the counter and turned toward the bedroom.

She was dead tired, but this was only a pit stop for a shower before she faced Henri if he was still at work. Yes, she was vain enough to want to look smoking when she walked into his shop.

He'd been the one to bail on their marriage.

She didn't have a lot of pride left when it came to doing

whatever was required to insure her father survived, but she would not suffer Henri's pity when she faced him.

Not when he was blissfully happy in his new relationship.

She unzipped her pants, stepping out of them on the way to her bedroom, and undid the buttons on her jacket. Second time wearing that outfit. She'd have to bite the bullet and drop it at the dry cleaners.

She tossed the clothes next to the dresser on her left as soon as she entered her dark bedroom, a place even more depressing than the rest of this dump.

She'd made two steps toward the bathroom and had reached around to unclip her bra when she heard, "Stop, Valene."

Her brain froze with instinctive fear for two seconds. That was all it took for her mind to sort through the voices she'd heard today and pin the tail on that donkey. "What the hell is it with you?"

When she turned around, her eyes had adjusted to make out a shape in the corner. He was propped against the wall with his arms crossed, just the way he'd been the last time she'd found him in her bedroom. That was a long time and a river of heartache ago.

Long enough that her body shouldn't go into happy-to-see-Dingo mode just because he was four steps away.

Four steps and seven years.

"I need to talk to you, Val."

She'd held onto her composure and a tide of emotions balled up inside her from the first time she'd seen him today, but he'd caught her off guard, showing up here.

"Now?" she said. "No. You had your chance *years* ago and you couldn't waste the time to call me and tell me you were leaving. No more talking. I'm so over this you have no idea."

She was so lying he had no idea.

Her throat was tight with wanting to yell at him for breaking her heart, even after all this time. She hadn't been nearly as hurt when Henri told her the marriage was over.

And no, she didn't want to think about how wrong that sounded.

"I'm sorry I didn't call you back then, but I couldn't."

She wanted to pretend this didn't matter, that just hearing his voice didn't brush pleasure across her mind the way his hands used to stroke her skin. But seeing him again, even in this crummy bedroom in her crappy apartment, stirred up memories she'd failed to bury after all.

But she had just enough pride left to shut him down.

"You know what, Dingo? I don't give a damn about you being sorry now. I don't believe you couldn't call me. I don't care what happened back then. I moved on."

The shadow shape of Dingo lifted away from the wall. "You got married as soon as I left."

"It was almost a *year* later!" Why had she said that? She wasn't the one who had to apologize.

"Didn't take you long to forget me."

The sound of longing in his voice struck hard, but he didn't get to question her choices, no matter how bad they'd been in retrospect. "It wasn't as though you ever wanted any more from me, Dingo, so what's your point?" she asked, sounding flippant to cover the pained sounds her heart was making.

Dingo unfolded his arms to tuck his hands into the front pockets of his jeans. He had to keep them from reaching for her to soothe the pain she kept trying to hide with her words.

He'd never forgive himself for what he did to her, but until now he'd fooled himself into thinking she might.

"What's the matter, Dingo? Cat got your tongue or don't you have a point to make?"

He had something to say, but if he started on that right now it would end with her calling him a liar, or with the two of them tangled up in bed like past fights always ended.

His gaze strayed to the bed again.

What had happened to her luxury apartment downtown? And all the beautiful antiques she'd constantly brought home to enjoy before she sold them?

Guilt chipped away at him, laughing at his honor for not

delving into Valene's personal life. Part of it had been that he truly wouldn't invade her privacy any more than he'd invade someone's mind if he could read minds.

The other part that would have stopped him even if he hadn't cared about her privacy?

Fear of turning what was left of his heart into a black stump incapable of feeling anything.

But damn, look at this place.

The only thing antique in this place might be that miserable lock he'd had a hell of a time picking. That reminded him he wasn't here to explain what happened when he'd disappeared years ago. Much as he'd like to deal with that now and clear the air, the one thing he'd learned from back then was to give Valene as little information as possible or she'd dig up a death sentence.

"You're right, Val. I admit that I never gave you reason to think any more was ever going to happen between us than late night rendezvous."

She looked away, squinting her eyes shut tight.

Still hurting.

Why couldn't he have Josh's silver-tongued-devil gift?

What could Dingo do to make this easier for Valene?

She turned back to him, chin jacked up and attitude following close behind. "Now that we have all that cleared up, what exactly do you want so I can get on with my life?"

Nothing had been cleared up, but he'd come here with a plan. Much as he hated to give credence to what Sabrina had said, he wasn't leaving without finding out about Charlie. "I was serious this morning. I'm worried about you, Val."

"Oh, puhlease! You can't pull this crap just because you don't like seeing me with another man."

Ouch. Who knew a heart could talk?

Was she with somebody else? "Are you involved with someone?"

"That's really none of your business is it?"

No, but that didn't stop the idea of her with someone else from eating at him. "Fine. You're right. None of my business who you're shagging."

"I didn't say I was–"

"You're not?" Damn. Had he really asked that?

She crossed her arms and squared her jaw. "You are so annoying. What do you want?"

You. He clamped his lips shut to keep from allowing that word to climb out and screw this up any worse. "I just want you to be safe. If you're, uh, seeing someone, then he might be at risk too." Like if the buggar touched Val when Dingo was watching.

"I knew it."

He didn't like the sound of that. "What?"

"You're stalking me and Charlie, aren't you?"

"Charlie? Who's he?" Dingo forced himself to stay put and not beat his head against the wall. That would be easier than encouraging her to talk about being with another man.

She doesn't belong to you. Got it.

"Charlie's my best client right now."

"How much do you know about this client?" Sure, he could pretend that he was hunting intel to do with his mission, but the truth is he was a sick bastard who wanted to know just who had taken his place this time.

That didn't mean he wouldn't know whatever Sabrina knew, and maybe more, the minute Dingo got a little time with his laptop.

"I know everything I need to know about Charlie," she stonewalled. "We work together a lot, or do you already know that by snooping on me?"

He wanted to shout at her that she was being too trusting, but then she'd turn that one on Dingo. He pushed off the wall. "How often do you work together? Like today?"

Valene must have taken his move as a signal for combat. She surged forward, shouting, "You can*not* come in here and ask me questions about my life or who I see for lunch."

Dingo didn't want her to throw him out, but if she pushed it, he'd leave. Then what? He couldn't tell her about Satan's Garden Club or she'd dive into that with both feet and draw their attention for sure. "I'm not stalking you, Val, but the group that Giuseppe was connected to has resurfaced. There's a chance they might snatch you off the street."

That got her attention. "Why would they come after me now when no one cared seven years ago?"

How could he tell her that he'd taken a bullet and suffered much worse so that Garcia would leave her alone? Then he'd have to tell her why he'd done all that. She'd be devastated with guilt because she'd feel responsible.

Hadn't he hurt her enough? "I can't answer that, because I don't know what this group is after. My people are hunting them." He let that sink in.

"I'll ask the police to make some rounds here."

"If they come for you, the police won't stop them."

"What about if they come for you?" She crossed her arms, giving him a look much like Sabrina's.

"I'm prepared, because this is what I do. But I'm concerned about *your* safety so I'm just asking how long you've known this guy."

"Long enough."

Dingo changed his tactics. "These people can infiltrate a lot of places. You don't want to find out you've been dealing with a criminal, do you?"

She dropped her arms and curled her fists. "Charlie is *not* a criminal. I investigated him myself and checked his references. Don't you dare come here threatening him," she closed the distance between them, getting right up in his face. "I'm trained in two different martial arts. I'm a damn good shot. This sounds like smoke and mirrors. Unless you have hard evidence to show me, do not screw up my relationship with this client or I will not be responsible for my actions. Do you get that?"

He got it. And he could ignore a lot of things, but seeing her all fierce and ready to do battle only turned him on. He'd spent many a night tweaking her temper just for the passion that followed.

His body came alive with her this close.

All systems go and target locked.

If he touched her right now, though, she'd try to break his arm or he might hurt her accidentally by defending his favorite parts.

Dingo backed up, but he was cornered. Not a smart place to be if Valene decided to make him pay for showing up here and breaking into her place.

Did that matter to his dick that was giving her a standing ovation? Not one bit.

She poked him hard in the chest. Val liked using that finger. "This has to stop. You're making me crazy, Dingo."

Welcome to my world.

She pushed again and his body begged her to use all those wild fingers on him.

When she jabbed a third time, Dingo grabbed her wrist, holding his breath that she wouldn't jerk it away.

He could feel her pulse racing.

His was doing its own version of heading for the checkered flag on a NASCAR straightaway.

Out of pure insanity, he started rubbing his thumb softly across her skin. He could smell her. He'd always been able to identify her just from her scent.

Now she vibrated with a mix of anxiety and anger, and her shallow breaths interrupted the silence piling up between them.

Dingo tried to remember why he was here, but the call of her body kept sidetracking him.

He swallowed and dug around for some way to reach past her anger. Words weren't his forte, but when he spoke it was in the same low voice he'd once used to wake her before daylight on mornings when he showed up unexpectedly.

"I don't want to fight with you." He wanted to kiss more than he wanted anything else at this moment, but he hadn't come here for that. Not as his primary objective, anyway. "I'm not trying to interfere in your life. You can hate me all you want, but please don't lock me out right now when I can't sleep for fear that I won't be here when you need me."

She'd either hear him out or kick him out.

What worried him was option three brewing behind those eyes that were showing no sign of surrender.

If he kissed her, would it thaw the ice formed around her heart, or would it destroy his one shot at staying close to her?

Or was he just rationalizing a way to feel her close to him after an eternity apart?

Yeah, he knew the answer to that one.

Chapter 10

VALENE SUCKED IN another shaky breath.

How could Dingo show up again in her life and wreck the emotional walls that she barely held together with willpower and fear?

She was determined to never hurt again as deeply as when he'd left without a word.

And she was terrified that the only person who could make her lose that battle stood an inch away, touching her.

Not really touching her the way she wanted, but just this small contact had her insides quivering for more. The feel of his hands dredged up memories of him waking her with tender kisses, holding her in his arms, in her bed, when she'd gone to sleep on the sofa.

She'd ask, *When'd you get here?*

An hour ago.

Why didn't you wake me?

I was content to watch you sleep. He'd kiss her and add, *I'm just happy to be with you when I can.*

He'd say those things, squeezing her heart until she couldn't breathe.

Damn him for what he'd given her then taken away.

Having him here, close enough to kiss again, had her emotions under siege. She couldn't afford to lose this war.

His free hand came up slowly until his knuckles brushed softly across her cheek.

She clenched her eyes shut. Had that last breath come out on a shudder? Way to hide her feelings. Her eyes burned, but no tear had better dare slip out.

Dingo had gotten all of the tears that she intended to donate.

"I can't go there again, Dingo." Yes, that was her pleading for him to stop. She clearly couldn't.

"I never meant to hurt you, Val."

"Little late for that." She didn't even try to hide the bitterness swimming through those words.

His fingers grazed her ear then swept down her neck.

She shivered and cursed herself. If she wanted to prove he no longer had a hold on her heart, then that had been a major fail. She wanted to touch him so much it hurt physically to stand this close to him. "Don't, Dingo."

"Don't what?" He leaned in and whispered close to her ear. His lips grazed her neck then her chin.

Now would be a great time to show him the new defense moves she'd learned since the last time they were this close. She used to come home excited to show off and impress him, but he wouldn't expect the one she had in mind that would bloody his nose and send him home limping.

Any time now she'd unleash Valene the Terminator on him.

Any minute now. Just as soon as he stopped kissing her neck.

God she missed his lips.

Her next breath came out with soft keening.

He paused.

Well, hell, now they both knew how much he was affecting her. If he leaned in any closer he'd feel the hard tips of her nipples that had thrown in the white flag without even trying to ignore him.

"I've missed you, Val." His words smoked through her mind and wrapped around her senses, warm and soothing.

It had been so long since she'd felt cared for, since a man had really touched her. And no man's touch had ever been anything close to Dingo's, to the way he sent her body screaming with need.

He let go of her hand and now had both of his in her hair, holding her carefully as he placed kisses in perfect spots along her cheek.

Years of anger slid away, leaving a raw yearning that had never disappeared. Was this his way of letting her know she meant more than he'd ever let on? Dingo had shown her he cared in so many ways, but he'd never uttered words that promised anything more than the moment he was with her.

How could she trust him now?

Trust that he was here only for her?

"I can't ever get enough of you, Val."

And with that admission, he must have decided he'd given her fair warning, and captured her mouth.

She reached around his neck and murmured, "I'm glad you're back."

"You and me both." He kissed her, taking her mouth and body prisoner.

When Dingo started to pull away, Val followed him, taking back the mouth he'd offered. He jumped right back in where he'd paused, running his hands up her shoulders and gripping her to him. It had always been this way with him. He let a woman know she was in the arms of a man who wasn't letting go, at least not while he was focused on her.

There was no place better than being under the intense scrutiny of Dingo when he had nothing but making love on his mind.

He had her bra unclasped and she shook it off, letting it fall to the floor. She gripped his arms and yanked, pulling him down on top of her when she fell backwards onto the bed.

Please don't break, bed.

They were draped half on and half off.

Her panties slid down her legs and his fingers took their place, stroking through the wet heat. He clamped his mouth on her breast and she clawed at his shoulders.

He still had on his shirt.

She was too far gone, headed for Oh-My-God Land to care about being the only naked one in the room right now.

His tongue tortured first one nipple, then moved to the other one. She grabbed his hair, loving that it was longer again. When his finger drove inside her she clenched it and lifted her hips, urging him to end this need consuming her.

He hadn't forgotten a thing about her. He stroked over the bundle of nerves waiting in a frenzied panic for him and sucked her breast at the same time, then touched her just the way only he knew how to do, and her climax ripped her in half, going on and on and on.

He never stopped kissing her while she slowly came back down to land on Earth again.

Lips danced over her breasts and she felt an aftershock buzz. She laughed. "Stop or I'll have cardiac arrest. It's been too long."

"Oh?" He held himself up with his arms, dropping his head to keep teasing her.

She was not discussing her sexual drought. His ego didn't need stroking, but that erection bumping against her did.

He said, "Your phone is singing a tune."

Really? She listened when the ringtone played. Henri's. That was a good sign and reason for her to be diving for the phone, but she was barely breathing. "It's business. I'll call him back."

Dingo peppered kisses across her face then stopped again. "Is it Charlie? You should let me check him out. Introduce me to him."

Charlie? She pulled her head back from Dingo. "Are you really going there with me?"

"Yes, I am. I want to know who he is and where he came from," Dingo said, stumbling over his words as if he was trying to figure out what to say.

Talk about a cold slap of reality. "You want to investigate Charlie to see if he's connected to this *other* group who you won't name but keep trying to convince me is a threat?"

Dingo's head popped up and via what little light permeated this darkness she saw some thought slide into home plate. Dingo nodded. "Actually, I do."

She shoved away from him, breaking the heated contact.

The past came roaring back again, but not the sexy parts. No, this was a reminder of how their connection had been all about her ability to research anything and anyone.

Was he here for her?

Was he here for work?

Was he giving her a line of crap so she'd let him back into her life again, and trying to drive a wedge between her and Charlie to make sure no other guy was in the way?

Or was Dingo telling her the truth?

She might know if she knew Dingo better, but she didn't. The one person in all this she had no reason to believe was him.

She'd spent years making herself accept that she'd been nothing more than a resource and convenient lay for him. One kiss and all that hard work to regain her sanity had gone flying out the window.

"What is it that you really want, Dingo? This visit is clearly not about me or us, but something you have cooking. Some project or mission or whatever the hell 007 crap you have going on."

"Val, you don't understand–"

"You're right. I don't understand and I'm sick to death of guessing all the time. Get up!"

He pushed to his feet.

It was hard to carry off dignified when she stood bare to the world so she reached over for her kimono robe that lived at the foot of her bed and pulled it on, talking as she did.

"You either come clean and tell me exactly what is going on right now, including names and specifics, or get the hell out."

He huffed a breath filled with exasperation. "I can't tell you some things–"

Talk about déjà vu. She yanked the tie on her belt and shouted, "Get. Out!"

"I'm not going to leave you exposed to a risk."

That again? Had he forgotten that when someone triggered her temper the best place to be was thousands of miles away? "Right now, *you* are the biggest danger in my life if you go near Charlie. He's very important to me."

Dingo wiped his hands over his face and looked around the room then back at Valene. "If he's such a bloody special client, what are you doing with the money? Why are you living here?"

Humiliation boiled up her throat. "Sorry it's not the plush apartment you frequented years ago."

"I don't give a damn what your apartment looks like, but

something has clearly changed since I was here last. What happened?"

She clenched her teeth. "If you really cared, you'd have been around to know the answer to that. Leave or I'm calling the police and you should remember enough about me to know when I'm not bluffing."

Chapter 11

DINGO DIDN'T SAY anything at first, but when he moved toward the door he paused to look back at Valene standing in the middle of this crappy apartment. He'd thought convincing her that Charlie might not be above board had been a bloody brilliant idea.

Evidently not.

He surprised himself by being able to talk with his heart lodged in his throat. "I do care about you, Val, and I *did* care before. There's a lot you don't know that happened in my life, too."

"Whose fault is that?"

"Mine. I can't change the last seven years, but I'm trying to do right by you now. I wish you'd believe me."

"When you're ready to tell me the truth, everything involved in you being here right down to names of the mystery group, then I'll consider listening, but that doesn't mean I'll believe you or dance around on your puppet strings. Not again."

She was no one's puppet, least of all his.

"You know it was never like that between us," he argued softly. "I never wanted to control you. Never tried to box you in or tie you down. I'm sorry I had to leave without telling you, but talking to you back then would have gotten you hurt ... or killed." He didn't want to leave, but if he showed up at the safe house now, he could slip away again before anyone figured out he hadn't been gone all night. "Are you in for the evening, Val?"

"That's none of your business."

True, but he waited silently on her answer.

She grumbled, "Yes. If I have any more unexpected guests, I'm shooting first and talking later."

He got that message loud and clear. "I'll try to end this threat as soon as I can and watch over you from a distance, but I won't promise to stay out of your life. If you put a restraining order on me, it will make it harder to protect you, but it won't stop me. Not if I need to get to you. Nothing can stop me from keeping you from harm."

The silence following that admission sucked the air from the room. That had to be the reason it hurt so much to breathe.

He was torn between walking out the door and walking back to her, but he knew her too well to believe he could patch the bridge that had just crashed between them.

He stepped out and closed the door silently behind him.

⸺⸺ ∾ ⸺⸺

Valene stared at the empty space Dingo had left. A moment ago, he'd filled up all the lonely parts of her apartment. Every breath dragged a reminder of Dingo back through her body.

She wanted to believe what he was saying, but once again he expected blind faith out of her and gave nothing in return.

Why couldn't you give me something, Dingo?

The distance between them physically couldn't be closed again until he was willing to meet her emotionally. She wouldn't survive another round of dropping her defenses and letting him back in for days or a month only to have him saunter off without a word again.

She just stood there, too drained to finish undressing or to fall on the bed in a heap of misery. She'd call Henri back and meet him in the morning.

Not because she'd told Dingo she was staying home, either.

She was tired and would be more up for facing Henri tomorrow.

Her phone played Bon Jovi's "*You Give Love A Bad Name*" ringtone.

She muttered, "Moment's over, back to the chaos." She got her phone from her purse and cut the second play of the ringtone short. "Did you get my message, Henri?"

"Yes, I did. I also received one from Aram. Any chance you two are after the same item?"

That son of a bitch. "Do not deal with him."

"I need the money, Va-*lene*," he said, treating her name like a rubber band he stretched for amusement. "You and I have not done business in a long time. I can't risk losing money by turning down what is a certainty over a maybe."

"I've got *the* deal of the year right now. Do not mess this up by talking to Aram."

"He said if he did not come by before I leave tonight, he'd be here in the morning."

That answered her question of whether Henri was still at work. "Meet me first."

Henri took his time responding. "It's late. I've had a long day and am still here only because I needed to sort through some inventory. Be here in thirty minutes. That's all I'm willing to wait and I make no promises. I'm calling you back only out of professional etiquette. Do not make me regret that by causing me to miss an opportunity to make money that I need."

Henri knew her father had been sick, but she hadn't told him about the recent bad turn of events or that she had to fork over ten grand for a special treatment plan, so she couldn't curse Henri for being self-centered.

She told him, "Just do me one favor and hear me out before you meet with Aram. Please."

"Thirty minutes." He hung up.

Showers were overrated. She cleaned up quickly and set a new land speed record for traveling through LA during the late rush hour. A competitive runner could have arrived ahead of her if not for the exhaust fumes that would have taken down the healthiest athlete.

She had a moment of guilt for telling Dingo she was staying in, but he'd lied to her time and again, if not directly, then by omission. She didn't have to explain her schedule to anyone.

When Highway 110 ended north of LA, it dropped her in Pasadena, a cozy area with history and panache.

A wave of longing hit her hard.

She didn't miss being married, which was odd to admit sometimes, but she did miss living here in her gorgeous condo with a view of the mountains. Their home had been filled with antiques she'd thought of as her children, and Henri had been just as attached. Each purchase had been chosen for a reason beyond financial value and came with history that told stories of times long past.

Her furniture had been more interesting than a lot of people she knew.

Henri no longer lived in luxury either, but he'd sunk all of his savings into a specialty shop with his new love, an expert on maps and rare documents, especially anything relating to Galileo.

If not for his expert, Valene wouldn't be preparing herself to beg her ex-husband.

She'd do it, though.

When she'd swung by to see her dad today, he'd agreed to the treatment program as long as she swore to him it would not sink her financially. A high power bill could do that these days, but she'd answered honestly when she'd told him she had a powerful client with an unusual request.

One that would not just pay well, but help put her back on top of her game again.

That news had brought light back into her dad's eyes.

She hadn't shared that she was hunting for a scroll practically no one knew about, but the main reason she didn't was because drugs affected her dad to the point that he babbled at times. In his right mind, she could've trusted him without putting herself at risk with Smith or the Vatican.

Pulling into a strip center, she parked in front of *Lost Adventura*, the middle business in a single-level building that also housed an insurance office on one side and a dog groomer on the other.

The only redeeming value to this place was the low cost per square foot.

Henri knew how important location was for antiques or antiquities sales, but he couldn't afford to be in the center of the Pasadena historic area where his operation might thrive. He'd sunk his savings into inventory of rare maps and documents. He was banking heavily on his new partner, who brought the kind of knowledge of those specific items that was a step beyond Valene's expertise, much as she hated to admit it.

Henri should be thrilled she wanted to tap into that cornucopia of information, right?

She took it as a positive sign that she didn't see Aram's car as she locked hers and walked across pavement that hadn't been maintained in so long the striped lines were gone.

She shook her head at Henri.

He'd tried to convince her to open a storefront with him when they were together. He wanted a place of business, because Henri needed the structure of going in to work every day at the same place and the same time.

That had been just one more issue between them.

It was clearly not an issue in his new relationship.

He'd never understood that Val liked having no idea where she was going to be from day to day or what her next contract would bring. Her conscience snorted at that.

She *had* liked that way of life at one time.

Back when she had people waiting in line for her services.

Gas lamps mounted on each side of *Lost Adventura's* entrance flickered light on the exterior wall. The front was covered with vintage bricks, giving the façade a timeworn appearance. Victorian trim ran across the top and down the sides, and around the two tall, narrow windows to the left of the door. The standard shopping center glass-and-metal door had been replaced with one made of weathered oak, bleached by age and carved with a lion's profile. It swung on black hinges shaped as tridents.

She pulled the door open using the curved iron handle, then stepped over the threshold, pausing to take in how the inside contradicted the outside beyond the brick fascia.

To Henri's credit, the minute she entered the shop it was as if she'd passed through a rift in time. She inhaled the rich fragrance of ancient history clinging to artifacts that had traveled across century upon century.

Light filled the space, glowing everywhere and nowhere.

Henri had an unmatched touch for subtle lighting that had complimented their vintage furnishings back when.

The room before her unfolded with eighteenth century bookcases placed strategically at intervals along the walls, and three sitting areas cordoned off with narrow burgundy curtains drawn back on each side. The closest alcove offered cushy sofas surrounding a beautiful red-lacquered tea table. Sixteenth century Chinese. At the rear of the room, a huge architect's drafting table had been placed beneath a spotlight where someone could unroll a fragile map.

Or a scroll.

Her gaze halted on the beautiful man who appeared next to the drawing table. His hair had once been bright red, but had turned more cinnamon as he'd aged. Sports had never been his calling, which left him with a trim body that could wear any suit with style and grace, such as the dark blue one he had on today. His eyes were the shade of green that reminded her of spring, but Henri's smile had been his best attribute.

Something he wasn't sharing with her right now.

His face was impassive as ever. The unflappable Henri.

"*Bonjour*, Valene," he said, strolling forward with that same lazy gait that had driven the girls in high school as crazy as when he spoke his smoky French.

Valene used to tease him that he didn't sound sexy to her. He'd scowl and threaten to give up their friendship until she admitted his voice was the ultimate.

Friendship. Such a simple word that, to a high school student, wielded great power, or great anguish, in equal measures, and still did. "Hello Henri. Your shop is beautiful."

He dipped his head politely in acknowledgment, but not before she saw how much her compliment meant.

She should have come by sooner, but she hadn't been in the best frame of mind for a while, and could admit she hadn't been up to seeing Henri happy when she was so miserable.

But she should have forced herself to be the bigger person for the sake of their friendship and might have done so if they hadn't been on bad terms for so long.

That was her fault, because of all she'd said to him in anger.

He waved her toward a sitting area that allowed them both a view of the shop. Once she was seated, he said, "I wondered when you would deem us worthy of a visit."

And here she'd been feeling glad to see him and beating herself mentally for not stopping by sooner. "I've been busy."

He flipped his hand in an I-suppose gesture.

She narrowed her eyes at him. "I sent you congratulations flowers when you opened your doors."

"They arrived as intended. I wrote you a thank you note."

He had a burr up his backside and she might as well deal with that so they could talk business. "Clearly I'm missing what I did wrong."

"It is not that I lack appreciation for the gesture, but there are two of us here and only one name was noted on the florist's card."

Is he seriously put out because I didn't include my replacement's name on the card?

Their breakup had been civil. Almost too civil. On his part at least. She'd had a hard time showing any restraint when it came to sharing her view on the matter.

To be fair, she hadn't suffered after he left, not like when Dingo had gone, but she'd lost her best friend since high school. For Henri to expect her to be chummy with his new love was a bit much even for him.

Don't lose sight of the goal. Her dad had told her that often.

"I didn't mean to slight anyone, Henri. I sent the bouquet for the *shop*, which should have encompassed you and everything in here."

Besides, you haven't kept up with my life either, she wanted to say, but that would only start an argument. Seven years ago, they'd shared grief and secrets. She'd promised herself on the way here that she would do her part to behave professionally, try to fix the damage to their friendship and not bring past history into this meeting.

Henri could help her out by meeting her halfway.

"It's neither here nor there," Henri said, dismissing her explanation with a handful of words.

Evidently he was content to remain business associates.

She shouldn't feel hurt, but why didn't anyone else miss having her in their life the way she missed them? With the exception of her father, they'd all left.

Maybe it's all me.

If that was the case, she was doomed to be alone, because she had no idea what she was doing wrong.

You have a temper with a micro fuse.

Right. There was that.

"What did you and Aram fight over this time, Valene?"

"Nothing, because Aram is not in on this deal. *I* have an exclusive." She sure as hell hoped she did. "He doesn't even know what I'm looking for and I've signed a nondisclosure so I have to be very careful with sharing information."

"He claims to be looking for a scroll."

Was it possible that Aram *did* know about the scroll, or had Mr. Smith gone to her sub-par competition to play both of them and see who came up with it first? That didn't make sense if Smith really wanted to keep a lid on this.

"What scroll?" she asked carefully.

Henri smiled, a dazzling vision of perfection from his pearly-white teeth to the shape of his mouth. She'd always appreciated how stunning he was physically, but when she compared him with Dingo, she'd never wanted Henri the way she'd wanted Dingo. *That* bordered on addiction.

Dingo's lips were completely different from Henri's. A mouth meant to burn away all inhibitions.

It took more effort than it should have for her to dismiss that thought, but Henri helped out when he snipped, "Ah, well, if the scroll is not what you seek then please continue as it can only benefit me to have two potential clients in urgent need of an item."

She counted to ten.

A total waste of time.

Dealing with Henri required the ability to count infinitely. It would only escalate once she dropped her next little bomb.

"I am looking for a specific scroll and I'll give you the details, but you'll have to sign a nondisclosure that covers you and anyone involved in the *Lost Adventura* shop."

His calm dissolved beneath a flat gaze. "Are you questioning my integrity?"

"Never."

"But you expect me to sign something to insure I don't break client confidentiality."

"Yes. I'm covering both my butt, and yours, because if anyone does leak word of this project it will not go well for the person who did. There's a lot of money at stake." Now was the time to spin the tables on Henri and make him come to her, plus ferret out whether Henri knew what scroll she was after. "If you're not interested, just say so, and I'll let you work out something with Aram."

He lifted a finger to his chin, thinking.

Not so quick with the comebacks this time, huh? If they were playing chess, she'd have announced, "Check," but gloating would be a dead giveaway that she felt on top of the negotiations.

Plus she was in no position to gloat when she was coming to him with her hand out.

Henri had known her a very long time, which meant he could pick up on a sign of what she was thinking, like flexing her jaw when she became anxious to get moving. Or when she tapped her fingers, even one, he'd know she was growing impatient.

Those were easy clues.

Dingo had learned her tells immediately and she was pretty sure he knew about some she hadn't figured out yet.

But she and Henri had no secrets when it came to reading each other. She hoped the time apart had dulled his memory, but in case it hadn't, she had to watch herself not to allow her pulse to race around him, because she had a vein in her neck that ticked with each beat of her heart. If she didn't stay calm, he'd realize just how important it was to wrap him up as her resource for this scroll.

But she was prepared for his scrutiny this time.

She'd trained hard in Krav Maga for the past three years by trading for consultation. She'd located and negotiated the agreement on a seventeenth century sword for a Krav Maga instructor who couldn't afford for her to handle the transaction if she'd charged him a fee. She hadn't actually needed more defense training, but she *had* needed the inner calm that she'd gained in the middle of an emotional apocalypse.

Henri said, "I agree to sign your nondisclosure if I find the money acceptable. How much are we discussing?"

With anyone else, that would be the first tilt toward capitulation, but not for someone as shrewd as Henri. His agreement to sign a nondisclosure was as good as his word, which was stronger than any document, so she could sprinkle some details if need be.

What would be Henri's flinch factor?

She would always treat him fairly, but it was clear he harbored as much resentment from the past as she did, though she couldn't figure out why when he was the one who'd thrown in the proverbial towel first.

Regardless, there had been a time that she would have asked how much money he needed, figured that into the mix, and made it work for both of them. But times had changed and she couldn't be cavalier with even a dollar.

Of the fifty thousand she'd received from Smith, ten was earmarked as deposit for the treatment. She could not touch that ten, but if she failed to deliver the scroll, that ten wouldn't get her dad what he needed. She had to have enough money for things she hadn't even encountered yet, that intangible unknown that could kill the best contract. "Five thousand now and five thousand later."

Henri became very still, eyes giving away nothing.

Evidently that hadn't tickled his money bone at all.

He stood. "You have wasted your drive and my time. *Au revoir*." He walked briskly towards the back.

She pushed up from the sofa and followed him. "No wonder you have no clients if that's the extent of your negotiating."

"We are doing just fine," he shouted, swinging around, eyes sparking with anger.

"Really? Is that why you're in a prime laundromat location instead of the historic district?"

That silenced him.

Dammit. She hadn't meant to snub his location.

Henri was brilliant, but he made decisions based on emotions. She'd always been the business mind in their partnership.

Somewhere along the line, they'd stopped supporting each other and started attacking each other.

This was not how she'd planned to reunite with him on a business level.

She took a breath and said, "I'm sorry, Henri. I think your shop is really amazing. I didn't mean to take a dig at it, or you. I'm just in a tight spot and I really need this contract and I wish you'd work with me on it."

She was not going to bring her dad's illness into this. Everybody had problems. She had no doubt that Henri had his own.

He put his hand at his collar, pinching it.

That was an Henri tell. He debated what to say.

His green eyes blinked away something she wanted to call moisture, but she had no idea why. He'd walked into their kitchen one morning just before their first anniversary and begun to calmly explain how their marriage had been a mistake and it was time that they both faced the truth.

How this change would be best for both of them.

Un-freaking-flappable Henri.

She hadn't been quite as sanguine upon hearing his announcement.

A few dishes had gone flying.

He'd stood like a beacon in the midst of a screaming hurricane, waiting for her anger to blow itself out, then he'd returned to their bedroom and started packing.

The Henri standing before her now had aged in the last five years. His body might not show it, but his eyes gave away the toll life had taken on him.

"I will work with you, Valene, but I need significant funds as well. We do want to move from here to the historic area, which is eight times the square foot rate, but they have the traffic. I have five days left to either sign a new lease on this location or give notice that we will move in two months. In spite of what you think, there *is* someone waiting to lease this space. I must make this move, because this place is causing me much grief."

Those were the most heartfelt words she'd heard from him

since he'd shared a secret with her in eleventh grade. She'd held his confidence and had protected him as much as he'd protected her from mean hormonal girls and pushy testosterone-loaded boys.

Her shoulders lightened as one of the chips she'd been toting around tumbled off. She reached out to touch his shoulder. "I want to help you and I will, but I need you to work with me. I've been offered a lot of money for this, but delivering the scroll comes with a very short time frame. If I don't come through, I could end up having to pay back money I've already spent."

Henri jerked his head and cursed vividly in French. "But why would you, someone who is revered in our business, do such a thing?"

Nothing to hide now that she felt exposed, but she warmed at his compliment. "I don't have a choice. I need the money for something personal, something important."

He angled his head in a thoughtful way. "Is your dad–"

"I'm not talking about him. This is business. I want you to make money, too. How much do you need to move to the historic area?"

"Thirty thousand, give or take some."

"Here's the God's truth." She drew a deep breath and hoped this worked. "I can give you five thousand now and, if I complete this contract successfully, then I'll pay you the other twenty-five. But I can't guarantee anything. I only committed to the second five thousand a moment ago because I'd sell my car before I'd stiff you any money I personally guarantee. This is a huge deal that might result in more referrals from higher up." He had no idea how high up. "I wasn't insulting you over the nondisclosure. I really am trying to protect you because of who I'm dealing with, but I can't share everything."

Now, she sounded like Dingo saying, "I'm doing this to save you but I can't tell you everything."

Did she really need to bring him into this? No.

Henri shouted, "*Sacré bleu*, Valene! Who do you make this deal with?"

"He's–"

Fifteen feet away, the door to the back room opened and a man said, "Are you all right, Henri?"

She turned with Henri to face a man who could be twenty-five or thirty-five. It was impossible to tell from his beautiful face that bordered on delicate and blue eyes that belonged in Hollywood. A head of blond wavy hair curled around his face.

"I am fine, Geoffrey." Then Henri's gaze flitted from Geoffrey to Valene. Silence and tension crackled in those sluggish seconds.

Valene's gaze locked with Geoffrey's, two warriors sending eye messages that they were ready to do battle.

Henri hurried to fill the void by saying, "This is my ... Ms. Eklund."

Valene had hurt Henri once and decided now would be a good time to be that bigger person, but words rushed up her throat and slammed to a halt behind her clenched teeth.

That man had stolen her one true friend in life.

Geoffrey's gaze danced from her to Henri. "This is the *one*?"

Henri appeared embarrassed when he muttered, "*Oui.*"

When Geoffrey's gaze swung back to Valene, she stiffened at his critical assessment. "What are you doing here? Slumming?"

So he did know who she was. "Thank you."

Blond hair bounced when he cocked his head. "Why are you thanking me?"

"I was searching for the right word and there you had it."

"Va-*lene*," Henri warned.

Her gaze snapped to him. "What? I was being nice. Your better half is the one with the attitude."

"I see why he left you," Geoffrey lashed out.

"Geoffrey!" Henri snapped before Valene could form a retort. "She is a client. We will treat her as such."

"You may be willing to lower your standards, but I'm not." Geoffrey slammed the door, sucking all the renewed friendship from the room.

She snarled, "You left me for *him*?"

Henri looked appalled. "Don't act surprised. You knew I was bisexual."

"That's not what I meant. I don't care if you married a him, a her, or a giraffe, but when you left you told me you couldn't take my outbursts. I got too emotional. I had a temper that exploded." He'd also said she was too distant, gone too much and too numb to hold up her half of any relationship.

Henri ran his hands through his stylish hair, sending the short, deep-red locks shooting in different directions, and muttering, "I ask myself every day what I was thinking. You drove me crazy. Now he drives me crazy."

Call it a character flaw, but for the first time since they'd separated, Valene felt better. Someone hadn't succeeded where she'd failed. She wasn't wishing for Henri to be unhappy, but she'd heard over and over through friends in the business that Henri was so full of joy and content these days.

All she could think was how he hadn't been happy at all for the last few months of their marriage. They'd spent the first part of that year consoling each other through the emotional hell of Henri's cousin's suicide and Valene's father being diagnosed with stage-three lung cancer, probably from the crap he'd inhaled on archaeological sites.

And Dingo had abandoned her.

She'd been a hot mess for a long time.

Henri brushed his hair back with a sweep of his hand. "I did *not* meet him while you and I were together."

"I didn't mean to insinuate that you had behaved with a lack of morality. I would never think that. It was...I was just... angry."

His chuckle rippled with sadness. "I know. It seems that I am without skills to make anyone happy no matter what I sacrifice."

She realized right then that Henri was desperate to move this shop to the historic district for *Geoffrey*. She wasn't at all glad that the two men were having issues and felt like scum on the bottom of a shoe for adding to his troubles.

"Let's make a deal to work together, Henri, so that with a little luck we'll both come out good on this."

The smile he gave her this time was the first sincere one she'd earned from him in a long time. "I will do whatever I can and I know that you'll be fair with me on the money."

"Thank you." She let out a long breath of relief. One hurdle cleared.

"I'll sign your form before you leave. Tell me about this scroll."

She brightened up at the first sign that this was going to work out after all. "You aren't going to believe this because I'd never heard of it in all my years of studying seventeenth-century writings."

His eyebrows climbed at that.

She nodded and grinned. The excitement of the hunt sent adrenaline rushing through her. "You know that Galileo was put under house arrest after he was brought before the pope for–"

Henri made a rolling motion with his hand. "Yes, yes. As you would often say, give me the bullet points."

She laughed at that and Henri's eyes twinkled. Maybe they could repair what their marriage had destroyed. She explained, "Galileo supposedly wrote on a scroll–"

"That is not news," he muttered, at once disappointed.

She put a hand on her hip. "This is why we butted heads before."

French curses spewed again then he motioned with his hands to keep going and ordered her, "Finish."

She grumbled, "Don't interrupt." After scratching her head for a moment to clear her thoughts, she explained, "This scroll was never out of the Vatican until now."

At his stunned silence, she gave him a look of *see*? Then she told him the one element that would fine-tune their search. "This scroll supposedly is what he wrote about visions he had associated with the Orion star configuration, best that I can figure from what I was told. And the scroll includes a star map."

"Galileo would not have admitted to having visions," Henri whispered, thinking out loud. "He'd been condemned for his beliefs about the solar system. This sounds like a fraud."

"You'll have to trust me that this scroll does exist and please don't ask me to tell you more than I have to, because–"

"I know, I know... you protect me."

"Yes," she admitted.

"This sounds risky, Valene."

True, but telling him she was just a little terrified would only make him nervous on top of his other problems. "I'll be the one taking any risk. Weren't you the one who said all great things come with risk?"

"Do not turn my words on me. What else can you tell me?"

"The name of the scroll is Profezia di Orione."

Henri's eyes flared for a second at that.

Valene asked, "Do you know about this?"

"No."

She would actually have been worried if he'd said yes. "Here's the kicker. I only have five days to deliver the scroll."

He lifted a hand to his forehead and walked around in a circle.

Valene began to have true concern. This was Henri's way of saying he had bad news. "What is it, Henri?"

"We have a gifted historian whose specialty is all things Galilean."

"I know. Geoffrey." She urged, "Don't you have some pull with him?"

"About as much as I had with you. I have a bad habit of choosing hardheaded partners."

"I am nothing like him," she said, then regretted sounding as if she'd criticized Henri's new partner. "What I mean is—"

Henri held up a hand. "Please. I know exactly what you mean, because you are correct. You two differ greatly in one point. I never worry that he will be off doing something dangerous."

She had no argument for that.

Henri had walked the floor many times when she was late returning from meeting a new client who could have turned out to be a mass murderer.

"Geoffrey is also sensitive and the jealous type. He has never been interested in women so my past relationship with you threatens him. He believes he will not meet some unrealistic standard he has envisioned."

What could she say about that? Her own insecurities had caused her to avoid any interaction with Henri once she heard he was involved with someone new, someone who made him happy. She'd been hurt more than anything when Henri left, but it wasn't as though she carried a torch for her ex-husband.

Henri kept talking. "I will talk to Geoffrey and convince him to use his skills."

"Thirty grand isn't enough to do that?" she quipped.

"It would have been if you hadn't pinched his ego. If I bring him to the table, can you mind your manners?"

She blew out a gust of air and ran fingers through her hair. "I'll even apologize."

An eyebrow quirked high on Henri's forehead. "I see."

And he did. She'd just told him how desperate she was, because Henri knew her pride could blind her at times. But her pride had been through enough battering over the past few years that apologizing to Geoffrey, snippy guy that he was, would be simple.

"In the meantime," Henri continued. "The key to this contract is finding potential buyers."

Valene had missed brainstorming with Henri.

She said, "Right. I wish someone on my gold list of clients could afford this scroll, but they're only millionaires. This deal is going to take a billionaire who has an obsession with Galileo."

The few seventeenth-century collectors who had the kind of money that could buy something even she couldn't put a price on were practically impossible to get in front of because they used agents to handle their purchases and sales.

And those agents were often just as secretive about their identities.

"You do know one who happens to be in LA," Henri said.

"They all come through LA at some point, but by the time we hear they've arrived, they're already locked away somewhere private or on their private jet headed somewhere else."

"I'm speaking of Jon Tinker."

She got excited, then slumped. "Getting to the president in five days would be easier."

"Ah, Valene, where is the woman who sent an exquisite seventeenth-century Oliver Cromwell shilling to a visiting duke as an invitation to meet?"

She was inside somewhere, buried beneath layers of worry over things like her father and fulfilling this contract, but she was there. "What are you saying?"

"I have an idea of how you might get in front of this collector. It's a gamble, but doable." Henri lifted both eyebrows this time and that meant there was more to it.

She already knew she wasn't going to like this, but that buried version of herself came crawling up from the dark place she'd been hiding when Valene said, "Point me in his direction."

Chapter 12

St. Moritz, Switzerland

THE GENERAL EYED the bane of his existence, Wayan, who was the second most powerful man in China and only the uninformed failed to recognize that. Wayan had a boyish face with the typical almond shaped eyes, soft cheeks and a mouth always pursed with disgust during these meetings. But where Asian women the General knew had beautifully shaped eyes, Wayan's were small, black and unattractive.

He looked like a man secretly planning the next world war, which might be exactly what he was up to.

Now that they were seated in a private salon of L'air Doré, an exclusive resort in Switzerland that catered to those who could pay for absolute discretion, the General began, "You said the scroll was safe."

Wayan propped his palms together with his fingers pointing up like a steeple. "The artifact was secure until someone unexpected got involved. We may argue and point fingers or we may take action. Which are you here for?"

To make sure you don't screw the powerful families who pay me well to protect them. The Rosso family was on edge and the General's job was to deal with the issue causing them stress. Admitting that to Wayan would be the same as the General exposing his jugular. "I'm here to make sure you understand that I'm not trying to snake the scroll out from under you, but I have to get my hands on it."

Wayan was a man of few facial expressions, but he allowed an eyebrow to float up. "You think I will assist you in gaining the single most valuable artifact of the five required to unveil Orion's Prophecy?"

"You said the panel from the Amber Room was the key piece."

Wayan's eyes smiled even though his mouth remained all business. "The scroll explains how all the artifacts work together. It was necessary that you believed the Amber Room panel was most important or you would have focused on the scroll too soon."

Deceitful bastard.

It wasn't as though the General trusted Wayan either, but Wayan could have been straight about all these damn artifacts. Orion's Prophecy was complete hogwash, but Wayan believed with the intensity of a fanatic. That alone gave the General reason to stay close to him. When it came to the warning about keeping your friends close and your enemies closer, the General only had to bother with the latter part.

He'd connected with Wayan when the Chinese nutjob sent minions trying to purchase a rare stater, a Greek gold coin used in trade during the fourth century. The coin had been in the General's family for generations.

It was locked away where Wayan would never be able to get his hands on it as long as the General was alive. He reclined and grimaced. Damn pain meds weren't doing it for his back. "Back to the scroll, Wayan. I meant it when I said I wasn't trying to screw you. If you help me find the person with the scroll, I want the thief and you can have the scroll. Fair enough?"

Wayan pretended to mull it over, but the General had known him for three years. Wayan made his decisions faster than many people drew a breath. He hadn't become the second in line to the leadership of China without being dangerously brilliant.

He was also a major ache in the General's backside.

And the little fucker actually believed that once five specific artifacts came together, Orion's Prophecy would come to fruition, revealing the final world conflict and who would win.

In Wayan's private fantasy world, a final conflict would be a world war that left only one country standing.

The General didn't buy into any of this shit, but six of the most powerful families in the world paid him well to keep his finger on the pulse of crazy internationals who might threaten *their* world—reality anchored by obscene amounts of money.

The scary part was that Wayan held a position where he actually *could* manipulate the launch of an international conflict.

Especially if the prophecy pointed to the US as the country that would come out on top.

Wayan lowered his steepled fingers. "I will contact you if I locate the scroll thief first."

Not exactly a commitment that left the General all warm and fuzzy. He clarified one point of the agreement. "I need the thief alive."

Wayan's head tilted forward only enough to acknowledge that he understood. "You wish to be sure he has spoken to no one of his deeds within the Vatican banking system on behalf of a prestigious Italian family."

I really don't like how this Chinese bastard always knows too much. The General shrugged with nonchalance. "Exactly."

"Then I see no reason we cannot reach an agreement, should fortune befall *my* people who search for the scroll ... as long as you are willing to make an exchange."

You sorry sack of shit. The General knew exactly what was being offered. Wayan would hand over the thief in trade for the General's artifact, one of the prized five.

Wayan already possessed carved jade art that he'd purchased on the antiquities market many years ago, according to what the General's people had discovered. A flat piece the size of a serving tray with gold Uyghur inscriptions, the accepted Mongolian writing. The art had belonged to Genghis Khan and had been sculpted to display one of Khan's belt buckles in the middle. It wasn't called a buckle back then, but the General couldn't be bothered to recall the term.

A German collector owned the coveted panel from the Amber Room. It belonged to Tsar Peter the Great in the eighteenth century, and Wayan was already going after that one.

That left the Galilean scroll from the Vatican and a Celtic cross belonging to Chatton, the number-two pain in the General's backside. The General groaned internally. That bitch had shown up unexpectedly, pushing her way into the Czarion, the code name Wayan and the General had chosen for their partnership.

The General had rogue CIA agents on his secret payroll, and he'd sent them hunting for Chatton, but they'd come up empty. She was a spook through and through. He and Wayan figured her to be MI6, but neither of their contacts in the British spy agency had anything on her.

"The time for fulfilling Orion's Prophecy draws near," Wayan announced. "We are entering the final days. The scroll will explain all."

Were those words written somewhere or just a fabrication in Wayan's twisted mind?

The General didn't know, but he was keeping a close eye on everyone to make sure Wayan and Chatton weren't teaming up to double cross him.

The General lifted his sixty-year-old scotch. "Here's to a new world order where we've agreed to continue our alliance."

Wayan's hint of a smile was the equivalent of someone else doing a fist pump.

The General did his own silent fist pump, because he had no doubt that Chatton knew all about the scroll being missing. With just a little luck, Wayan and Chatton might cancel each other out.

Best case scenario? One of them would go down for sure.

Chapter 13

DINGO MADE A full turn, taking in what he'd consider a nightmare to keep secure if he didn't know this party could double as a security convention.

The Slye team had arrived early this morning and were now spread through five hundred guests who had paid over ten grand apiece to be *invited* to this charity event.

Dingo passed groups of bone-thin women in clingy dresses and men wearing tailored tuxes that might be more comfortable than this straightjacket outfit he had on.

A front was moving in and had dropped the temperature to the mid-sixties by lunch, saving him from sweating like a whore in church.

He maneuvered around people mingling throughout the tiered garden area of Savoir Faire West, the luxury hotel hosting this event. The four-story Mediterranean structure had a sweeping circular drive that had been busy since noon when the first limos and flashy rides arrived to deposit their riders. Someone had remodeled this place. To Dingo, it was now done up like a silver-screen star from the 50s. Based on the team's intel, the current owners had bought adjoining property to expand the garden patio from postage-stamp size to one that stretched forty yards deep and half as wide.

Keeping all the plants and flowers alive had to be a full-time job.

None of the guests seemed to notice all the work that'd been done to turn this into a fairytale party, or the army of wait staff running around in black tuxedos determined that no champagne glass remained empty and everyone got a bite of the funky little snacks on their silver trays.

"What's the ETA on Perdido?" Dingo asked, speaking in a harsh whisper–just loud enough for the other five members of Slye's undercover team to hear through their comm sets.

Nick replied, "Approximately eight minutes out."

"Roger that."

Blade appeared nearby carrying a tray filled with bubbling champagne just as Nick's voice came through Dingo's earpiece again.

"Wait staff all set?"

Blade beamed a bright smile at the couple he'd paused to serve before strolling past Dingo and replying, "Affirmative. Identity confirmed on each staff member. Doors are locked and the house security is to notify me if anyone new shows up or if someone asks to leave."

Dingo continued weaving his way through a cluster of designer dresses that ranged from ankle length to nothing more than butt trim, all while listening to the team's communication.

Music floated through the balmy ocean air along with the hum of conversation, but Nick's voice calling for reports came through clear. "Exterior positions set?"

In a smooth tone, White Hawk replied, "Ready at north exit." As soon as she finished, Ryder's deep voice acknowledged, "Good to go at the south exit."

That put White Hawk outside the front entrance of the hotel and Ryder at the far end of the outdoor setting. With the exception of trips to the lounges for men or women, all of the guests should be in sight around the terraced patio.

Tinker had his own security force, and the hotel had another eight set up as guards around the perimeter, plus two inside the hotel. In addition to White Hawk and Ryder, Slye had four more highly skilled agents overseeing the gardens enclosed by a security wall. Trees and foliage lined the inside of the wall, hiding it from view.

Dingo shook his head at this overkill.

Six deadly Slye operatives on site under the guise of nabbing a stalker. That's what Perdido's people thought.

Wonder if her campaign manager had a cosmetic surgeon on hand in case she broke a nail?

Sabrina would have found that amusing at one time, but she had no sense of humor when it came to Dingo these days.

At least she'd relented and agreed that leaving Dingo at their temporary headquarters would have been a waste of personnel, especially with Josh on hand. Dingo normally accepted the desk jockey position because Josh would rather be in the field, but Josh saw the wisdom in keeping Dingo and Sabrina apart as much as possible right now.

Dingo had to mend the rift with her. They'd been friends too long to allow this to continue.

He'd tested that friendship when he brought Valene in on his last op a month ago.

But Valene had stepped up when he'd asked.

Nick said, "Target's transport just arrived. Perdido and Caddy exiting vehicle with four guards."

All thoughts of personal issues were shoved from Dingo's mind. Go time.

Lt. Governor candidate Emilio Fontana had joined Perdido as her running mate, surprising his celebrity family. The Slye team had tagged him *Caddy* because Fontana was the youngest son from a family of pro golfers, but had shied away from earning his living on a golf course, swinging his clubs only at corporate outings. Still, he was well liked among the press even if he tended to play second string to everyone around him.

Nick updated the team. "Perdido and Caddy on the move. Handing off."

Tanner's voice rumbled. "I have eyes on Perdido and Caddy. Crossing through center of crowd."

Dingo caught sight of the political duo. They were surrounded by four of their own security and passing through a gap in guests as Tanner updated his report. "Perdido and Caddy intercepted by Daddy and Lady Warbucks."

Lady Warbucks was the code name for Jon Tinker's bombshell wife, June, who still turned heads at sixty. She had a smile that charmed the press. The reclusive billionaire she'd married had underwritten this charity event to *Save the Hollywood Pacific Theater*, a spectacular relic from years gone by that several investors had tried–and failed–to bring back to life more than once.

Protecting California treasures was just one of Tinker's pet projects.

Perdido had jumped on that bandwagon by issuing a bold statement that, if elected, she would guarantee that California reclaimed its history by maintaining some of the monstrous old buildings.

There had been an outcry about wasting tax dollars, but Perdido had smiled in victory when she gained Tinker as a major supporter. Perdido used her physical attraction to her advantage when playing up to fat wallets, but her abrasive attitude and ability to stir up opponents had cultivated many enemies.

And now a stalker.

One that would be easier to spot from a high point, if the billionaire hadn't screwed that option.

Stashing Ryder in a sniper position on the roof, where he'd have been right at home with a scope, would have offered the best set of eyes for this afternoon. But Nick couldn't even put Ryder on a balcony of the twelve-story hotel towering between the garden event and the street, because Daddy Warbucks's people had trumped Nick's request. Two of Warbucks's security detail were homesteading on the roof right now.

Lots of manpower.

But with no new intel on the assassinations, tonight would likely turn out to be nothing more than a surveillance gig for some obsessed stalker.

Simple, right?

Nothing more dangerous than an overzealous fan who wanted his ten minutes of fame. Not as deadly as an Uzi-wielding terrorist.

So what was causing the hairs on Dingo's neck to stand up as if he faced down a jihadi guerrilla?

He couldn't put his finger on what was wonky, but he felt it. He moved through the sprawling gardens laid out on two tiers, with white-linen covered tables and massive ice sculptures that didn't even seem to be sweating. Tossing quick visual sweeps, he took in every person speaking, staring, yawning, glaring ... all were suspect, and none were suspect.

Nick ordered, "Update on Perdido."

"I've got eyes on Perdido near the stage," Blade confirmed, which meant he was on the upper tier of the garden where a raised stage had been positioned alongside the fountain. A small orchestra was perched nearby, sending out soft melodies fit for Hollywood royalty, or for those who believed they were.

Nick said, "Maintain that position."

"Roger that," Blade replied.

Dingo blew out a weary rush of air. Other than a couple of quick combat naps, he'd had no sleep last night. He'd checked in before midnight, making sure Josh and Nick had seen Dingo come in, then he'd slipped out to spend the rest of the evening and early morning watching over Valene's apartment. He'd shown up with donuts at headquarters before daylight this morning, and ignored Sabrina's suspicious gaze. They hadn't spoken since their argument and probably wouldn't sort their issues out until they returned to Atlanta.

Dingo stifled a yawn and shifted around just as a man blinked in and out of his line of sight, just long enough to send a chill racing up his spine. Dingo squinted, but the face was gone. Even so, his mind had snapped a shot and slammed it up front and center.

Had that been Len Rikker?

Wouldn't Nick, who was panning everyone coming through the entrance, have recognized Rikker? Or Josh, who was back at their LA safe house headquarters feeding visuals from video feeds into facial recognition software, have caught Rikker's?

Dingo had only seen a partial view from the side. Rikker played through many of Dingo's bloody dreams.

Had he just imagined the wanker was here?

Adrenaline shoved all weariness from his system.

He swept a sharp eye over everyone in the area where he thought he'd seen Rikker.

Nothing out of place. No one moving with purpose.

Dingo rubbed his neck, willing himself to settle down. Boredom and fatigue had him imagining things.

Overactive mind without enough to do.

Sabrina would go ballistic if Dingo reported a *possible* sighting of Rikker. Josh would be just irritated. Everyone would doubt anything he said at that point. No announcing phantom visions without evidence. Got it.

Dingo gave himself a quick pep talk made up of mostly four-letter words and focused on his job.

Catch the damn stalker. Stop an assassination.

Check.

The good news about Nick being in charge of tonight was that a completely objective person was on top of everything, leaving Dingo free to infiltrate the crowd at will.

If only he had an idea who would kill for money in this sparkling group of LA's movers and shakers.

In California's bling capital, a high-dollar hit could be anything from a grudge attack to a spouse wanting out of a marriage the easy way.

Between the in-house security and that of Daddy Warbucks, which rivaled protection for a king, this place was safer than the White House right now.

A number of guests held tickets that cost twelve thousand dollars, which allowed them one minute of Daddy Warbucks's time. The philanthropist sometimes acted on requests made through the private meetings.

Dingo wouldn't pay the ten grand required just to walk through the door much less twelve thousand to talk to someone, but then he wasn't trying to squeeze cash out of the guy.

He scratched his chin, sweeping a glance over the crowd.

This was a perfect example of why Dingo would never settle down. He wasn't cut out to work something dignified like corporate security and damn if Sabrina didn't have more of those contracts coming in faster and faster.

That's what happened when you had someone with Sabrina's savvy running a company.

She was too freakin' good at business. If she ever wanted to give up all this smoke-and-mirrors fun, the corporate security side of her Slye agency would keep her financially secure forever.

She should do it.

Then maybe Josh would stay in Miami or wherever he planned to build a home for him and Trish.

Dingo saw only one problem with all that.

Josh and Sabrina would both expect Dingo to quit the black ops contracts if they did, but Dingo wasn't cut out for a normal life.

Too many rules.

Too much standing around.

Too much time to think.

A young bloke standing by himself in a shadowy corner snapped Dingo out of that depressing line of thought. This guy had a suspicious air about him.

But as Dingo watched without turning his head in that direction, the guy brightened when a young woman stepped over to speak with him.

She hugged the pimply kid. Not really a kid at mid-twenties, but after all Dingo had seen and done, he felt twice as old.

He dismissed the pair and turned to do a three-sixty sweep of the area just as a head of wild blonde locks bounced past him. The golden hair flitted around a slender neck on a curvy female in a slinky blue dress strolling away from Dingo and causing his heartbeat to stutter.

What the bloody hell? Was his mind going?

He rammed his attention back on track with ruthless discipline and mentally slapped himself for allowing any distraction to interfere with an operation.

Even her.

That was *not* her.

Valene Eklund couldn't be at an event that cost a minimum of ten thousand dollars just to walk through the front door, when she lived in a place that was one step above poverty housing.

And why the hell was she in that shitty place?

If you really cared, you'd have been around to know the answer to that.

Valene's words had rambled around in his head all night.

To avoid thinking about that and to clear up who the fuck Charlie was, Dingo had spent his surveillance time outside her apartment hammering on his laptop to find out what he could on Charlie. Basically, the guy checked out as an antiquities and rare artifacts dealer, but that was before Dingo pushed past online business listings anyone could get. Nothing of value and nothing too high profile. But anyone could find that much. Dingo had gone deeper on Charlie and the guy still looked upstanding until Dingo did a bit of stealth hacking to find what Josh had run across. Charlie's background was buried in layers that would take a shovel to dig through.

There were holes here and there. Given enough time, Dingo could track Charlie electronically and find just who might be Charlie's black market art dealer overseas.

Dingo could see why Sabrina's hackles were up and, yes, he agreed that Charlie was suspect, but the team hadn't come out here to stop the illegal art trade.

Plus, holding Valene responsible for Charlie's criminal behavior was a serious stretch, since Valene would have no reason to go deeper than a normal background search on Charlie.

If you were still in Valene's good graces, she'd have believed you when you cast suspicion on Charlie.

He didn't need another reminder that he'd been MIA when she needed him.

Bottom line? Charlie had nothing to do with Slye being in LA to catch an assassin, which meant his relationship with Valene was still none of Sabrina's business. He'd find out what Valene had agreed to do for Charlie and deal with that when he had time. Like when he wasn't watching for a threat.

A young couple strolled past Dingo, the happy pair jogging logic loose in his mind.

Valene *could* be here if she came as someone's date.

Shit. But he had no say so, no reason to be fighting this unreasonable spark of irritation.

All that flood of logic did nothing to stop him from heading in the direction he'd last seen those golden locks.

"Nothing suspicious so far," Nick reported to the team from the two-story glass entrance.

Dingo paused.

Team members were expected to report *anything* suspicious, but there wasn't anything technically suspicious about him seeing his former...what?

Girlfriend? He'd never had one.

Before meeting Valene, he'd been more of a one-night-friends kind of guy, who went for casual encounters with a woman who never expected to see him again.

Valene didn't fit into *that* category.

He had no idea how to categorize her and he had a feeling that *not* knowing made him a dick.

Good thing Sabrina wasn't here, or she'd be in his face asking why he was so worried about a woman who he couldn't even define what she was to him.

He forced his breathing to slow down, anything to slow the fist punching his heart over how he'd hurt Valene. And the other fist slamming his gut to complete the repeat one-two punch, because she'd up and married someone while he was gone. The guy Dingo had seen with her looked like he modeled on the side.

Could he blame her?

No.

There'd been no words to bind them to each other. It wasn't that Dingo didn't care for her, but that he was not the man to be home every night. He'd been on the run from all that since getting tossed aside at eight.

He still cared, but he'd get over it.

Every time he closed his eyes, he saw her smile and heard her laughter. Uninterrupted sleep was never going to happen again. His heart hadn't let him forget.

But he'd taught that damaged organ to live without love the week his mother committed suicide and his stepdad dumped Dingo at an orphanage. He'd retrain his heart again just as soon as he found the damn stalker, insured Valene was safe and got the hell out of Cali-*fucking*-fornia.

He searched the fair-haired women he could see. None of them were Valene.

Because he was losing his mind. She was not here.

This city was full of hot blondes who were not Valene.

He had to stop imagining he saw her every time a sexy woman showed up.

Tanner came into view wearing a frown and heading Dingo's way.

Nick's deep voice reported, "Arriving guests are down to a trickle. Handing off the entrance surveillance to Josh. I'm making a pass through the crowd."

Dingo had installed video feeds, and one covered the entrance that Nick referenced.

Nick would move through everyone without drawing the least bit of attention, since these people bled the same blue blood he did. At least that's what Dingo always figured about the crazy guy.

Crazy, but the loose wire you wanted on a team when your back was in a corner.

Tanner moved his hand up to his throat mic, deactivating it as he passed by Dingo and murmured, "Just saw Valene."

She *was* here?

How had she gotten inside an event that cost as much as her car for an invitation? He'd questioned Sabrina's claim that Valene had received suspicious funds, but he couldn't deny something was up.

Dingo looked around. Who the hell could she be with if she was here as someone's date?

What do you care if she's not your ...

Fuck. He really had to figure out what she was to him. But first, he had to find out what she was doing here, which meant he had to talk to her without getting caught on one of the ten lipstick cameras he'd hidden throughout the event complex.

Chapter 14

NICK FOLLOWED A woman who hadn't come through the party entrance to Savoir Faire West.

He'd have remembered that one.

And he'd wager his favorite Ferrari that she hadn't inserted along with the other wait staff, since Blade had forwarded every face to Josh with credentials that all matched up.

Nor did Nick think she belonged to any one of three security groups. There were so many people guarding this place and their respective celebrity bodies that they were falling over each other.

Those two men of Tinker's on the roof had the best positions of all.

The woman Nick followed turned a corner too soon, instead of heading out to the tiered gardens where he would have expected someone on the wait staff to go with a tray full of hors d'oeuvres.

He knew that body.

Chin-length brunette hair, wire-framed glasses, pale makeup, black and white wait-staff outfit. Everything about her packaging advertised average female, all except her height.

Disguising a *lack* of height was easier than hiding the fact that a woman was statuesque.

Two more turns and he entered a hall on the east side of the building that led to a door at the end. He ran the plans for the hotel through his mind. This was the service corridor to a supply room on this end.

Nick spoke quietly for the benefit of his team. "I'm going silent for ten to fifteen max, but I'll still have ears on while I check something out on the east side. Might be nothing."

Blade came back. "Need backup?"

"Not for this."

When he reached the door, he knew she was in there.

His training warned him to think twice before walking into a place that would be the perfect ambush.

Life without risk was just clocking time.

He grinned and put his hand on the knob, which turned easily. When he stepped inside it wasn't completely dark, but security lighting forced him to wait for his eyes to adjust.

Once he could see, he moved past rows of rolling carts for the domestic engineers. A mix of smells assaulted him, but the one that tugged an old memory from him was fresh laundry.

As a child in Sicily, he'd follow old Jemma around as she delivered clean clothes and changed bed linens once the rest of the family was up and out. He'd been a late-in-life accident that nobody knew what to do with, so Jemma was the one who'd made him breakfast and read him bedtime stories.

A noise turned his attention to a dark shadow where the security lights didn't reach.

Correction. Those security lights had been shut off.

He took the bait and walked over there.

If he was wrong about his hunch, it wouldn't be his first knot on the head.

Or knife wound.

Or bullet wound.

He reached the leading edge of the shadow and stopped. Waiting a beat, he leaned against the wall with his arms crossed. "Been a while."

A figure emerged from the shadows, wearing a tuxedo that handled curves the way a high-performance car hugged switchbacks through the mountains.

She said, "Only you would walk into a bloody ambush setup and smile while doing it."

"I had an idea I followed someone I knew, even if she isn't willing to give me a name yet."

She hadn't yet shown him her true face, either, but while she might actually be a brunette, he had no doubt she was far beyond average. The latex mask she wore now was that of a woman who could be twenty-eight or thirty-five, which was easy to pull off with a figure like hers.

He'd met her a while back when she'd shared information that had given Slye teams a hand up and saved lives. She had to be trained by some country's international spook division. If he went on her British accent alone he'd guess MI6, but that could be something she affected just for him.

Did it matter?

Not a bit.

He grinned at her. "I would say we have to stop meeting like this–"

"–but you'd be so disappointed," she finished for him.

"Actually, I was going to say that you'd risk never getting that debt I owe you paid."

"Debts. Plural." She smiled and crossed her arms over her chest.

He'd seen enough of her body before to know she hid a beautiful décolletage beneath that tuxedo. "Is that why you're here?"

"I do like working with someone who doesn't waste my time. No, I'm not here to collect. Yet. I'm in LA because a rare scroll is being shopped and I need to get my hands on it."

"I haven't heard anything about a scroll," he told her.

"I figured as much, but when I saw you here I thought maybe we were after the same thing."

Nick listened to each word she shared with the same care someone decoded a message from the enemy. Every word counted. "Why would you think that?"

"Because the Orion Hunters are after this scroll."

That upped his interest.

She quirked an eyebrow. "What *are* you doing here? Looks like a convention for We Be Security out there."

He laughed. "It does."

She wouldn't have missed that he skipped over her question.

He debated on sharing intel for the slow seconds she stood patiently waiting. This operative had brought way more to the table in the past without asking for anything in return. Except the debt she kept refusing to tell him how to repay.

Sabrina wouldn't like him sharing mission details with anyone, but his willingness to take a risk with this woman had paid off heavily in the past.

Slye had nothing but Perdido for assassination targets so far.

Nick wasn't one to tiptoe into anything. "We're here under the cover of hunting for Perdido's stalker, but in truth we have reason to believe three assassinations are going down in California. We just don't have targets."

"So you're pretending to be Blinkin' in *Men In Tights*?" she teased.

"Pretty much." Nick laughed at the image of Blinkin', a blind character put on watch for Robin Hood's hideout. When Robin Hood stopped by to check the guard on duty, he asked Blinkin' what he was doing.

Blinkin' had his hand shielding his eyes even though he was wearing sunglasses and said, "Guessing."

Yep, that summed up what Nick and his team had been doing all night. "We think the Orion Hunters are involved, but that's only because of a tattoo on someone who killed a snitch in Atlanta."

"Bergman? He's dead?"

"Yes to both."

She seemed mildly surprised. "I thought he was gone, then I heard a rumor that he'd come back to Atlanta and was slashed."

"Bergman belonged to one of our people."

"That's too bad. He was useful."

Nick had one more crumb to toss out. "What about Satan's Garden Club. Hear anything on them?"

She frowned and thought on her answer, then uncrossed her arms and lifted a finger to her lips. "South American group. Man named Garcia. Thought he was dead, too."

"He is, but someone has started up a new operation and is using that moniker."

"Bloody criminals have no originality. It's bad taste to use another buggar's name." Her eyes twinkled. "But it does keep things interesting."

Her demeanor changed from talkative to a look that said this meeting was over. She walked forward the three steps required to close the distance between them.

His dick stood up faster than a launched heat-seeking missile. One day soon, he intended to find out the real person beneath that latex mask, and exactly what her tuxedo hid.

But he didn't make any quick moves around this woman. She reminded him of a wild leopard who might change her spots, but was just as deadly in any camo.

Sweet Jesus, that just turned him on more.

He'd never been much for the tame ones.

She lifted a hand to his face, long fingers toying with his cheek then his lips. "How's the chest wound?"

"Healed." He sucked a finger in and let his tongue do his speaking for him by showing her finger what the rest of her was missing.

She must have liked what he said, because she didn't hide the heat burning in her gaze before she withdrew her fingers. "One of these days."

"Agreed." He liked a woman who didn't pretend getting naked wasn't going to happen.

She leaned close and whispered, "I don't know who all three targets are, but I have a hunch that one of them won't happen for another day, maybe two. If I pick up anything else, I'll let you know."

"Thanks." He let that hang in the air, testing to see if she'd give another inch.

"You can call me Chatton."

He let her walk out first, not the least surprised when she'd vanished by the time he slowly turned and strode to the door.

Chatton, huh? Interesting. Seeing her here was good news and bad.

On the positive side, she had access to intel that he doubted even the CIA or MI6 could match.

On the negative side, every time she showed up, the game stepped up three levels and the players came locked and loaded.

Just the fact that she was at this event meant there was something else going on that she hadn't shared, but allowing him to recognize her had been Chatton's way of telling him to watch his back.

Chapter 15

DINGO WOVE HIS way from the upper tier of the garden level where more guests had crowded in to speak with Daddy Warbucks, Perdido and Fontana. Once he dropped down a step and had the rear access to the hotel in sight, he said, "Find anything, Nick?"

"Nothing to do with our assignment. I'm taking a spin around the perimeter."

With the team listening, Dingo kept his next words to a minimum. "Taking ten to hit the head and walk the west corridors." Because he had a hunch where Valene might be if she wasn't out here clamoring for Warbucks's attention.

That had to be the only reason she was here.

Right?

His logic was suspiciously silent. Maybe because that meant she held a ticket worth twelve thousand dollars.

Nick said, "Roger that. I'll take your position outside."

When Dingo spotted Tanner, he waited until he had Tanner's attention to send a subtle hand signal that translated into *cover me*.

Tanner nodded and continued patrolling.

With Nick mobile, the rest of the Slye team on watch, an eight-man event security force and Daddy Warbucks's personal squad of guards, Dingo could probably leave for a half hour and not be missed.

He wouldn't do that, but he could justify a brief break to pin down Valene.

Things were finally falling his way, because he saw bouncing curls heading inside through the left set of doors that led to the ladies room.

That was in the west wing.

Walking with determination that sped up his steps, he hung a left in time to see her enter the last lounge on the right.

When he reached the ladies room, a tall brunette slipped out. Dingo went for his serious business voice and said, "Security check. Is anyone else in there?"

The brunette swept an appraising look over him from head to toe. "One more, but I'm in if we're talking a full body search."

That woman clearly fit his *other* category. One whose gaze and tone offered screaming sex.

Right idea. Wrong woman.

Dingo gave her a not-this-time half smile and she shrugged, then walked away.

The minute she turned the corner, he eased the door open and said, "Security."

"Stay out. This is the *ladies* room."

That was definitely Valene's voice, one level before it hit full-blown pissed-off mode. Dingo stepped in and twisted the lock on the door. Not wanting to embarrass her, he eased around the corner.

She was leaned close to the mirror fixing her lipstick. He took another step in.

Her gaze shot to his in the reflection of the mirror and went from fear to shock to ready for battle. "What. The. Hell?" She swung around as she stomped out each word. Hand shoved to one curvaceous hip, she made hornet-mad look sexy. "What are you doing here?"

"Me?" Dingo asked, eyebrows lifting because they both knew she hadn't been referencing his presence in a ladies room, but at this event. "I'm on the clock. What are *you* doing here?"

"I'm a ... guest." But she hadn't looked him straight in the eye when she'd said that.

Just the fact that she answered rather than blast him backwards with a jolt of Valene fury told him she was hiding something.

"At ten grand a pop?" Dingo argued. Evidently, his sense of self-preservation had taken a break, too, because he also asked, "How can you afford to come here when you're living on ramen noodles?"

Yes, he had no grounds for asking how she ended up here, but suspicion about Charlie haunted his mind. He hated the unknown. He wanted clear-cut answers.

"How I came by the ticket is none of your business." She snapped her purse shut and slung the silver chain over her shoulder, staring him down.

There was his take-no-crap Valene.

Not his.

How many times was he going to have to keep reminding himself? He needed to keep his mind on coming up with a believable lie that would get her to explain her presence. Inspiration struck. "It *is* my business since I'm here to insure no one enters the event unauthorized. I'm sure you've heard about Perdido's stalker."

Her face lost it's healthy pink. Something was definitely off.

He asked, "Do you *know* anything about Perdido's stalker?"

"No, of course not. I have no idea what's going on in Perdido's life. Everyone is news in LA. Politicians have to stand out for their sound bites to reach the top of my online news feed. I'm here to see Tinker about a potential project and you're holding me up."

She was here.

Orion Hunters or the SGC might have sent an assassin.

No matter how many ways he added two and two, he kept coming up with someone dead. He didn't want it to be Valene.

She took two steps to leave.

His gut was pitching a fit that something was definitely going down and he didn't want her anywhere around it. Did he have any grounds for trying to get her to leave? No, but that wouldn't stop him from trying.

Words were his worst ammunition so as she took a step to pass him, Dingo caught her around the waist and swung her around, pinning her back to a full-length mirror.

Eyes wide and blinking, she said, "Are you crazy?"

Evidently.

"Let me go."

He wished to hell he could. "Not yet. I want you to listen to me just once, dammit." Where was the calm and control that got him through every situation? It shattered in the face of anything happening to Valene.

She snapped, "This is ridiculous. I warned you once. I'm putting a restraining order on you tomorrow."

"Dammit, Valene, I'm not stalking you and you know it."

She leaned in, nose-to-nose, and clutching his biceps with sharp fingernails. "Really? Showing up unexpectedly yesterday. Breaking into my apartment last night. Now I see you at an event I'm attending. I think the police would side with me."

"Do it and I'll drag you away to a safe house before I call my team to get me out of lockup."

"You wouldn't dare."

"You know I would."

She sucked in and breathed out harsh breaths. All that lung action put her girls on display, but Dingo was not looking down no matter how much his DNA demanded he show them some appreciation.

When she started trembling, he took stock of her and realized she wasn't intimidated, not in the least. She snarled, "If I didn't have to walk out of here looking fresh, I'd kick your ass all the way across this room."

Ah, hell.

She used to threaten to kick his ass on a regular basis and finally admitted it was because she missed him.

Hearing that shot lust straight to his groin. The last time she'd yelled those words at him, they'd made love for six hours straight.

Dingo kissed her, really kissed her and then some.

She dug her fingers in.

He grunted at the pain. Bring it. Because she was digging in to pull him close. She kissed him right back, reaching up to grab a fistful of his hair, holding on for the wild ride any kiss between them turned into.

His hands found their way to her breasts and he made up for lost time with the girls, rubbing his thumbs across the sheer material barely covering the hard tips.

"I'm wet," slipped from her lips when she took a breath.

"I miss that. Miss you. Everything." The words were out before he knew he'd said them.

She stopped kissing and let go of his biceps.

His dick was shouting, *"What?"*

But his brain knew she'd stepped over some line she'd drawn since he'd left her last night, and she had not intended to cross that line again.

He lowered his forehead to hers, lungs begging for air, and moved his hands to her arms. "I'll make you a deal," he said, finally conceding that he was getting nowhere by pushing her for answers. "Tell me what you're doing for Charlie and I'll leave you alone."

"No."

Dingo couldn't tell her what he'd found out on Charlie, because if he did manage to convince her that Charlie might be dealing in illegal antiquities, Valene would confront Charlie. That could end with either Valene being harmed or Charlie getting away, which would send Sabrina over the edge.

No good choices.

"Let's get one thing straight, Dingo," Valene told him, sliding sideways to get away. "I signed a nondisclosure agreement that I'm not breaking for you or anyone else. That should end this conversation."

Dingo took a stab in the dark, arranging his question so that he didn't reveal intel. "How have you vetted your projects with Charlie to be sure you're not looking for something stolen?"

She went rigid and shut down, quick to answer, "I'm not and I'm insulted you think I don't do my homework."

In the past, she would have considered that her client might be doing something illegal. She'd have started pumping Dingo for information, even if she wasn't going to share what she was looking for. But not this time.

Why was Valene stressed and shading the truth?

It wasn't out of fear over what he'd think or say. She'd never been afraid or cautious around Dingo. Never hesitated to get up in his face and give him what for, which he'd loved about her.

He didn't intimidate her.

He never wanted to.

But something, or someone, had his rambunctious beauty acting as if she were operating under a microscope.

Had to be the money.

"I hate fighting with you, Val," he told her and stroked his fingers along her face, trying to calm her. Maybe to calm him, too. He'd missed touching her so damn much, that just standing this close shook his body to the core.

She closed her eyes. "Why are you doing this to me?"

"Doing what?" He lifted his head so he could see her and try to figure out what she was hiding.

His radio clicked twice.

That would be Tanner signaling him to head back.

She shook her head and opened her eyes. "I have to go. I'm here on business. I can't waste this opportunity."

Fuck it. Her showing up here meant Dingo was taking a bigger risk by *not* telling her about the new Satan's Garden Club. And if he was straight with her, she'd be more open to talking with him about this client. She'd never hidden anything in the past, not back when she'd have welcomed Dingo's input.

But she was protecting someone and he had to find out if it was Charlie. He had to figure out whether Valene either suspected, or knew, that Charlie was dirty. Dingo said, "Neither one of us has time for this now. Let's meet later."

⌘

Valene had to take her eyes off Dingo's mouth.

Actually, she had to mentally block out what he'd done to her last night with that mouth.

Dingo stepped away, "Did you hear me?"

No, she was too busy thinking about finishing what he'd started. "What?"

"I said, let's meet later."

"Why?" Meet Dingo? Bad idea because clothes would come off and she'd regret having opened herself up to a level of pain she wouldn't survive again.

His face gave up nothing. Classic Dingo. He said, "Because

you want answers, right? You'll get them, but I have to get back to the event, too."

Should she believe what he said? That he'd give her answers? "Uhm..."

"Yes or no, Val."

Who was she kidding? "Yes. Where? When?"

"The cove. Midnight."

He *would* pick what used to be their spot at El Matador Beach, where they'd watched sunsets blaze over the Pacific and made love to the sound of the ocean crashing against huge rock formations. One of her all-time favorite LA locations.

Meeting him was probably a mistake, but she'd been born with an insatiable curiosity that had gone into overdrive around him before and was even stronger now. "Fine. But come prepared to answer my questions first. Don't be late or you'll miss me." She walked out ahead of him.

"I miss you already," he muttered.

She heard him, and the longing in that one sentence had her wanting to turn around and jump into his arms. To hear him say he couldn't live without her. That she was his world and all he'd ever want.

Dream on, Eklund. She kept moving toward the event, sounds of conversation and music growing louder as she reached the garden area.

When Dingo didn't pass by her as she'd expected once she was outside, she looked around and he was gone.

Maybe he didn't want to be seen with her.

That stung, even if she had been concerned about him talking to her in public.

Valene snagged a glass of champagne and strolled around to keep from being conspicuous by standing in one spot. When she recognized a former client she'd heard had recently contracted with Aram, she smiled politely.

Once she put this Vatican deal to bed, she would be back in the driver's seat again.

Aram would not get a chance to snake another client.

She had no issue with competition, but she'd never gone after a client who was already contracted on a project, and that was Aram's standard modus operandi.

Valene stepped past one of three gurgling fountains, impatient for her meeting with Tinker.

Her ticket insured she would get sixty seconds to pitch whatever she wanted to Tinker. Most attendees were here to convince him to throw a few million toward their personal charities.

Valene only wanted to pique Tinker's interest enough for him to have a second meeting with her and to make him think twice about dealing without her expert consultation.

If he hadn't already been contacted by someone helping the thief.

A rare item such as the scroll would make any collector of those artifacts salivate, but they also knew the extent of fraud in the business. She couldn't calculate the value of that scroll, if it was certified as genuine, but the thief would be more focused on getting fast money. How much would that be?

Ten million? Fifty million? A billion?

Would that even put a dent in Tinker's bank account?

Perdido, Fontana and Tinker drew everyone's attention when they stepped onto a low, flower-draped stage that put them a head above everyone else. Perdido said, "Emilio and I appreciate the invitation to join my dear friend, Jon Tinker, in support of saving the..."

Valene tuned her out.

She'd have sixty seconds with Tinker.

She'd come prepared and only needed twenty.

Henri had really come through with this ticket. Of course, he'd first explained that one did not trade for an invitation to a celebrity event only to dispose of said ticket with the nonchalance of selling an item on eBay.

That was hardly different than selling antiques at a flea market, in his opinion.

But he'd had no qualms about negotiating with a treasure hunter, who had mentioned the ticket in passing while inquiring about a set of maps and other documentation related to a sunken sixteenth-century Egyptian trade vessel.

The treasure hunter had no interest in hobnobbing at a party. He'd gladly handed over the invitation plus another two thousand dollars to get the maps.

A man just ahead of her made a surgical move to keep from being stepped on by a woman who'd enjoyed a few too many free drinks.

Valene chuckled at the comical sight.

But lost her smile when the man turned as if he'd felt her watching him.

Her mouth fell open.

Was that Smith? What the hell was he doing *here*?

She started toward him, but the crowd filled in and he disappeared. It took her a moment to realize he'd looked different than he had just one day ago, with his hair a lighter shade, wearing tinted glasses and a tuxedo, but she'd developed a keen ability to match up images and shapes from years of searching for items–and people sometimes–who she might only see once in her hunt.

If she hadn't just spent time studying Smith yesterday, he wouldn't have been quite so clear in her mind, but that was him.

Had he been here checking up on her? How would he have known she was here? Or had he also come to the party with the idea of talking to Tinker?

Had he seen her with Dingo?

No, because she had a feeling Dingo had dissolved into the crowd and surroundings the minute he'd exited the ladies room.

The ladies room. Valene had left her lipstick in the damn ladies room. She could not afford to replace it.

With Perdido still grandstanding about how she was going to save California's treasures, Valene had time to get the lipstick and return to the gardens.

Behind her, Perdido introduced Jon Tinker who said, "Thank you for coming today and donating your pocket change."

A ripple of laughter ran through the crowd.

That opening meant Valene had eleven minutes until she could meet with Tinker.

Now if only Henri could convince Geoffrey to help by tossing a bait out to his tight-knit community of Galileo experts and gain her an introduction to the other two potential buyers in New York and Seattle.

Geoffrey *might* do that for Henri, if Henri could convince Geoffrey it was for the greater cause–their relationship.

Geoffrey sure as hell wouldn't do it for Valene.

Too many ifs to keep worrying over. The plan was good.

"Just keep telling yourself that," she muttered.

Chapter 16

DINGO PASSED TANNER, sending a finger signal that all was fine. Tanner nodded, but that only meant Tanner would have questions later.

Blade broke in to inform the team, "Caddy keeps checking his watch and glancing around. Looks to me that he's anxious to be on the move."

Tanner replied, "Can you blame him when he doesn't have a speaking role?"

"Roger that, cowboy."

Nick interjected, "Everything look good up top, Ryder?"

"Roger that. Sniper cover still in place." Ryder had been keeping tabs on the rooftop security, because for one thing he had the best view of the rooftop from where he stood at the back of the gardens, and for another, the sniper in him would force him to constantly watch Tinker's men on the roof, whether Ryder was ordered to or not.

Fifty feet away, on the opposite side of the garden from Dingo, a man was moving around the perimeter. Side view. Pale brown hair, trimmed goatee, and a tuxedo covering a body that moved with purpose, but that nose and his chin...

Bloody hell.

Dingo's mind locked down and all the sounds around him receded, leaving a vortex of disbelief in its wake for the third time today.

Rikker?

In the blink of an eye, the bastard disappeared. Again. Had that really been him this time, or was Dingo *actually* losing his mind, hallucinating about the person he'd rather be hunting? If he was truly seeing Rikker where Rikker was not, he was in serious need of the downtime Sabrina had been pushing on him.

But if that *was* Rikker…

He took a step toward the empty spot, determined to find out. If it was, he would hunt down that miserable piece of humanity and drag his carcass back to Josh and Sabrina before leaving tonight.

Shit. He had to tell the team about Rikker and then he had to tell Sabrina about Valene being here. That was his duty.

Dingo spoke in a whisper, for his mic only. "I just—"

Blade broke in fast, reporting, "Possible Tom showing an interest in Perdido. Nineteen, maybe twenty, five-nine, hundred and thirty, black suit, bowtie, snub nose, short brown hair, curly, fingers twitching like a smoker needing a hit."

Tom was the code name for a stalker.

And that description fit the guy Dingo had seen smooching the young woman earlier.

The minute Dingo mentioned Rikker, the team would be distracted, choosing between who went after the stalker and who focused on Rikker...who Dingo only *thought* he saw.

Josh had no intel indicating Rikker was here.

Dingo hadn't seen the spook in years.

Everyone had a doppelganger, a twin version of another person with no DNA connection.

Dammit, he'd never questioned himself like this before. Lack of sleep was shredding his mental stability.

Blade added, "Tom heading north."

That was Dingo's area, the lower tier of the garden.

The op always came first.

Dingo took a quick turn to step up on the main level that led into the double doors at the rear of the hotel. From here, he had a wide view of the gardens.

There was Perdido, Fontana and Daddy Warbucks, who was saying, "In closing, I want to thank you again for your generosity..."

"Disregard," Blade amended. "Tom is leaving with parents."

Dingo caught sight of the pimply young man following his elderly mother and father. A late-in-life baby looking miserable and lonely.

At least his parents had wanted to keep him.

Dismissing the possible stalker, Dingo took advantage of his position to scope the crowd for Rikker so that he could at least give a position when he alerted the team.

Ryder spoke as calmly as if noting the mild weather when he said, "The eagles are out of the nest."

Dingo's pulse took a major jump. He swung his head around and twisted to look straight up, but Ryder had the superior view of the rooftop security coverage.

Where were Tinker's guards who were supposed to be up there?

Nick sounded as if he was moving fast, maybe running when he asked, "How long?"

Ryder answered sharply. "Twenty seconds. Ten seconds too long. Still gone."

Nick ordered, "Lock down the elevators. I'm heading up the east stairwell."

Josh broke in from where he kept eyes on them through the webcams. "Copy that. Elevators now inoperable."

The only place they'd been forbidden to access was the roof since Warbucks's men had said no.

Dingo swung back around and in the next second he took in the entire garden scene, mapping everyone's position as if they were on an oval-shaped clock face.

Daddy Warbucks, Perdido, and Fontana stood at the center of the clock. Dingo held the six o'clock position. Closer to the celebrities, Tanner anchored the number three position with Ryder at noon and was walking toward Blade who stood ten feet off the raised stage.

Dingo rushed forward, but life often changed in a matter of seconds, as it did now.

Fontana and Perdido leaned toward Daddy Warbucks as if to hear a secret.

Blade could be heard ordering one of Warbuck's bodyguards, "Your topside guard is gone. Get on that stage and–"

One of the in-house security guards near Tanner shouted, "*Gun!*" drawing everyone's attention to the left where a guy was backing up with a weapon pointed at the stage.

A rifle report blasted at almost the same instant the back half of Fontana's head exploded.

A second shot followed, taking down the guy waving the gun.

Nick cursed, "East entrance to the roof is locked."

Dingo could hear Nick grunting as he slammed up against the door, then the pop of Nick shooting the lock.

Screaming and shouting erupted. People raced in all directions, unsure where to go for safety.

Bodyguards dove to protect the bodies they were still responsible for, but every Slye agent would be headed to their respective positions that had been assigned in case an attempt was made on Perdido.

Dingo raced for the doors to the hotel, catching sight of Tanner and Ryder moving to cover any escape route through the garden. Running ten steps behind Dingo, Blade had been assigned to cover the front entrance in case White Hawk picked up someone leaving that way and had to follow.

They all knew the layout of the hotel.

Nick continued, "I'm on the roof. One guard down. The other missing. West exit is unlocked but door blocked."

Inside the marble and glass lobby, Dingo plowed through frantic guests crying and yelling, running in all directions. When he reached the stairs meant to be a fire exit, Dingo reported, "I'm at the west stairs, heading up."

They all knew it was him since this was Dingo's pre-assigned position.

Nick replied, "I'm backtracking to back you up."

Dingo acknowledged Nick, then stopped to quiet his breathing before drawing his Sig and taking the steps, but nothing would slow the pace of his body mainlining adrenaline. He started upstairs quickly, treading silently with senses tuned to red alert as he sorted through what had already happened, planning for what might happen next. Stairwells like this were every agent's nightmare place to get caught in a firefight.

The person behind this hit had used the gun in the crowd as a distraction to give his sniper an exit strategy.

One of Warbucks's men had made the hit.

What *was* the exit strategy?

And why hadn't Dingo seen the guy in the lobby first? The shooter was ahead of Nick coming down, and wouldn't have risked the elevator, not with Warbucks's men aware of the extra security. But they thought Nick and his team were here only to watch for a stalker.

On the second landing, a sharp metallic smell singed the air. Blood.

As Dingo turned to step up, he saw a hand dangling at the landing of the midway point to level five. Moving faster, he searched the stairwell for threats, then came face to face with the dead eyes of a man dressed in the dark blue suit of Tinker's security, and with a case that probably held a dismantled rifle.

A double tap to the head had killed him, but instead of being in the forehead, the two shots were through the eyes.

Dingo called out, "Body in west stairwell looks to be our shooter."

Nick said, "Heading up those stairs now."

Footsteps pounded up toward him now that there was no reason to be quiet. When Nick reached Dingo and the body, he frowned. "What the hell?"

Dingo stepped over the body to stand on the opposite side of the landing so they could both study the body and watch each other's backs. "Have no idea, mate." He noticed something odd on the dead man's neck, and squatted down, using the muzzle of his Sig to turn the guy's head, exposing a scarred marking. "He's got that Orion Hunter tat."

Nick crouched down. "What's on his wrist?"

Dingo reached over and picked up the sleeved arm, easing it back to see something that should only be in his nightmares. He worked to keep his breathing steady and his voice even as he told Nick, "It's a Satanic design wrapped around three letters."

"What are the letters?"

"S. G. C." Dingo swallowed then added, "That stands for Satan's Garden Club."

"Shit," Nick murmured then raised his voice. "We thought the Orion Hunters were tracking information down on SGC to kick them out of Orion territory, like a gang war."

"Nope." Dingo stared at evidence that the two groups were working together.

Valene had been exposed to both groups.

Was she in danger? Or was she somehow connected to all this?

It was time to climb off the fence and choose a side.

Chapter 17

"Get my team out of there now, Barry!" Sabrina ordered her contact for this government clusterfuck-of-a job. "We had a deal. I send my people in undercover and you guaranteed me access. Fontana got hit and that might not have happened if my people had been on the roof. You assured me I could yank my agents out fast if I had to, well news flash–*I need them. Now!*"

"Give me a break, Sabrina. I had no control over Tinker's guards. He's got political friends in places you can't imagine and they don't want him crossed."

"I don't care. I've got a few friends of my own. Trust me when I say you won't like which way shit rolls downhill if I'm pushed to call them. Get. My. Team. Released. My next call will be to someone who can do it, but it won't be pretty." She thumbed the end button on her cell phone as hard as she could.

It just didn't have the same effect as slamming a receiver down on a landline phone.

She strode across the conference room in the basement of their safe house in LA and stood over Josh, who was monitoring the four video feeds from ... wait a minute. "What happened to number two camera at the event?"

"Lost it right before everything went down. I did everything I could to bring it up, so I'm thinking it's a glitch in the camera itself."

"Dingo's cameras don't have glitches," she argued, but not with Josh. Just thinking out loud.

Sabrina's cell phone buzzed. She looked at the caller ID on the display. "Be right back."

Not waiting on him to reply, she walked across the conference room and entered the private office she used when on site then closed the door before answering. "Did you hear about the hit on Fontana?"

"I more than heard about it. I have something to show you and you're going to have to make a choice about where you stand after you see it."

Chapter 18

"YOU DIDN'T GET the scroll, Perdido?" Rikker had waited for her to be dropped off at home before he inserted into the estate she'd built on her smoking looks, sex and manipulation.

The perfect mix for politics.

Her nostrils flared when she turned a black gaze on him. "I did what I could. Did you miss that I was almost killed tonight? One hair closer and it would have been me instead of Fontana. You tell your boss I am not pleased with any of this."

Rikker could imagine the eye roll the General would give her in reply. And, just to be clear, the General was not Rikker's boss, but since the General thought he held sway over Rikker, there was no reason to let him or this bitch think differently.

Not yet.

Making himself at home, he stepped over to her private bar and lifted a bottle of whiskey with his gloved hands, pouring two fingers into a crystal glass.

A bar in her bedroom? Was it too much trouble to walk to another room for a drink?

Guess so.

He turned to her, swishing the drink in his glass. "I'm here for the scroll. You made a deal. You haven't delivered. That means my boss won't fulfill his end either."

"What?" She went into a tirade of cursing fluently in her native South American language. When the noise died down, she said, "What about the assassin?"

Rikker took a last sip of his drink and dropped a piece of paper on her bar. "He'll come for you and he won't miss this time. He's your problem."

"The General can't leave me exposed like this."

"Apparently he can, unless you want a dossier released on you to the press."

That took the red rage out of her cheeks and washed the crazy from her eyes.

"Calm down. The General had a secondary plan in case you did not deliver. You have four days left to deliver the scroll. If not, the General has a way for you to make amends, but I've seen his makeup tests and I don't think you'll pass."

She would do as told with no argument or it would be her last argument. Perdido was a narcissistic bitch who took care of *número uno* first.

He took her silence to mean they had an understanding.

Setting the glass down, he walked out.

Chapter 19

DINGO TRUDGED BEHIND Nick into the meeting room at the safe house where no one was happy. Least of all Dingo.

Sabrina had ordered him to return.

Ordered.

Dingo had texted back to say he might run a little behind, maybe an hour, which should have gotten him a "be careful and stay in touch," not a curt reply that unless he could explain why he had to be late he was expected to return just like everyone else.

Yes, Sabrina led the teams and everyone needed to debrief after that goat rope security detail, but Dingo had wanted to follow Tinker's entourage when he left.

And, to be honest, Dingo wanted to make sure Valene was okay. He hadn't seen her when the shooting went down and just wanted a minute to be sure she got out of the interrogations and went straight home to sit tight until he got there.

Orion Hunters were involved.

So was Satan's Garden Club.

All right here in LA. Coincidence? Not likely.

Valene had still been inside a private room at the hotel, being questioned when Sabrina sent out her get-the-hell-back-here-ASAP text. It hadn't been those exact words, but the phone had practically steamed from that message.

Of course, if Sabrina had known Valene was on site, Sabrina would have gone from zero-to-pissed in seconds.

Or maybe *that* was the problem.

Sabrina had seen Valene on the video feeds.

If so, Sabrina would have made the leap that Dingo had wanted to stay to see Valene out of purely personal reasons.

Dingo paused next to Josh, who stood from where he'd been monitoring the video feeds from the event. He handed Josh two fingerprint samples he'd pulled off the killer and did a double take at video two. "Where's the feed for number two?"

Josh said, "Lost it."

"Before or after the hit?"

"Right before."

"Is that what has her jacked up?" Dingo asked, not needing to clarify that he meant Sabrina.

"Maybe. She's got something crawling up her spine and won't say."

If she wouldn't tell Josh then it probably didn't have to do specifically with Dingo.

Everything is not all about you, dumbshit.

Dingo dropped onto a seat on the opposite side of the big conference table from the door, glad to sit down for a moment even if he hadn't wanted to come back. The room smelled of frustrated agents who had been working for hours on end.

Sabrina stepped in from her adjoining suite and moved toward the head of the table.

She liked her privacy no matter where she was.

He understood. They'd been packed into bedrooms like tuna into cans as kids back at the orphanage. He and Josh were the same way. The three of them would hunker down in tight quarters for as long as it took if they were on a mission, but the minute they returned, everybody went to whatever they called home.

For Dingo, that was a company apartment since he kept nothing more than the few changes of clothes he could fit in a small duffel, which allowed him to use any place for home.

Sabrina's gaze slid over to Ryder as he found a chair on Dingo's left, then it skipped Dingo completely and jumped to Josh, who took a spot at the end of the table on Dingo's right. That must have suited her because she glanced over to Tanner sitting across from Dingo, Nick who was standing up, then Blade and White Hawk sitting between Tanner and Sabrina.

But she'd avoided any eye contact with Dingo.

Maybe he'd been right all along about what had her on edge. Either way, he was going to have a talk with her after this.

Just the two of them.

But Sabrina had to let him deal with his own life. She thought she could save him from himself, keep him from making another mistake with Valene, but she had it wrong.

Dingo still believed Valene had done nothing wrong beyond being too enthusiastic when it came to life in general.

If not for the danger it put her in, he loved that about her. But now she might have put herself in trouble by her association with Charlie, and Dingo had to get her out of it. Once he did, he'd have to thank Sabrina for alerting him to Charlie. Then he'd remind her that the end does not always justify the means.

If their friendship meant anything to her, she'd never betray his trust again.

Sabrina's heart was in the right place, but she needed to butt out of his personal life.

He was also going to tell Josh and Sabrina about seeing Rikker. They could decide whether anyone else knew. He would never hold out information on Rikker from those two.

Eyeing every agent in the room, Sabrina asked in a voice that could ice over hot coals, "Anyone want to tell me how someone got sniped with six of my people on site, and we have no suspect?"

All but Nick had settled around the table.

Nick stood just inside the door, over six feet of tension coiled tight from the look of his stiff shoulders. He let out a rush of breath and began spitting out a report.

"Two Warbucks guards on the roof prevented any Slye coverage there. Evidently one was the assassin. Dingo found him in the west stairwell dead. My guess is that whoever killed him was part of the assassination plan and simply clipping any loose threads immediately."

Sabrina's gaze ticked back in Dingo's direction again, but wouldn't stay.

What was that look all about?

Tanner leaned back in the office chair, still alert and ready to go. "Killer had scarring that I think is the Orion star configuration we discussed earlier. Ties this to the Bergman killing."

Connecting a dot with the Bergman killer sent tension rippling around the room.

Sabrina asked, "Have you confirmed that marking as a hunter identification yet?"

"My source says the marking was on the elite agents of the Orion Hunters, but now that I have a photo I'll get an absolute confirmation." Tanner didn't look happy about this connection with the hunters. He'd defied death to keep his resource and future wife, Soo Jin, out of the hands of Orion Hunters. But she was the best intel the team had on the elusive fanatics. Jin had been a captive research specialist in North Korea when she'd shown up unexpectedly on Tanner's mission to extract two physicists from the country last month.

The physicists had been connected to an Orion Hunter terror plot and Jin had been instrumental in preventing it.

Dingo asked Sabrina, "Did you get a photo on the Bergman killer's tat?"

Had he not been studying her closely for any change, he'd have missed the slight tensing of her shoulders before she shook her head and said, "The report I had was a visual ID. I've avoided asking APD in case there's an Orion Hunter on the force. Based on everything we've learned from past encounters, we have no idea where they might have infiltrated."

That figured. She just accepted Laughton's intel as valid, but questioned everything Dingo did right now.

Josh leaned forward with his elbows propped on the conference table. "I fed every face that entered as a guest, security and wait staff at the event through our facial recognition contact and there were no suspicious hits."

If Josh had seen anyone resembling Rikker he'd have told Dingo while the team was still on site.

That meant Dingo had been wrong.

But his gut still argued that he'd been right. Nick scratched his back against the wall then paused, arms crossed, deep in thought–or so he'd seemed–staring down at nothing. He said, "That entire scenario was off."

"Because the assassin missed Perdido?" White Hawk asked from where she sat closest to Sabrina. She said very little unless she required information at that moment or had assimilated something she didn't understand.

Ryder answered, "Maybe, but that would depend on the assassin being an amateur. A really bad amateur at that. Do we have anything back on the fingerprint?"

Josh cleared his throat. "It's sent in and they'll ping me as soon as they have something."

"It's one of two things," Ryder went on. "If it was an amateur who blew the mission, that begs the question of why he stopped shooting, because someone without experience would panic and shoot again."

"He did," White Hawk argued. "He shot the guy who was down in the event who had a handgun."

"That's another issue. What I meant was that someone sent to make a kill who thinks he's missed would try to take a second shot right behind the first one. It could be as you said, that Fontana knocked Perdido out of position for a second shot or if the sniper was a pro, then that means–"

"Shooting Fontana wasn't an accident." Dingo stated what they all had to be thinking based on the simple fact that the assassin had infiltrated Tinker's security, which meant he'd been in place for a while and that his background check for that job had been above reproach. A freakin' sleeper cell.

White Hawk tapped a finger on the table surface. "Fontana leaned toward Perdido just as he got hit and he fell, knocking her to the ground. That would explain not taking the second shot at Perdido."

"Maybe," Ryder conceded, but his tone said he didn't think so and as the resident sniper on their team Dingo went with Ryder's gut reaction.

"Then who was the target?" White Hawk said, pursuing the point without being obnoxious. "The initials were F.E.P. Francine Eva Perdido."

"If it wasn't Perdido, then the hypothesis we built around the initials is wrong," Josh offered.

Dingo shook his head. "I have a feeling we were at the right place and the right time, but the intel is skewed in some way. There were players on stage that we weren't expecting."

Tanner rubbed his eyes with the heels of his palms and slapped the table. "I suck at cryptic shit. We need Margaux. She loved damn puzzles."

Sabrina told Tanner, "True. I tried to reach her but she and Logan are out of pocket for another six days."

Margaux Duke, aka "The Duke" had been a Slye agent, and still was as far as the team was concerned, but she'd gone rogue to find the person who killed her FBI agent cousin and landed in a South American jungle prison with Logan Baklanov who had been after the same person.

They survived when Dingo wouldn't have given either of them more than single digit odds, and she was now part of Logan's HAMR Brotherhood operation.

"What about the other guy with a weapon," Blade inquired of the room.

Tanner frowned. "That clown on the ground?"

Blade lifted a finger. "That one."

Dingo gave his opinion. "I'm with Nick. I think this whole thing was shonky."

"*Shawn-kee*? What the hell is that?" Tanner Bodine's deep Texas drawl purred around the room.

"Shonky is Aussie for only-an-idiot-would-consider-the-evidence-as-it-appears," Josh explained. At least he pronounced Aussie correctly as Ozzie, the way Dingo had taught him when Josh was just a punk.

"Back on point," Sabrina ordered everyone.

Dingo arched an eyebrow at her short fuse when she normally would have ignored the occasional jab or quip to break the tension.

She sent a subtle look back at him that said, *Don't push me right now.*

Yep, they had to talk soon for the benefit of everyone.

Dingo got them back on track. "I'm saying I think the shooter on the ground waving the gun might have been there as a distraction."

"As part of the hit?" White Hawk asked.

"Right." Dingo caught a nod of agreement from Ryder and continued. "Plant a handgun long before the event. Buy him a ticket and send him in convinced that he'd be snatched out with the assassin then paid well."

White Hawk said, "Killing him on site would have been part of the plan from the beginning."

"Right."

"Then who killed the assassin?"

Nick snorted. "There's the sixty-four-thousand dollar question."

White Hawk cocked her head, looking totally confused by that old saying.

"What else do we know about the assassin's death?" Sabrina asked, keeping the debriefing moving along.

"Dingo found him first," Tanner replied.

Nick added, "Assassin had been popped twice and looked like he knew who killed him, because he had his rifle packed in a case, but he also had a Glock on his hip that never got drawn."

Blade slouched back, listening in quiet speculation. "Basically someone double crossed someone and double tapped him in the head. Sounds like a professional hit."

"Not the forehead," Dingo corrected. "Shot him through each eye."

Sabrina wasn't often surprised, but from the way her face lost its sharpness and her eyebrows bounced up for a second, she clearly hadn't expected to hear that.

Why? Dingo had never had this tough a time reading Sabrina.

"And there was a second tat," Nick concluded.

"What was that one?" Sabrina was shifting her attention between Tanner, Nick and Dingo.

"It was a satanic ink design on the shooter's forearm with three letters. S. G. C." Dingo met Sabrina's stare, daring her to stop him from protecting Valene.

"How sure are you it's related to Satan's Garden Club?" she asked.

Here we go. Dingo said, "That would be a reasonable assumption based on those I saw years ago."

Josh had covered his eyes with his hand as if he didn't want to see the blood bath building.

In for a penny... Dingo added, "If I hadn't been ordered to return immediately, I could have stayed long enough to gather more intel." Dingo could have hunted for Rikker.

Sabrina unfolded her arms and dropped her hands down on the table to support her body when she leaned forward. "What specific intel?"

He wasn't about to admit seeing Rikker in front of the team. He'd tell Sabrina and Josh later. "Hard to say since I didn't have the opportunity."

Her jaw flexed. Furious.

She stood up. "Nick, please take everyone except Dingo and Josh to the other war room and let's get started on figuring out what our next step is and take another look at all three sets of initials. Clearly there will be more than one assassin going after targets at this rate."

Nick said, "Will do, but before I leave, I picked up a tip tonight on one of the artifacts the Orion Hunters are after." Sabrina's gaze whipped over to Nick. "You had a resource at the event? Was it someone inside the hunters?"

"No."

"Then how do you know the information is reliable?"

Drawing in an uneasy breath, Nick said, "You don't want to hear this, but we've had help from this person on a number of missions and the only way I'm given intel is by protecting the identity of this resource. This person suspected something was going down at the event, told me what could be shared and offered to share more later if new information became available."

Sabrina's chin moved like she was grinding her teeth. She said, "Thank you. We'll discuss that later."

That was Sabrina's way of saying she expected Nick to come clean about how much he was sharing of Slye intel in return.

Once everyone had vacated the room and the door to the hallway snapped shut, Dingo waited on Sabrina to get her piece said first.

He'd learned back during his early years that remaining quiet often meant being spared a beating. He had no fear of Sabrina, not physically, but words were often more deadly than getting slashed with a knife. They would both regret anything said in anger. He sat back, the vision of cool and calm.

The door to Sabrina's private quarters opened and Dingo knew right then that it was going to get ugly.

Gage Laughton walked in.

Chapter 20

JOSH GLANCED OVER at Dingo, then back at Sabrina. "What the fuck is he doing here?"

Glad to see that Josh wasn't in on this, Dingo muttered, "Took the words out of my mouth."

A mix of emotions formed in Sabrina's face, but worry and guilt stood out the strongest. She held up a hand. "You know that Gage has helped with intel in recent months. He gave us the image of Rikker in DC. He's also the person who told me about Bergman's killer being an Orion Hunter so it would be wrong for me to ignore his intel."

"Because he's so bloody honest, right?" Dingo quipped.

"At least I don't lie to Sabrina," Gage countered.

Josh said, "What the hell's that supposed to mean?"

"Hold it!" Sabrina's black eyebrows pulled tight at the bridge of her nose and her voice turned hard as granite. "Gage has some disturbing information and I want him to get it out first then we'll talk. Give him a chance to explain what he told me just before everyone returned."

How long had that bastard been camped out in her private area? Just the fact that he was here, this close to the team and the mission soured Dingo's stomach.

When Dingo caught Gage and Sabrina exchanging a quick look, hair danced along his neck. He had that hinky feeling, the kind a person got right before they stepped on a land mine.

Standing with hands in the pockets of his black cargo pants, Gage lifted his chin and fixed his gaze on Dingo. "I heard what was said in here during the debriefing. I've gone through all the videos up to ten minutes ago. I know who killed the sniper or who wants credit for the killing."

That was definitely news and from the lack of surprise on Sabrina's part, she knew too.

Josh jumped on Gage's words. "Who?"

Sabrina said one word that cracked the silence. "Rikker."

Josh stared in disbelief. "No fucking way. We'd have seen him."

Gage argued, "He had to already be inside the event before any security or your team was on site. Whatever exit strategy he had was the same one the assassin had intended to use, because he didn't come out of the hallway to the stairwell after he killed the sniper. And you don't have that surveillance tape, do you?"

"We did but–"

"Your camera died," Gage finished. "Don't you find it odd that one of your cameras was out of commission at a critical time?"

All through this, Dingo watched Sabrina whose eyes wouldn't meet his. "Why aren't you surprised to hear Rikker's name right now, Sabrina?"

She drew her chin up and held her body as if fortifying her backbone. "Rikker was here ten days ago, but there was no sighting of him again until now."

"Is that what Gage told you?"

"Yes."

Josh was a ball of energy waiting to burst. "Is this another Rikker crumb thrown our way?"

Dingo said, "Because we aren't in the loop."

Sabrina's voice was on edge. "He's sharing information with me that the agency isn't getting."

"Why?" Dingo asked, sending that straight at Gage.

"Because of all that's happened recently to convince me that the Orion Hunters are a dangerous group and I have no way of knowing where they might have infiltrated the government."

Dingo lifted his hand and counted off fingers in Gage's direction. "You knew Rikker was in LA as recently as ten days ago, but we're only just now finding out." He paused to check Sabrina's rigid mask that didn't change then continued. "You're now saying there's a connection between him and the hunters, but even *if* that's dependable intel we don't know if Rikker's behind these killings or working against the hunters and last, but not least by any means, you've insinuated the camera on the hallway was disarmed intentionally."

When Sabrina did not say a word, Dingo pinned her with a hard glare. "Have I got that about right? If so, now you can clear up the muddy parts like who you think disarmed a camera when I was the only one dealing with it, and why Gage is here now, since *you* could have told us all that?"

"He's got more to show you," she offered.

She'd said "you," as in for Dingo and Josh.

Gage waited while Sabrina also said, "Valene Eklund was at the event."

Dingo was so busy trying to pull these crazy threads together in his head that he said, "Valene? What's she got to do with this?"

"But you know she was there, right?" Sabrina questioned.

"Sure. I saw her."

"Did you know she'd be there?"

"No, but it's not that surprising. LA *is* her stomping ground." But now that Gage had pointed out Valene to Sabrina first, he'd kiboshed Dingo's chance to tell Sabrina and Josh about seeing Valene tonight. In fact, he wasn't about to admit to seeing anyone in front of Gage-fucking-Laughton.

Gage's eyes narrowed, judging Dingo and questioning his words with a steady look. "Did Eklund tell you *why* she was at the event?"

Dingo dodged that question by countering, "Why should she? Last I checked this was a free country."

"Did she meet with anyone while she was there?"

"What is this, a fucking inquisition?"

"Just answer him," Sabrina pleaded softly.

"Why? When did he become part of our missions?"

Gage said, "When I started filling Sabrina in on what her people were hiding from her."

Josh shoved up to his feet, all semblance of the cultured veneer disappearing under a whip of fury. "So this fucker has you convinced that *we're* lying to you?"

Sabrina was quick to say, "No, Josh."

Dingo caught the single reference. "Not *Josh*, but what about me, Sabrina? Do you think I'm lying to you?"

She hesitated a second before looking at Dingo. That had been all the answer Dingo needed even though she was shaking her head and saying, "I just want you to tell me what's going on with Valene."

"What the hell do you think is going on?" Dingo asked right back.

"Stop answering me with a question," she snapped at him. Her phone buzzed. She eyed it and made a sound under her breath then looked at Dingo. "Do me one favor, Dingo, and listen to what Gage has to say. He's helped us out in the past when it counted."

"If that's all the criteria you need then what about Valene? She pulled markers everywhere to help us stop a terrorist attack. Doesn't that count for something?"

Silence must have sucked the oxygen from the room, because no one said a word.

Dingo had never been put in a position of defending himself or his actions. That Sabrina would stand there and allow this ripped the fabric of their relationship. Dingo crossed his arms and decided to see this through, then give her a chance to explain herself.

Gage was the only man she'd ever gotten seriously involved with and the UK mission had screwed badly with her head. As her friend, Dingo would allow her the opportunity to fix her mess, and he hoped she took it.

Dingo said, "I saw Valene talk to different people and I understand that she had a ticket that would have allowed her sixty seconds to meet with Tinker. Everyone in this room knows that Valene's expertise is in antiquities and Renaissance antiques. Now show me why you're standing there in support of this prick, Sabrina."

The prick in question asked, "Are you sure Valene had no ulterior motive for helping the last time you were here?"

Dingo turned to Josh whose fingers had scrambled his hair that had been nicely styled a moment ago, and he saw no clue in that gaze so Dingo asked Sabrina, "Are you suggesting Valene found the Korean doctor treating the physicists brought over here for a criminal reason? What kind of screwed up question is that? Valene has always been on the right side of the law."

"Maybe in the past," Gage agreed. "But things have changed."

"Like what?" Dingo's temper rarely showed up, but it was boiling closer to shooting over the edge every second.

"Like the fact that her client list has fallen off significantly over the past three years and that she desperately needs money for her father's medical expenses? For a special treatment because he's got a rare lung cancer?"

No. Dingo didn't know that, and the fact that he didn't punched him in the gut. Valene had always wanted to know more about him, but he'd intentionally kept some distance with her, or he thought he had. Based on the sick feeling flooding him, he hadn't been as smart as he'd thought, and the result was that she'd been in trouble and hurting and he hadn't been around to help. Could the woman he thought he knew so well actually be committing a crime willingly?

All these pieces were piling up against Valene.

Had he lost all perspective on this?

Or had he spent that much time with someone who'd been playing him all along?

Dingo answered in a weary voice, "That should explain why she was at the event tonight. She was probably networking for new clients."

"With a ticket that cost twelve grand?"

Dingo *had* questioned that and even more so now, but he wouldn't admit it to Gage. "She's connected in her field, and that means she knows a lot of high rollers. Knowing Valene, she made some deal for it." The words hurt coming out, but he added, "And she's gorgeous. This is LA. Could be someone she's dating gave her the ticket."

Sabrina had listened quietly to the back and forth play between Dingo and Gage.

Josh must not have been dealing with this any better than Dingo, because he said, "Wait a damn minute. That's why you wanted me to review Valene's bank account. You two have been investigating all this and you didn't bring me or Dingo in on it?"

"Thanks, mate." Dingo could still count on one person in spite of Josh snooping around in Valene's records.

The look Sabrina gave him came with a shade of remorse that colored her voice. "I only found out for sure about Valene tonight, so no. I have not been investigating her behind your back. I only told you about Charlie because... "

"You were looking for something to make me back away from her," Dingo said, finishing her sentence. "But he *has* been investigating Valene." Dingo lifted his chin in Gage's direction. "Before, it was just about me, but now that Laughton tells you something you're convinced Valene is dirty. Why?"

Gage said nothing.

Sabrina asked Dingo, "Do you realize how hard you're working to defend Valene? So much that you might not be seeing everything clearly?"

He had one code and that was to take care of everyone who mattered to him, because that number was small and everyone in his circle was worth dying for. He'd never meant to get involved so deeply with Valene, but the truth was that he couldn't be objective.

But no way was he saying that out loud.

He *would* get to the bottom of all this and find his own answers on Valene. He said, "Want to know what I see, Sabrina? I look at your boy there and I see betrayal that kept him at arm's length for a while but that distrust is gone on your part," Dingo pushed back at her. "He's got you thinking that I'd cover for Valene if she was doing something criminal? And you just believe him? Is that it?"

Sabrina's answer came out with brittle edges. "Are you telling me you wouldn't help Valene if she got into trouble?"

"Define trouble."

"Criminal activity."

Had he fallen down some rabbit hole into an alternate universe? "What evidence do you have of her doing anything illegal?"

Dingo had expected Sabrina to look embarrassed at this point, not as if he'd asked the one question that was going to cut his heart out.

Gage fished a small remote from his pocket and pointed it at the large monitor behind Sabrina.

An image came to life with a frozen shot of Rikker in a restaurant having a meal. The silent screen images clicked by one at a time in a slide show of Rikker, then a woman meeting with him. She signed a tablet with a stylus and viewed something on that tablet. The last slides showed them both exiting the restaurant.

The next shot was another closeup of the woman that had every muscle in Dingo's body twisting like a cable being tightened.

And there came the facial recognition software engaged, flashing images until it stopped on a perfect one of Valene.

Blood pounded so loud in Dingo's ears it drowned out everything.

Chapter 21

DINGO HEARD GAGE'S voice at a distance saying, "You were in LA yesterday during the same time period that Valene was meeting with Rikker. Were you aware of that meeting?"

Rikker? Sabrina's private office spun for a moment then Dingo shook it off.

"No." Dingo's voice had thickened with emotion. She couldn't be in league with Rikker. "Unlike Sabrina, I'd have told her and Josh right away."

Sabrina ignored the jab. "Valene might be in the middle of all this voluntarily. You came flying out here thinking she's at risk from Satan's Garden Club, but you're the one who could be in jeopardy. Valene was here seven years ago when the SGC were in business. Yes, she found leads on the Orion Hunters in a matter of hours a month ago. Satan's Garden Club is back in business right here in LA again and involved with Orion Hunters, but they haven't touched her, have they?"

"Yet." He bit out the word.

Josh heaved out a deep breath and sounded sick to ask, "Okay, I'll play devil's advocate. Why haven't they gone after her, Dingo?"

Dingo sorted through all the evidence at hand and laid it out in his mind. He didn't give a flip what Gage thought, but Sabrina was balancing on a fence between her loyalty to Dingo and Gage on the other side.

Dingo would never put Sabrina or Josh on the wrong side of the law, no matter what.

He just couldn't accept this.

He knew Valene. Something was wrong with all of it.

Gage clicked his remote again and a new video played.

Dingo watched as the back of Valene's wavy blonde head of hair and shapely body went strolling down the hall to the ladies room at the event. Next came the back of Dingo's head, then the brunette he'd talked to who exited the hallway.

Dingo turned to Gage and Sabrina, holding his hands out. "Guilty as charged. I did talk to her. But I already told you that."

Gage said, "Keep watching."

Dingo turned back, pointing out, "Josh said the Slye camera went down right before..."

"This video isn't from a Slye camera," Gage clarified.

That meant this should show if anyone went down that hall right before the hit was made.

Dingo's heart thumped faster the closer the time on the video got to the hit. Twelve seconds before the hit, Valene returned to the hallway that remained empty until twenty-three seconds after the two shots were made.

There she came hurrying out before Dingo then went down the hall.

His heart clenched so hard he thought he was having a heart attack. She couldn't be involved. He didn't care what his eyes were telling him. Then he swung around to find Josh shell-shocked quiet, Gage wearing his usual stone mask and Sabrina's silence damning him.

"Thought you said Rikker killed the sniper," Dingo launched at Gage.

"You said the assassin tonight was shot through each eye. That's Rikker's MO, but based on this he might have given instructions to someone else to make the kill in his signature style."

"You think Valene is a cold blooded murderer?" Dingo asked Sabrina in a voice vibrating with fury.

"I don't know her and I don't think you do either."

Gage interjected, "Just so we're clear. I'm going to make sure no one sees your image going down that hallway, but not for you. However, I want whatever you have on SGC."

That message was clear.

He wouldn't burn Dingo for Sabrina's sake.

Sabrina and Gage might have had something going on at one time back before their team got burned, but Dingo had no reason to believe that Gage was here in Sabrina's best interest.

Dingo might as well get this out on the table to make it clear that Sabrina and Josh were not a part of what he took on his own to do. "Seven years ago, I went inside Satan's Garden Club to stop them from going after Valene because she'd found information that led me to them, but it also made her a target. I hadn't wanted her to dig that deep, but she did, with no idea of what she had brought down on her head."

After a pause, Gage asked, "Why didn't they kill her?"

"Because I took a bullet to protect Garcia just to get inside his circle fast. He asked what I wanted for saving his life–"

"And almost losing yours," Sabrina muttered.

Dingo kept talking. "I told Garcia I'd work for him if he'd leave Valene alone, that she was just a convenient piece when I was in town and it was my fault she'd stumbled on Giuseppe, which was how I found Garcia. He bought it. Not right away, but he made me a deal that if I double-crossed him he'd skin her slowly in front of me." Garcia *had* allowed Dingo to heal before he was put through the Satan Garden's Club initiation.

"Garcia died along with his three top men," Gage pointed out. "No one was left to carry on the legacy. Why is the SGC back in business and why LA?"

That's what Dingo wanted to know, but Gage was going for a connection. "I don't know, but it doesn't mean they're linked to Valene."

Gage shrugged. "The reason I mentioned Valene's financial straits earlier is because she had a fifty thousand dollar deposit dropped in her account from an offshore bank. That deposit dropped at the moment Rikker was seen walking away from the restaurant.

"Maybe she took him on thinking he was a new client," Dingo suggested, but his voice sounded unconvinced even to his ears. He wanted to rub his head but he'd be damned if he'd show any weakness in front of Gage. Dingo's headache had started six hours ago when he found Orion Hunter and Satan's Garden Club markings on Fontana's killer, and it wasn't letting up.

Fifty thousand dollars would buy a lot of things, like a ticket to a twelve thousand dollar event. That had to be a deposit Valene took for work to be performed, but what the hell could she be looking for that brought that kind of deposit?

The knowing smile on Gage's face said no one believed the new client angle any more than Dingo did.

Valene had been building a strong business, but even then she hadn't dealt with the level of artifacts that came with a fifty thousand dollar deposit.

Dingo had another set of suspicions as long as they were pointing fingers. "How is it you have this film of Rikker?"

Gage took his time answering. "I have someone watching for any sign of Rikker. We've been catching him on traffic cams, but that does us little good when he's already gone each time. However, this time, the traffic cam picked him up leaving the restaurant. I got lucky that this restaurant runs surveillance cams on all their operation."

Dingo would agree that it had been a lucky break if Valene hadn't been the woman meeting Rikker.

Gage clicked his remote and new pictures loaded on the screen. Bloody and gruesome torture of two men, but the woman in the third picture was stomach-turning bad. Nude, bleeding everywhere, even from between her legs, she was hung with sharp hooks pierced up through under her arms.

It wasn't just bloody.

Parts of her body had strips of skin literally peeled away.

Too macabre to look away from and so sickening Dingo wouldn't be able to eat for a while. "Who are they?"

"What's left of the man on the top right is the person who alerted Bergman that Satan's Garden Club was coming after him."

Dingo swung around hard. "What do you know about them?"

Calm in the same way a predator waits patiently for his prey, Gage asked, "So now you want my intel?"

"Not particularly, but I want to know what you're feeding Sabrina."

"Dingo–"

His gaze locked horns with hers and he warned, "Don't Dingo

me. We're talking about a woman who put her life at risk to help us and save this country, and she gets no consideration for that."

Acting oblivious to the standoff, Gage said, "The second man and the woman tortured and killed were the closest friends of the man SGC thinks betrayed them. They didn't care that neither the man nor woman had anything to do with any of the operations, only that they wanted to send a message to anyone who crosses them."

Sabrina's phone buzzed. She held up her phone, closed her eyes in frustration, then opened them and said, "I'll be right back."

The minute she stepped out, leaving the door ajar, Gage dropped his voice to a deadly level, addressing Josh and Dingo. "Let's get something clear. Regardless of what you two think, my number one concern is Sabrina. I will not stand by and let her end up in pictures like those. If that happens, I'm coming after everyone involved, friend or foe."

Dingo shot back, "Like you protected her in the UK?"

"I'm working on what happened there."

"I'll tell you what happened, Laughton. Your agency fucked us and you still play ball for their team instead of coughing up some names."

"There's more to it than you know."

Josh said, "We're all ears."

Gage's lip curled ahead of a snarl.

Sabrina walked in. "What's going on?"

Voice smooth and easy, Gage said, "I was just filling them in on how the State Department is after anyone connected to Satan's Garden Club and they have their own videos that confirm everything I'm telling you. Valene was seen at the event, and my contact in the State Department tells me that right after Valene walked out into the gardens during the event, with Dingo following at a safe distance behind..."

The bastard paused long enough for Josh and Sabrina to look at each other then over at Dingo.

Then Gage finished, "That as soon as Dingo was called aside, Valene went back into the hotel, which is where you saw her re-entering that hallway on the video. She had enough time to meet the assassin in the stairway and end up in the middle of the guests with no one the wiser once panic broke out."

And Dingo was now sure he'd seen Rikker. He asked Gage, "Why hasn't Rikker been caught yet?"

"For the same reason I asked Sabrina not to mention any of this yesterday. Rikker is just a lead to much bigger fish. This is the closest we've come to him since he escaped with whoever freed him in the UK. If you spook him now, not only will we risk losing Rikker, but we'll lose the person who really did pull the strings on the UK mission."

Gage had sold Valene's guilt all the way through.

Dingo realized exactly what he had to do for any chance of proving Valene's innocence and protecting Josh and Sabrina.

Once Dingo made peace with what he had to do, he turned to face Sabrina. "So now you trust this buggar over me?"

"I didn't say that," she said, insulted and hurt at the same time. She never broke down. Never shed tears, but she hurt just like anyone else.

Josh sighed. "Come on, Dingo. I don't like this rat bastard CIA agent any more than you do. Sabrina just wants you to tell her that you're on our team no matter what. The same team we've had since childhood."

Dingo turned on him. "Now *you* want me to manipulate her the way Gage does?"

Josh scowled. "Shit no. Of course not."

Sabrina's throat muscles tightened and flexed. "Gage is not manipulating me."

"How would you know?" Dingo countered with the same argument he'd just been slapped with.

"She *knows* I'm not manipulating her," Gage said, "because she *knows* that I'm the objective one here."

"Can't talk for yourself, Sabrina?" Dingo taunted, a professional when it came to which of Sabrina's buttons got maximum response.

Her eyes flashed with threat of injury. "I have no problem saying what's on my mind and no one manipulates me. Let it go, Gage!"

"Why? He's clearly hiding something."

She turned on Gage. "Stop it. I brought you in here to explain, not to divide us."

There came the Sabrina that would scrap as hard as someone twice her size.

But Gage did have to divide them.

Dingo chuckled, a nasty sound he intended to let everyone know that he'd finally reached his limit. "That's precious coming from you, Sabrina. Valene stepped in with no questions when I asked her to find a Korean doctor. She then backed me up when Tanner and I were on our own. She played a significant role in preventing a national disaster and you can't even get Gage to give you one fucking name of who was involved in the planning of our UK op."

Sabrina flinched at the verbal hit and Gage cursed him.

Josh said, "Stop acting like a dick and just talk to her."

Dingo hated forcing Josh to take a side, but Josh was choosing correctly. "I'll stop acting like a dick when she stops cutting Gage slack and trusting him over me."

"I'm not cutting *anyone* slack, including Gage, when it means putting the team at risk, but you can't make the same claim or you'd have told me about Valene."

True that. "Oh, and he told you about Rikker yesterday, but you're only telling us now? Explain that to me...*pot*?" Dingo pushed his expression to cold fury and said, "Just never mind. Since I'm so bloody non-objective, untrustworthy and lacking, you clearly don't need me on this team."

Sabrina's face washed out a shade. "What are you saying?"

Josh echoed her words, "Yeah, what the hell?"

Dingo lifted a hand. "I find it rich that you tell me I'm not objective when you're standing next to the man you wanted to gut two years ago. That's where your loyalty lies, fine."

"You're twisting this around," she shouted at him.

"Me? I'm just giving you a look from my side of the room. You don't trust Valene even though she's never done anything but support us, yet you want me to listen to *his* shit? No!"

"Everyone just calm down," Josh said, trying to mediate an agreement that was not going to happen.

Dingo told Josh, "You've got a place here. She trusts you, mate."

"Dingo!"

He talked right over her. "But me? I'm not staying where I'm not trusted. I'm going to find answers, because I'm the best bet at getting close to Valene. Even though no one in this room believes me, if I discover she's in league with Satan's Garden Club, the hunters, Rikker or the Grim-fucking-Reaper, I'll drag her back here in cuffs myself."

Please, God, don't make me do that.

Dingo speared Gage with his next words. "But if I deliver evidence otherwise, then you'll have to make a choice, Sabrina, between me or him."

"Stay away from Valene. I had her released from the questioning."

"To make her your damn bait," Dingo accused him, knowing he was right.

Gage's only acknowledgement was to say, "If Rikker goes to ground, I'm holding you responsible."

"Dammit, Gage," Sabrina shouted.

Dingo pointed at Gage. "Fuck you." Then he strode out, not slowing down when Josh roared at him to stay and Sabrina alternated between shouting Dingo's name and cursing somebody.

He hoped she was unloading on Gage. Fat chance, that.

Nick intercepted Dingo on the way out, asking, "What the–"

"Leave off, mate. I'm done with this shit." Dingo stormed out, got in his rental and drove off in a spin of tires.

He fought to draw a breath. *I did the right thing.*

He'd walked into Satan's den to protect Valene. Dingo could do no less for the two people he'd admit loving if he had any idea how to love someone.

Dingo had to find out just who was lying and who was not.

Sabrina had been right to accuse Dingo of lacking objectivity, because with Valene in the middle of all this he couldn't do his duty.

The agency was leaving Valene dangling just to use her to pull in Rikker. Gage hadn't denied it.

No one wanted Rikker more than Dingo, unless it was Josh and Sabrina. But none of them would put an innocent woman in harm's way to get revenge. Gage, on the other hand, was another matter. Before Sabrina's team had gotten burned in the UK on a CIA mission directed by Gage, Dingo had followed her lead by giving Gage the benefit of the doubt when any issue arose.

Now? Dingo believed Gage would turn his own mother over to the devil if it served his agency.

Sabrina's head was not on straight. Laughton had her emotions twisted into a pretzel.

Dingo couldn't fault her since he was fighting just as hard not to accept what the evidence presented. The best he could do was keep emotions out of the mix.

If he came up with proof that Gage was setting them up again, he'd get word to Josh, who would at least listen to him.

But if Dingo discovered Valene was truly working with Rikker, of all people, and that she was involved with Satan's Garden Club...

 Then he'd have to make a decision that was going to destroy what was left of his soul after walking out on the only family he'd ever had.

Chapter 22

MAXX NAVARRO GAVE the "leave me" look to the two men, his close *compadres*, who had just reported to him on the Jon Tinker fundraiser hit.

He asked his uncle, "Please stay, Tío."

At forty-nine, Tío was still an intimidating man who carried two hundred pounds of muscle and a loyalty to his late brother that was second only to Maxx's own. Maxx *would* avenge his father.

If not for Tío convincing a devastated sixteen-year-old boy that justice was better served by cold calculation, Maxx would never have waited so patiently to avenge his father's death.

Death was too forgiving a word for what was done.

Santori Garcia had been murdered, and the only way that could have happened was through betrayal by those closest to him.

Just as someone thought to betray Maxx today.

Two contracts completed twenty minutes apart, but the first one had not gone as planned.

Maxx's uncle took a cigar from the humidor on Maxx's desk. The desk was Brazilian Rosewood, and he'd had it shipped into LA. Tío mused, "Your papa would be very proud of you, Maxx. I had promised him you would be ready to stand at his side by the time you reached thirty. But look at you. At twenty-three, you have done well. Even your papa did not control so many resources at your age."

Maxx waved off the compliment, but deep inside he appreciated the encouragement. "Gracias, but I have much yet to do." He lowered himself into the office chair that was oversize to accommodate his six-foot-three frame.

His father and uncle were big men who had descended from Arawak ancestors who lived on the island of Curacao when Spanish invaders had thought to take the women as slaves. That was until the tribal men who showed up were six to seven feet tall, giants to shorter Europeans. Maxx had been blessed with the blood of his forefathers, the same thick, black hair, plus the devastating Navarro smile that had drawn women into their web back when selling whores was worth his time. Any attractive woman who wore revealing clothes and strutted her stuff was a whore in the making, if she wasn't one already.

He'd brought them in and his uncle had handled placements through contacts Tío had made when he worked with Maxx's father. That was before Maxx had developed a relationship with someone in the Orion Hunter network. That relationship opened the door to even better resources for what he had in mind.

No, he was not bigger or better than his father, but Maxx was just getting started. "I have my father's hard work and reputation to thank for what little I have gained in the two years since we moved here."

Tío lit his cigar, drew on it and released a puff with a sound of satisfaction. "I will not argue over my brother's accomplishments." He held the cigar, staring at it in thought. "If Garcia had entertained even a *thought* that he was under threat, he would have moved the bulk of his money to the account he funded for us while you grew up."

Eighty-seven million dollars gone.

"I will find every man who betrayed Papa and when I am through, no one will dare cross a Navarro again."

Nodding at that, Tío said, "What of this new associate of yours?"

"He will be fine," Maxx said, brushing off a potential argument.

"I don't like this man."

"We don't have to be his amigos to take his money, Tío."

"You know I support everything you do and I also wish to make those pay who killed your father, but this Smith is not being straight with you. I don't want your hunger for revenge to lead you into a trap."

"Smith is not capable of tricking me." Maxx preferred not to cross his uncle, but they were in agreement on who led Satan's Garden Club. And that hadn't been decided simply due to a sense of entitlement on Maxx's part, but Maxx had surprised even Tío with the ruthless determination he'd shown to reach this point, and brutal punishment of anyone who got in his way.

That was why Mr. Smith, a ridiculous alias, would be no problem.

Maxx owed his uncle respect so he did not pursue the discussion. He did not want to be forced to prove who was right.

Tío had raised Maxx from the age of four when his father's long-time companion had died. For that reason, when Tío told Maxx he had to finish the job Garcia had tasked his only brother with–to raise Maxx to become Garcia's second in command and deadly enforcer–Maxx had listened.

Then he took to his training like never before, attacking his studies, because an ignorant man could not lead. He built his body into hard planes of muscle and developed his marksmanship skills.

Now he was strategically rebuilding Satan's Garden Club, which would once again be great and control far more than his father's empire had.

His cell phone buzzed with an incoming call. Maxx lifted it from the desk, noted the unidentified caller, and answered, "I've been waiting for you to call and explain why my man was killed tonight, Mr. Smith."

Tío's eyes narrowed. Maxx lifted his free hand in a request to wait. He hadn't told Tío about their shooter being killed. Not until Maxx heard Smith's side and decided whether he would allow Smith to continue breathing.

Smith said, "Someone saw him. That would have left a loose end for both of us."

"I find it hard to accept that one of the Orion Hunter elite would be that careless."

"Calling me a liar is not in your best interest, Navarro. Not if you want to continue as one of my contractors."

"Neither is losing my people in my best interest. If there is a loose end, I handle it."

"Fine, next time I'll tell you, let you hunt someone who will go to ground the minute they're made and let you clean it up, but you'll wait on your money while you do. As it is, the money is already in your account."

Maxx knew the money had been transferred. He'd checked. "Only for the first kill. Not the second one."

"I'm waiting on confirmation of the ONC hit."

"The evidence has been delivered, so the delay is not on my end. Additionally, you are to supply names as part of our agreement."

"I gave you Bergman. He was the number one snitch who fed information on your dad."

"The agreement was one name per hit in addition to the money," Maxx reminded him. "Plus I now have to make amends for losing an employee of someone with whom I have a business relationship. I'm reconsidering the last contract I have to complete for you."

"That would be unwise at this point."

"Only in your opinion, Mr. Smith." Maxx allowed the silence that followed to speak the loudest for him.

After a moment, Smith conceded. "You're right, but only to a point. I'll tell you what I'll do. I've got more than the name of someone who was tight in your father's circle. This man was the one who saved your dad's life ... then ended it."

Maxx sat forward, gripping the phone. "That one. I want that one." Because he'd known it had to be someone very close to his papa, and the only other two who could have possibly given up his father had been killed with Garcia.

"Are we still on for the third contract?"

Tío caught Maxx's eye and gave him a tiny headshake, warning Maxx not to continue with Smith, but if Smith delivered on what he'd just offered, Maxx would kill the next one for free. "Yes, we still have an agreement."

Tío grumbled something that Maxx ignored, intent on hearing what Smith had to say next.

"Your dad knew this man by an alias, but his real name is Dingo Paddock. And as a bonus, I'm texting you his photo. He's even in Los Angeles right now."

Maxx's phone buzzed. He pulled the phone away to open the text. There was the picture, and it resembled one his father had sent to Tío with all the other photos of everyone in Satan's Garden Club. Until now, every dollar Maxx had paid to find this man had been spent in vain.

"Hey, Navarro," called to him from the cell phone in his hand. "Happy now?"

No, but Maxx lifted the phone back to his cheek. "I will take care of the third one as scheduled." He ended the call and drew in a deep breath to explain to his uncle, but a hard knock on his door interrupted.

His uncle shouted, "Qué?"

The door opened and Dominic said to Maxx, "He's back."

Maxx lifted his chin, ordering Dominic to send in his man.

Vincent had arrived in Brazil years ago, and had been with Maxx ever since. He taught Maxx English that could be spoken in business dealings so that Maxx would not sound like he'd just crawled across the border from Mexico. His father had trusted Vincent, but it had taken Maxx a while to warm up to the guy whose soul had been created from a block of ice.

Now, he held Vincent in the high regard someone with such expertise deserved. Maxx pointed at the chair next to his uncle. "Please have a seat."

Once the office door closed, Maxx asked, "Any problems?"

"No." Vincent had a deep, authoritative voice even when asking for the salt at dinner. "Should I have expected any?"

Tío spoke up. "Our associate on the first job did not survive the mission, but Maxx will have to give you the details."

Maxx buried his irritation. Tío would be Tío, regardless of who was in charge. "The client claimed our project was compromised, that someone saw the shooter leaving."

Vincent took his time thinking on that. "Odd."

A man of few words. Maxx agreed, "Yes, and for that reason we will take extra care on the next job by sending in eyes."

That gave Tío reason to smile.

Vincent pulled out a phone and placed it on the desk. "I took a few moments to chat with this one before fulfilling my obligation."

"Oh?" Maxx had learned far more than English from Vincent. This man had also taught him the fine skill of psychological warfare, especially when it came to withdrawing information. But in this particular case, the target had been some weak-kneed antiques dealer. "What did you bring us?"

Vincent took his time lifting the phone again, and while he did, hc said, "Evidently a very valuable item is up for grabs and some high rollers are after it."

Maxx took that in stride. There was always something of value that could be had. He couldn't waste time or resources on anything that did not bring a sizeable payday. "If I wanted rare antiques, I would send my man to Sotheby's."

"Oh, this is rare, but not what you're imagining," Vincent murmured. He paused and lifted his wrinkled gaze to Maxx. "This man I spoke to knew about the big fundraiser, the location of your first contract from Smith. This man said he'd help me obtain the prize if I'd allow him to live."

That was interesting. "What prize?"

"A scroll so rare he claims that the Orion Hunters would give all they owned to gain it."

"*Ridículo*," Tío growled, sitting upright.

"What?" Maxx said, leaning forward and agreed it sounded ridiculous. "Why would the Orion Hunters want this scroll?"

"You know about the Orion Prophecy, correct?"

"Yes, yes." Maxx waved his hand to the side, dismissing the crazy beliefs of the hunters. "The leaders are after artifacts, five in fact, so what makes this scroll so valuable?"

"This particular artifact is key to the prophecy and the most important piece of their puzzle."

Maxx cursed in Spanish, the only time he broke from his discipline of speaking English. He had learned the language of his enemy so that he would have no weakness when he hunted his prey. "Tell me why I should care, Vincent. Our business is not of antiques."

"Perhaps your client's business is, though."

"Why would you say that?"

"Because my target mentioned a Mr. Smith during our chat.

He said he did not have Smith's number, but he would be happy to introduce me to him as soon as Smith called back because Smith had offered him money to stay away from this scroll. That was the end of the information. There was much begging and crying at that point."

Tío cursed. *"A man should have cojones!"*

Vincent lifted his shoulders in a polite shrug. "I had a knife staking one of his to his kitchen chair at that point."

Maxx and Tío both flinched, but Vincent continued. "I find it a bit coincidental that we are dealing with a mysterious Mr. Smith in LA at the same time someone else is communicating with a Mr. Smith who told this antiques dealer to not attend the fundraiser where we also had a contract."

"Good point." Maxx had the patience of a gnat, where Vincent could take days to make a point if allowed. "What do you have for me?"

"I have the last four calls on this man's cell phone. Evidently he was obsessive about clearing his phone, but when I first found him he was ranting about a woman. Valene this and Valene that. Lot of anger." Vincent pressed the keypad as he spoke. "He thought I originally came to warn him away from her project, just as Smith had. Before I dispelled that notion, he told me Valene had no more claim to the scroll than he did. He called her to make an offer to split the proceeds with her and she did not even return his call."

Maxx nodded for Vincent to continue. "He called this Valene a few disrespectful names, then when he finally realized I was not there for the scroll, he told me the scroll is worth more money than what is sitting in any of the Federal Reserves. It's priceless."

Maxx clarified, "And he thought Smith was after the same thing?"

"Yes."

Maxx glanced at Tío, who chuckled softly. Grinning at his uncle, he told Tío and Vincent, "Smith owes me still. Perhaps we can renegotiate the last contract if we can obtain the scroll. First we need to find out who has it."

Vincent smiled, looking like someone's grandfather, which worked to his advantage on close up kills. He turned the phone to face Maxx and said, "We can start with Valene Eklund. I took the liberty of locating her."

Chapter 23

VALENE HURRIED FROM the assisted living facility where her dad was a resident, into the dark skies unleashing a storm as fast and hard as it could. Of course, she had no umbrella, so she used her hand to shield her eyes from the rain.

She ran for her car, sparing a look up. "Would it have been too much trouble to have held off another ten minutes?" Probably a good way to catch a lightning bolt.

She unlocked her door and sank into the driver's seat of her T-bird.

The seat that immediately started forming a puddle from her soaked clothes.

Wet hair hung in front of her eyes. She swatted it off her face, cranked the engine and backed up slowly, then pulled onto the quiet road. It had to be after ten by now.

Dad had looked bad.

By Monday, she'd either have the money for the treatment, plus extras like an air ambulance service that would fly him to the clinic outside of Seattle, and her expenses for staying with him ... or she wouldn't.

It was all or none.

She had four more days, but no meeting with Tinker after all that Henri had gone through to get that ticket. How would she explain not meeting the billionaire? What was the chance Tinker would see her if she contacted his office and politely mentioned the missed opportunity?

Would they consider it a huge faux pas on the heels of Tinker and his wife watching Fontana get his head blown off?

Valene would.

Smith hadn't called. He had to know what happened tonight.

Had he been detained like everyone else? She'd never seen him again after that one glimpse.

She slowed as a stoplight changed to red.

Cold metal touched her neck and she froze. Then the trembling started. She dragged her eyes to the rearview mirror where a face covered in a black ski mask stared back at her.

If that was Dingo...

"Dammit, I'm sick of this shit."

"Shut up, bitch and drive where I tell you."

Not Dingo. He would never call her that. Her heart did a bang-up job of trying to jump out of her chest. Why couldn't this have been Dingo again?

It was official. She was insane for first cursing Dingo for being in her face every time she turned around, and now wishing with all her soul that he was sitting here to deal with this kidnapper.

Her passenger said with a Spanish accent, "Drive straight. You have a tail and we will lose it."

She glanced up at her side mirror, but all the lights behind her looked the same. Who was following and how was she going to lose someone capable of tailing her?

Ski Mask said, "I will tell you when to turn. Do not reach for your purse. Do not stop, put on your flasher, or do anything without my direction. *Comprende*?"

She couldn't draw enough air to talk so she nodded.

Dingo had tried to warn her, but she hadn't believed him. Now he was gone and she had no idea why anyone was after her. Damn him for being so shut off from her. Why couldn't he trust her just once?

He said he was going to give you answers tonight at the cove.

Still, he should have told her everything long before now.

Hadn't she helped him every time he asked?

You also did things he asked you not to do, her wisecracking conscience reminded her.

Shut. Up.

She clutched the steering wheel, turning carefully when ordered and making soft stops, which were hard to do with her knees banging together. Her kidnapper had her at a disadvantage right now, but the minute they were out of this car, even if she couldn't get to her gun, she'd find her opening and make him think twice about grabbing another woman.

The windshield wipers swatted water back and forth. Headlights blurred her vision as they passed and lightning spread across the sky in jagged bolts.

It took until she turned onto San Pedro Street to realize he had her driving to Skid Row, an area of downtown Los Angeles that had earned the name honestly.

She never came here. Self-defense training was no good if you were too stupid to stay out of dangerous areas.

After two more turns, he told her to turn left immediately.

The only driveway she saw led into a closed overhead door on the bottom floor of a four-story building that had broken glass and graffiti on the brick exterior.

She said, "But there's no..."

The garage door began lifting and she had no choice but to drive into the dark abyss on the other side.

She swallowed, realizing there was more than one person involved and this was not a simple kidnapping.

Her headlights faded into the deep recess of what might have been a parking garage or a warehouse. It went forever.

Of all the reasons she had to panic right now, the one hitting her hardest was that her father would be left alone with no one to help him.

Losing her would kill him. She regretted not making some plan in case anything happened to her. Dingo had once accused her of thinking she was invincible. He'd called her arrogant.

He'd been right.

"Stop," her passenger ordered. "Turn off the engine."

She put the car in park and reached for the key with trembling fingers. Her second regret hit her in the chest, a power punch to her heart.

I should have told Dingo the truth.

I should have told him I loved him.

"Get out," Ski Mask ordered her.

Dingo wiped water off his face as he eased over the second-floor balcony of an apartment at the opposite end of the building from Valene's. Gage might have someone watching the front and her windows, but he wouldn't have someone at this end because there were better exit routes than this one.

He hated to waste the time, but it was this or drag a tail forever.

Dingo had driven up ten minutes ago in the same rental he'd been using to travel around since arriving in LA. He'd turned on a small light in Valene's bedroom, grimaced at the place again, then turned on the lights in the bathroom. Let Gage's people think Dingo was inside Valene's apartment taking a shower, waiting for her to return.

That would keep them content until he got away.

He lowered himself as far as he could until he had no choice but to drop to the hill falling away from the unit. He hit and rolled, biting down on a grunt, but who would hear him over rain pounding the ground?

Damn, he was getting too old for this shit.

Either that or less than ten hours sleep in three days was catching up with him.

When he stopped sliding, he continued to follow the rain that flowed to a concrete culvert, a large one that tunneled under a paved road. The round opening was tall enough for him to crawl through for fifty feet. It was nice to be out of the water bullets beating down, but this pipe was full of sludge and debris that slowed him.

When he exited the other end, he was a block from his new ride, a 1968 GTO he'd seen earlier, parked on a used car lot. He'd either return it or send the money next week, more than they'd get for it at fair market value.

The newer cars were more trouble to hotwire.

He withdrew the slim jim tool he'd shoved under his shirt and hidden with the windbreaker he'd put on before getting out of his rental car. The rental still had a go bag and assorted things inside, so it looked as though he intended to come back to it.

Sabrina and Josh would know better.

Dingo had always run lean and mean, carrying only what he

needed in the immediate moment. But Gage's agents wouldn't know that.

Once he had the door open and was snug inside from the rain, he wrinkled his nose at the stale odors of cigarettes, booze and carpet cleaner. In another minute, he had it cranked and let the engine warm as he pulled out his smart phone, then booted up the tracking program on Valene's car.

She'd been in west Los Angeles right before he'd reached her apartment, but now she was driving on ...

"No!" He pounded the steering wheel. "What the hell are you doing in Skid Row?"

Fuck. He answered his question as fast as he'd asked it. She was driving down the road that played through his nightmares.

A dark, potholed street through LA's own corner of hell.

The blip kept moving slower and slower until it turned off the street into a building. And stopped.

He stared at the blinking light, begging for her car not to be where it was.

All the wishing in the world wouldn't change reality.

Years ago, seven to be exact, one group had owned that turf and based on what he'd found out tonight, they were back. Gang activity had moved deeper into south LA, but the blip on his map was the home of Satan's Garden Club.

Sabrina's words banged around in Dingo's head, questioning his ability to be objective. If she stood here now, she'd be in his face, because she cared that much about him. Because she didn't care who she pissed off if that's what it took to protect the people she called family, and the crazy woman would bleed for him or Josh, which was the reason he'd forgive her for what happened tonight with Gage.

But Gage? Not so much.

Dingo studied the blinking light on the map.

Had Valene gone there of her own free will?

Was she, at this very minute, laughing about the kill that went down at the fundraiser?

Or had he made a huge miscalculation by coming back to LA, so bloody sure he could protect her, when all he'd done was lead Satan's Garden Club right to her front door?

If he called Sabrina and Josh, they would back him up to find out, but if Valene was part of the organization, Dingo would be walking two of the people he was trying to keep alive into a sure death.

Gage already believed Valene was guilty as hell. He didn't want anyone to tip her hand while his people stalked her. Calling Sabrina would force her to choose between supporting the State Department's interest and backing Dingo.

If he did bring Sabrina in on this and it went bad, he might destroy the only chance Slye had of figuring out who was going to die next. Sabrina would end up catching the brunt of the backlash because the State Department would have to blame someone.

Dingo revved the big engine and let the bruiser growl a minute while he debated which direction to drive.

Go back to the safe house and pick up a team or head to downtown LA and face his past alone?

Adjusting the rearview mirror, he cracked his neck and put the car in gear.

Chapter 24

"I DON'T KNOW ANYTHING about a scroll..." Valene saw the hand flying at her face, but her hands were tied behind her. All she could do was give in to the force when the hit landed ...

Crack. The sound was as vicious as the pain ripping across her cheek and her body hitting the hardwood floor. Even with her training that allowed her to roll with the hit, her head still bounced. That rung her bell.

She blinked, trying to see past stars.

Boots standing on a polished floor filled her watery vision.

She was no longer trembling.

She'd passed from terror to a numb level of acceptance a half hour ago. The man in the ski mask had walked her up three flights of stairs to this designer office that was as out of place in the decrepit building as pearls on a ragdoll.

A hand grabbed her arm and yanked her up then shoved her into a cushioned chair. Her aching hip and shoulder appreciated the reprieve even if it was only for a moment.

"Leave me," the bastard called Navarro said.

She watched as the man who had delivered her, and an old guy this one had called Tío, left the office. Both of them looked like they crushed bones for exercise and grinned the whole time.

Silence fell over the room like an unwelcome guest.

She moved her jaw and hissed softly at the pain.

"There's no reason for making this difficult," Navarro offered conversationally. He had ink-black hair, stood an easy six-three, and had honed his body to be a chick magnet. Black lashes, deep-bronze skin and perfect teeth, he was a walking version of a Latin god come to earth, but it was only skin deep. There was nothing powerful about a man who beat someone when they were tied up, especially a woman.

She tasted blood where her teeth had cut the inside of her lip.

Navarro leaned a hip on his desk, not a speck of her blood on the pale blue dress shirt tucked into black jeans that fit him as if he'd been shrink-wrapped. Nails too clean and neat to do real labor. This man had others do his dirty work. Except for when it came to abusing women with their hands tied.

He waited for her to say something.

She spent hours with potential clients. It was the only time she could be patient and still. He would need a walker for getting around by the time she talked.

"I see." He stared off into infinity for a few seconds then said, "I know about the scroll. There is no way for you to gain it now without me, so accept that your life has changed and now belongs to me. Spare yourself the pain and tell me what I want to know."

She just stared at him, waiting for his next strike.

"Don't you wonder how we found you?"

Actually she did, but she wasn't going to let on that she cared.

"Ah, I see that you do want to know."

Had she totally lost her poker face? Evidently, since she hadn't played poker in six years. "I'd play your silly game if I knew what you were talking about."

"You spoke to someone about the scroll earlier today by phone."

She'd spoken to a number of her contacts about the scroll, but they shouldn't know that. Regardless, she wasn't giving this slimeball any names. Still, he'd pricked her curiosity enough for her to ask, "Who are you?"

"I am Maxx Navarro, head of Satan's Garden Club."

Was he serious? "Never heard of you or this twisted version of a garden club."

"This is no joke." He said that the same way a doctor would tell you he couldn't save your leg.

Dead-freaking-serious.

"I didn't mean to insinuate that I thought this was funny in any way." She could do contrite, but if he gave her any opening he'd find out she could do bust-your-balls, too.

Literally.

Her feigned apology must have appeased him.

Navarro dialed back the death glare. "I got your name from the person who spoke to you about the scroll today. Not actually from him, but from his phone. I have it. He won't need it anymore."

Henri had called her.

Air backed up in her lungs. What had they done to Henri? "Show me the phone."

Navarro frowned at that order but reached around behind him and lifted a phone that ...was not Henri's. *Thank you, God. I know we haven't been on good terms, but I owe you one for saving me that nightmare.*

She made a point of squinting as she studied it, trying to figure out who had called her from that phone.

Could it be Dingo's? No. She didn't think he knew anything about the scroll or he'd have brought it up when they talked.

That ruled him out. She hoped.

Wait a minute. How would Navarro have any idea what someone called her about just because he found her number on a phone?

Geoffrey wouldn't call her if someone paid him a year's rent for his and Henri's building.

She mentally ran back through the calls to the doctor, her bank and the assisted living when Aram had called and she'd ignored...

Aram? He'd left a voice mail and she'd ignored it. "What's the name of the person who owns that phone?"

"Aram Pavlovsky."

Navarro came after her because of *him*? Val scrunched up her face in a way she hoped was convincing. "I don't know what Aram told you, but he's just your standard scumbag who's so full of shit his eyes are brown."

Navarro's eyes were brown. Oops.

Those eyes narrowed at her. "He said nothing about you."

She let out her breath. Aram could have screwed this up royally.

"But," Navarro continued. "He did tell my man about a very rare scroll, and he said you had the inside track. He offered to split the proceeds from this scroll with us."

"Aram? He never splits anything," she said before she could stop herself.

"Let's say he was motivated by having a knife pinning his family jewels to a chair."

Oh, dear God. What had they done to Aram?

She never liked the guy, but neither would she wish him to be harmed. "I don't understand what's going on."

"It's very simple. Your friend died a painful death, but it was fairly quick once my man got down to business."

"You killed him for a scroll?"

"No. He was merely number two on my list of bodies to put to rest. We found out about the scroll because my people are thorough and I will not be fooled even though someone has gone to a great deal of effort to keep this secret. I will gain the scroll before he does, and you will help me. Slow deaths are so unnecessary unless there is information to be gained. You, however will be offered a swift death unless you continue to make my life difficult."

Her skin was suddenly clammy and she fought to breathe. This was not a good time to pass out. Stars danced in front of her eyes. She had to get a grip.

He stood up. "Very well. I take your silence to mean you have opted for the difficult route."

"No, that's, uh, not what I want. I'm just lightheaded. I need a minute to catch my breath." She was rambling, but it was working because he seemed happy with that declaration.

Or not. He walked to the door and called to a Dominic who came in, but he was so thick he had to turn sideways to do it.

Navarro said, "Take her into the next room. There's no point in making a mess in here."

Dominic grabbed her and started pulling her toward the door. She pulled back. "No, what are you doing? I can help you."

Not to find the scroll, but with a little time she might figure out a way to get them to take her out of here. That would give her a chance at escaping or drawing attention.

Navarro said, "Wait a moment, Dominic." Then Navarro took her gently by the arm and moved her over to his desk where he shoved her face down on the desk and gripped her crotch. "If you give me another moment of trouble, I will rip these clothes off and take you while every man here watches."

That didn't sound like an empty threat. She closed her eyes against the degradation and pain in her limited future.

"*Comprende?*"

She was starting to hate that word. "Yes."

As he lifted her and started to turn her around, her gaze landed on a printed photograph on the desk and her mouth fell open.

Dingo. Why would he have a picture of Dingo?

Navarro noticed her reaction.

She realized her mistake too late and tried to hurry to get back in sync with him turning, but he'd caught her staring down and picked up the picture. "You know this man."

"No."

"You're lying."

True, but she felt certain that admitting she knew Dingo would be a mistake.

A huge mistake.

Navarro shoved her over to Dominic who dragged her away to what would've been some kind of reception area *if* this had been a real office building.

She was shoved into a chair in the center of the room, on display for him and his hombres.

Navarro stepped into her line of vision and held up the photo again. Dingo had the short blond hair she'd seen a month ago when he'd shocked her by calling after so long. He'd let it grow out since then and now his hair was back to the silky brown locks she'd loved so much.

Someone had captured that shot without him knowing it.

Navarro said, "You must have realized by now that I know how important the scroll is, and from what I understand it is worth too many millions to estimate. One might say even a king's ransom."

She considered that a valid estimate for Galileo's scroll.

He spoke as someone who wanted to make his meaning very clear. "To put my interest in this man in the photo into financial perspective, I would trade ten of those rare scrolls your friend Aram told my people about for one minute with this man." He waved the photo of Dingo in front of her.

She'd never been a genius at math, but she added two and two pretty fast to come up with exactly what Navarro was after.

He wanted to kill Dingo.

He'd do a lot worse than rape her in front of his men to learn what she knew about Dingo.

Chapter 25

A BEHEMOTH GUARD CARVED with muscle and with straight black hair was protecting the entrance to the Satan's Garden Club building. It was only two blocks from where Garcia had run the first one on Skid Row.

Since Dingo couldn't just walk past the guard, he had gained entry to a building next door to the one where Valene's car still dinged on his tracking software. Getting in was no trouble, but it had taken ten minutes to find enough rope and wire to make a line he could use to rappel down three stories from a window on this building to the roof on the four-story one he'd come to get into.

At the moment, he hung from the window, getting battered by the storm off the ocean. Maybe going through Godzilla next door would have been easier.

When Dingo's feet touched the roof, he whipped the rope-wire combination twice and it fell to his feet. He wiped water off his face. In the distance, the city glowed in a steamy mist, but not much light fell across this area.

It took only another minute to pick the lock on the roof access door and he was in.

Pitch black everywhere.

He dug out his headgear and popped his night vision monocular in place. Bam. Everything came to life in shades of gray-green. He moved carefully across the concrete floor that led to a stairwell, which should enter somewhere on the top floor of the building.

His boots were waterlogged and squishing. He took them off and carried them down the stairs, pausing in a room encased in concrete. He kept his distance from the breaker panel for the power that had been jury-rigged with half the guts hanging out. Just past that was the entrance door to what would be office area in most buildings.

A quarter rotation of the doorknob confirmed ... unlocked.

He noted the carpet, put his shoes back on and leaned in to listen.

Muffled voices.

Easing the door a fraction open, he snuck into the dark hallway.

Garcia had always remodeled everywhere he went, no matter what the building looked like. He'd have had a gold-plated trough in a pigpen if he declared that to be his current office.

Dingo's brain still refused to believe that Garcia was back, but his eyes kept picking up evidence.

He slipped down the hall until the voices became louder.

"Look, I do know what Aram was looking for, but I was forced to sign a nondisclosure agreement. That's why I didn't volunteer anything, but I don't know that man," a female said.

Valene. She was in negotiating mode.

The sound of a hand slapping a face reached him right before Valene's gasp of pain.

Dingo felt the strike through every muscle in his body. She clearly wasn't here by choice. He was going to kill the scum who hit her right after he cut the bastard's hand off.

Forcing himself to stand still and figure out a plan of attack was killing Dingo. But rushing in and getting holes blown through him would make the bad guy's day and leave Valene alone.

Dingo struggled to gain control of his emotions and locked them down tight. Now was the time for ice in his veins.

"I will not tolerate any more lying," her interrogator snarled.

"I'm trying to answer your questions." Her voice shook. "M-Maybe if you explain who he is I'll recognize something and tell you. I meet a lot of people. I'm not good at remembering everyone I meet."

"You want to know who he is? He killed my father. He is a dead man."

Dingo couldn't have heard that right. First of all, it sounded like a bad version of Inigo Montoya's famous line from *The Princess Bride.*

You killed my father. Prepare to die.

This man couldn't be Garcia's son, because Garcia had said he had no family.

Then again, Garcia had been a lying rat bastard.

"The man in the picture," she said as if trying to clarify. "Do you have a name?"

"Dingo Paddock."

The walls rushed in on Dingo.

He'd never given Garcia his real name and Bergman had never known it the whole time he'd been Dingo's contact.

Who was this guy abusing Valene?

Needing to get a look at him, Dingo maneuvered to a closer vantage point. He risked being discovered, but moving another step closer to Valene was worth it, plus he had to get a look at who had come after Bergman, Dingo and Valene.

"Dingo Paddock," she said quietly. "That's an odd name. I'd normally remember that. Did he have a middle name? Something else he went by?"

That was his Valene. She'd still be asking questions to ferret out information at the pearly gates, but that wasn't going to happen. Not on his watch.

"Did all that about your father happen here?" Valene asked then added, "Please. I'm really trying to understand. Did that happen recently?"

"No. This man Paddock saved my father's life seven years ago, then stabbed him in the back a year later."

Technically, Dingo had cut Garcia's throat.

He leaned near the edge of the doorway to see Valene sitting in the middle of the room with her right side to him.

Three men stood in front of her.

He couldn't see the face of the one in the middle who had curly black hair, but the old guy on the other side of him looked too much like Garcia not to be his brother.

Son of a bitch.

Garcia's son had Valene and she was doing her best to talk her way out, but there was no way out except dead.

The old guy said, "Enough of this, Navarro. We are losing time."

"This will only take ten minutes, Tío. She knows something about this man Paddock and she is going to tell."

Tío. Spanish for uncle. That confirmed Dingo's guess.

Navarro's uncle scratched the stubble on his cheek. "We have not eaten. Get what you can out of her and put her in the box while we have dinner."

Shit. Dingo backtracked fast to the panel inside the concrete room shielding access to the roof. He scanned the panel, trying to figure out the squiggly Spanish writing and hoped he didn't fry himself with what he had in mind. Two breakers were marked with big asterisk-type stars.

That had to be important, right?

He pulled his wet sleeves back and grabbed two breaker switches, flipping them off, on, then paused. Off again for five seconds then back on. Another pause, then he flipped them off permanently. A buddy at the power company had once explained how the system worked, and that if the lights didn't come back on the third time, then no power until the service personnel figured out what had caused the outage.

Now, to see if that had convinced Navarro and crew.

"Fix the lights, Dominic!" someone in the room with Valene yelled.

Dingo was hurrying back down the hallway when the man he assumed was Dominic turned the corner heading Dingo's way. Adrenaline slammed through his veins.

That was one way to get rid of a crushing headache.

But Dominic was brushing a hand along the wall, because he didn't have night vision gear.

Dingo ducked into an empty room, then stepped back out behind Dominic, who had probably made this walk in the dark too many times to count. That explained why the door to this floor had been left open for easy access to the gut-shot breaker panel. Just as Dominic stepped into the concrete utility room and flicked on a tiny LED light from a key ring, Dingo followed him in and used his weapon to bash the guy at the base of his skull.

Dominic uttered a groan and slid down.

Dingo relieved him of his keys and the Colt .38 Super on his hip. He pulled off the guy's belt and tied his hands behind his back, then yanked his boots and socks off to shove a sock in his mouth.

If Dingo got word to Sabrina before this group disappeared, she could take this one in alive.

Another quick trip down the hall allowed Dingo to hear Tío grumbling, "Dominic is an idiot."

Navarro said, "Agreed, but we'll discuss this later when we have privacy."

That translated into, "We'll decide who replaces him and how to dispose of the body later." Dingo had done Dominic a favor.

"While we're waiting, you should start talking," Navarro said. He had to be addressing Valene.

Dingo slipped around the corner and flipped up his monocular, because Navarro had a flashlight on Valene, whose cheek was already bruising.

She said, "I've been thinking hard and I don't recall–"

Navarro slapped her so hard she fell sideways in the chair.

Navarro would beg for death when Dingo was through with him. He pulled out his knife and took a step, heading for the uncle first, then Navarro.

He'd kill the uncle, but Dingo needed Navarro alive to find out how Navarro had gotten Dingo's name and picture. Without that, Dingo had no way to kill the snake this time from head to tail.

Shots erupted down the hall toward the elevator and stairs. What the hell was going on now?

Tío cursed and yelled into a radio, probably calling his goon downstairs, but if someone was up here shooting, that meant the doorman was already down.

Navarro and Tío turned away from Valene, palming weapons and fanning the flashlight toward the hall. Tío gave Navarro a hand signal and as Dingo sucked backward into the room next door, they both snuck down the hallway toward the noise.

More shots popped. Deep voices shouted.

Navarro yelled, "He's getting away. Catch him and don't kill him. I want that bastard!" Abrupt shouts in Spanish then more shots.

Dingo made it to Valene's chair where her head leaned over the arm. He gently cupped her mouth and whispered, "It's me. I'm getting you out of here."

Liquid ran down his hand from where tears pooled on her cheeks. He released her face to cut her ankles free first then her wrists, grabbing her arm and turning toward the hallway and the roof access.

Navarro was shouting, "How dare they try to hit us. That gang has not learned my name, but will by tomorrow morning."

Dingo hurried Valene down the hall.

Tío shouted, "Dominic! Get the lights on!"

When Dingo reached the access door, he pulled Valene up the stairs with him. They opened the door onto the roof that was still under attack from the storm, and Valene said, "How are we getting out of here?"

"Hold on." Dingo pulled out his lock picks and set about relocking the door from the outside. The last thing he did was pull out a special tool he'd had made just for jamming the tumblers. He latched onto her fingers and hooked them into the waistband of his pants. "Keep your fingers there and follow in my steps."

"Got it." The words had come out through chattering teeth. Probably shock more than cold.

He lifted his makeshift rappelling rope and led her to the back of the building, then freed her hand so she could stand by herself while he tied a lead on the rope around a steel vent structure. This building was from an era when every part of the roof was built to be heavy-duty.

Valene waited silently in the pitch dark, a trooper all the way.

He stepped up to her, wanting to pull her into his arms, but pounding started on the access door. Shit. He tugged Valene over. "We're going to the next floor, Val."

"How?"

"I've got a rope tied off. I'm going to climb off first, then you follow me so that I'm beneath you."

She couldn't see his face, but he could see the doubt in hers.

The door pounding changed tone.

Then Dingo heard a crack. They were using an axe.

She asked, "Will it hold both of us?"

"Yes." Unless they delayed any longer and that axe blade got a shot at his rope.

"Okay."

He got her to the edge and put her hands on the rope then dropped below her. She'd just climbed over the edge when Dingo heard shouting getting more distinct. They'd have the door hacked all the way through any minute.

"Keep coming down, babe," he encouraged.

When his feet touched a window ledge, he stepped onto it and bumped his boot against what was left of the glass. He stomped it down, all the while keeping his hand on the rope then on Valene's leg, guiding her foot to the ledge "Stop right there and hold the rope."

He climbed into the room and found clothes scattered around, probably rags someone had slept on, but they'd cover any glass edges that might slice Valene's back or legs.

When he had that set, he leaned out to hear Valene say, "They're coming."

Chapter 26

VALENE SQUATTED ON the six-inch-wide brick window ledge, hanging onto the rope that Navarro's man would chop any minute now. She could hear them yelling and pounding around the roof, searching for her, because they didn't know about Dingo.

And she wasn't going to let them find out he'd been here if she could help it.

Dingo hooked an arm around her and said, "I've got you. Let go."

She did and banged her arm, but she was inside the room as lights beamed down from the roof, shining outside the window. She stood still, listening to them shout at each other in Spanish. She translated it in a whisper for Dingo.

"Navarro is yelling for the guards to come around back when they get down to street level. Tío is arguing that I couldn't have made that last drop. That it had to be ten feet to the ground. Navarro said I could have fallen on the garbage piled back there and gotten lucky..."

She listened then added, "Tío is shouting at Dominic, demanding to know how I got loose and where I found a rope."

The light outside disappeared and the voices withdrew.

Dingo said, "Time to go."

"Where?"

"If I said I knew, I'd be lying."

"Good enough for me." And it was.

She could hate him for leaving her broken in half.

She could curse him for coming back without a word of explanation.

But she would never fool herself into believing she didn't trust

Dingo one hundred percent in this moment. She had no question that he'd find a way out of here, because this was what he did for a living. She didn't know who he did it for, but everything about him told her that he was a skilled operative of some sort.

So why did you always blow him off when he was worried for your safety?

Okay, she'd face that music. But this was not the time.

He wound his way through the building and found the stairwell going down.

They didn't encounter anyone until Dingo had led her out of the stairwell and past the door to the garage she'd originally entered through. He cracked open a door to the street running in front of the building and pulled back, saying, "One bloke outside."

She leaned close and smelled the warm musk of Dingo's exertions, a scent she remembered waking to in the middle of the night when he'd appear like her fantasy come to life. Her mind was a scary place right now if she could think about being naked with Dingo.

She said, "They brought me in through the garage. Last door we passed on our right."

"Good."

They backtracked to the garage that opened to the cavernous room she remembered as stretching the length and width of the building. There was only the elevator shaft and a small office structure at one end.

She whispered, "My car is here."

"We can't get it out. They'd gun us down first."

"Just show me my car," she demanded in hushed voice.

Dingo muttered something unintelligible, but towed her over and put her hand on the car. She carefully opened the door and the light inside came on.

Dingo cursed lividly.

But thank God, the guy who'd carjacked her hadn't been the sharpest tool in Navarro's shed, because her purse was still there on the seat. She snatched it and closed the door just enough to kill the light, but without making a noise.

"You didn't get your matching shoes," he grumbled.

"I needed my purse," she hissed low at him. "It has my phone and gun dammit."

"Shh."

She wouldn't have let him shush her but their lives were at risk after all.

Dingo towed her along, guiding her away from anything she'd fall over. When he stopped again, he said, "Pull out your Walther. I need both hands to open this overhead door slowly."

"They'll hear you."

"Only if they're standing on this side of the building."

"That's a big only."

He kissed her cheek gently. "That's why you're holding the gun so you can cover me while I handle the overhead door. Just be ready, and if I don't take down whoever might be out there once my hands are free, you get the second shot at him."

"I might shoot you. I can't see shit." She fished out her gun and held it at her side.

"Don't shoot unless I tell you. If it comes to that, I'll hit the ground before I tell you to shoot."

No he wouldn't.

Dingo would stand between her and a wall of bullets. How had she ever convinced herself that she'd stopped loving him? Being with Henri had been a Band-Aid on a deep wound, a cosmetic attempt at patching up her emotions.

Dingo positioned her exactly the way he wanted her standing and trusted her not to kill him.

Or maybe it wasn't trust, because Dingo didn't trust.

He probably thought allowing her to cover him gave her a comfort level, but she'd bet his first concern was making sure she was in a position to defend herself in case he died.

Oh, God, don't let him die.

She had to stop thinking and just pay attention.

This overhead door sounded smaller than the one she'd driven her car through, but it still made a soft metallic whine as he pulled it up slowly. Sounded like he'd only moved it maybe a foot, not high enough to get a vehicle through.

She could hear him moving and then he was up against her ear, talking so low someone standing on the other side of her wouldn't hear. "The door is up two feet. I see a man seventy feet away toward the rear of the building and facing the back corner. The street access is ten steps away on our right. We need to get out of here fast and silently."

She hoped he had some plan once they were outside this building or Navarro would catch them before they made a mile.

Rolling under the door when he told her, Valene pushed up on her knees, one palm in squishy stuff. She hoped it was only mud that she wiped on her pants.

She'd been moving blind until they reached the street where light fought its way down through the rain driving sideways.

Looking over to the right, she saw men crowded around the entrance to Navarro's building. More men than she'd seen when she first arrived.

Navarro was calling in reinforcements.

How did Dingo expect to get past that?

Dingo tugged her to the left and they were off again, hugging the front of the next building and sidestepping to minimize their profiles. Then Dingo dropped out of sight, yanking her with him into an empty parking lot.

She squinted to make out the hulking silhouette of some vehicle.

Dingo opened the unlocked passenger door, tucked her in and ran around to climb in behind the steering wheel.

The inside smelled old, really old, and a smoker had owned it, but she'd had to clean that smell out of her T-bird when she bought it. "What is this?"

"'68 GTO." He said it with pride. Men.

The car was almost fifty years old. "Are we stealing it?"

"I did that earlier." He cranked it and the old engine rumbled to life.

"That's just wrong."

"I'm not keeping it, Val. I won't screw the people who owned it." Then he made her day when he said, "No one will question this car driving through the hood. Lie down so there's only one silhouette."

She eased her way down onto her left side, since that side hadn't hit a hardwood floor with nothing to block her fall. For the first time since getting carjacked, relief flooded her, and her tight muscles started griping from the abuse her body had been through.

Dingo drove slowly down the street.

She wanted to see where they were going, but not enough to struggle back up to a sitting position. His hand came down on her arm and he started stroking her, soothing thc tremors that still hadn't stopped. Her eyelids fluttered once, twice, then she was gone.

⚯

Dingo watched for headlights running up behind him, but none came.

Valene's chest rose and fell with gentle breaths. She no longer shook like a leaf in a hurricane. He couldn't take his hand off her. Needed that connection of knowing she was here with him. Alive. Safe.

What the hell had she gotten herself into?

He should have been here to help her with money and figuring out how to deal with her dad. Hard to do that when he'd avoided the very person who needed his help, too afraid that seeing her happy without him would have stomped on the last pieces of his heart.

Still, coming back around with no intention of staying would have given her false hope. He'd done that before and then sworn he wouldn't do it to her again. Bad enough that she'd married some bloke less than a year after Dingo had left. The time they'd spent together before that had been ... hell, he didn't know how to label that time since he'd never stayed around anyone else that long, but he hadn't expected her to grab the next guy she met and marry him.

He wasn't bailing on her this time. Not without making sure she was in a better place than she was right now.

She needed someone to depend on.

He was going to be that man and damn the consequences.

She slept for the next seventy minutes while he drove northeast to the only place he knew would be safe for both of them.

He was yawning by the time he pulled off the main highway,

drove another ten minutes to a gravel road and grimaced when the GTO bottomed out as the road climbed for a quarter mile.

When it ended, he lifted his phone and entered a code into a text then hit send. In six seconds, what appeared to be an old fence gate with a rusted chain fanned open. Vines and weeds hid the machinery.

As soon as Dingo passed through, the gate returned to its nondescript position.

He drove a twisted path through trees until he reached a hill camouflaged with overgrowth that would make it pretty impossible to detect from the air. The garage door opened the minute a sensor picked up his approach.

He'd written the computer security programs for these buried safe houses, and the garage door would rise at this point only if the gate code had been entered correctly one time. He'd intended to talk Valene into hiding out here the minute he arrived in LA this week, so he'd rewritten the program during his flight. If he hadn't, opening the gate would have alerted Josh or someone else at Slye keeping an eye on their assets.

Sabrina had four safe houses closer inside LA, all better equipped for missions. This was one of ten special ones she'd set up during the two years she'd gone underground after the busted UK job. She wanted to know she had places her people could hide that were fully stocked and hidden from the air if things got too hot.

When Dingo parked the car in the garage and turned it off, the quiet jarred Valene awake.

She sat up as the garage door was closing. "Where are we?"

Here came the questions.

He'd disengaged the interior light on his way to find Valene, so it was dark as a tar pit. "Sit still and I'll come around to get you."

On his way around the car, he flipped on a light that hung over a worktable and turned to see her door open.

He met her at the car door when she pushed to her feet. Right as her knees buckled. He caught her and she hooked her arms around his neck.

Finally, he could pull her close and hold her next to his chest, feel her heart pounding. Very much alive.

After a couple of long breaths, she eased away and stood on her own. "Back to my first question."

"We're safe." He tried not to be stung when she pushed away from him. He still wanted to hold her. Instead, he opened the door to a contemporary kitchen with white cabinets and stainless steel. With a couple of switches flipped, lights came on under cabinets and into the great room on the other side of the kitchen. Big overstuffed sofas and chairs covered in tan leather were strewn around with an eye to decorating that Dingo had never had.

Not a lot of call for it when there was no one place he called home.

Valene strode past him and entered the big room. "How many people live here? This is huge. You could easily seat fifteen with everyone slouching."

Four big-screen TV monitors hung in different places and the ceiling peaked, held up by thick teak beams. Dingo said, "It sleeps twelve comfortably in six bedrooms." Three large bedrooms with two oversized single beds in each one plus three master bedrooms with king-size beds.

Taking in every nuance of the room as she turned in the center, Valene said, "I don't understand."

"It's built into the ground, we're on the top floor..."

She shook her head. "No, I mean you. This. Everything." She followed that up with a look that waited for an answer.

His voice held a gentle warning. "Val–"

"Never mind. We'll never get past your secret life. I don't know why I do this to myself. Are we still in LA?"

"Pretty much. We're on the outskirts."

She smiled with a look of someone who just realized she'd been fooled. "But you're not going to tell me exactly where, are you? I'm surprised you didn't put a sack over my head."

He should have.

If it'd been anyone else, he would have, but she'd been through enough for one night and thankfully slept the whole way. "Would you like a shower?"

"Yes."

After setting her up downstairs in one of the master suites that came with an assortment of new clothes, he backed out and stood there with his hands on the doorframe, staring at the closed door and wanting to shove it open again.

Chapter 27

VALENE DRIED HER hair on a towel that belonged in the Ritz and tossed it on the closed bidet. This place was as spacious as any mansion she'd been in and she had a feeling that on the outside it would look like somewhere a hobbit lived.

Not a window in any room so far.

She'd avoided the mirror since stepping in here and finally gave in to see the damage.

The bruise on her cheek smarted, was purple and blue, but would turn lovely shades of yellow and green by tomorrow. That hadn't concerned her.

She ran her tongue over the split inside her lip. Tolerable. Not as bad as it had felt earlier. She'd suffered her share of dings when training.

None of that had stopped her from facing the mirror.

All the damage along her side and sore shoulder could be overlooked.

She'd been avoiding peering into the eyes of the woman who had wounded Dingo upstairs. "He risks his life for you and you still complain. What's wrong with you? Yes, you're hurt. Yes, you want him back the way it was before. Yes, he's still elusive and distant."

Her conscience thumped her between the eyes, forcing her to admit, "But he never misled you, Valene Eklund." Dingo might not have told her who he was or what he did, but neither had he pretended he was any more than what he presented.

Would admitting the truth hurt?

Maybe. If she told him what she really felt, everything she'd tried to hold inside and keep hidden would be out. She'd have to accept that no matter what she said, he was going to leave again. One of her panicked thoughts during the kidnapping had been that she'd failed to tell Dingo she loved him.

The mirror blurred from fog billowing out of the shower and she closed her eyes, seeing her dad's face in her mind.

You're no coward, Hot Shot.

I might be, Dad.

Always remember that there is nothing more important than this moment.

He'd said those words to her all the time, reminding her that she was in charge of her own destiny. How many times had her dad tried to get her to lighten up and go with the flow?

Not her. She ran straight ahead, bulldozing her way through life and expecting everyone to think the way she did.

In a moment of frustration with her, Henri had pointed out, "You can't force the world to fit your plan. No one can. Confucius said, 'As the water shapes itself to the vessel that contains it, so a wise man adapts himself to circumstances.' You expect a man to shape himself to the vessel *you* choose and be happy while he's doing it. I'm not able to fit the confining image you have of marriage and, to be honest, I don't want to be the man who does."

Henri had closed the door on their marriage the next day.

She was hurt, but not the soul-crushing pain of when Dingo never returned. Henri had been her friend since high school. They'd been confidantes.

In hindsight, she missed that more than she missed the marriage.

Was it so wrong to be passionate about life and expect others to step up their game?

Or was Henri right when he accused her of masking her flaws by thinking of them as righteous dedication when a more accurate description would be stubborn and inflexible?

She ran her hands through her damp hair and opened her eyes. The mirror had cleared and the same unhappy woman stared back at her. When was the last time she'd been genuinely happy? Seven years ago.

What she wouldn't give to be as carefree as Henri, to take life as it came at her.

She had responsibilities. Henri did, too, but he ignored his business goals, left them sulking in the corner, while he built a world around Geoffrey.

But Henri was happy when he gazed at Geoffrey.

Grabbing her hair, she stalked to the bedroom. She'd love to let go of everything, just climb into Dingo's lap, tell him how much she missed him, how amazing he was, how all she'd like to do was spend the night tangled in sheets and warm in his arms.

Her father had tried to teach her how to let go and throw her cares to the four winds on occasion, but she was too driven to be so casual. Bad things happened when she let go of the reins as she had in the last few months she and Dingo were together. Her father became very ill without her realizing it. Everyone gave up on him, said he would be gone in six months.

Not her. She didn't walk when the going got tough and she wouldn't give up on her father.

Then don't give up on Dingo whispered through her mind.

But how long was she supposed to hold out hope? Seven years? Ten years? A lifetime?

Enough of this. Dingo would never change and neither would she. Two powerful forces on a collision course would destroy everything around them. If nothing else came of being in this seclusion, she was not leaving without answers.

After digging around in the closet where clothes had been shelved, she pulled on sweats that fit and a T-shirt she could sleep in later.

A teak chest of drawers held unopened packages of underwear for both sexes, but she was picky about hers and would just have to go commando until the freshly washed pair dried.

She looked like hell and shouldn't care, but she'd pictured being with Dingo again many times in her head and she'd envisioned being irresistible when he walked in.

Not a battered wet rat wearing someone else's frumpy clothes.

When she made it back up the stairs and across the great room, she inhaled an aroma that had her close to drooling.

Wouldn't *that* be attractive?

Dingo had on a pair of jeans and no shirt. Three scars marred his toned back. She'd known about the one on his shoulder and on his lower back, both knife wounds from what he'd told her, but the obvious bullet wound was new.

Not raw new, but new enough for her to wonder if that came from when Dingo had gained the attention of Navarro's father by saving his life.

Some men worked out to the point of bulging muscles that were hard as the slate floor she stood on, but Dingo had developed muscles that were powerful and fluid at the same time. She'd seen plenty of attractive male physiques back when she had time to surf often. None of those bodies had drawn her the way Dingo had the first time he'd shrugged out of his clothes.

What woman would gain Dingo's heart some day?

A streak of jealousy a mile wide slashed through her.

He should be hers. No one would ever love him the way she would, if only she had a chance. But that would happen when hell became the new Antarctica.

Dingo was busy stir-frying something in a wok that looked as if someone had beaten the metal with a hammer. Two glasses of red wine waited on the center island, with a bottle of merlot.

A rice cooker steamed on the counter.

Where had this domestic version of Dingo come from?

Not a recipe book in sight. Bottles of spices and a half can of green curry paste crowded near the stove, all waiting their turn.

He whipped around to check the rice cooker and caught sight of her.

Time stilled, stretched and turned clumsy.

He cleared his throat. "Hi."

"Hi."

"Grab a wine." Then he was back to cooking.

But not before she saw the uneasiness in his eyes.

Or had that been sadness?

Valene reached for one of the wine glasses the way a drowning man went after a life preserver. With enough wine, she could convince herself she hadn't put that forlorn look in Dingo's whiskey-colored eyes.

He talked to her without looking her way as he stepped over

to stir the rice. "Have to let the coconut milk cook down a little then we'll eat."

He was putting a lot of effort into sounding casual.

If they kept this up, tonight would be worse than the years she'd spent watching for him to return.

She put her glass down.

Enough was enough. "What were you doing at Navarro's tonight, Dingo?"

Snapping the lid down on the now warming rice, he stood still, eyes on the counter, then turned and leaned back against the sink.

He crossed those guns he called biceps and said, "I had a tip."

"Your evasive answers worked once," she said, moving around the island to face him. "I'm not as accepting as I was years ago."

He covered his eyes with his hand.

She'd started this. She would finish it, even if it meant getting her heart ripped out and stomped on again. She'd been twenty-two back when they met and far from naïve, but forgiveness and acceptance had come easily when she'd been caught up in lust.

Then she'd figured out it was more than wanting his body.

She'd wanted the man. All of him.

And stupid, stupid woman, she still wanted him even knowing he was no one's keeper.

Truth hit her like a lightning bolt as she stood there looking at him. If she couldn't have him all the time, she refused to live without him at least some of the time.

You have to take what you can out of this world when you can, Hot Stuff.

I'm finally hearing you, Dad.

"Navarro talked about you," she continued, watching Dingo. "He said you saved his father's life–"

"Yes," he admitted, dropping his hand to his folded arms.

"–then betrayed him," she finished.

"Yes."

"Why did you join up with his father and later betray him?"

"His father was running a massive criminal organization with a string of profitable endeavors from drugs to gun running to white slavery."

She waited for more, but true to nature, she had to prod him. "Is that why you disappeared without a word? To join that group?"

"Yes."

She hated one word answers. He'd joined a deadly group of men. She had a sick feeling building in her stomach about what had prompted that move. "Why, Dingo?"

"It doesn't matter."

She slapped the counter. "It does to me! I'm asking for the truth. One. Time. Is that too much? Navarro told me a lot before you got there." Not really, but Dingo had no way to call her on it. "I've waited a long time–*too long*–to find out what happened back then. Just tell me."

A debate raged in his gaze that sparked with gold flecks, then he looked away.

She added, "Please. You owe me that."

When he turned back to her, she wasn't ready for the pain in his face.

He said, "When I asked you to locate any family or childhood friends of Giuseppe, I didn't consider how far you'd dig. When you showed up with everything from three addresses to personal banking to the 9mm he'd hocked plus the places he frequented and a bartender who had just seen Giuseppe that week, I saw the connections between him and Satan's Garden Club that I'd been investigating for a long time."

She recalled that moment when she'd been expecting to be showered with affection as her reward and Dingo had raged instead, then left, saying only that he had to check on something.

That had been her last vision of him. Angry with her.

"When did you save Navarro's father?"

"Two in the morning on Labor Day after I left you."

She'd seen him on Saturday night. "You still haven't told me why."

He dropped his hands to the counter on each side of the sink and cupped the ledge. "I can't tell you about what I do."

"That isn't good enough anymore. Not on this. Why. Did. You. Do. It?" She would not lose her temper. Not now.

Dingo didn't look as if he could make the same claim. "Leave off on this, Val," he ground out between clenched teeth.

She walked all the way around the counter and stopped an arm's length from him. "No, I won't. Why, Dingo?"

"It doesn't concern you," he lashed out.

"I think it does and you're lying," she yelled back. "Why, dammit!"

His grip on the counter had turned white-knuckled. He didn't shout but the growl in his voice should be shaking the room. "Some things are better left unknown."

She was too close to snapping that control he clenched with all his might. She poked him and couldn't stop the hot tears rolling down her face. "Tell me why you couldn't have cared enough to tell me goodbye! Why?"

He grabbed her shoulders, shaking her only because his body thundered with fury. "I couldn't risk any contact with you once I went deep undercover. Not after I walked away to keep Garcia from touching you, dammit! Giuseppe worked for him and talked too much, which was why you were able to find some of the things you shouldn't. Garcia tortured Giuseppe's daughter and killed her baby in front of her and Giuseppe before cutting their throats and throwing all three bodies in a bloody dumpster."

Oh, God.

He'd rushed into danger to keep her safe and she was bitching him out for it.

Valene lunged up and kissed Dingo, clutching at his shoulders that were tight, ready to battle.

Dingo vibrated and she knew it was from the effort of not stepping over that line again. Screw that. She deepened the kiss and said, "I want you."

He backed her up to the island and lifted her, never breaking the kiss. She held his face, finally content. This was what happy felt like.

No, this was ecstatic.

Happy was watching a shooting star.

This was like being in the center of the universe.

His hands pulled her to him until she wrapped her legs around his back. "Missed you so damn much."

"No more than me missing you, babe." His lips devoured hers, pulled her out of time and place as quickly as being dragged underwater into a different world.

Everything sharpened with Dingo in hers.

His skin tasted salty and clean, smelled musky and warm.

His hands ... found her breasts, thank you, Universe. Heat rushed and coiled, twisting. She needed more. Lifting her head, she panted, "Here. Bedroom. Don't care, but I have to have you inside me."

"Jesus, Val. Good way to make me lose it before I get there." Dingo could feel his heart trying to jackhammer its way out of his chest. If he died now he'd be pissed.

At least give me one more time with this woman.

She laughed and his heart flipped over in his chest.

He'd said he missed her.

Missed? Could a word be more deficient in meaning? How could he explain what walking around without any hope of ever holding her again felt like? That he woke up at night calling to her. Wishing he could come back and change everything just to have another minute with her.

She leaned in and he kissed her tenderly, careful of her bruised face. Dingo would find Navarro. When that happened, Navarro would pay in ways he could never imagine, but Dingo could. One thing about the life he'd led was that he had plenty of experience to draw on when it came to payback.

He'd never been one to go after vengeance, but he couldn't allow Navarro to get away with hurting Valene. Dingo would do this world a favor and wipe out Navarro's organization, starting with the head of it.

He'd never kissed much before Val, because kissing her had been more intimate than sex with women before her. She stole a piece of him every time her lips touched his and he'd given it up willingly, knowing the day he had to walk away there'd be a bottomless hole inside him.

But he couldn't stop himself back then.

He'd never touched anything habit-forming... until he held her.

She kissed his face and hair, murmuring, "I like your natural color. Looked strange as a blond. Like a pretty boy."

He rolled his eyes. He'd never been called pretty in his life. Leaning close, he nipped her ear and whispered, "This is crazy."

She scooted forward, backing him away from the counter until he had to grab her as she slid off. She took advantage of the move to tighten her legs and stole his breath when she pulled herself up against his dick that was so hard one more move like that would ruin everything he had in mind.

His conscience started yammering about how he wasn't going to do this again. He cursed the little bastard but it wouldn't shut up.

Dingo dropped his head to hers. "I hurt you once. Didn't mean to, but I sure as hell don't want to do it again."

She clamped a hand over his mouth. "Whatever idea you have about being honorable and passing this up because tomorrow you'll be gone–which I pretty much have figured out–that's not stopping us from doing this. I could have died tonight and so could you. Every second you stand here talking, is one less second you get to feel my mouth on you."

He swung around with her hugged up against his chest, flipped the knobs on the stove to off, and had made it to the great room when she reached down and cupped him.

"Fuck, Val, keep that up and I won't make it to the bedroom."

"Screw the bedroom. I can't wait that long. I'm wet and ready. What's wrong with here?"

She would be the death of him. No question. He was panting so hard it hurt to laugh. "No condoms."

"Oh. Get moving. What are you waiting for?"

"For you to let go of my dick so I can walk, babe." He kissed her and she relinquished her grip on him. He'd run full obstacle courses with less effort than it took to stride across that room and down one set of stairs with Valene doing everything she could to make him blow a gasket.

He tossed her on the first king-sized bed he found, then snatched a condom from the top drawer on the closest dresser where he'd stashed them when they set up this place. He tossed the unwrapped condom on the bed.

She pushed up on her elbows. "It doesn't work unless you wear it."

"Smartass." Holy hell, he'd missed her. He grabbed the legs of her oversized sweat pants and yanked, pulling them down far enough to find out she had no underwear on.

His mind blew two fuses trying to hold back after seeing that. He warned her, "Don't do a thing or I'll be the first one to have fun."

Velvet brown eyes twinkled with a wicked thought. She lifted her T-shirt over her head and pinched a breast. "You mean like that or..." His mouth dried out when her nipple turned into a hard little nub. Her other hand slid between her legs and she gasped, "Or like ..." Her head fell back. "Hurry up, Dingo!"

Somehow, he had his jeans off, the condom on and landed on top of her in ten seconds. He couldn't remember pulling down his zipper. "You're torturing me."

He eased down and pushed her hand away from between her legs to make room for him to nuzzle all that sweetness. One lick and she came off the bed. He licked again and she grabbed a fist full of his hair.

"Stop torturing *me*," she yelled at him.

"You can take it." He chuckled then got serious about kissing and teasing her with his lips and tongue, taking his time driving her to the edge of insanity then bringing her back. He loved the sounds she made. Loved her yelling at him. He pushed his finger inside and she arched, trembling.

Val was always strung tight as a well-crafted bow and he lived to make her snap, lived for the one moment she was all his and nothing in the world could reach her but him.

He eased his finger inside her with his palm turned up, slowly bending the tip of his finger and stroking gently. She whispered, "Oh...yes ... "

His girl knew what he was looking for and wanted him to find it. Her G spot.

One brush of his fingertip over that tiny rough area deep inside her was all it took for her to shout, *"There! Right there!"*

He stroked her with his tongue at the same time his finger played across her G spot.

She let go with a wild scream. "*Yessss!*"

He didn't stop until she finally fell back against the bed, limp. Now he could take his time without her berating him to stop fucking around.

Yep, that'd been one of her favorite orders.

But he had a few favorite commands of his own that he'd get around to before he was done with her. Running his hands over her silky skin would make a blind man not care about seeing. He reached her breasts and sucked on one, running his tongue over the tip that puckered, happy to see him.

Missed you, too.

She had perfect breasts because they were attached to the perfect body because it belonged to the perfect woman. When you started with a woman who could turn you on with just a smile, make you happy just to be alive and rock your world with just a kiss, you knew you'd found perfection.

She pushed herself up and stared at him with the languid look of a cat who had fallen into a barrel of catnip.

He paused, kept his eyes on her, and leaned forward to kiss each nipple.

That's all it took for her to rejoin the party. She shoved him over onto his back and climbed on him. His balls throbbed. They were worse than a mutt waiting to be given a treat.

And she was a killer treat.

Grasping his erection, she lifted up and brushed the tip back and forth through her wet canal and started moaning. "This is so good. Don't you wish you were me?"

He laughed, because if she didn't slide down soon he'd cry. If his dick could talk, it'd be begging and offering her anything she wanted.

She guided him in slowly then buried him inside her so fast he sat up sucking air. His hands held her still. "Don't move."

She was stifling another laugh. Damn her.

He heaved breath in and out. Every nerve in his body had locked onto the feel of her wrapped around him. "I'm telling you, Val. Been too long."

"We could fix that if you'd let me move."

He started laughing. He had never laughed during sex like he did with Val.

Maybe because it was always more than just sex with her.

Don't go there. Just stay in the moment. No past. No future.

Releasing her shoulders, he said, "Go for it."

Oh, she did, squeezing gently as she slid up and down, tightening her muscles more each time. He gripped his forehead, but it might as well be empty since all the blood had headed south the minute she'd played with herself.

He lifted his hips, picking up her rhythm when she changed the tempo. She dropped her hands to his chest and he clamped his on her hips, driving into her over and over. Muscles corded in his neck and he gasped. "Do it."

She reached down to touch herself and arched.

He was a goner.

The inside of his head exploded with blinding light. He kept pumping until he was milked dry. When his brain fog cleared, he had her in his arms, tucked as close as he could hold her and was kissing her hair that had dried into blonde spirals.

She didn't move and he was content to just feel her skin against his, letting his thoughts drift to the times they'd spent the night in their favorite beach cove with a bottle of wine and a blanket. He'd wake to the ocean rolling softly along the shore and Valene curled up against him.

If he had to define contentment, those moments would be the closest he'd ever come to putting it into words.

She lifted up on his chest and grinned. "I felt that at my G spot."

"You feel everything there."

Her face took on a mellow expression and her eyes softened. "I feel everything *you* do there. Only you."

See? A woman like Valene made a man feel powerful enough to conquer worlds. He'd never wanted to conquer a world, but damned if he wouldn't go hunt one down for her if they lived during the dark ages.

So many people wanted power and money.

All he'd ever wanted was to be wanted ... for more than right now.

No matter how much someone said they cared, they eventually tossed him aside. Val cared. He knew she did, but their worlds might as well be in two different solar systems. He'd stayed too long the last time and almost got her killed. Just being associated with him had her in danger this time.

He'd know when the time came to leave, but this time he'd tell her goodbye if he lived long enough to have that choice.

Chapter 28

CHATTON SAT NEAR a tall window where she could watch airplanes take off at Los Angeles International Airport. In her other hand, she held a burner phone for calling Wayan. He should know better than to try triangulating her position since this phone had no GPS, but that wouldn't stop him from putting every resource at his fingertips on it when she called.

He answered, "Few people know this number and none call from untraceable numbers. What do you want, Chatton?"

"I've got good news."

"You have located Soo Jin?"

"I told you, Wayan. She's dead. She went up in a small airplane with someone who was trying to release a poison into an aquifer in the US. Something went wrong and the airplane crashed. She has no fingerprints on file anywhere, but the woman who died was definitely Asian." There was enough truth in that statement to stand on its own. Soo Jin had helped a man called Tanner on Sabrina Slye's team stop the terrorist plot, and both of them almost died in the plane crash, but they'd had one working parachute and survived.

Jin's sister, on the other hand, had been marked as disposable and jumped with a sabotaged chute. That meant a female Asian body was recovered but not identifiable.

"I do not accept that as truth."

"What would be the point in my lying to you, Wayan?"

"To keep me from uncovering the reason you sought out the General and me. I also do not believe that you are sincere about Orion's Prophecy."

Where was a hammer when she needed something to beat sense into the voice in this phone?

"I'm as invested as you and the General, but I'm not calling to argue who cares the most." If she tried too hard to convince him she was in all the way on the prophecy, he would definitely not believe her and she'd throw up in her mouth by the time she got the words out.

"That has yet to be seen. Why are you calling, Chatton?"

She let a pause build, knowing he was pressing the phone closer to his ear because he would never take this call on a speakerphone. "Like I said, I thought I'd share good news. The scroll you and the General tried to get out of the Vatican a while back with that bombing attempt is out in the open. I'm on the trail to it."

Now the pause was on his end. Was he trying to determine if she was jerking him around or not? Maybe, but he couldn't risk losing the scroll. He might even be behind getting it out of the Vatican this time, but if that was the case, something had gone very wrong for it to be floating around the US.

He finally said, "I know who possesses the scroll."

"Okay. In that case, we won't need to discuss any arrangement." *Come on, Wayan, take the bait.* She had to keep him from going after her secrets. When she allowed Sabrina's agent, Tanner Bodine, to spirit Soo Jin away and hide her forever, Chatton had crossed Wayan by not delivering Soo Jin. He threatened to find out what she was after and to take it from her.

She was hunting for the person who was systematically killing off everyone in her Macintosh bloodline. She would find the person who had killed first her mother, then her father.

Chatton was now convinced it had to do with a damn Celtic artifact passed down through generations of her family that had roots all the way back to when the Picts ruled Scotland.

Wayan said, "I am willing to discuss an arrangement if you take possession of the scroll before my representative acquires it."

At least she had him talking. "What sort of arrangement?"

"I want the scroll and you want to remain a secret to someone."

Just like Wayan to slide in a threat. "You also need my artifact," she reminded him, just to keep all the cards on the table.

"It would be unwise to think you may hold that over me forever, and you should know that I am quite close to discovering who you hide from and why."

She'd spent enough time around Wayan to pick up the slightest change in his voice and she caught excitement. She'd buried her identity as an MI6 agent who hadn't survived a bombing when she'd been in the right place at the wrong time.

But when determined to take down an enemy, Wayan was as lethal as the strike of a black mamba. Chatton had been his enemy since the day she'd informed him she had the Celtic cross he needed for his Orion Prophecy project.

His belief in all this Orion business was absurd. She saw it as a pet project with deadly consequences if those five artifacts came together. She didn't think spirits would rise up and start a war, but Wayan might.

She kept her gaze on a 747 coming in for landing, flaps set. All clear. "Tell you what, Wayan. I'll bring you the scroll if that will clear our debt about Soo Jin. I can't produce a body that doesn't exist."

"I have one offer for you. Bring me that and the General's artifact if you wish for me to keep your secrets. You have precisely six days." He ended the call.

Wayan was a psychopathic killer, but from what she'd learned about him, if he made a deal he was good for it.

The only problem would be getting her hands on the General's artifact, but it was that or hand over Soo Jin, and Chatton wouldn't fool herself into thinking Wayan didn't already have someone else hunting for the woman. There was no way Chatton would hand any human being to Wayan with the exception of the General, who was cut from the same cloth as Wayan.

If she got her hands on the scroll, she'd very likely run into the General's man Rikker, which could give her leverage for gaining the General's artifact.

Everything came back to finding that scroll.

Wayan waited through the clicking sounds associated with a secure call, something Chatton never worried about. Careless woman. When the new call went through, he spoke first, "Report your progress."

His man said, "Targets one and two have been successfully eliminated."

Wayan asked, "Have you reported to the General as well?"

"Absolutely. You said to make sure he thinks I'm his man on this end."

"Very good. I believe we have an opportunity to corner Chatton, who is presently in your area of operations."

"Think she's working with the General?"

"No, she operates on her own. She believes she can retrieve the scroll and deliver it to me."

"Do you want her to do that?"

"Absolutely not. What I want is for you to deliver *her* to me. Alive."

"I may not be able to arrange that until I have the scroll in hand."

"That will be satisfactory, Rikker. Leave no trail whatsoever."

"Yes, sir."

Chapter 29

FEW THINGS COULD drag Valene from a deep sleep like the one she'd dropped into, but the smell of fresh coffee was one of them.

Guess it was morning already, which shouldn't be a surprise since Dingo had brought them to his secret hideout a few hours ago.

She cracked an eye open to find Dingo standing at the end of the bed, thumbing his phone with one hand and holding a steaming mug in the other.

Not a stitch of clothes on.

She amended her list of things that could keep her from sleep and put that image of him on top of the list.

He didn't look her way or give any indication he'd noticed her when he said, "Stop ogling me."

She smiled. "Don't walk around looking like a centerfold for women, and I won't."

Finished with his phone, he tossed it on the dresser and sat next to her. "You want this coffee?"

"Is a frog's ass watertight?" She pushed up to where she could lean back and dragged the sheet up under her arms.

"Don't hide the girls."

She ignored that and reached out. "Give."

He handed her the mug. "Demanding woman when you wake up."

Not when she woke up to him. "How long did we sleep?"

"You were out about two hours." Dingo got up and crossed the room, pulling on his jeans.

Which meant he probably napped less than a half hour. "What have you been doing?"

"Been online looking for information on last night's event." He zipped and padded back across the floor.

Evasive as always. She raked her fingers through her hair. "Has my phone rung?"

"No. I'd have gotten you."

"What's going on, Dingo? I can't take this polite conversation. It's not like we're planning a day at the beach. Nothing has changed in two hours, right?"

He walked back over and scratched his forehead. "That depends."

"On what?"

"How much you're willing to tell me."

"About what specifically?" She could do evasive, too.

"Who are you working for and I don't mean Charlie?"

Acid churned in her stomach. What was he talking about? "I told you I can't share anything about the project I'm on."

"I heard Navarro mention Aram. Who is he?"

"Aram Pavlovsky is in the same field as me, but not in my league, and I say that with no ego. He's a hustler who closes deals like a demon. He does outperform me right now in that regard."

"How'd you meet Charlie?"

"He was referred to me a month ago by someone in the northeast. I spent a lot of hours checking him out. He's very highly respected. What is your interest in him?"

"But he's not the client you're contracted to right now."

"Where are you going with this, Dingo? If I tell you my client's name, what are you going to do with that information?"

"Depends."

"I hate that word. I hate everything about this moment, because it feels like we're right back where you're feeding me a line of shit and I'm dancing around your lies." She put the mug down and threw the sheet aside, standing. She headed for the shower, grousing, "We never get past this point."

"I can't tell you things that have to do with national security, Valene."

She stopped and turned. "Who are you, Dingo? What group do you work for?"

"I'm an operative. I'm not with any alphabet agency, but I'm on the right side of the law."

"Is there somewhere I can call to confirm your identity?"

He hooked a hand on his neck. "There's a number and if you called you would be convinced that person was me, but it's bogus. I'm not in the system. I don't want to lie to you. I'm on a case and I'm trying to keep you safe from Satan's Garden Club, but I need information specifically about you."

"Why?"

That got her the thousand yard stare.

She could scream but it would only hurt her voice and his ears. It wouldn't make him give up anything. "I need to think. Let me shower and we'll talk."

She stepped into the bathroom and shut the door before he could irritate her any more. Once the water was on lobster-boil-hot, she climbed in and started scrubbing while she figured out her next move.

Smith had been at the event, but he hadn't spoken to her, so what did that mean? She'd missed her chance with Tinker. Henri was going to maim her even if it wasn't her fault, but Henri hadn't contacted her with any information from Geoffrey about the scroll either.

Satan's Garden Club would come after her again.

Why had that Navarro guy killed Aram?

Poor Aram. She put her head down against the tiled wall and let water blast over her. He'd been a pain in her side, but not someone who deserved to die that way. Had he stuck his nose into the wrong spot?

Navarro hadn't seemed well informed on the scroll, which meant Aram had lacked information to give Navarro. She went back to scrubbing. Maybe Navarro went after Aram for another reason and lucked into the scroll information.

How had Dingo known to find her there?

Who was Dingo and what was he after? He kept asking about her client, but not the scroll. Smith had warned her Orion Hunters were after the scroll, but Dingo hadn't really known who they were when he came to her a month ago.

Or had he known and just kept her in the dark, like usual?

He couldn't be with the Orion Hunters, could he?

She stomped on that thought. Dingo had been working to stop the hunters from destroying this country, and his friends had almost died trying. Dingo might not ever tell her the truth about who he worked for or what he did, but she knew *what* he was–a man with an ironclad moral code.

If she could only get him to level with her on everything else.

She finished showering and toweled off, struggling with one question.

Do I tell Dingo about Smith or not?

What was the worst-case scenario if she did?

Smith finding out and demanding the fifty thousand dollars back. That gave her indigestion.

How would Smith find out?

If Dingo told whoever he was working for.

That simplified her decision. She knew what to do.

After pulling on a pair of jeans, a pink cotton blouse she rolled the cuffs up on, and sneakers, she actually found a small stash of makeup in a vanity drawer, and *score*, there were three shades of concealer. She managed a decent job of toning down the ugly bruise so she looked a little less battered before she made it up to the kitchen.

Dingo had finished dressing in a black T-shirt, scuffed up jeans, a gray hoodie and boots. He sat at the island and looked up from his phone when she walked in.

She said, "Let's talk."

He shoved the phone into his pocket. "About?"

"Everything." She refilled the mug she'd brought from the bedroom, turned and leaned back against the counter.

He offered, "You start."

"You keep asking about my client. If you want me to tell you who he is, then you have to explain why you need to know and what you're going to do with that information. If you give me the I-can't-tell-you sound bite again, we're at a stalemate."

"What if I told you I'd use that information to keep you and other people safe?"

"The only person threatening *me* right now is Navarro. I did not hear or see anything that connected my client and him. Are you saying they're connected?"

"Possibly."

At least he hadn't lied when he could have, but then she'd have made him prove it to her.

He said, "What else did Navarro tell you?"

Her conscience was taking her to task. Dingo had clearly made good on his claim to be here to protect her. But she had no idea who he would tell about Smith if she gave him information. "Give me something, Dingo. Anything. This client is important to me. Tell me why you're so interested in him."

"I'll tell you what I can, but you can't share it or go running off to confront someone."

She considered that and nodded. "Okay."

"And you can't get mad at me."

"I reserve that right."

He looked up to the ceiling in a show of seeking patience, took a moment and brought his gaze back to her. "It was brought to my attention that Charlie is suspected of illegal operations."

She pushed off the counter. "Your people are investigating my client? Why?"

"Charlie wasn't on our radar, but after what happened with Navarro, I'm looking at everything connected to you."

"I told you Navarro only came after me because Aram had called my phone and then he blabbed to Navarro's man about an artifact that might be the one I'm hunting."

"Why did Navarro kill Aram?"

"I don't know. I asked and he said it was just a body he had to put to rest. How is Navarro connected to what your people are investigating?"

Dingo went deathly still. "Let's get back to–"

"Don't you dare clam up on me," she said, slapping the counter. "You can't trust me, but I'm supposed to believe all this and answer all your questions?"

"It's not like that, Val. There's a chance this is all tied together. Your client and Navarro's group."

"That's a leap. Navarro didn't know about me, or what I'm

hunting for, until he found my name in Aram's phone. Speaking of Navarro, what about your name? Is it really Paddock?"

"Yes."

"But you couldn't tell me that seven years ago, could you? You said it was Paddington."

"I was shielding you–"

"*Stop it!*" she shouted. "Stop shielding me. Stop hiding everything from me. Stop taking risks for me and then saying you can't trust me! Don't you get it? I–" She caught herself before she blundered and said she loved him.

She'd regretted not telling Dingo that when she thought Navarro was going to kill her, but if she said it now she'd regret telling him when he couldn't give her love back.

He saw her as a responsibility, someone to protect.

Not someone to have as a partner.

Dingo needed no one. Least of all her. The time had come to stop just *telling* herself that and start accepting it as truth.

He looked lost and lifted a hand to her, but her phone rang with Henri's tune, extinguishing the chaotic tension that had been ricocheting between them.

She reached for her purse.

Dingo put his hand on the purse, stopping her. "Who is it?"

"My ex-husband..." Her words stalled at the look on Dingo's face.

"What's your ex got to do with this?"

She was an idiot because her heart did a little dance at the anger in Dingo's voice. "He's in a business related to mine and helping me with this project."

The phone kept ringing. Dingo's gaze narrowed with suspicion. "He knows what you're hunting for, but you won't tell me?"

She should have said *a* project. It did sound bad when he put it that way, but he was not going to make her feel guilty. "Yes, he does. He's been with me for a long time and I need to take this."

"No. Wait until you see if he leaves a message."

"Why?"

"Because someone could triangulate our position."

She snatched her purse away, but waited for her phone to stop ringing. She punched her button for the voicemail and got, "Valene..." Noisy racket. "...the shop in half an hour."

"What's wrong?" Dingo asked.

"The message is broken up. He must have had a bad connection." She tapped Henri's number and got a message that the cell phone customer was not answering.

It should have said the cell tower was taking a break.

She ended the call and pointed the phone at Dingo. "You're taking me to Pasadena now."

"To see your ex?"

"Yes."

"How long were you married?"

"I don't have time for this. I need to go!"

"Answer me, Val." Dingo wasn't budging.

She made a sound of disgust and irritation balled into one surly growl. "A year, give or take a few days. Satisfied? Can we leave now?"

That drew a frown on his face as if confused, but only for an instant, then he produced a set of car keys from his jeans pocket. He walked to the door for the garage, slowing to lift a black duffel bag from the floor before he opened the door.

"Do I get luggage, too?" she quipped.

"This isn't luggage. It's a go bag and if you want to go with it you need to get your ass moving. Wouldn't want to keep your ex waiting."

What?

Dingo–the man who shared nothing, wanted no ties and acted as if he was here just to keep her safe–had a burr up his butt about her being married?

She clamped down on the sudden rush of happiness she felt at what sounded like a spurt of jealousy. *Don't be stupid.* Allowing that idea to take root was the road to misery.

Chapter 30

HER EX, AS in ex-husband.

Dingo could feel Valene's eyes on him from the passenger seat.

She didn't do quiet, except when she was asleep. He'd liked that about her, the boundless energy that drove her as hard as the Energizer Bunny.

She'd give the rabbit a run for its money.

But she was quiet now. Bad sign that.

He'd been deliberating all morning on what he was going to do with Valene. Locking her up somewhere safe would have made *him* happy, but with Rikker in play she had to be available or Rikker would get suspicious and hightail it.

Hard to imagine, but Dingo didn't give a rat's ass if that meant losing Rikker. Valene was not anyone's bait.

But he did care about Rikker coming back for Valene later. Dingo couldn't keep her locked up indefinitely, not with her father seriously ill, and having no idea when Rikker would return was far riskier than keeping her with Dingo until this ended one way or another.

She made a sound like clearing her throat then asked, "It's dawned on me that you said I was married as soon as you left. How would you know when I got married?"

Her favorite word was anything she could stick a question mark after. "Lucky guess."

"That won't fly."

When he said nothing more, she asked, "How about talking to me with straight answers for once? You want me to trust you, to answer any questions, because in your world any question you ask is vital to national defense."

Most of the time, it was.

She kept going. "You started this by asking about my past and you know way more about me than you've ever shared. Would it be so hard to talk about us?"

She had no idea.

He functioned best in a world when he could keep everything that had the potential of distracting him at a distance.

Valene had the ability to distract him just by sitting here smelling freshly showered. The idea of her being with another man distracted him. The fact that Dingo was on his way to meet the bastard she'd married might cause his head to implode from trying to maintain a calm appearance.

But she had a valid point. He had started this by asking about her ex-fucking-husband. Not that he cared who she'd married or that she had married or ... shit it pissed him off.

"Dingo?"

"Right. Sure. I'll talk. We got another ten minutes to kill. Why not?" Might as well spend it doing the equivalent of shoving a sharp stick in his eye.

At least he was driving, which saved him from having to face her while they talked. He hated talking.

Crap came out that was better left shoved out of view.

But for Valene, he found himself saying, "What do you want to know?"

"How did you find out I was married? The truth, please."

Here we go. "I saw you two and the ring you had on ... at the time. I never dug around in your life. I don't do that with friends. But I figured if you were married, it was public knowledge. Looked it up on the Internet and realized you'd been married a week."

The barrage of questions he had expected didn't come.

Should he look at her or not? Not would be safer.

But she wasn't making any sounds.

He had to look just to reassure himself that she was still breathing so he cut his eyes over, intending to be quick about it.

The devastation rocking her face held him prisoner for long seconds until he had to pay attention to the crazy LA traffic. Quiet had never made him uncomfortable. He'd spent days sometimes without any interaction because the less he engaged the easier it was to get through life.

Look at how well talking had gone during his last conversation with Sabrina.

But this silence started eating at him, biting him with worry that he'd somehow managed to hurt Valene yet again.

When he risked another glance, she was staring out the windshield and her profile carried sadness in each slow breath she took.

He couldn't stand it any longer. "What's wrong, Val?"

"Nothing."

That was the single most dangerous word for every man living, equal in significance only to the word "fine." "You're the one who wanted to talk. Why aren't you talking?"

She turned her head, catching his eye as he stole another look. For a moment, he thought she was going to cry. If she did, he'd find a tree to beat his head against. He hated making her unhappy and damn if he didn't seem to be a professional at it.

After another drawn out moment, she said, "I spent that first year sure that you were dead. I couldn't imagine how you could be alive and leave me that way, with no word of what had happened to you. I was so alone. My dad had been diagnosed with cancer the first time and you had vanished. If not for Henri, I'm not sure I'd have made it through."

If not for Henri...

Dingo had no reason to feel torn up over that even though he couldn't have been there for her, but it felt like a spinning blade had been turned loose inside him and a dagger kept stabbing his heart over and over.

Valene had been alone and needing a shoulder to lean on.

His shoulder had been healing from a bullet wound.

She'd turned to some guy who had been able to give her all the things Dingo never could and that punched him dead center.

She wasn't through with him. Her voice was raw and thin. "You came back a year later and didn't even call? Couldn't have just picked up the phone to say hi, I'm not coming back but I'm still alive?"

"Val, I..." Jesus, what could he say? *I saw you with that guy,*

Henri, and went back to Atlanta where I holed up alone for months until Sabrina and Josh dragged my ass back to the real world?

How could he tell her that, then leave again when the time came?

She'd never understand and she'd just keep on hurting.

Wouldn't it be better to deal with this now so that once he'd dealt with Navarro and company, Dingo could take off with a clear conscience?

His conscience might be at peace once that happened, but his heart wouldn't. Not after having her in his arms again.

Don't get close to anyone.

He'd lived with that golden rule and it had served him well. Sure, he got close to Sabrina and Josh, but that had been back when they were all young and they'd needed his protection. Over the years, he just got used to being with them and they lived in the same world he did. He hadn't brought them into it.

He would stay this time to make absolutely sure everything was fine before he left, but he could never be with Valene.

Not like two people in a normal relationship.

Just *knowing* Dingo had her in danger right now, and he was willing to bet that Rikker had found her because of what she'd done to help Dingo a month ago.

He saw the sign for the street where Henri-the-ex had a business and made the turn.

"You've got nothing to say?" Valene said. "Why doesn't that surprise me? You tell me you joined Garcia to take him down to protect me, but you don't trust me enough to tell me the truth. I'll tell you what I think the truth is. You can't face what you feel about me so you give me this whole song and dance about how you're keeping secrets to protect me. You left to protect me. Now you're not telling me what happened to protect me. Bullshit. All of it. So don't go acting put out that I married Henri quick or something. There was nothing quick about it."

Dingo pulled into the parking lot of a crummy location for high-end antiques and picked a spot close to the street where he had two easily accessible exits. Not a problem since there were only two other cars and both were parked near the building.

Were Friday mornings slow for the antiques business or just at this place? He turned the engine off and sat there.

Valene was angry.

That was better than hurt. Better for her in the long run, because she'd turn her back on Dingo the first chance she got instead of waiting for him like she had last time.

You still owe her something, asshole.

He didn't look at her when he said, "You're right. I should have called you at some point, but you looked happy and I wasn't going to interfere. And you're also right that I have no place asking anything about your ... marriage. Every time I show up, I cause you problems. Just being near me puts you in danger. Let's get through this and I swear to you I'll never contact you again."

Pushing the door open, he climbed out before he screwed up that fine little speech by reaching for her and wrapping her up in his arms so he could hold onto the one woman who had given him a moment of happiness in his life.

She was out of the car just as fast and walking slowly ahead of him. Toward her ex. Henri. Sounded French when she said it like, "Ahn-ray."

The man who'd taken Dingo's place the minute he was gone.

Dingo had wanted to stay with Valene back when they were first together and that longing had terrified him.

So he'd been twice as angry when she put herself at risk to find information for him. He'd decided the best way to protect her was by removing the threat, which hadn't been a bad plan. Sabrina had railed at him to never do that again.

Surviving Garcia had been one step from insanity, but he'd healed. Seeing Valene married and happy had shriveled his heart. It wasn't her fault, but losing her had broken something inside of him that he'd never gotten back. He'd gone through life perfectly content with no ties beyond his commitment to Sabrina and Josh. No place he really called home.

Nothing to lose.

No one to ever toss him aside like yesterday's trash.

Never again.

Then he'd met a funny, sweet, hot-tempered, intelligent,

beautiful woman and he'd fooled himself into believing he could dabble at life. Have a day here and there.

But one day turned into two that turned into a month ... then a year had passed and he woke up one day to find he wasn't happy when he had down time anywhere else in the world but Los Angeles.

He'd been battling himself for weeks back then, trying to figure out what to do. The simple answer had been to just tell Valene it was over and he was leaving, but he'd gotten caught in the magic of Valene and had kept making excuses for staying.

Then she'd drawn Garcia's attention.

Dingo would do it all again, but in hindsight he had to admit that he could have gotten word to her at some point. He just couldn't bring himself to say he was never coming back, so he'd held on to the fantasy of returning to her arms and picking up right where they left off.

But someone else had picked up where Dingo left off.

Reaching the sidewalk in front of the stores, Dingo moved ahead of Valene and opened the door for her, preparing himself to meet her ex.

They must still be on good terms. Just how good?

If her ex kissed her, maintaining professionalism might be tough to do while Dingo shoved Henri's face down his neck.

"Henri?" Valene called out as soon as they were inside.

A door to what was probably the back room opened and a man appeared. Not overly tall, but Dingo recognized the man he'd seen walking with Valene six years ago.

The model-worthy guy.

"Valene. Have you heard about Aram?"

She strode quickly to the back, saying, "Yes. What did you hear, Henri?"

Yup, that's what Valene had picked as marriage material, which meant Dingo never had a chance. But he never planned to get married anyhow. Women wanted a man who was home cutting the grass and cooking steaks on the barbie.

Not someone like Dingo.

Nobody had wanted him as a kid, and kids were like puppies.

If you weren't adorable enough to keep when you were a kid you sure as hell wouldn't be as an adult.

"What? When?" Valene's shout brought Dingo out of his thoughts.

"What's going on, Val?"

She turned around, looking embarrassed. "I'm sorry. Dingo this is Henri." She addressed her ex. "Henri this is Dingo, a... an associate of mine."

Associate? Did all of her *associates* break into the headquarters of known killers to save her cute ass?

Henri stepped around her and gave Dingo a full assessment, and if Dingo had to guess at his rating he'd put it between slug and mutt.

Not much better than being called an associate.

Henri's eyes were loaded with suspicion. "What is *he* doing here, Valene?"

"What's your problem, Frenchie?"

"This is my place of business. You will show me respect or I will have you removed."

Valene muttered, "For crying out loud, Henri."

Dingo crossed his arms. Yes, that was showing off his guns, but those hard-earned muscles had convinced more than a few men to think twice about laying a hand on him.

He'd suffered at the hands of strangers as a kid and had never allowed anyone to touch him uninvited again.

A sound slipped out of Valene that sounded like a pissed off teakettle. "Enough! Stop it, you two."

Henri said, "We have business to discuss, Valene. Private business. In my office."

"Okay, I'll just–"

Dingo put his foot down. "No."

"What do you mean no?" Henri frowned first at Dingo then at Valene. "Does this man speak for you?"

"This is important, Dingo," Valene said, sounding like a mediator.

Dingo didn't care whose feathers he ruffled. "I want to be able to see you."

She rolled her eyes at him, but smiled at ex-Henri. "Wait for me in that far alcove, please."

Henri sniffed at Dingo then softened his voice when he told Valene, "But of course."

When Henri walked off to a cozy area all decorated as if the queen was coming for tea, Valene rounded on Dingo.

"What's wrong with you?" she hissed with her back to where Henri sat far enough away not to hear her words.

"Me? What'd I do?"

"I need Henri to help me and you're acting like a caveman, which you have no grounds for doing."

Maybe so, but Dingo didn't like the proprietary way Henri watched Valene. "I'm acting like someone trying to keep you alive."

"This isn't the hood and Henri knows I'm under a confidentiality agreement. If I talk about this in front of you I might as well say all bets are off. Tell anyone you want, even the news. I have to talk to him alone."

"Because you can't trust me?"

"No, because you don't trust *me*," she ground out. "Henri does. The back of this building has a steel door with a heavy bar across it in addition to the locks and alarms. The Hulk couldn't get in that way. You're standing between me and the front door. I'm as safe as I can be, but I'm also under a time crunch. Can you stand down long enough for me to do my business?"

No. Maybe. Hell, he didn't know. Eyeing Henri with the perfect hair and eyes and clothes, Dingo considered the pretty boy and what happened when women married men who were used to a lot of attention.

He asked, "Who called an end to the marriage?"

Her face flushed with color. "That's not relevant right now." She swung around and walked away.

Why had she looked guilty? Like she'd done something to cause the divorce.

Dingo tracked the sweet swing of her hips as she walked over and sat down in the alcove. Even with Dingo's limited knowledge of antiques, he could tell this guy had a wad of money tied up in inventory.

He didn't even pretend not to watch every move Henri made. Divorcees sometimes got back together.

What better way to do that than to be Mr. Helpful with Valene's special project? And what did Rikker have her hunting for? Short of forcing her to tell him how to find Rikker, Dingo had to wait for her to meet with Rikker again.

The same thing Gage's people were waiting on.

The difference was that Dingo would not allow Valene to be anyone's bait.

She smiled at Henri and Dingo felt a cramp in his chest.

If Henri made a move on her, Dingo was going to rearrange Henri's pretty face.

That wasn't caveman, just proactive.

"This is not funny, Valene. He's a brute," Henri said, waving his hands as he talked. "He looks like a barbarian with that hair and he's unshaven."

She couldn't help the laugh that bubbled up. Dingo and Henri couldn't be more opposite and, yes, Dingo might have a barbaric side to him, but in a very hot way. Maybe she could talk Dingo into wearing a Conan outfit and...

Down girl. Take a left off Fantasy Lane.

"That was awful about Aram," Henri said, mournfully. "He was unpleasant to do business with, but I wish no one to be mugged."

"Oh, yes. Damn. That's what I wanted to tell you when I got here. Aram wasn't mugged. He was murdered." She'd debated how much to tell Henri, but this was not information that Dingo gave her so she was not breaking a confidence.

Henri's eyes were wide and round. "Murdered?"

"Yes, and the people who killed him used his phone to find me. Have you called his phone since yesterday morning?"

"No. I would not undermine my agreement with you. Was he involved with the scroll?"

"Not exactly, but he'd heard about it, so when they came after him he told them he'd help them get this valuable scroll, so they came after me."

"Were you harmed?"

"No, but that's why I've got a bodyguard."

Henri cut another look at Dingo. "Now I understand bringing a Neanderthal with you." Then Henri got very intent. "I saw the news about Fontana. Does this mean you went in vain?"

She let the Neanderthal comment pass and grimaced at his question. "I'm sorry. I had a pitch down. I was ready."

He blew out a breath and rubbed his forehead. "This is disastrous."

"What has Geoffrey found out?"

"He is making progress, but he is gone on several errands. He said he would be back later today. He made calls to his best people who deal in rare writings and they made inquiries and so on. He has been very busy and seemed happy with his progress."

"I would say tell him thank you, but I doubt he'd accept it from me."

More innocuous hand motions from Henri. "It is what it is." His gaze went past her in the direction of Dingo. "I see how you look at him. Tell me you will not attempt marriage again with one such as that."

"It's not like that between us."

"Only lust. Good. I would not like to see you go through a second divorce."

Valene snarled low and quiet, "At least I was willing to stick it out."

Henri huffed impatiently. "I will say this one time and be done. You still blame me for quitting. You want to know why I ended that farce we called a marriage? Not because I wanted a man more than I wanted you. I wanted someone who was completely in the marriage *with* me. You may not have been the one to leave, but you never really committed to us."

"How can you say that?"

"*Shh!* The barbarian is staring as if he intends to pummel me. I will not tolerate that in my own shop!"

Valene calmed down and turned around, giving Dingo her I'm-okay smile then waved him off as if he'd been standing too close. He nodded and walked toward the front of the shop.

She swung back to glare at Henri. "I was there day and night."

He scoffed. "You might have been physically present, but not in spirit. You couldn't really love me, not the way I wanted, because you loved someone else. You *still* love someone else. Do not get me wrong. I wish you would tell me who the man is that left you. I would go find him for you and you would be happy again, as you were before we ruined a perfect friendship by getting married."

Was he right? Had she failed to do her part from the start?

"We were good friends, Valene," he said gently. "We just weren't good spouses."

"I do love you Henri." She blinked away tears. "I really tried…"

He leaned forward and took her hand in his. "I love you too, but not the way I love Geoffrey and not the way you loved some crazy guy who let you get away." His Adam's apple moved with a hard swallow. "Your father had just been diagnosed with cancer. My cousin had overdosed. I'd lost my closest family, the only one who not only accepted me but loved me, and you were terrified of losing the one person who you lived and breathed for."

That was a horrible time. A dark smear of misery they'd both suffered through. "I wouldn't have gotten through that without you."

"Nor I without you, but somehow we confused comfort with love and both of us were terrified of being alone so we insured we would not be. You must admit that what little sex we had was not memorable, and I say that even though I had much experience with women and am a skilled lover."

"And humble. Never forget how humble you are."

His eyes twinkled at the jab, then softened with remorse. "The worst part of all that was after our divorce, I missed my good friend. Geoffrey is my best friend and all that I could ever want for a partner, but you and I? We go back to high school when you were my first real friend. I hated losing that most of all."

She swiped at a tear, nodding. "I'm an awful person. I've been blaming you all this time because… well …"

"Because you didn't want to admit the truth about loving someone who left you. And you thought I'd left you too."

She did love Dingo in a way she'd never felt about Henri.

At least, this was what she'd expect love to be, but Dingo was not someone who would allow any woman to love him. Without that acceptance, all the love in the world was nothing but heartache on her end.

"I'm sorry, Henri. So sorry for all the time I've let bitterness damage our friendship."

"You're forgiven only if you promise to be my friend again." Dingo cleared his throat.

She twisted around to find him eyeing Henri's hand on hers with a black look in his gaze as if Henri's touch might contaminate her with a deadly disease.

Henri removed his hand and leaned back. His phone buzzed. "About time. I have been calling Geoffrey for an hour. He is normally much more considerate about calling back."

Valene shot Dingo a back off look that he ignored.

She sighed and turned around to find Henri making a call, which must not have gone through because he was texting next. He grumbled at the phone, "Why aren't you calling me?"

"What's wrong, Henri?"

"Geoffrey. He hasn't returned a voice mail I left a few minutes ago, but he sent me a text that he left me a surprise on my desk." His smile was intimate when he spoke of Geoffrey.

"Go see what he left you or you'll obsess."

"I do not obsess."

"Yes, you do. Go," she chided him just as she once had when they'd studied together and he'd obsessed over whether he should ask someone out who had grabbed his attention.

"I shall return promptly."

While Henri was gone to his office in the back, Valene walked over to where Dingo glowered. She angled her head in question. "What?"

"Are you two still together?"

Dingo *was* bothered by Henri.

The imp in her said, "It's been an amicable divorce."

"What the hell does that mean?"

"We're still friends." Just saying that felt good all the way to her toes. She'd missed Henri so much, but she craved being with Dingo. Henri had been spot on.

She'd never been *in love* with him.

She'd just needed someone to hold on to in the shit storm her life turned into the week Dingo vanished.

Dingo's jaw muscled flickered. He kept looking at the door to the back then at her as if he'd just figured something out.

Valene hooked her thumbs in her jeans. "Spill."

"Did you divorce him because you figured out he was gay?"

"No, I knew that."

"Huh?"

"Henri left me."

"For a guy?"

"Not really. Henri is bisexual and we became friends back in high school. He's always been comfortable with either sex and became involved with a man named Geoffrey sixteen months ago, but that had nothing to do with why he left me. We married for the wrong reasons."

"What reasons?"

She didn't think she could handle explaining that to Dingo, because she might slip and say something she'd regret.

"Valene! Valene!" Henri rushed toward them from the back. He was ghost white.

"What's wrong?"

"Geoffrey's note. It says he is speaking to someone who asked Geoffrey to validate a Galileo scroll for which he wishes to find a buyer."

Valene should have known better than to trust Geoffrey just because Henri did. "He was supposed to tell *me* so I would meet with the seller." She wanted to strangle Geoffrey *and* Henri now, because Henri had opened his big mouth in front of Dingo.

But first she had to keep Henri from going into full drama mode.

Henri was babbling. "Geoffrey's not answering my call. I sent our emergency code of 999 that means to call *immediately*. I can't reach him."

Valene grabbed Henri's shoulders. "Calm down. He's fine.

The cell connection might not be going through. Your call to me was all jumbled up."

"You don't understand." Henri's eyes were wild. "Geoffrey is going to meet this man. Geoffrey said he wants to prove to me that he is just as tough as you. He found out the scroll is rumored to be an Orion Hunter artifact so he told this man he was with the Orion Hunters. Geoffrey said the man who called him got the referral from Aram!" Tears poured down Henri's face.

Oh, shit.

Dingo stepped in. "Give me Geoffrey's cell number."

"Why?" Henri stared at Dingo as if he'd forgotten anyone else was present.

Dingo's entire demeanor shifted from his earlier adversarial one to a tone used to talk someone down who was hysterical after a catastrophic accident. "Finding him requires information. Everything you can give us from that note, to anything else he told you and his cell phone number is a good start."

Henri still panted in panic but he started nodding. "Yes, yes. I will get everything. The note is in the back."

Valene still had a grip on Henri's shoulder that she used to hold him in place so she could look him in the eye. "Look at me. We're going to bring Geoffrey back."

Henri's eyes floated in tears. "Please. You have to. He is everything."

She hugged him. "I know what it is to lose that one person. I won't come back without him." Then she let him rush off to gather what Dingo needed.

She hadn't made an empty promise.

Dingo had connections with people capable of stopping a national disaster. Surely all Dingo had to do was call the secret bat cave phone and Arthur would locate Geoffrey.

Chapter 31

DINGO THUMBED KEYS on his cell phone as he led Valene from Henri's business, across the parking lot toward the car he'd have to swap tags on soon. He had two more in the trunk of the GTO.

Valene's footsteps tapped close behind. "You can find Geoffrey, right?"

"Maybe." He sent the text and crossed his fingers that this was one of those times Nick being an unorthodox black ops player would work in Dingo's favor. With Nick, you might have to dive through the jaws of a whale to rescue the key to a mission, knowing the only way out depended on getting shot out of the whale's blowhole.

"What do you mean maybe?" she snapped. "Don't you have people you can call?"

"I'm not on good terms with my people right now. I'll do what I can, but there's no guarantee that I can find him." Dingo reached the car and unlocked both doors from the driver's side.

She argued with him over the roof of the car. "That's bullshit. You work with some agency that can track GPS and crap like that, right?"

"I did and it's not something I want announced to the world. Can we discuss this in the car?"

She had the decency to look chagrined and glance around, then dropped into the car.

He slammed the door. "I'm trying to get some help, but this situation might not have happened if you would just trust me enough to tell me what you're involved in."

That buttoned her up.

What the hell did Rikker want with the scroll? Or did the

scroll even have anything to do with Rikker? Dingo thought back over the meeting right before he took off from Sabrina and the team. Nick had gotten intel that the Orion Hunters were looking for an artifact. An important one.

A scroll and something to do with Galileo maybe?

History had not been Dingo's strong suit in school. He'd majored in getting into trouble and the only school record he'd ever set had been for the most suspensions.

But he did not forget details when it came to a mission.

He said, "I know you're hunting for a scroll." Then he made a wild guess based on the way Henri had described why Geoffrey was at this meeting. "A rare one from Galileo."

Still she said nothing.

This was his chance to convince her to tell him what was going on and break through to get her on his side. He hated to go after her weak point, but Valene had few and one was clearly her relationship with Henri, as a friend.

She didn't explain the wrong reason she got married, but Dingo could pursue that later. First he had to figure out the connection between the scroll and Rikker.

He asked her, "Why are we going after Geoffrey?"

She looked at him like he was delusional. "He's in danger. Why are we still sitting here?"

"I'm waiting on someone to contact me with a fix on Geoffrey's location, *if* my friend can do it," Dingo explained, then went right back on point. "Why is Geoffrey in danger?"

Here came Tornado Valene. She leaned forward and he was pretty sure she was straining to keep from lunging at him. She shouted, "Didn't you hear Henri? Because the man Geoffrey's meeting said he got the referral from Aram and Aram is dead. *D.E.A.D!* Navarro killed Aram so Navarro might be the person meeting Geoffrey."

"And why does Navarro care about this scroll?"

She opened her mouth and clamped it tight.

"*Godammit, Valene!* I'm trying to find Geoffrey and keep you alive!" Dingo had his arm pressing so hard on the console that it should have cracked when he shoved up close to her. "Now is the time to be straight with me."

"Why are you interested in all this? You wouldn't even have known about the scroll if not for Navarro and Henri."

Because Rikker was in the middle of this whole fiasco, but Dingo couldn't breathe Rikker's name or tell Valene that he knew about their meeting in the restaurant. "The bottom line is that I'm here right now and I'm–"

His phone buzzed.

The energy inside the car stilled with a mutual truce as Dingo read the text that had Geoffrey's location as of six minutes ago. He shoved the phone into his lap and put the car in gear, peeling out of the lot.

"Did you find him?" Valene asked, voice coming back down to earth and riddled with anxiety.

"Maybe."

"Enough with the maybe already!"

"Look, Val. I'm trying to tell you the truth. I need you to trust me to do my job. I have a location from six minutes ago, but his phone is moving. We're headed west. I'll get updates as long as the signal is moving. That's all I'm telling you until you meet me halfway on this."

She flopped back against the seat, elbow propped on the door and her head against her hand. "I have everything on the line with this deal. I need this, Dingo. You have no idea how much."

Because her dad was sick. "Then tell me."

"Why? And before you get cranky, I'm asking why because you don't want the messy part of being involved with someone. You want to come and go. I get that, but you can't expect me to share everything that's going on in my world just because you decide to drop in out of thin air and you need the information. You want to know why I married Henri?"

Talk about a switch in topics, but Dingo couldn't stop himself from saying, "Yeah, I do."

"Because the week you disappeared, my dad was diagnosed with lung cancer, stage four. He's living with one lung right now. Henri and I have been best friends since high school, but you didn't know that because you didn't want to know that. Henri's closest family member was a cousin he loved dearly who died of a drug overdose the day after I heard about my dad. We were both hurting and had nobody except each other."

Her words cut over and over, slicing deeper each time.

Dingo had always been there for Sabrina and Josh.

He'd never stuck around any female long enough to learn her last name, much less meet anyone in her life. But in fairness to him, those women hadn't wanted anything else from him. They wanted someone who made them feel like they were playing with fire and forgot about him before the door hit him in the ass. If he'd stuck around, those women would have left first.

He was not being shoved away again. Ever.

But then he met Valene and she screwed up his wiring.

Or maybe she untangled it and he didn't know how to be with someone who acted as though she wanted him to stay.

His cell phone buzzed. He pushed the button to hear the text from Nick. *"Your target is still heading in the same direction and you better have something to tell me after you find him. Sabrina's turning into Attila the Hun and Josh looks like the Grim Reaper. My next text is going to be coordinates for saving my ass after I go off on one of them."*

Dingo put the phone down and drove from memory of the area, but he had at least another seventeen or eighteen minutes to get close to Geoffrey. He had to say something. "I'm sorry I wasn't here when that happened. If I could have been here, I would."

"How can you say that when all I've ever had were temporary numbers for you? I called your number back then. A lot. Your phone should have exploded from the texts blowing up on it."

"I told you I–"

"I know. You went undercover with Garcia. There were no phones undercover, right? Because you were off on another mission and you couldn't risk contacting me."

There was a lot of truth to that. "There was more going on than I can tell you, Valene."

"Exactly. And that's why I ended up marrying Henri. I was terrified of losing my dad who has been the only constant in my life besides Henri. But more than that, you became a part of my life and I wanted you there. Even though you couldn't give me anything back that I wanted to give you. I still wanted you there.”

“Why want someone who isn’t worth keeping?”

“Is that what you think, Dingo?” she asked with soft sincerity.

“Think about it. You just said I couldn’t be depended upon and I wasn’t there when you needed me.” Now he was getting jacked up.

“But you care about me. Whether you can admit it or not, you do. I just don’t understand why you came back and never told me.”

He slowed to get off the interstate and make a right into a busy flow of traffic. “I saw you two walk out of your apartment. You were smiling and laughing. He had his arm around you.” It hurt all over just seeing that in his mind. “I was trying to figure out when would be a good time to drop into your apartment when your finger flashed. Left hand. The only ring you used to wear on that hand was a black onyx carved with hieroglyphs or something.”

“From my dad,” she whispered.

Right. Another thing he hadn’t known. “Once I knew for sure you were married, I saw no point in interfering.” He’d figured one of them might as well be happy.

“We were hardly together. My dad required a lot of time. Henri was busy keeping up with my clients and trying to develop his rare map business. He told me today that I was never in love with him and he was right. I love Henri as a close friend, but I didn’t hurt as bad when he packed up to leave as I did when I realized you were never coming back.”

Dingo’s heart pounded like a boxing match going on in his chest.

Was she saying what he thought she was saying?

His phone buzzed and he fumbled it, lifting the phone to hear the text from Nick telling him the signal was stationary and giving him information on the mall where the phone was parked. Dingo dropped the phone and wheeled hard to cut left against traffic and lurch into the mall parking area that spread out forever.

Horns blared.

Valene shouted, "What's wrong?"

"Found him. We go in together only if you will do exactly what I say. If I tell you to get out of sight or to hide somewhere specific, it's to stop you from taking a bullet."

He waited on the argument, but she surprised him by saying, "I'll do it. I don't want to make any mistakes with getting Geoffrey back safe and sound."

Dingo parked the car and climbed out, shoving his 9mm inside the back waistband of his jeans where it was hidden by his loose shirttail.

Valene came around to his side, but kept her voice down. "Why would he be at a mall?"

"Either Geoffrey or the client set the meeting location. Whoever picked this spot wants to be in the open and around a lot of people."

Could be Rikker.

Could be Navarro and his merry band of Satan's Garden Club.

Could be someone with the FBI or Gage's people looking to nail Dingo's hide to a wall.

Nothing good could come of any of those possibilities, especially with this guy Geoffrey playing at being an undercover agent. He did not want to take her in with him, but the only way to prevent that would be by putting her in the trunk. That would certainly smooth things out between them.

Wouldn't that make it easier to cut this off clean with her later?

No. He had to stop thinking about the future, because he didn't do future, and he had to deal with right now if he wanted to keep her out of harm's way.

He shed his hoodie. "Come here. You got your Walther?"

"In my purse."

"Good." He pulled the hoodie over her head to hide her face and all that glowing blond hair. Then he reached into his go bag and pulled out a Dodger baseball cap he yanked down over his ears. He gave her a pair of sunglasses too big for her face and put on his cheap pair.

She adjusted the glasses. "They'll think we're celebrities incognito."

Only in LA. He tugged on the hoodie, hiding her as deep in it as he could and she licked her lips. *Don't do that.*

"What?"

Had he really spoken the words? At a loss for what to say, he gave her a brief kiss and covered by saying, "Don't fiddle with the strings on the hoodie. Makes you look nervous."

"I was not fiddl–"

"You're at a mall. Just act like you're happy to be here."

"I will be happy if we find Geoffrey. This is a good location, right?" she sounded as if she was trying to convince herself more than Dingo. "He'll be around all these people until we get to him."

Dingo hated to destroy her comfort, but he wanted her to know the score. "No. Being in a busy area only means innocent bystanders might die if this gets ugly."

Chapter 32

WHAT WAS GEOFFREY thinking to pull this stunt? Valene kept her head down and stayed close to Dingo as he walked them into the newly remodeled mall. She'd seen a spot on the news about it opening again, where the reporter followed the developer through new service areas and the open-air mall that offered seating outdoors where people could have coffee or eat.

Her anger at Geoffrey had shifted into worry on the way here once she realized he wasn't trying to snake her deal on the scroll. Based on his note to Henri, Geoffrey was playing "superhero like Valene" and trying to impress Henri.

Geoffrey had it all wrong.

She was not a superhero by any stretch of the imagination. She might have thought she was pretty badass at one time. But Geoffrey hadn't seen the wreck she'd become when her dad first got sick and she'd wandered through an apartment where smells and sounds of Dingo ghosted through the air.

When this was over, she had to make Geoffrey understand that she was not a threat to his relationship and not someone to emulate.

But that wouldn't happen unless she delivered him back to Henri in one piece. Henri would never forgive her if Geoffrey got hurt, even if his significant other had landed in trouble only because he was a big fat wad of insecurity.

Dingo slowed as they passed around an enormous circular fountain. He said, "If I was meeting someone and wanted to do it in public, it would be as out in the open as possible."

"There are areas to sit on the next level up."

He nodded and led the way to an elevator instead of the

escalator. He didn't explain and she made a quick guess that it was to avoid *them* being exposed on an escalator.

When they exited on the top level, Dingo's gaze moved over the crowds and the people seated along the rail, eating and visiting.

"We got company," he murmured.

"Who?"

"Have no idea." He gave her a judgmental glance. "If I knew who all the players were I might be able to make a guess."

"Point the person out to me." She started to look around, but he grabbed her and spun her to look in the opposite direction.

"You can't just stare at him or he'll know he's been spotted. Sort of blows the whole disguised approach." Dingo tinkered with her hoodie and leaned in to kiss her, just as a boyfriend might do at a mall.

One more kiss and she'd go up in smoke. She warned him, "Stop that."

"Why?" The devil grinned at her.

"Because there's no reward at the end of that tunnel."

He hooked his arm around her shoulders and turned her to walk, whispering. "There's plenty of reward at the end of that tunnel. You just have to take the gamble and come after it."

That sounded like the Dingo she'd known a long time ago. She'd missed his joking around. He had her halfway around the top floor when she realized he'd distracted her from looking.

"Okay, I won't stare."

"Good because I think I found your friend and his client." He caught her cheek before she turned her head.

This whole surveillance business was too confining.

She liked action more than watching. "I'm not turning."

"You're sure this time?"

"Yes."

"Keep your head facing straight ahead and cut your eyes to those two men in suits sitting at a table to my left. Do you recognize either one?"

"Yes. The slender guy with the black frame glasses in the hairpiece that looks like a bad Saturday Night Live skit is Geoffrey. Guess that's Geoffrey's idea of going incognito. I don't know the bald guy who could stand to lose thirty pounds and looks like he could be a chain smoker the way his knee is bouncing and he keeps touching his mouth."

"Let's get close enough to hear what they're saying first."

"Why not just break it up?"

"Aren't you curious to know if Geoffrey has found the scroll?"

She'd been so focused on finding Geoffrey and thrown off balance when Dingo said someone else was here, she'd forgotten about the stupid scroll for once.

What about the other guy Dingo had called company? She asked, "Is someone still watching?"

"Yes, but he's keeping an eye on these two and hasn't noticed us yet."

"I don't care who anyone else is or what they have. I want to get Geoffrey out of here."

Dingo squeezed her shoulder and she took that as a sign that he liked her answer. That didn't mean she wasn't going to make Geoffrey tell her everything right down to phone numbers, but she wanted him out of harm's way first.

"I'm going to ease my arm off your shoulder and we're switching into angry-at-your boyfriend mode."

"Do you want tips? Oh, never mind. You have that down pat."

"Very funny. Just keep walking no matter what we do."

The two men were positioned in the middle of a patio with plants scattered around. The client opened his trench coat–could he be any more stereotypical?–and showed Geoffrey a small tube he had stuffed into an inside pocket.

Valene's quick intake of breath gave her away.

Dingo had just removed his arm. "Is that the scroll?"

"Could be." Had that guy really brought the scroll here? Or was he trying to pawn off a copy on Geoffrey? She could not risk anything happening to that tube in case it was the real deal.

Dingo grabbed her arm, his hand and fingers looking like he clenched hard, but he was not hurting her. He growled a noise and said, "Stop flaunting yourself at every asshole in this place!"

It took a second for the shock to pass then she snarled, "Let go of me. You're hurting my arm."

Dingo barked, "Shut up."

They sounded just like two people without any grooming in etiquette, who would air their dirty laundry in the middle of a beautiful mall.

As they got closer to the two men, Dingo kept a clamp on her arm and she struggled for real, trying to break lose. He was pretending, but she knew he could hold her as long as he wanted. He was coiled power waiting to unleash, and she pitied the person who dared to threaten her.

Geoffrey and his client looked up as Dingo and Valene continued arguing.

Valene changed the sound of her voice to keep Geoffrey thrown off just in case he recognized it.

But Geoffrey turned to watch them, perturbed over their abominable behavior.

Just as she was sure she knew what Dingo was going to do next, he whipped her around and grabbed her other arm, shaking her. "You want to act like that? I'm done with your shit."

He shoved her and she landed in Geoffrey's lap.

The shock on Geoffrey's face would be comical if not for worrying over how the unknown observer was taking this.

"Get out of here," Geoffrey's client shouted. He started looking all around. "Go away."

The man was having a serious panic attack.

Valene grabbed Geoffrey by the collar and pulled up close to his face to say, "This is Valene. You're in danger. Go with my friend."

Geoffrey didn't show any appreciation for her effort.

He shoved her off his lap and yelled, "You stupid bitch. You're screwing up everything."

Dingo said, "Shut up, Geoffrey." He ordered Valene, "Get out of here. Head out the same way we came."

She was not leaving without either that scroll, or the guy who had it.

Chapter 33

DINGO CHECKED ON the guy who had been pretending to be just another mall rat and not surveilling Geoffrey and his scroll client. The guy keeping tabs leaned forward, but had not moved yet.

That meant Dingo had a chance at getting these two men and Valene out of here alive, if she'd do what she promised and follow his orders.

Or he might have had a chance if Geoffrey's client hadn't panicked.

Scroll guy had jumped up and was looking all round.

He took off running back the way that Dingo and Valene had come, which meant...

"No, Valene!" But she was gone, racing after that damn scroll.

Now the guy who'd been spying headed this way, plowing through people and turning this into an official clusterfuck.

Worse? Dingo recognized the guy as one of Navarro's men and the bastard was angling in the direction that Valene and scroll guy had just gone.

Geoffrey stood there like a dumbass, which might be due to a bad case of shock.

Shit. Dingo had one play to keep that goon away from Valene, but he had to get Geoffrey onboard for any hope of making it work.

Dingo put on his death face and pointed a finger at Geoffrey who took one look at Dingo and Geoffrey's expression corrupted into terror. Perfect. Now that Dingo had his attention, he said in a tone meant to shrivel a man's balls, "When I shout, if you don't run for the exit behind you *immediately*, I'm killing everyone who slows me down from reaching Valene before she gets hurt."

That drained the blood from his face.

Navarro's man broke out of the congestion and sprinted.

He was almost close enough...

Dingo backed away from Geoffrey and shouted, "I don't give a shit about them. I did my part. We got the scroll. Fuck 'em. Let's go. *Now!*"

That did it. Geoffrey took off for the exit like a scalded piss ant.

Navarro's man skidded at that and did an about-face.

Dingo put on his best Oscar-winning face of someone surprised to see one of Navarro's goons.

Navarro's man shoved his hand into his jacket.

Dingo tore off after Geoffrey, who had just reached the exit door and flung it open.

Gunshots boomed.

Two bullets struck chairs Dingo passed. He zigzagged until he could dive for the open door and yank it shut. Geoffrey sounded like a herd of buffalo pounding down the emergency exit stairs.

If buffalos screeched like their hair was on fire.

Dingo still reached Geoffrey before he hit the bottom landing.

A door banged open above them and shots pinged off the metal stairs and concrete walls. Footsteps banged in fast repetition on the way down.

Getting out of here alive would be easier if Dingo didn't have to drag Geoffrey, but at least he wasn't dead weight.

Yet.

He let Geoffrey run out the exit that set off alarms and held the door open as if it was stuck.

Navarro's goon was too intent on the hunt to realize his mistake until Dingo bashed him with the door. That only stunned him. Dingo caught the goon's gun hand, slamming it against the metal railing, then cold cocked him.

He opened the door, breathing hard.

Now, he had to catch Geoffrey, who was still racing away. Then he had to figure out how to find Valene.

Chapter 34

VALENE RAN AFTER the man with a cylinder that just might hold the priceless, one-of-a-kind scroll everyone was after. She'd bet he was the thief who had stolen it from the Vatican, because everything he did screamed amateur.

He was not an expert at this espionage stuff like Dingo.

She had no idea how she was going to find him or Geoffrey again, but she trusted Dingo to get Henri's honey bunny out safely.

The thief shoved his way past everyone and started running down the escalator, stretching his lead.

She hooked the shoulder strap of her purse across her body to keep from losing it and pushed her way down past people first complaining at the guy with the scroll, then cursing Valene for being just as inconsiderate.

Someone jammed an elbow into her ribs. Ouch.

She was losing him. Valene yelled, *"Get out of my way! He's got a gun."*

Moses couldn't have parted the Red Sea any faster.

People sucked to each side of the escalator with faces frozen in fear. Valene dove forward, thumping down the moving steps as her target reached the bottom and speared his body into a crowd.

But she was in better shape and she was starting to gain on him.

The crowd got into the spirit and raised voices everywhere, shouting about a guy with a gun.

Screams ripped through the throng.

An opening formed behind her guy as they realized someone running might just be the man with a weapon.

Valene stretched out her stride and tackled him, taking him to the ground. People scattered. She reached in and grabbed the aluminum cylinder that was cool to her touch. He latched onto her arm with both of his, yelling, "No. You can't have it."

She shouted back, "It's not yours to keep."

"Fuck you, bitch." His eyes were small and dark, glittering with rage as he struggled to get a hold on the tube.

"Is that any way for a priest to talk?" she said too low for anyone else to hear.

His eyes widened.

Bingo.

People went in all directions as she fought him for the tube. He kicked her leg and rolled sideways, but she kept her grasp on the cylinder while they rolled around. He let go long enough to grab her throat, covered by the hoodie still pulled tight, and choked her. Stars burst in her vision. She hit him hard in the gut, but he was in better condition than she'd realized for a bishop or whatever he was.

Did they even work out? His elbow whacked her in the jaw. Lucky punch, but it still hurt because he hit the bruised side.

All the frustration she'd bottled up over the past months came roaring to the surface.

She hit him hard in the nuts and he let go.

She might feel bad about doing that to a guy, but anyone who had stolen from the Vatican and tried to strangle her deserved it.

He made gargling noises, but he wouldn't die. Hopefully she'd crushed any chance he had of donating a mini-me, thieving bastard sperm.

Men sounding like mall security shouted nearby. "Clear the way!"

Police would be here any minute and she'd lose her chance to escape.

She didn't need to capture this guy, just get the scroll back.

Valene snatched the tube and jumped up, yelling, "He said he has a bomb. *Runnn!"*

She was going to hell for all these horrific lies.

Pandemonium broke out with everyone heading for an exit.

That should keep security off her back. She yanked the hoodie down tighter over her face and hoped she wasn't headlining the security tapes.

The chaos gave her the break she needed to run.

"Police! Halt!" yelled behind her.

She had a choice of stopping and getting caught with a rare scroll that she had no way to explain or making a run for it, which would turn her into fair game for any law enforcement who got close.

Some choices just weren't that tough.

She picked up her pace and hoped they didn't decide she was a terrorist and shoot her. Using what she recalled from the report on the mall remodeling, she headed for the closest exit that would dump her out far from the main entrance to the mall.

If she got out of here without being arrested, her next hurdle would be to find Smith before anyone figured out that she had the scroll. Charlie should have a hotline to Smith.

Of course, Smith said he'd find her.

How was he going to do that with her running for her life?

She raced around and found the door she'd been hoping to locate. The door had a bright yellow and black sign warning to not exit that way.

Probably because of the hideous alarm that triggered the minute she shoved it open.

Sirens cried in the distance, getting louder as police headed for the mall.

Her heart tried to fight its way out of her chest. She shoved the tube inside her hoodie and looked around, trying to choose the best direction, but the sirens sounded as if they were coming from everywhere.

Tires squealed and a muscle car came roaring up on her right.

Dingo slid the GTO to a stop with the passenger door in front of her and yelled, "Get in!"

She was inside and pulling the door shut when he hit the accelerator.

"Are you hurt?" Dingo asked.

"Few bruises. I'll survive."

"Don't do that again. Scared the shit out of me."

"I was following directions."

Dingo shifted a wry look her way, telling her that he knew she'd only followed his orders once the guy with the cylinder ran in the same direction.

He slowed the GTO's speed, motoring out the back parking lot as if they weren't part of the fiasco going on inside the mall. The police hadn't figured out to block the exits yet, but they would soon.

Valene heard raspy breathing behind her.

She turned to find Geoffrey, and she had a bone the size of Texas to pick with the man, but one look at his pasty skin and the way he trembled toned back her anger. Shock probably gave him the chills. She thought about pulling off her hoodie to give him, but that would expose the tube she had tucked against her right arm to hide the bulge. Once things calmed down, she wouldn't fool Dingo with that placement.

She offered to Geoffrey, "If Dingo's okay with the heat, I'll turn it on to warm you up."

Geoffrey tossed a look of disdain at her and talked around the shudders racking his body. "Leave the heater off. I don't want anything from you. Ever."

He was going to be that way, huh?

In that case, she had something to get off her chest, too. "Why did you go to meet this guy without saying a word to Henri? I was supposed to negotiate the scroll exchange."

Geoffrey bared his teeth, tarnishing his pretty looks. "You ruined everything. The scroll is lost to us now. Raul will never meet with me again. You caused me to fail. This is all your fault."

Dingo pulled onto the interstate into light afternoon traffic. He lifted a warning gaze to the rearview mirror and told Geoffrey, "Let's get something clear right now. She actually saved your life. There was a third party waiting nearby to take the scroll from you and he wouldn't be giving you a lift home. That level of muscle works for some very nasty people who expect him to deal with loose ends without leaving a bloody trail."

Geoffrey twisted his face into a pitiful grimace and argued, "If that's the case, then *you* saved me, because she abandoned both of us to do what she always does ... racing after the next big deal." He had no problem glowering at Valene. "But you blew it this time or you'd be waving the scroll in front of me, showing off how you got it without having to give up anything. I've heard about your phenomenal skills when it comes to hunting something down and negotiating, but I still don't see what Henri ever saw in you."

After that verbal slap, he turned to look out the window in sulk mode.

Dingo looked over at her and she could see the question in his face. "Want me to drop him at the next exit to make his own way home?"

Geoffrey looked at Dingo and his lip trembled.

Valene said, "No. I promised Henri we'd bring him back safe."

Dingo gave her an if-you-say-so shrug. "What happened to the guy with the tube?"

"He was faster than I expected." She gave a little shake of her head that she hoped Dingo took to mean she came up empty-handed.

The rest of the ride was made in silence, which allowed her to consider how she was going to move forward. If she opened this cylinder and the Galileo scroll was inside, she'd give Geoffrey a chance to redeem his miserable butt by certifying it. But she couldn't do that until Dingo was out of the picture, because the only valid reason she could find for his interest in her client Smith was if Dingo's people had been informed of the theft and were trying to return the scroll.

Which might mean that Orion Hunters had infiltrated Dingo's people and he didn't know it. If that had happened, the hunters were pulling strings to get the scroll found for their own benefit. Dingo wouldn't be a part of that willingly, but he just might be trusting the wrong people without knowing it.

What other reason would he have for wanting information on Smith?

Dingo made a quick stop at a gas station because she asked, claiming her bladder wouldn't survive the bumper-to-bumper traffic they'd be stuck in on the way back to Pasadena.

She kept expecting LAPD to come roaring up with lights

flashing every minute that passed, but they reached Henri's shop without getting stopped.

Geoffrey barely allowed Dingo to park before he leaped out of the car and strode ahead of Valene and Dingo.

She'd gotten two steps inside the shop when Henri shouted at the sight of Geoffrey and rushed to hug him. Geoffrey was mumbling an apology for losing the scroll and that he almost had it in his hands, and if Valene hadn't interfered ... then he babbled about having shots fired at him and almost dying.

Henri glared at Valene over Geoffrey's shoulder.

When Geoffrey's string of woes tapered off, Henri stepped out of Geoffrey's grasp to address Valene. "Someone shot at him. You *never* said a word about this being dangerous."

She took a step. "It wouldn't have been, Henri, if–"

"The police are after him." Henri pointed at Dingo who didn't flinch at that news. "His face is all over the news."

That's because Dingo had given her his hoodie to protect her identity. She'd deal with that in a minute, but first she needed to know how bad this was. "Did they mention Geoffrey on the news?"

"No. Not yet."

"Okay, good." Her relief at one person being safe was short-lived.

"No, this is not good!" Henri shouted. He sliced his hand through the air. "I'm done with your devil-may-care attitude! You go too far this time. *Leave!* I'm done with all of this. Do not call me. We have no reason to do business anymore."

Taking a bullet to her chest would have to hurt less than hearing him say he never wanted to see her again, and she knew that was exactly what Henri meant.

She stood there, torn between begging Henri not to walk away again and wanting to rail at Geoffrey for destroying the fragile friendship she and Henri had been mending.

She refused to cry, but holding back was a strain.

Not here. Not now.

She wouldn't give Geoffrey that satisfaction.

Dingo made a move and she knew it would precipitate an angry exchange of words, but this wasn't his fight.

Besides, she had to get him somewhere safe.

What a mess she'd gotten Dingo into.

Unable to talk past the knot in her throat, she put a hand on his arm and turned away to leave. He stayed planted. Moving a tree would be easier.

She avoided looking at Henri's face, not wanting her last view of him to be yet another that was angry and hurt. When he'd ended their marriage, he'd been considerate and polite, but now he believed she'd put the person he loved at risk.

A part of her understood, but that didn't make the pain any easier to handle. She squeezed Dingo's thick arm and managed to whisper, "Please don't."

He turned and fell into step with her when she continued outside.

She'd lost Henri.

The minute she handed over the scroll to Smith without telling Dingo, she'd lose Dingo, too. Henri might hate her at this point, but she still owed him for all he'd invested financially and personally on this project, and her father still needed treatment.

Dingo told her to trust him to do his job finding Geoffrey and she had.

She wanted to tell him to trust her to do her job, but with Navarro looking for her, an empty-handed thief running loose, and Dingo a wanted man, she had to unload the scroll as quickly as possible and without involving Dingo.

During the gas station break, she'd checked and even with her limited knowledge of the scroll, she could tell the ancient parchment appeared genuine and Galileo's signature looked like the ones she'd seen over and over. Her niggle of worry came from knowing people like Geoffrey were skilled in creating masterpiece copies.

If not for what she'd just gone through to get this scroll, she'd be less certain. Raul, as Geoffrey called the guy, had reacted to her dig about being a priest and acted as if he ran with the most important item in his world.

Thankfully, the tube was lightweight aluminum, airtight and waterproof.

Charlie hadn't called back after she'd texted him. Dingo had said not to call anyone, but she needed to find Smith fast, unless Smith really could find her first.

Then she'd have to sneak away from Dingo, which meant her being the one to leave him this time without a word of goodbye and no way to tell him. Once she was out of his hands he'd have to use his amazing skills and vanish for real.

Chapter 35

DINGO COULDN'T DRIVE around Los Angeles until dark while he thought, but neither did he want to go all the way back to the safe house he'd taken Valene to earlier. Sabrina might have sent someone there to watch for him by now.

He'd motor around until he found a store big enough that he wouldn't stand out when he entered. He'd put a knit skullcap over his hair until he got a chance to cut it, and shoved on a pair of aviator sunglasses. Valene had looked into his bag, asking if he had any rabbits in there.

He spared her a quick look, but she was too focused on talking quietly into his cell phone to notice which way they were going.

She'd gotten a call from the facility where she'd put her dad, and he'd given her his phone to make the call back.

He had a plan and hoped he ran into no roadblocks.

With Navarro's group on the prowl, no idea what that incident in the mall had shaken loose, law enforcement after him–that was going to piss off Sabrina to no end–and no timeline or target for the other assassinations, Dingo had to get answers now.

Valene had said Navarro found her name in Aram's phone.

Navarro had killed Aram, but not because of the scroll. Navarro hadn't known about it until Aram told him. Why had Aram been killed?

The tattoos on the shooter at the charity event said Orion Hunters were committing the assassinations. If he took the evidence at face value, that at least was clear.

Satan's Garden Club and the Orion Hunters were connected, which might mean Navarro was also involved with the hits.

If that was the case, then Navarro might be contracting hits for Rikker, but that made no sense if Rikker was killing the Orion Hunter assassins.

Nick said the Orion Hunters were after an artifact. The scroll Valene had? Is that what Rikker was paying her to find?

Based on that, Navarro, the Orion Hunters and Rikker were all after the scroll that Valene had in her possession.

Not that she'd admitted as much.

She'd had a bulge under the hoodie when he picked her up outside the mall exit and hadn't fooled him one bit when she asked for a pit stop on the way to Henri's.

She'd returned to the car with the hoodie off and wadded up, but the wad had been in a distinctive shape. She had the cylinder and the way she was hiding it meant the cylinder held something of value.

She was key to figuring out this mess.

Valene wouldn't be happy when he pinned her down, but if she had the scroll, she'd disappear the first chance she got to find her client, aka Rikker, because Dingo hadn't told her she was working for an international felon.

He couldn't tell Valene without betraying Sabrina and the team's trust.

Valene was speaking softly. "You're sure that's the only change in his condition and he doesn't need to go to the hospital?" she asked someone on the other end of her call. She nodded to no one in particular and said, "Please tell him I called and I'll be by soon. And call me at this number if anything changes." She paused. "I know you will, but please make sure everyone knows. Thanks."

She dropped his phone into the cup holder in the console and rubbed her eyes, then looked around. "Where are we going?"

"The only place no one knows to look for either of us. We've got maybe an hour and a half until sunset."

It took her a minute then she said, "Our cove."

Those two words held sweet memories for him. He hated to go to their spot on El Matador Beach, but he was on short time and might have to disappear altogether now.

He needed a place he felt relatively sure no one would be waiting to ambush or arrest them.

She rallied a smile, but it took effort. Henri had hurt her. Her fingers twisted in the folds of the hoodie she clutched in her lap. "What are we going to do about the police looking for you?"

"I'll figure out something by daylight," he said, rather than give her an inkling of what he might have to do. He put on his blinker and pulled off Highway 101. "We need to get a few things from Wal-Mart. Blanket, electric light, food, scissors ... "

She'd grabbed a piece of paper and jotted notes as he finished the list. "I'll go in. No one is looking for me."

He hesitated to agree.

"No one knows us out here," she argued against his silence.

"Okay, but you're in and out in twenty minutes or I'm coming in."

"That's not enough time."

He pulled alongside the front entrance and fished out enough cash for anything she'd buy. "Twenty minutes starting now."

Snatching up the money, she opened the door with the hoodie in hand.

"Leave it, Valene. You'll be faster."

She stalled, thinking, and he saved her the effort of wondering. "I know you have the scroll. I'm not going to take it from you. I swear on what honor I possess that I'll be here when you come out. I wouldn't leave you alone out here."

Totally flummoxed, she dropped the hoodie bunch on the floorboard, grabbed her purse and rushed into the store, but managed a last quick look over her shoulder.

While she was inside the store, Dingo used his cell phone, since it couldn't be traced, to contact Nick who answered, "What?"

"It's me," Dingo said just in case anyone was close enough to hear the conversation.

Nick said, "Hold on." Then the sound of a door closed. Nick asked, "Looking for a way out of town?"

Dingo's kind of team member. One who got right to the point. He said, "No. Well, not yet. I'm working on an angle that might mean a connection between the killings."

"Have you told Sabrina that?"

"She doesn't listen so good when Gage is the room."

"He's not here."

Hmm. Dingo wasn't sure what to make of that. "Why?"

"Have no idea other than a lot of loud cursing went on right after you left. I passed Gage leaving as I walked into the conference room. Sabrina didn't say a word about you, but she did say she'd shoot anyone who got in our way, including CIA agents."

Dingo wasn't in any position to revel over Gage leaving with his own nuts in a vice. "You mentioned at the end of the meeting that the hunters were looking for a specific artifact. What is it?"

"A scroll."

Some days it sucked to be right. "Do you know anything about Rikker being in California?"

"Nothing's been mentioned."

That screwed Dingo telling Nick about Rikker. That damn Gage was interfering with this operation.

Sabrina might want to shoot Gage, but she clearly wasn't sharing anything until she decided she had no other choice. Dingo might give Sabrina reason to make that choice if he convinced Valene to give up what she knew.

Not if, but when.

Dingo asked, "Where are we with the initials? Anything firm on a new location and target?"

"Not yet. We've got three major events going on in LA over the next two days. Nothing that pings with any of the three sets of initials, but we're spreading out resources to cover all three events."

"What's your gut telling you?"

"My gut tells me a lot of things, but I'm waiting on intel from a friend."

"The same one who told you about the scroll?"

"Yes."

Dingo thought back a month ago when Nick was laid up in the hospital after taking rounds in his chest. He'd come up with crucial intel then. "Would this be the same informant who fed you information on the North Korean physicists and the Orion Hunter attack on the aquifer?"

"Yes."

Dingo didn't wait for more. Nick's mind ran nonstop, but he only said what he felt someone needed to know at the moment. "Did Sabrina mention anything about Valene Eklund?"

"Yes."

See? Getting information out of Nick was possible. You just had to ask the right questions. "Such as?"

"She's the woman you contacted the last time we were in LA. Eklund is being watched by the FBI and may be connected to Satan's Garden Club and the Orion Hunters."

"She's not, but I don't expect you to choose a side."

Nick said, "I make up my mind as the plan unfolds and it so happens my informant believes Eklund could be a pawn in all this. My informant thinks Eklund might have been pulled in because of getting on someone's radar after finding the Orion Hunter doctor in Chinatown for us."

Dingo cursed hard. He'd had a bad feeling about that. Just another confirmation that he was bad news for Valene. "Have you told Sabrina what your informant says about Valene?"

"Not yet. Sabrina's not particularly receptive on that topic right now and it's only speculation on my informant's part at this point."

"Got it." Dingo considered what he knew and what he could share. Much of what he had was speculation, too, and Sabrina wouldn't listen to a word he said about Valene. "Look into a guy named Aram Pavlovsky."

"Who the hell is he?"

"I'm not sure yet. I'm working off my phone right now and can only research so far. Pull everything on Pavlovsky you can get and see if he had a recent deposit from an offshore account. Satan's Garden Club killed him and by the way, Maxx Navarro is Garcia's son and is now running the SGC. I'm still working on all this, but don't tell Sabrina I called yet. Tell her you got the intel from your mysterious snitch."

"Works for me. Keep your head down."

"Will do. Keep this line open."

"Done."

Dingo ended the call just as Valene stepped out of Wal-Mart with huge bags hanging from her hands and the straps of a backpack hooked over her shoulders. He pulled up just past the entrance, got out and loaded everything in the trunk while keeping an eye out.

She was right. No one should know they were in that spot at that moment, but shit just happened sometimes. Thankfully, they made it out and were back on the road in minutes.

He told her, "Go ahead and get comfortable. I'm taking the shortest path, but it'll be crooked and winding through the mountains."

She groaned. "I hate being carsick."

"Then go to sleep before I get there."

She laid her head back and started to drift off then sat up. "The scroll."

"It's in the back seat. Were you going to tell me you had it?"

"No."

"At least you're truthful."

"You can't take that scroll from me, Dingo."

"I don't intend to."

She let out a tired sigh. "Good. Wake me when we get out of the mountains."

He wished he could tell her what he had in mind was good, but he wasn't going to lie to her either.

Chapter 36

VALENE WOKE TO the sound of Dingo outside moving around and unpacking the back of the car. She had to blink again to clear the groggy feeling away after that deep sleep.

He'd left his door open, but no interior light was on and twilight was setting in.

Salty air stirred through the interior and the easy churn of waves rolling along the shore reached her.

He stuck his head inside and she noticed the dark sweatshirt he'd put on. His eyebrows jumped in question. "You up?"

"Mm hmm."

"But are you awake enough to navigate to the beach and down to the cove?"

In answer, she opened her door and stepped out, stretching.

He said, "I'll take that as a yes. Get your sweet buns back here and load up."

She hadn't had a reason to smile, really smile for a long time but hearing Dingo say the same words he used to tell her on beach trips lifted her spirits. "Okay, grumpy one, who has had no sleep."

"Yeah, yeah, yeah."

She took two plastic bags he'd repacked, because they had been heavier when she'd carried them out. By the time he hoisted the backpack on his shoulders and slammed the trunk shut, the sun had disappeared below the horizon.

Dingo flipped on a flashlight and handed it to her. "Shine this ahead of me and stay close."

They were almost to the steps that would descend thirty feet to the beach when she slammed to a halt. "Wait."

"It's in the backpack," he told her, answering her panic about the scroll. "So is the hoodie if you're cold."

"No, I love the ocean air. It's soothing." Her moment of comfort dissolved at remembering the scroll, which reminded her of the mall and Dingo being a hunted man. "Maybe we should be making a run for it."

He'd gone down two steps, but turned around, coming back up one to be eye level with her. "You are not going on the run, no matter what. We're fine for now. Okay?"

"I'm going to say okay, but I don't feel it."

He caught her face and pulled her lips to his.

The kiss took her back to when life seemed too good to believe. She'd found out how true that could be.

When he finished, her arms and the bags she held were wrapped around his neck and back. She whispered, "I want to stay in this minute. Right here. Forever."

"You'd get tired after a few weeks." He touched her nose. "Get moving."

She managed to keep the light ahead of them as they made it down to the beach, then walked along the shore caught between the ocean and rocky bluffs.

Their cove was a sixteen-minute hike.

She knew it by heart.

The water never reached where they stayed inside the cove even at high tide, but at low tide, which it was right now, they had to wade barefoot through six inches of water to find their spot, then climb up the sandy incline that leveled out at the top, insuring they'd stay dry.

Dingo had the blanket spread out and the electric lantern on by the time she'd unloaded cubes of cheese, sliced smoked sausage and fruit along with a bottle of wine.

He tossed her the hoodie, and she was ready for it with the temperature cooling off.

With so much hanging over her head and Dingo's, this impromptu picnic felt like a last meal for the condemned.

At least it came with wine.

Her phone buzzed her pocket. She pulled it out to an unknown number.

Dingo paused. "Remember, if you don't know who it is, don't answer it."

This could be Smith.

She let it go to voice mail then listened to the message. *"I will assume that you were the woman fighting at the mall today and the man you were seen wrangling a cylinder from is our thief. I have a small window of time to meet you. Don't be late."* Smith gave her the address of a coffee shop to be at by no later than eleven in the morning.

Then Smith said, *"If you fail to deliver the scroll, I'll find you and take back my deposit in one form or another."*

One form or another did not sound like payments on time.

Could Dingo be right about Smith being connected to Navarro? How? Why? She had to get him to talk to her so they could put their heads together and figure out all of this.

She put her phone away. Fourteen hours until she had to meet Smith. If she got her hands on transportation, it would take her an hour to get there. She wouldn't leave Dingo stranded, but neither did she want to risk him being in the city with his face plastered on the news. She didn't want to meet Smith alone, not if he was connected to Navarro, but that was also why avoiding Smith scared her.

What would he do if she didn't show?

Dingo sat next to her, leaning back, looking relaxed to anyone who didn't know him, which was why his words surprised her. "It's time to put all the cards face up, Valene."

She angled herself back, resting on her elbows, mimicking him. He wanted the cards face up? Then he had to show his first. She shrugged. "We've been around this tree more times than I want to count. You don't trust me enough to tell me the truth. I'm not giving up my client or the scroll. You're going to have to tell your people you didn't find it."

"Is that what you think I'm after? The scroll?"

"I have no idea what you're after but that at least makes sense. I'm guessing your people were tasked with returning it, but the man I'm working with is going to pay me to return it. And he's getting a hell of a deal. The scroll is priceless. Let me make the meeting, hand over the scroll and get paid. I need the money and I owe Henri his part. If you want, I'll tell whomever that you helped me return it."

Dingo sat up and put his head in his hands.

It wasn't that bad of an offer.

She sat up and put her hand on his shoulder. "I'll lose two hundred and fifty thousand dollars that I need to get my dad into a treatment program and to get back into business, plus pay Henri. What will it cost your people to show up empty-handed?"

He lifted his head. "I'm not after the bloody scroll. I'm trying to stop assassinations and your *client* is connected to all of this."

She'd caught the way he'd said client as if she'd made a deal with a terrorist. "How is that possible? He works for the Vatican."

"No, he doesn't."

What he was not saying hit her between the eyes. "You know who my client is. You've been spying on me this whole time and now you want me to believe you aren't interested in the scroll?"

"I'm not. I couldn't share his true identity with you because there's more at play right now than a missing scroll and the man you think is with the Vatican is an international criminal."

Her body shook from blood coursing fast and hard through her veins. "None of this makes sense. He told me the scroll had been stolen and negotiated a contract for me to return it."

Dingo rubbed his forehead. "I have to make a choice and I'm going with my gut."

"A choice about what?"

He turned to her and light from their lantern reflected in his hazel gaze. "The reason I haven't told you anything about what I did in the past or what I'm doing in LA now is because it's my job to manage intel and not let it leak out. It's my duty to find people who threaten national security and to protect lives any way I can. It's also my duty to keep you safe and those duties are in conflict."

She waited, because Dingo had never opened up to her and she didn't want to stop him now that he was talking.

He said, "I can't tell you the real name of the man you're

dealing with, but there are people very high in law enforcement such as the FBI, for one, who have a video of you meeting with him in a restaurant two days ago. I shouldn't be telling you even that much. I haven't been investigating you, but others have and I've been doing my best to do damage control and keep you out of all this."

She put her hand down to stabilize her body when she felt light-headed. Why would the FBI be watching her? "I didn't do anything wrong."

"I know that, but right now I'm the only person who believes you're innocent in this."

She recalled him saying he might be able to find Geoffrey because he was at odds with his people at the moment.

Wait a minute. She'd asked Dingo, *You work with some agency that can track GPS and crap like that, right?*

And he'd said, *I did.*

She'd been so upset over Geoffrey missing, the scroll at risk, people chasing them, and Dingo being evasive that she'd missed the point of his comment the first time.

Valene touched his hair, drawing his attention. "What happened with you and your people? Why are you not with them now?"

"Because someone had to come prove your innocence."

She mentally ran back over the events of the last thirtyish hours. "What did you do? Just walk out?"

"Yes."

"Was that before you found me with Navarro?"

He nodded. "I was coming for you regardless of what happened, but I had a difference of opinion with my people on your involvement and ..." He just let his words trail off.

She'd accused him of not trusting her, but he'd put faith in her she hadn't been giving him back. "I'm sorry."

"I'm not." He leaned over and kissed her tenderly then pulled back. "You keep telling me I don't trust you. This is me trusting you. I'm going to tell you as much as I can, but I need you to give me information, too."

If what he was saying about Smith was true, she'd walked into a trap and he was trying to free her. "Fair enough."

"What name is your client going by?"

"Smith."

"Figures."

She snorted. "I know it's an alias. What's his real name?"

"Don't get angry, but I really can't tell you that."

"I'm not angry. This is me trusting you." She smiled, but didn't feel it in her heart where all this was crashing in on her. She heaved a deep sigh. "Charlie set up the meeting and Smith convinced me he was with the Vatican security. He made it very clear that it was imperative to keep this confidential."

"Why?"

"Because the pope is under attack by some people who don't like how he's aggressively pursuing fiscal responsibility. Smith said that these same people would use the missing artifact as a way to divert attention from what he's after and focus on his not being responsible with Vatican treasures." She ran her fingers through her hair and stared out at the dark ocean constantly in motion. "He said he believed the thief would be caught in the pope's dragnet, which would expose the thief and anyone he was connected to, so this guy Raul stole something worth enough that he could unload it and disappear. Sounded logical."

"Yes, it does," Dingo agreed. "This man–Smith–is a master at what he does. He was in the CIA at one time and went rogue."

On a scale of one to ten, this level of disaster ranked in triple digits. What had she gotten herself into? "And the FBI thinks I'm working *with* Smith? Why? Didn't anyone investigate my background? Doesn't it count that I helped your people in Chinatown and Nebraska?"

"Those were my arguments. The FBI had no information on the Vatican theft or what this man–we'll just keep calling him Smith–is up to," Dingo explained. "Another agency is tracking Smith and they don't want to alert the Vatican to the theft yet in case they tip off Smith and risk losing him after he's been linked to at least three terrorist attacks in the last year."

She thunked her head down on her knees where they were drawn up to her chest. Could this get any worse? "I was sitting in that meeting with Smith, and every instinct I had was throwing up red flags, telling me something was wrong." She curled her hands into fists and shoved them against her forehead. "But I needed to help my dad."

"I know, babe." Dingo took one of her fists in both of his hands and uncurled her fingers, one at a time, stroking his thumb across the back of her hand, soothing her. "There's not a person alive who doesn't have an Achilles heel. A soft spot about something–or someone–that keeps them from being objective." She wrapped her fingers around his and he continued. "Smith is involved in one assassination that just happened in LA."

She lifted her head. "Fontana?"

"Right. That's why I was at the event that night, but we were protecting a different primary. We have information that indicates three assassinations, including initials. But none of the initials we have correspond with Fontana's."

Valene's curiosity kicked into high gear. "What are the initials?" When Dingo hesitated, she said, "In case you forgot, flushing out information is my business."

"I haven't forgotten. You're one of the best researchers I've ever known. That's why I had to leave." He snapped his jaws shut.

"Whoa. You are not going to say that and shut down on me. What do you mean by 'that's why I had to leave'?"

He rubbed his head again and she felt bad about adding to his misery, but he'd been holding back forever on her.

She prodded, "If you tell me, I'll stop hounding you about it."

"Your hounding doesn't bother me."

"Then why won't you tell me the truth about when you left?"

"I did. I told you I had to go undercover to get Garcia."

"Now, tell me the rest of the truth you've been holding back. I'm talking to you about Smith and I'll give you all I have *if* you will do the same."

"Blackmail?" His mouth twisted with a wry quirk.

She shrugged. "Call it what you like. It's the only currency I've got for trade right now. You're not going to throw me off track like you usually do. It's just me, you, and the ocean. No distractions."

He sat there silent for a moment then said, "You were enthusiastic about your research on Giuseppe."

"I was trying to help," she said defensively.

His fingers covered hers again, where she'd dropped her hand onto the blanket between them. "I know, babe. You never failed to amaze me, but this time you dug too deep and went for things I hadn't specifically asked for. By the time I realized what had happened, Garcia had been alerted that someone was tracking down Giuseppe's family members. That was an open path to Garcia. I realized it as soon as I reviewed the extra information you'd dug up. I connected the dots."

"The night we had the fight."

"Yep. I was blind with worry over how to keep you away from Garcia. I knew you'd pitch a fit about going into the WITSEC program and I couldn't trust that you'd stay in it, so the only other choice was to stop Garcia from coming after you. I had constant surveillance on him. It was a matter of setting up an attack on him and taking a bullet."

"You risked getting *killed* to get inside his organization? Were you crazy?"

Dingo thought on that. Was he crazy? When it came to Valene, yes. He told her, "You have to be a half bubble off to do what I do."

"What happened with Garcia, that was ... all my fault."

He turned to her. "No. This is exactly why I didn't tell you. I knew you'd try to take the blame. This was all my doing. I'm the one in this business, not you. I made that choice."

She wheeled around on her knees to face him and leaned forward, putting her hands on his shoulders. "I would have done anything to have prevented that. Even going in the WITSEC."

"Your dad would have had to go in, too, and he might not have fared as well. And you would never be happy in that life. I couldn't have done it to you."

"Would you have done the same for another woman?"

No. He'd have put anyone else in WITSEC. "I haven't had to make that choice."

"You should be a damn politician the way you avoid giving a straight answer. Why did you do it?"

He felt walls closing in on him, forcing him to admit something he couldn't. If he told her it was because he couldn't live knowing she was either in mortal danger or miserably unhappy, she'd ask for more. For things he couldn't give. "Let it go, Val. Please."

She dropped her head down close enough for their noses to almost touch. "When are you going to admit there's more between us than casual friendship? Tell you what. I'll start. I love you and I'll do whatever it takes to keep *you* safe. I love you enough for both of us so you don't have to say anything. But you need to know that I'm not letting you just walk out of my life again."

What the hell could he say to that?

She loved him.

She wanted to keep him.

She was just as insane as he was.

The words were inside of him, pounding to get out and tell her how much she meant to him, but saying them then abandoning her would be worse than last time. As soon as he got Rikker out of the picture, Dingo had to go to ground and figure out what tomorrow brought.

Whatever it was would not include Valene.

Just admitting that to himself was squeezing the life out of his heart.

He wanted her. More than anything he'd ever wanted.

And he believed her when she said she wouldn't let him go.

This sucked. He finally had someone who really wanted him and he couldn't have her.

She kissed his forehead and cheeks. "I don't know why you think you're destined to go through life alone, but you're not. I will fight to keep you. I will never let you go. If you leave this time, I'll find you."

His throat was too tight to get a word out so he kissed her back and color came into his dreary world again. Holding Valene was as close to perfect as a man could get.

She reached down and found his erection.

Okay, there might be one more place just as perfect and that was inside Valene.

Clothes came off in a rush and he helped her get her panties down. Then he scooted out of his jeans, the whole time keeping his mouth on her.

"Hurry up," she ordered.

Pure Valene. Demanding and eager. He loved that about her. Loved *her*.

Those words struck him as hard as lightning. He'd fought to keep that inside, not daring to let the words creep up into his world, because once they did he'd never get them stowed away again.

Her fingers curled around his dick the minute he freed the happy part.

A primal groan crawled up his throat.

He filled his hands with her breasts, brushing both nipples at once and she tensed.

"I need you inside me."

"Say that again and you'll miss the best part."

She laughed and brushed herself across the tip of his penis. "Then hurry the hell up. Screw it..."

She impaled herself and Dingo shouted, locking every muscle to keep from losing control. "Don't. Move."

"I keep trying to tell you that it works better if I do."

"Need a condom."

"I'm on the pill and ... I trust you. No more argument."

He growled, chuckling at the end. It was that or grind his teeth over the pain of holding back. "What about foreplay?"

"What about next time?" she countered then lifted up. "Ready or not, here I come."

And she did... right before he did.

Chapter 37

L OOSE HAIR TICKLED her nose.

Valene blew it away and it came back. She woke up slowly. She was stretched over the top of a warm, muscular chest. Dingo had an arm wrapped protectively around her back. He'd covered them up at some point with half the blanket.

The hair grazed her nose again. She swatted and hit his hand. "Stop it."

He laughed softly. "Time to get up. We've got a little over an hour to daylight. Need to be out of here while it's still dark."

"Good, because I need coffee." She pushed up and smiled at him.

He said, "Hello, beautiful."

"You are definitely a keeper."

His grin faded.

What had she said? She brushed her fingertips over his scruffy cheek. "What?"

"I've just never heard that."

She tried to wrap her head around what he was saying. She asked, "Where's your family?"

"My mum's dead."

That was it for his family? "I'm sorry."

He made an attempt at shrugging, which was not easy when lying down. "Long time ago."

"How old were you?"

"Eight."

"No dad?"

His chest rose and fell with each deep inhale and exhale. "The man who got my mum pregnant left her in the outback as soon as he realized she was knocked up. She met a man when I was six. He moved us to New York. Mum didn't adjust well. Didn't understand the city and started thinking my stepdad was being unfaithful. Don't know if he was or not, but she thought so and went downhill. Lost weight. Cried all the time. I came home from school one day and my stepdad was the only one there. He said she'd died. Taken pills. Then he told me he wasn't cut out to be a father and I wasn't his kid. He had a bag packed for me and dropped me at the children's home."

She was too stunned to speak at first, but she got her voice back quickly. "What kind of a son of a bitch does that to a kid?"

He stroked his hand over her hair with a soothing touch. "It was a long time ago, babe."

"I don't care. My dad kept me when I was a lot younger than you and he'd lost his arm."

Dingo frowned. "What about your mum?"

"She fell out of love with my dad when he became damaged goods. Her family's a bunch of socialites in the Northeast. Big money. She got her divorce, then packed up my brother and moved back."

Dingo's fingers stopped on her hair. "Why didn't she take you?"

"Even though I was only five, my father asked me where I'd rather be and I said with him. I had no idea just how hard it was going to be on him to take care of a little girl alone, but he never let on. When I was older, I looked back and realized what all he did. My mom sends cards and gifts. I don't really care if I ever see her again, or my older brother, because neither one even called when dad got sick. What he did for me? That was true love. Not words. Not gifts. Someone who showed up every day no matter what."

His fingers slid over her hair again, back and forth, in a rhythm. "He must be some kind of man to have raised a woman like you."

"He is." She couldn't hide the haunted sound in her voice. "I'm just trying to keep him alive."

"I know."

To keep from thinking about failing her dad if Smith really was the criminal Dingo had described, Valene said, "We never finished talking last night. By the way, thank you for trusting me to share what you did. I won't betray that trust."

"I want you to if you run into trouble with the law. I'm going to do my best to keep you off their radar, but if you get in any situation where that information will help you, use it."

"I hear you."

"But are you going to do what I said?"

She grinned. "Why should I start now?"

"Va-*lene*."

"*Ding*-o!" She laughed and asked, "Where'd you get the name Dingo?"

"It's a nickname. Dingoes are wild dogs in Australia. Some people try to domesticate them. That's not always a wise idea with an animal that's been wild for thousands of years. I was a hellion as a child. Like a half-domesticated dingo. My mum used to joke that I'd come from the dingoes. They just dropped me on her doorstep." He was quiet then added, "I think it was easier than thinking she was at fault for saddling herself with an unwanted child."

"Don't say that. I'm sure she loved you."

"What makes you so sure?"

"Because I love you and any woman in her right mind has to love you."

He studied her a bit. "That's what I call Valene logic. It's a brand all your own."

"It's true." She wanted him to tell her that he cared as much as she did, because she could feel it and see it in everything he did. But she also sensed his hesitation to take that risk. To allow himself to care for someone again after he'd been taught that love didn't exist.

He said, "You were going to tell me more about Smith."

She conceded to his change in subject. "I've been trying to rebuild my business–"

"What happened to it?"

"I dropped everything to take care of my dad and the next thing I knew I was out of funds and out of circulation. But I've managed okay." One step from being on welfare at times, but she'd kept going. "Anyhow, I'd lost a lot of contacts, especially when Aram showed up in town."

"Does he know Smith?"

"I don't know. I would have said no, but someone clued Aram in about the scroll and Navarro killed Aram. Navarro was talking about some man who he was going to one-up by finding the scroll first."

"Did they give a name?"

"No. You're wondering if they were talking about Smith, right?"

"Yes."

She went on. "Navarro didn't mention anyone else." She thought back over his interrogation. "I don't understand why he killed Aram. Navarro's so cold blooded. Aram was just a number on a list to him."

"What'd you say?" Dingo's body tensed beneath hers.

"Navarro is cold-blooded."

"No, about Aram being on a list."

"Oh. Navarro made a snide remark that Aram was merely number two on his list of bodies to put to rest."

Dingo sat up, jostling her, but he stopped to carefully lift her up and place her beside him. "I have to get that information to someone."

"What's going on with the assassinations?"

Dingo ran his hand over his head and back again. "I wish I knew."

"Remember when you were telling me how good I am at what I do?"

He smirked at her. "Yes."

"Then why don't you give me what you have and let me see if I can figure anything out?"

"Hell, it couldn't hurt. My people are running out of time to figure out who to protect."

"Would that be the same people not willing to help you right now?"

"It's complicated, babe."

She let that roll off her list of concerns, but only for now. "Tell me what you've got."

Dingo shared the intel he'd gotten from someone in Atlanta on three hits, and gave her the high points of what happened at the charity event. He concluded by saying, "They have you going back into that hall we exited after I saw you in the bathroom."

"I went back to get my lipstick. I'd left it on the vanity."

"They think you had time to meet the assassin who came down the emergency exit stairs on that end of the building."

She said, "What? They think I *killed* the guy you found in the stairwell?"

"Right."

"Oh my God. How could they think that?"

He lifted his hand and counted off fingers. "You have weapons training that proves you're capable of making the kill shot, especially at close range. You're skilled in Krav Maga. You received fifty thousand dollars from an offshore account and you were seen meeting with ... Smith, whose signature kill shot was used on the assassin at the charity event."

"Then Smith is the one who killed him."

"That's my bet too, but they have no confirmation that Smith was at the event and they believe he had you use that signature shot so others would know he was behind it."

"He *was* at the event."

"I thought I saw him, too."

"No, he was *definitely* there." She realized she was wringing her hands and stopped. "Tell me what else you know about the assassinations."

"We have three sets of initials. F.E.P. O.N.C. P.G.C. We thought F.E.P was Francine Eva Perdido, but they killed Fontana."

She agreed that the initials didn't work. "Aram's last name is Pavlovsky, so he can't be O.N.C."

"And there's been no high profile second hit," Dingo said. "So we have no idea who O.N.C. is."

"Navarro said Aram was the second hit. If his list is the same as yours, then the initials might mean something other than a name." Valene turned to get Dingo's reaction. He was studying on her suggestion so she kept brainstorming. "You say Smith is a criminal. If he's behind Fontana's assassin's death then whose side is he on?"

"I don't know. And why does he want that scroll?"

She went after that angle. "Could Smith be an Orion Hunter?"

Dingo cocked his head, chewing on that. "It's not outside the realm of possibility, but it's more likely that he's the front man for someone pulling strings in all this. Someone who is connected to the hunters. We won't know until I get my hands on him."

"How are you going to do that if you have to get out of town?"

He gave her a sly grin. "I'm not running. I have a job to do and Smith is not getting away again."

"That sounds like history between you two."

"It is. He's the reason my team almost died in another country three years ago. His debt is piling faster than he can outrun it."

Smith was former CIA. "Are you CIA?"

"No."

She knew even less about Dingo than she had before, and hadn't thought that was possible. But putting off the one thing she hadn't told him yet was wearing a raw spot in her stomach.

Valene admitted, "I heard from Smith last night."

He didn't react unless turning still as a stone sculpture counted. "And?"

"He gave me a time and place to meet him."

"Where is it?"

She gave him the directions for the coffee shop. "I don't know of any event significant to that location, but he said he was on a schedule and had somewhere to be right after that."

Dingo's gaze focused on somewhere distant as he spoke. "Smith has been on site for one kill, but we can't assume that Fontana was the actual target. If Smith's on site for the next one, then maybe he's picking up the scroll before he goes, so that gives us a guesstimate time frame."

"I have to be there at eleven. Gives me about six hours."

"That's tight but I can find someone who looks like you to make that drop."

"No. Smith has made it clear that if I am not there with the scroll on time he'll come after me for the deposit he's paid."

Dingo squeezed her hand. "He's not going to pay you the balance."

She forced the tears back. "I know."

"And I'm not going to risk losing you. He's too dangerous."

"But what if ... what if he really is willing to pay for the scroll?"

"That's not how he operates for one thing, and the scroll would be used for something bad."

"Oh, hell, besides it has to go back to the Vatican and from what you're saying he isn't working for them." She pounded the ground with her free hand. "What does he want with killing these people? I mean Fontana might be part of a political deal that went bad, but Aram is not connected to this."

All the information tumbled around in her mind.

Not connected. NC.

One Not Connected. O.N.C.

"Dingo!" she grabbed his arm. "I have an idea. Remember I said the initials might not be people?"

"That's a tough logic angle because they're assassination targets."

She got excited, waving her hands. "Hear me out. What if O.N.C. is One Not Connected? As in someone to throw law enforcement off the trail?"

His eyes narrowed as he concentrated on that. "What would F.E.P. be then?"

"Francine Eva Perdido. Fontana's Eva Perdido. Fontana's End Place. Fontana Eliminated ... Permanently?" She pushed to her feet and jumped around. "That might be it! If so, my theory is right."

"That's another dose of Valene logic," Dingo quipped.

She grinned at him. "Admit it. Pretty brilliant, eh?"

"I always think you're brilliant. Okay, based on that logic, what is P.G.C.?"

Hmm. She slumped. "I don't know. Let me think on it."

"Think while we head back to LA." He stood up and stared out at the horizon, which was barely visible.

She hugged his waist, enjoying the peace filling her from the ocean whispering along the shoreline. "Someone might recognize you."

"Stop fretting. You have no idea how good I am at disguises."

"Okay, but we have to make a stop before we meet up with Smith."

"For what?"

"I've got another brilliant idea, but it's going to depend on my convincing Henri to speak to me again."

Chapter 38

DINGO WAITED FOR Valene outside the hole-in-the-wall restaurant where they'd had a late breakfast on the beach drive back. He'd told her to take her time in the ladies room where she wanted to freshen up. That allowed him time to talk to Nick, who needed to hurry up and answer his cell.

"I'm here," Nick said, coming on the line.

Dingo turned to watch the entrance to the restaurant, a humble shack that dished out great food. "I've got information and maybe a theory on the initials."

"Good. We need it. Nothing is breaking loose and Sabrina's chomping at the bit for answers."

"Has she mentioned me yet?"

"Oh, yes. She said if anyone heard from, and I quote, *fucking* Dingo, she wanted to know immediately."

"She cursed? That's bad." Dingo didn't have much time and jumped back on track. "The initials might mean Fontana Permanently Eliminated."

"Heh. What about the other two?"

"If that theory holds true, then O.N.C. might mean One Not Connected, because we think Aram Pavlovsky, the antiquities broker, was the second hit even though I wouldn't call it an assassination."

"We?"

"Yes. We. Mention to Sabrina that I'm with someone at your own risk."

"Not me," Nick assured him. "I like my head where it is right now. What does the third set of initials stand for?"

"Don't know yet. Still working on that, but I did find out that Rikker is after the Vatican scroll." Dingo was going on raw gut instinct and believed if Sabrina was wearing his shoes, she'd want Nick to know about Rikker, especially with this mysterious contact of Nick's. Pissing off Gage was too far down Dingo's give-a-shit list to worry about.

"Rikker? No shit?" Nick paused then said, "That fits. I'm not sure how, but I know it does. The question is whether that means Rikker is working for the Orion Hunters."

"Why kill an Orion Hunter hit man if Rikker's working with them?" Dingo said, playing devil's advocate.

"Good point. I'll ask my source and see what else I can come up with. By the way, LAPD has an eyewitness that saw you leaving a building in south LA where a gang fight went down with one dead. This supposed eyewitness has identified you as the shooter. That would be bad enough, but we got the report and the LAPD have reason to believe based on past history that you've joined up with Satan's Garden Club again."

Fuck.

No wonder Sabrina was on a tear. She'd want him to come in so she could make him vanish faster than a bride's panties. If he didn't send Nick back with something, Sabrina would focus on Dingo when she needed to keep her attention on more important matters.

"Nick, tell Sabrina I called and I'm fine. Don't send anyone out to bring me in. But this is very important. I need you to tell her I've confirmed that Valene Eklund had no idea who Rikker was when she met with him. Eklund thought Rikker was with the Vatican and contracting with her to get a stolen scroll back. Make sure everyone on our team knows Valene is not a target. If she gets hurt, I'm not going to be calm about it."

"I'll tell Sabrina. She's still going to want to know where you are."

"I'm at the beach." Dingo told her a long time ago that if he ever had to really disappear and didn't want to be found that he'd send word he was at a beach.

"I'll tell her. Are you going to try to take down Rikker alone?"

"No." When Nick didn't respond, Dingo adjusted his answer. "I can't say."

"You need backup?"

"Not right now."

"Let me know when you do."

Dingo wouldn't ask anyone for backup when they might end up being bullet meat just by associating with him. "Roger that, mate." Just not in this lifetime.

Valene came out as he shoved the phone into his pants pocket. She studied him with each step that drew her closer and tapped her chin with a finger.

When she reached him, she said, "The two days of beard, rose-colored John Lennon glasses, bad haircut by yours truly, baggy pants and the padding around your shoulders does change your whole look." She straightened the bandana tied at his neck. "Nice square knot."

"What'd you think I was going to do? Put on a toupee and fake mustache?"

"You've kept so much from me that I've never seen you in action until this week. You're really something."

"Don't be impressed. It's a dirty job most days."

She grabbed the scarf knot and jerked his face to hers and said, "You listen to me, Dingo Paddock. If I say you're impressive you are and when I say I'm not letting you go, I'm not. Get used to it."

"You're hot when you get all fired up, but these pants aren't baggy enough to hide a hardon for long."

Her eyes widened and she looked down then back up. "Get used to me loving you, too. I love you."

He would never get used to hearing that.

His whole body came alive when Valene said those three words. He'd never felt anything this amazing before. His throat was tight with needing to tell her what he felt, but he couldn't.

That idea led to too much pain down the road.

Instead, he caught her by her shoulders and drew her in for a kiss that he hoped would show her how much she meant. These tiny moments with her were like small gifts he tucked away to give himself later when memories would be all he had.

She had a mouth that begged to be loved. Sweet. Sensual.

His... for now.

When he had her breathless, he explained, "You're hotter than a fireball. Just kissing you makes me want to lay you back over this hood and strip you right here in the sunshine. If we weren't in a hurry, I'd have your legs around my shoulders and the hell with anyone watching."

Did that scare her?

No.

Crazy woman just smiled. "Save that thought. Ready to catch a killer?"

Going to meet Rikker was not what he wanted to do, but she'd made a valid point on the way here. Rikker had not been present where anyone would see him connected to the killings. Dingo believed Rikker was paying Navarro to make hits, which technically meant Valene should be safe in an open coffee shop.

Technically didn't soothe Dingo's gut one bit.

He'd always thought when the time came to take Rikker down that Sabrina and Josh would be with him, but from what Nick had said, Sabrina and Josh were stretched thin trying to cover three venues and still had no idea who the next target would be.

Plus, if the FBI nailed Dingo for aiding Valene since they were investigating her, Sabrina and Josh needed to be as far away from him as possible.

And if that wasn't enough incentive to keep them miles away, Dingo couldn't risk anyone giving Rikker a reason to take out Valene on the spot.

Rikker had not survived this long by making mistakes.

Dingo lifted an arm to check his watch. "We've got enough time to make our detour before the meeting with Rikker and still arrive twenty to thirty minutes early. Can you depend on Henri?"

"I hope so. He's not happy with me, but once he makes a deal, he stands by it."

"How much did you have to offer him?"

"Enough."

Dingo didn't know what it would take to get her dad in the special treatment program, but he was pretty sure she'd cut a deal with Henri that bankrupted her new stash. Dingo would help her once this was done, but he wasn't going to say so and start a new battle with his independent hellcat.

He liked her soft and accommodating right now.

He liked the wildcat who had raked her claws over his back last night, too, but the kitten was sweet to hold.

She must have sensed his concern and backed off, looking around as she said, "Let's go. I want to meet Henri then get to the coffee shop ahead of Smith."

Smith, aka Rikker, would already be there, which was why Dingo intended to have her let him out of the car before they reached their destination. That way he could arrive on foot to find a spot and observe undetected once she showed for the meet. Rikker had specified a table on the patio.

What if Rikker did something to Valene before Dingo could reach her?

He had to stop second-guessing.

Either she did this or they called off the meeting and that would only result in her meeting Rikker without Dingo knowing.

That ended the second-guessing. This happened now while Dingo could watch over her. If Rikker touched Valene, it would be the last mistake he made.

Chapter 39

"HOW DID YOU know this place is a favorite of mine?"

"I like to think I'm astute when it comes to what a woman likes," Nick answered, turning away from the street vendor and smiling at the sound of Chatton's voice.

She was close enough for him to catch a whiff of *Eau de Hadrien* as he turned. He remembered that smell. She'd worn it when she came to see him in the hospital and somehow the scent of Sicilian lemon had stayed on his pillow. He'd refused to allow anyone to change the pillow, then paid one of the hospital's housekeeping staff a hundred dollars to include the cloth in his belongings when he was discharged.

To the casual observer, she didn't stand out as she waited on food from *Kogi*, Nick's favorite street vendor, too, but she had to work at not standing out, because she was a powerhouse.

Any man with half a brain could see that.

She played it low key today in a vintage outfit of khaki pants and a matching jacket loosely laced up the front with leather cords. The high collar showed off her soft neck and the jacket flared for ease of motion. He'd guess 1960s era and she pulled off the look like a runway model. The Annie Hall hat and sunshades hid all but the pert nose and finely-sculpted lips.

Nick said, "I'm having kimchi quesadillas."

"Works for me."

Once he had what they needed, he walked with her to a nearby memorial park to sit on a bench in the shade.

"Fast food in a cemetery," she said with a chuckle in her voice. "You really know how to show a girl a good time."

"Let me know when you're ready for a better time."

She didn't look up but her lips twitched. "I'll keep that in mind, but it's not going to pay off your debt."

She'd helped him out on a couple of missions and had told him she'd call the marker due at some point. His peace of mind was in knowing he still owed her. Otherwise, Chatton would blink out of existence. He didn't need a background file on her to know she had the skills.

Nick suggested, "Looks like my debt's going to get higher after this. I may need to start making installments at some point."

"I'll think on that."

Once they'd finished off their lunch, he stuffed the remnants into the bag and said, "I've got some news on your scroll."

She turned her face up to him with sunglasses hiding her eyes. "I do too. You go first."

"I know someone specific who's after the scroll."

"Besides the Orion Hunters?"

"Yes and I'm hoping you can help me figure out how everything is connected. The hunters killed Fontana then someone killed the hunter assassin."

She released a whispered breath. "I tried to get to him, but there were too many people on that side of the hotel. Have any ID on the hunter or who killed him?"

Nick nodded. "Ever hear of an operative called Len Rikker?"

"Yes."

"Do you have anything current on him?"

"Maybe."

That evasive answer might put off someone else, but Nick had figured out that if he gave Chatton time to decide it was worth giving up the information she had, she would. He continued, "Rikker's pretending to be security for the Vatican and that he's tracking down a stolen scroll."

She cursed softly. "That makes sense."

"Want to enlighten me?"

She stared forward for a bit then said, "Yes and no. I'll share what I have, but not right this minute. I need to stop him from getting his hands on that scroll."

"What's so important about it?"

"Galileo wrote many things. Some got him into trouble and he ended his days under house arrest at the Vatican."

"I remember years later a pope made a public apology."

"Right. Not that it did Galileo any good by then, but everyone cleared their guilty consciences. Anyhow, while living in the Vatican, Galileo continued his theories on stars and the planets. But he also had a vision that he wrote down, and it's the central piece to Orion's Prophecy."

"The prophecy the Orion Hunters are rabid about?"

"That one. It's believed that once this scroll is with the other four artifacts, the final conflict will be revealed."

"I've heard all about their World War III theory."

"Some of the believers are your garden variety fanatics, but some are powerful fanatics. One in particular, someone on another continent, wants that scroll and will kill for it."

He considered that. "Are you saying this person who wants the scroll is behind the assassinations?"

"Not necessarily, because I don't see the connection, but Rikker represents this man and one other powerful player who happens to be in this country. Is Rikker involved with the killings?"

"We think so. Two Orion Hunter assassins were killed in Rikker's signature style of shooting through each eye for a double tap."

She leaned back, relaxed, but thinking. "Do you know where the scroll is?"

"I know where it might be very soon. The person Rikker paid to find the scroll is on her way to meet him."

"Bad move," she warned. "Rikker won't leave any loose ends."

"She'll be covered."

Chatton tilted her head in an if-you-say-so motion. "No leads on the other two assassinations?"

"There may only be one more."

She cut her head around fast at him. "Who was number two?"

"My associate who is watching over the scroll exchange has a theory that the initials aren't specifically people, but acronyms such as F.E.P. might be Fontana Eliminated Permanently."

She rocked her head back and forth as if she tried to accept what he told her. "I'm not sold on the F.E.P. one. What about O.N.C.?"

"If he's right about the first one, then O.N.C. might mean One Not Connected, to throw everyone off."

Her profile froze. She said, "I think he might be right about the second one. Making a hit that isn't tied to the others would be wise. If that's the case, then any guesses on P.G.C?"

"We have three high-profile targets, none of which have initials that correspond to P.G.C."

"The pope's in town. What about him?"

"Nothing that points at him. The last time they had a pope in LA was during the 80s, and the crime rate actually went down that week. We'll have a small team on site just because he's on the list of high-profile targets, but hard to see him as trouble."

"True. I'm just tossing out ideas that start with P."

"I'm always interested in your ideas."

She stood, indicating the meeting was over. "I'm glad. Here's one to consider. Why steal a scroll that rare from the Vatican?"

Nick gave it consideration. "Someone wants enough to retire on … in some remote part of the world."

"Right. The man from the mall attack was found floating in a Marina Del Rey hotel pool with a bullet through each eye an hour ago. His name was Raul Brambilla. He was an administrative person within the Vatican. He stole the scroll. I'm certain of it."

"That was an expensive theft."

"True. Why take that risk?"

"Makes you wonder." But Nick understood that she had a point to make and kept thinking out loud to see if he hit on where she was going with all this. "The pope has been on a push to clean up mishandling of finances. Think this guy Raul was going to get caught in the pope's investigation?"

"If that was his only concern, why not just run? He could have taken enough money or small artifacts to disappear. Things that would have been easier to unload. Why take this particular scroll?"

He got what she was saying. "Raul might have only been a front man for someone more powerful. If I was that person,

I wouldn't want to leave a weak link that would expose me, especially if we're talking millions in embezzlement."

"Correct, which means Raul needed enough money to hide from some very powerful people. If you were his employer, what would be your next step to protect yourself if Raul disappeared and is now dead?"

Nick grinned. He was, indeed, Italian, and not everyone in Nick's family tree had been the forgiving type. He knew what powerful people did to protect their hides. "The people I have in mind would take measures to stop the problem at the root." He looked up at her. "They'd kill the pope and make their problem go away, plus send a message to the next one."

"Thank you for lunch." She stepped away, paused, and turned back. "The woman in the hoodie who fought with Raul in the mall is Valene Eklund. She must have the scroll. If she does, Rikker will not allow her to live once he has it in hand. Rikker is a servant of two masters, but he's loyal to only one. Allowing Rikker to end up with that scroll will put it in the hands of a person capable of starting a third world war."

Chapter 40

DINGO PULLED TO the curb a quarter mile from where Valene had to meet Rikker. "Give me time to get into position. You're twenty minutes early."

She'd been fidgeting with the cylinder since they left Henri, who'd delivered one pretty damn close to the original cylinder, along with a reproduction scroll Geoffrey had made from shots of the original that Valene had taken with her phone, then emailed.

Not good enough to pass a professional authentication process, but it should work if Rikker wasn't some damned closet artifact specialist.

If.

The safest bet was not allowing him to walk away from here with that reproduction.

Valene had sounded impressed when Henri delivered the fake scroll. Dingo studied her as she pulled herself together. She had her blonde waves covered with straight dark hair past her shoulders, a wig that looked like shit up close but would work in a pinch. She had wrap-around sunglasses to wear over those big brown eyes and bright red lipstick on lips that needed no decoration. She'd covered the ugly bruise on her face with makeup again.

Reaching over, he put his hands on hers. "Let me take it. Smith will not know who I am until I walk up to him."

"No. I'll do this. I don't know how to back you up in this situation. You're the one with skills, so you do what you have to do and I'll do what I have to do." She gave him a tight smile. "I've been thinking on the initials."

He let her shift the conversation. "And?"

"This Smith is looking for a scroll stolen from the Vatican and the pope's in town so maybe it's the pope."

He gave it serious consideration, just as he would any potential lead. "The only letter that works is P. You think the P.G.C. acronym stands for Pope Gets Canned?"

"No, and I'm rethinking the Fontana one, because that's a stretch. But I started digging on everything related to this scroll when I got the job. Pope Lando is a descendant of Pope Goffredo of Castiglione. He was actually born Goffredo Castiglione and there was some speculation that he'd call himself Pope Celestine the sixth."

"Papal names make no sense to me. Why would he call himself Celestine?"

"Because that's what his ancestor had called himself."

"Oh. So you think P.G.C. is Pope Goffredo of Castiglione?"

"Maybe. That would be a good code name for an assassin. No one would figure it out easily."

Dingo shook his head. "Why kill him?"

"I don't know. He's shaking up the church. Whenever you do that, there's a domino effect."

"The only reason that doesn't fit is there've been no death threats. Nothing that would alert the FBI here and the Vatican's security team haven't reported any concerns."

She lifted her shoulders. "Just a thought because he's in LA right now doing some visits to schools and low income areas."

"I'll pass it on."

He kissed her quickly and held her chin. "Don't do anything to give Smith a reason to react. Don't ask questions, nothing. Promise me. Just text me as soon as you walk out."

Exasperation and nerves came through when she snapped, "I promise."

He waited for the next group of people walking down the sidewalk and slipped out into the loose throng as Valene climbed into the driver's seat. Then he moved forward with a purpose. First he texted Nick a message to add the pope to the potential list.

Nick texted right back. *We've got two different pieces of intel pointing at our original target, which means the first action was a miss and FEP is back on again.*

Nick was saying that they had information indicating Perdido *had* been the target. Dingo texted, *What about PGC?*

Still working on it, but we think it's related to the first P.

This was all about Perdido? Dingo sent back, *Keep me posted.*

Roger that.

The urge to go help his team rode Dingo's shoulders.

He would be a liability if he was caught with them, but that didn't stop his drive to be there.

Just as soon as he dealt with Rikker, he'd call Sabrina.

Life was too short to leave things on bad terms with the people who mattered to him, especially when those people had deadly occupations.

If today was Dingo's day to grab a break, he'd get a shot at Rikker before Valene met with him. If Dingo intercepted the bastard first, he could give Rikker a go-to-sleep tap with the butt of his gun. Then he could load the unconscious and secured body into the GTO trunk and deliver him to Sabrina.

If not, Valene had the scroll that Geoffrey had produced. Geoffrey had even added details that would strengthen the case for its authenticity. The final product was a testament to his talent.

From all that Sabrina had learned on Rikker and shared with the team, Dingo saw no reason that Rikker would be able to identify the scroll as fake on his own. But assuming anything about Rikker was dangerous.

Valene had said over and over again that she hadn't gotten to know Dingo the way she wanted.

The way things were playing out, she never would get to know him, and if that meant she was never under threat again then that had to be okay.

Valene thought Dingo would just be close by to observe. That she'd hand off the scroll and walk away.

If she did know him the way she wanted, she'd realize there was no way Dingo would allow her to hand off the reproduction scroll without some plan to take out Rikker if the meeting went bad. If Rikker realized he'd been played, he wouldn't just kill Valene. He'd punish her brutally first.

Rikker had to go down for Valene to ever have a chance at a life without someone stalking her.

Chapter 41

VALENE WALKED THROUGH the coffee shop carrying a big patchwork purse that matched her bohemian looking, ankle-length cotton skirt and sandals, plus the ridiculous wig that she wouldn't wear for Halloween. The oversize purse hid two scrolls, the real one in a false bottom. She'd crafted a new inside liner from materials Henri brought when he delivered her fake scroll. As long as Smith hadn't been trained to recognize parchment three centuries old, he wouldn't know he wasn't receiving the real one.

Geoffrey had delivered a damn good reproduction. Even *she'd* given it a double take.

Henri was still angry with her, but he'd lowered his standards to accept the money she'd offered him. She'd have to find a way to face her dad come Monday, when she didn't have the money to get him into the treatment program.

But even though she could sell the scroll, she wouldn't. It didn't belong to her. It belonged to the Vatican and the church's people.

Hoisting the bag higher on her shoulder, she passed through the door that connected the main coffee shop to a patio wrapping the building on two sides in an L shape. She envied the people sitting outside, just enjoying their Saturday morning. One of these days, she'd have that life, too. She hoped.

The other patrons sitting outside were further down on the long side of the building where the breeze was better.

She found a table near the front corner of the patio close to the door, because Dingo had said to plan a second exit that didn't include scaling the waist-high wrought iron fence, and to keep her back to a wall.

She would normally have chosen a place closer to the black railing, but she wanted to prove she trusted him and could do what he asked.

An elderly woman in a purple warm-up suit, who looked to be seventy going on ninety, finished drinking her tea two tables over beneath a wide umbrella. She tucked the used teabag into her cup, then gathered up a chunk of newspaper sitting in front of her.

When she looked around, so did Valene.

The closest garbage receptacle outside was at the far end of the patio, and the woman would have to navigate through people sprawled out and visiting.

Shrugging to herself, the lady tottered toward the door to the coffee shop.

Valene jumped up and stepped over to open it for her.

When the woman finally made it there, she smiled. "Thank you dear."

Her good deed for the day done, Valene sat back down and found the woman's newspapers piled on her table. Valene rolled her eyes. Nice thought to share the paper, but she didn't need one more thing to deal with while she was waiting.

She wanted a clean surface so she scooped up the papers and paused. A phone had been left on the table face up.

The screen had a message.

Valene – Do not look around. Do not react or your boyfriend dies. Pick up the phone with the papers and walk inside as if you're throwing the newspaper away, then walk out the back door of the coffee shop. You have exactly sixty seconds and I will see any attempt if you try to signal someone visually or with your phone.

She couldn't get air. Her lungs seized up. Her fingers turned icy.

The phone dinged with a new message. *Tick. Tock.*

Oh, God. She had to get moving. She lowered the papers and

bundled them to her, with the phone inside, all without looking around for Dingo.

Walking took effort. The message had turned her legs to wobbly sticks.

She would have to face Smith alone.

Would he be able to recognize a fake scroll?

Chapter 42

DINGO WATCHED HIPPIE Valene open the door for the old lady, who showed her appreciation by dumping her newspapers on Valene's table. That wouldn't fly.

Valene wouldn't stand for all that crap on the table.

Just as he'd expected, she picked up the stack and stared down. Had she dropped a piece or was she reading an article?

Maybe she was trying to look in character.

She finally bundled it all up and walked inside where she probably had just passed a garbage can.

He gave her thirty seconds then stood up and started texting her as he walked. *Go back outside. Now!*

By the time he'd taken four steps he was running from where he'd been waiting twenty yards away on the other side of the street. He shoved the phone in his pocket and leaped over the black railing, drawing shocked looks from patrons on the patio. Dingo didn't give them a thought, snatching the door open and rushing inside where the atmosphere was calm and sociable.

He hurried to the back and knocked on the ladies room door. It yanked open, exposing a single room with an annoyed middle-aged woman.

"Wrong bathroom, buster."

Dingo was already running for the back exit that opened into the parking lot behind the coffee shop.

Empty.

He grabbed his hair. "*Nooo!*"

His phone buzzed. Valene's number came up. Thank you, Jesus. Dingo answered, "Hello. Valene? Hello! Talk to me."

Then he listened. The phone line was still connected but he couldn't even hear background noise. She had it on mute.

You brilliant, beautiful woman.

Snatching out his phone again, he called Josh. He didn't give Josh a chance to speak past, "Hello."

"I need you to track Valene for me. Now."

"What the fuck is going on?"

"Josh, please man. I'm begging you to help me. Rikker has her."

Heavy cursing then tapping was going on. "What have you got?"

Dingo gave Josh his location, Valene's cell phone number and his burner phone as he raced to his GTO that Valene had parked in the rear lot. Dingo was at home hacking and moving around in any direction on computers, but when it came to electronic forensics or tracking, that was Josh's territory.

Work your magic, mate, Dingo wished silently.

"Got it. She's not far ... shit."

"What?" Dingo had the driver's door open and reached for the wires to start the car.

"She's going in the direction of where we have a team inserted into a public event with Perdido."

"Give me an address."

"You can't go. Perdido is with the pope dedicating a newly reclaimed building in Skid Row. That place will be crawling with law enforcement. They'll have you down and cuffed the minute they see you. And that's *if* someone doesn't get trigger happy."

"Skid Row is the home of Satan's Garden Club. Rikker is working with them. Give me the fucking address!"

Josh did and Dingo's heart climbed up his throat.

Her phone's position was only three buildings away from where he'd pulled Valene out of Navarro's hands.

He squalled the tires, leaving a trail of blue smoke and asked Josh, "Where's Sabrina?"

"On site overseeing this operation herself."

"Don't tell her I'm coming."

"I take it that you're disguised. You can't go on site without her knowing or you risk getting hit by your own team."

Dingo wove through people determined to slow him down.

"I'm not going to do something that will get me shot." He hoped. "After she's off this op today, tell her I called and I'm sorry for the crap I've caused her. I don't hold her responsible for anything and I understand the stress she's under from the UK op and her relationship with Gage."

"Stop talking like you won't be able to tell her yourself."

"I will if I can, but I need you to know that."

"Your ass had better be on time for the damn tux fitting."

That was Josh's way of saying Dingo was scaring him and Dingo got it, but he was pretty sure the only fitting he might have coming up would be for a casket. "Stop giving me shit. I'll be there."

That mollified Josh who said, "I'm holding you to it. No marriage without you and that's me saying it, not Trish. Call me when you find Valene. I'm calling Sabrina to let her know that Rikker might be coming and that he might have taken Valene hostage."

"Thanks, mate." Dingo hung up and made the last turn that put him half a mile from the event that had the street blocked off from this side.

He didn't waste the time to hunt a space closer and just pulled down a side street to park.

Chapter 43

VALENE HAD FOLLOWED directions on Smith's phone that had directed her to a sedan sitting outside the rear door of the coffee shop. She'd driven it, using his directions that sent her to the Skid Row area of downtown LA where a celebration of some sort was going on.

She parked along a curb as close as she could to where the street had been closed to traffic for two city blocks. In the middle of that area was an intersection where a crowd and news crews congregated.

She headed down the street on foot. The only thing keeping her upright was the phone in her pocket that she hoped was still calling Dingo's phone. She didn't know how he'd use that to find her, but she was praying he could.

Looking around, she recognized this particular area.

She wasn't far from the building where Navarro had held her. Was he still there? Or would he have left now that someone knew his location?

She'd meet with Rikker. Give him the scroll and leave.

If he recognized her.

He'd said to meet him at the first corner where she could see the celebrities speaking.

That worked for her. Nice and public. Lots of police around and there were always the news crews.

Someone waved a cross the size of a hammer.

Was this one of the pope's stops?

The minute she handed the scroll off, she'd planned to call Dingo and explain what had happened, but she had to tell him now. If Rikker was here, someone was going to die.

A hard object jammed against her back and a deep voice with

a Latin accent said, "Make one sound and I'll shoot you, then I'll kill those children standing in front of you."

She knew that voice. Navarro.

Two little girls and a small boy were clustered around their mother, holding hands.

Valene fought to see through stars in her vision.

He said, "*Comprende?*"

She nodded. That word was officially out of her Spanish vocabulary.

He guided her back to a narrow walkway that stank, but she could barely breathe anyway, from the anxiety choking her. She'd pass out if she held her breath. When they reached a door on her right, he kicked it open and shoved her down the stairs into the basement floor of a building that appeared to be having work done. The Skid Row revitalization project. If the pope was actually here, that had to be why.

"Give me your phone," Navarro demanded.

When she turned, he had a .40 caliber Glock pointed at her. She hated that her weapons training had taught her how big a hole that would make. Better to hand over her phone than give him a reason to make her. She took out her phone, thumbing it off as she did, and tossed it to him.

He caught it, dropped it on the ground and crushed it under his boot.

Navarro said, "You thought you would make a fool of me, but you are the fool."

"What do you want?" Valene heard muffled voices, carried from microphones, but blunted by the brick wall between her and the speakers. Screaming probably wouldn't help her since it would take a while for someone to hear her and Navarro would kill her by then.

Navarro's phone hummed. He had it hooked on his belt and thumbed the button that turned it into speaker mode. "I'm busy. What?"

A woman answered, "Are your people ready?"

Muscles in Navarro's face twisted with hate. "Do *not* ever question me."

"I can't afford for this to go wrong."

"The only way it will be bad is if another one of my men gets killed. If you screw this up, you still owe me for the first one *and* this one, Perdido."

Had Valene heard that right? Navarro was working for Perdido?

F.E.P. For Eva Perdido? "I'm ready to settle my debt today." She sounded terrified and angry at the same time. "Just remind your man not to miss when I lean in."

"Give your speech and do your part as we agreed. My man will do his. And stop calling me. Do not give me a reason to kill two birds with one shot." He ended the call.

His eyes were full of crazy. Something had pushed Navarro to the edge of sanity. Or maybe he was just insane to begin with if he was killing high-profile targets.

Valene had to get him talking. Anything to buy time and figure a way out of this. "Just tell me this. Why'd you kill Aram?"

"Talk, talk, talk." He waved his gun. "Shut up and tell me where the scroll is."

He didn't know she had it with her? "I could show you better." And have more chance of drawing someone's attention outside.

"No. You tell me and I'll send someone while I hold you."

Dingo had speculated that Smith and Navarro had some connection. "If I do, Smith will come after you."

"So you know Smith? You know Dingo Paddock, too. You're a popular woman. I may need to keep you around. I'll find Dingo and when I do I'll send him a picture of you ... under me."

Over my dead body. She didn't say that since she didn't want to give a man holding a gun on her any idea about her capabilities. Speaking of ideas, she had one. "I'll give you the scroll. Right now. Just let me go, please."

He laughed. "I should have realized you'd have it with you. Hand it over."

"I have to reach in my purse and pull it out very carefully or it will be damaged."

"You pull out anything that is not a scroll and you will lose that hand first. I need you alive for a while, but I don't need all the parts."

She kept up the act of being nervous, which didn't take much acting, and slowly dug into her purse, fingering around to open the lid on the cylinder. "The scroll is fragile. I'll make you a deal. If you tell me why you killed Aram, I'll give you a tip on how to sell the scroll."

"I can *make* you tell me."

That froze the blood in her veins. "But it would be easier just to trade information."

"Very well. Aram was not of any consequence. I have three people to kill. He was merely someone to throw off investigations trying to tie the kills together."

"So you didn't go after Aram because of the scroll?"

"No, just another job for your Mr. Smith. How did he find you?"

She'd love to know. "Have no idea. Just my bad luck."

"Your luck is going to be much worse if you stall any longer."

"Got it." She pulled out the reproduction scroll as she stepped forward, and tossed the roll at him.

He grabbed for it.

She attacked him and made a well-placed kick that knocked the gun flying, but she wished for her boots. He caught his balance and came at her, but she was ready and pummeled him with Krav Maga strikes, adrenaline super-charging her hits.

She spun and kicked him backwards into a big wall cabinet. The hit stunned him and he slid to the ground, shaking his head.

She'd taken note of the room on her way in and lunged to grab a bucket of paint. Two steps and she whacked him across the head with it, turning out his lights. She grabbed the fake scroll and turned to find her way out.

The crowd outside was applauding someone.

Construction material blocked Valene's way to the front of the building, so she ran back up the stairs, out the side door. When she reached the street, she slowed to catch her breath and straighten her wig.

She'd almost lost the scroll. Looking around, she saw the perfect place to hide the real one and eased her way over to a detached gutter downspout. She fished the cylinder out of the false bottom in her purse along with the roll of paper she'd planned to use as a clean surface to roll the scroll out on.

Everyone was so focused on whatever was making news that Valene managed to wad up the paper and shove the lightweight cylinder up inside the broken gutter, then push wadded paper in behind it as a blocker.

Then she wormed her way through the crowd, ignoring the ugly looks and grumbles. Everyone she'd passed was wearing a cross.

She didn't want to go to the corner on this side after what had happened.

Instead, she'd watch for Smith from here. If he was so smart and knew her every move then he'd have to come look for her, right?

When she'd pushed her way near the front of the crowd, she could see Perdido stepping away from the microphone so the pope could talk behind a protective clear shield that had to be bulletproof.

Whatever Navarro had planned wasn't going to happen right now. Not with that shield up.

The crowd was still shouting and clapping for the pope.

Eva Perdido had just sat down when she said something to the pope.

He looked her way.

Eva stood and took a step, then the pope cupped his hand to his ear and leaned past the shield just as the crowd noise subsided.

Just remind your man not to miss when I lean in.

Valene realized what was happening and screamed, *"Gun! Get the pope down!"*

Security jumped in front of the pope as Perdido jerked up, then back, with red blooming on her shoulder.

Pandemonium broke loose.

Police were everywhere.

Valene saw scaffolding on the opposite side of the crowd. She jostled and pushed her way there then climbed up to get a look at the crowd.

Where was Rikker?

She didn't see him, but she did see Dingo running up the street toward a sea of bodies between them. When he gave her a sign he saw her, she knew he'd want her to stand still. She climbed down and stepped back to wait.

Steel fingers locked on her arm.

Not again.

Smith said, "Move it or I'll drop Paddock right here in front of you."

She started walking as he dragged her down the street away from the crowd.

Sirens were shrieking.

LAPD, the FBI, everyone in the area would be here any minute.

But Smith turned a corner and had her half a block further away by the time the sirens cut off when the police vehicles stopped at the street with the action.

"You better have that scroll with you," Smith said.

She wished she'd never heard of this scroll. "I do. Stop and I'll give it to you."

He didn't answer. She asked, "How did Charlie really find me?"

"I gave him your name and address."

"So he's working with you."

"Past tense. Charlie had the same flaw you have."

Charlie was dead. Valene didn't want to end up the same way so she asked, "What flaw?"

"He talked too much." Smith stepped up to the front entrance of the building Navarro had held her in before.

The door was snatched open by one of two men inside who were armed with automatic rifles. They nodded, which Valene took to mean they worked for Smith and not Navarro.

He dragged her to the stairs and started up.

Dingo would come for her, but he'd end up dying here.

She said, "Let me give you the scroll then you let me go. I know you're not going to pay me."

"You're right about not getting paid, but the scroll isn't all I need you for."

Chapter 44

DINGO PLOWED THROUGH people.

Someone in a uniform grabbed his arm and Dingo had to keep himself from snarling. He affected a high voice and grabbed the cop, whining, "Where is Jean Pierre? He was here. Tell me he did not get shot."

That got him shrugged off and Dingo kept bulldozing his way through the mangle of bodies until he burst through the side of the crowd where Valene ... was gone.

Navarro had her.

Dingo ran all out toward the next street.

He would have thought the police activity around Navarro's building after the gang attack and now this event would have cleared him out, but maybe not.

Criminals continually surprised Dingo when they did stupid things. Good thing. It helped law enforcement thin the herd.

He made it to the turn as more police rolled in, and waited behind garbage piled in and around a large can as the cars emptied out and officers raced toward the shooting.

Had to be fucking Rikker, but Dingo had given Josh everything he could. Sabrina and Josh would have to take down Rikker without Dingo.

He had something more important than vengeance.

Valene.

By the time he reached the building, he had his Sig out and rammed the door open, dropping two guards whose shots went wide.

There'd be more upstairs.

He lifted one guard's rifle, plus the two extra mags he found on the guy, and started up.

Shots came from the top of the stairs.

He didn't have time to play hide and seek with Valene up there. He raised his Sig and the rifle, opening fire with both, going at the shooters with a determination that would make Rambo proud.

A bullet caught him in the arm. The wound burned, but apparently no bone was hit because he could still use that arm. With adrenaline rushing through him he gritted his teeth and lunged forward, shooting everything that moved.

His pistol ran out of ammo first.

He sucked back against the wall, ejected the mag on the rifle and reloaded, prepared to continue, but it was quiet above him. Had he really gotten them all or was someone waiting to snipe him the minute he reached the top floor?

He heard a distinctive whomp, whomp, whomp.

A helo.

Shit.

Chapter 45

VALENE STRUGGLED AGAINST Smith's hold as he dragged her past men guarding the building, but it was just the two of them heading to the stairwell she and Dingo had used to escape.

She tried again to stop him. "Why won't you let me go? You can have the scroll."

"Because I'm not stupid enough to risk flying this scroll to China without knowing for sure I have the right one."

China? Did that mean he meant to take her, too? She said in a hurry, "I told you I've never seen that scroll before, but I have it on good authority that it's genuine. I have nothing more to offer."

"Then it won't be a problem when our specialists test the paper and compare the scroll with the photos, since the only way there could be a reproduction was if you used the original to make one."

Her mouth dried up. Not a drop of spit. She didn't have the original scroll. She'd tucked it away where nothing could get to it but rats.

Could a rat chew through that cylinder?

She'd run out of things to ask. That might be a flaw, but Smith wasn't going to kill her before the scroll was tested, so anything she said now might slow him down.

"What does someone in China want with the scroll?"

"That's not your concern." He started up the stairwell to the roof.

Shooting erupted in the building.

Boom. Boom. Boom.

Sounded like cannons were going off inside.

Smith paused to listen.

Shooting was blasting back and forth, a rapid fire of bullets pinging hard surfaces and glass breaking.

At this point, she'd welcome a gang attack. She'd have a better chance of surviving that.

Then silence. Smith smiled. "Let's go."

That's when she heard a helicopter approaching. They stepped onto the roof into sunshine and wind. The helicopter was coming down.

Smith walked her halfway to where the helicopter would land.

"*Let her go, Rikker!*" yelled over all that noise.

Smith was Rikker? She'd never been so happy to hear Dingo's voice and turned to see him pointing a rifle like the guards had been holding. Dingo repeated, "Let her go and I'll let you walk."

Wind buffeted her with the helicopter blades spinning closer.

Rikker yelled back, "Not without the scroll."

"Give him the scroll, Valene. The real one."

She stared at Dingo openmouthed. Then she shouted, "Seriously? You know who he is, right?"

"I know," Dingo assured her. "If he leaves without harming you, he can have it."

Rikker called out, "I like dealing with reasonable people."

She reached into her purse and pulled out a scroll in a clear plastic holder. The parchment looked as old as time. "Careful, it's fragile."

Rikker took it and started backing toward the helicopter, but he still had his hand on her arm.

She had to give Dingo a shot at him. Valene stumbled and let her dead weight fall forward, pulling Rikker.

He must have realized what she was doing and shoved her forward, then leaped up into the helicopter.

Dingo ran forward, shooting at the helicopter, but Rikker was firing back. Dingo yelled, "Run for the stairs, Valene." He kept ripping off rounds as the helicopter engine powered up. She ran to where four walls surrounded the stairwell access and dove behind one, turning as one of Dingo's shots killed the helicopter pilot.

Rikker hung out the side, shooting back, but Dingo was darting right and left, backing up to her.

She turned to run down the stairs and saw a body enter the stairwell. She turned back to grab Dingo when he reached her. "Someone's coming up the stairs.

The helo wobbled two feet off the roof, tilted and the blades slashed into the stairwell access that stuck up from the top of the building. Metal screeched.

Dingo grabbed Valene's arm, pulling her away from the stairwell and the helicopter that was chewing up the top floor of the building.

That left them one corner before a four-story drop.

One of the rotor blades caught and stuck into the roof, making a loud grinding noise. The whole helicopter body twisted and burst into flames.

"Is it going to explode?" Valene yelled.

"If it does, we have nowhere to go but down ... ah, shit."

"What?"

Dingo shoved her down to the rooftop and fell on top of her.

When the blades got jammed, the motor kept turning and sent the tail section flying around. The rear rotor was coming straight for them like a buzz saw turned sideways.

She screamed and Dingo covered her with his body.

Then everything went deathly still.

She peeked out from under his arm.

The blade had stopped inches from her face. Dingo's heart was beating hard enough for both bodies. He grabbed her to him and kissed her. Nothing would ever get her to let go of him again.

"FBI. Put your hands up. You're under arrest."

She dropped her head to his and turned. The moment was over.

Chapter 46

D INGO HUNKERED ON the ground, handcuffed. His arm hurt like a bitch, and he'd lost at least a pint of blood, but the bullet had gone through without hitting anything important. The paramedics had bandaged him up after the FBI cuffed him. He'd have been dragged off to a hospital if Sabrina hadn't interceded after determining he was stable.

That meant she didn't trust anyone to take Dingo out of her sight.

Sabrina stood twenty yards away speaking to the FBI SAC, Special Agent in Charge, who looked over at Dingo then nodded his head. She strode over to where Dingo had been placed, near the stage where the pope had almost been killed.

Sabrina's voice vibrated. "What the hell did you think you were doing coming into this mess and with no backup?"

"Protecting Valene."

"You could have died."

"She could have too."

Irritation lit Sabrina's eyes. "Does everything come back to her?"

He thought on it and nodded. "Yeah, it does. She's the one thing in this world that makes life worth living. She's the only woman I'll ever want."

"Really?" That took the fuel out of Sabrina's rage. She sat down next to him.

"Yeah, but I've screwed that with this." He raised his wrists that jangled. "Valene was only trying to keep her dad alive and they targeted her because she helped us with that last mission."

Sabrina stared down at the ground then nodded. "Nick told

me everything and I had planned to discuss it with you." She gave him a severe look. "If I could have found you."

"Staying away from you and Josh was the best thing I could do for you two. Staying with Valene was my only hope of keeping her alive."

Silence spread between them until Sabrina released a heavy sigh. "I've been thinking on things and I wasn't being objective either. I saw Valene as the reason I could have lost you. She was a convenient target the minute I saw the picture of her with Rikker. I'm sorry we didn't shield her. We will from now on."

Dingo believed her. That was as close as Sabrina ever came to admitting feelings. He said, "I'm going to hold you to that commitment to protect Valene if I end up in prison."

"I'm not letting anyone take you away."

If only it were that easy, but he wouldn't argue with her when this might be the last chance they had to talk.

Nick walked up, silent and listening.

Dingo said, "I know Rikker did a fine job framing me for the gang killing down here. I was here. My fingerprints are in the building. Going to be hard to get me out of that."

Nick crossed his arms. "You want the scoop?"

Sabrina cocked her head. "How can you have information already?"

"Friends in low places, and three hours is not that quick." Nick grinned. "It so happens that they found the head of Satan's Garden Club, Maxx Navarro, unconscious in the building next to where the shindig was going on. Valene told the Feds she knocked him out and said she heard a conversation between Perdido and Navarro."

Dingo leaned over to look at where Valene was being interrogated by the feds. She saw him and held his gaze for a long moment before the FBI agent snapped something at her.

She gave him her can-we-move-this-along cocked eyebrow.

Dingo smiled. That was his girl. *His*. He'd found the one woman for him and ... better not to think any harder on that. *Live in the moment.* That was going to be his future from now on because it would probably be spent inside a ten-foot square space.

Nick kept talking. "Valene also said from what she heard around Navarro that FEP might mean For Eva Perdido and, when the feds hit Navarro with that, he started spilling his guts on Perdido and Smith, aka Rikker. P.G.C. originally stood for Perdido's Gubernatorial Challenger, but that changed today to Pope Goffredo of Castiglione."

Dingo said, "Valene was right. She called it and said the third one was the pope."

"But the pope's hit wasn't ordered until today, based on what Navarro said," Nick clarified. "Perdido owed Smith for not delivering the scroll. I'll get to that in a minute. Smith gave her Navarro's number and said she had to work out her debt with Navarro, who was calling for blood after his assassin was killed. Everyone believes now that Rikker killed him. Navarro told Perdido that he had to make the hit on the pope look like an accident and that if she did her part to get close so that when the pope was shot everyone would think it was another hit on her life, he'd kill her opponent for a discount."

Sabrina said, "Are you sure? Perdido was behind all this?"

"Yes, but not entirely. From everything that Valene has shared, Dingo has said, that we found out, and that Perdido and Navarro have said, it sounds like Smith, aka Rikker, was coordinating everything. If Valene hadn't been grabbed by Navarro who was trying to snake the scroll from Rikker, the pope would have died today."

Sabrina nodded. "That's why Valene yelled when Perdido moved toward the Pope."

Dingo hadn't been close enough to see all that. "What did Valene yell?"

"Gun. Get the pope down," Sabrina explained. "Perdido got hit in the shoulder."

Nick picked up the thread. "Perdido was screaming 'he missed, oh my God, he missed, he hit me, the son of a bitch swore he wouldn't miss,' which coincides with what Valene has told authorities. Detectives are at the hospital now talking to Perdido."

"Why would they kill the pope?" Dingo asked.

Nick thought a moment then continued. "The minute Navarro

heard that Perdido was fingering him, Navarro rolled big time. Navarro said the killings were all for Perdido. He was to make Fontana look like an accident. The FBI had actually been working with Fontana, who came to them with evidence that Perdido was accepting illegal funds from outside the country."

Sabrina lifted her eyebrows. "She got him out of her way and picked up the sympathy vote."

"Right," Nick said. "Perdido claims she was supposed to get to Daddy Warbucks during the charity event, to get help finding an artifact Smith wanted that was part of the payment for her two kills, but right after the attack, Tinker went into seclusion again. Perdido is claiming Smith set her up in all this. Rikker contracted with Navarro for the kills and qualified that he wouldn't pay unless Navarro used Orion Hunter assassins."

"Why is Perdido giving up so much?" Dingo asked. "I get that she wants to cut a deal but she's running off at the mouth."

Nick grinned. "Not all of this information came from the feds and LAPD. No one realized Perdido was guilty of anything at first, so they rushed her into an ambulance and I climbed in as an FBI agent."

Sabrina groaned as if she had severe indigestion.

Nick tended to give that to everyone when ops went FUBAR, but Dingo grinned back at him. "She get some happy drugs?"

"Oh yes. She babbled about Smith being her contact to someone high up in government. Someone she'd known since she was a kid. A general in the Pentagon."

Sabrina and Dingo both sat up and said, "Who?"

"I pressed her for a name and she mumbled that it wasn't a real general, just what he liked to be called. Then we reached the hospital and there were FBI agents waiting to intercept her."

"Real ones," Sabrina clarified.

Nick shrugged. "Their badge looked like mine."

"Tell me they didn't see you flash that?"

"No one knows. I convinced the EMTs that I was on a high-level clearance case, and that the local feds weren't privy, so they needed to keep anything they heard to themselves or I'd come visit them."

Dingo shook his head. Nick could be a scary mother when he needed to be.

"Something's strange here," Sabrina mused.

"Just something?" Dingo asked. "Not the whole crazy deal?"

"Who is Rikker working for?"

Nick looked at Dingo then at her. "Rikker contracted the hits. Perdido owes someone in the government for the hits. Rikker came out of CIA. He could be working for the same person."

Dingo held up a hand. "Valene said Rikker was trying to take her with him because he didn't want to risk showing up with something less than satisfactory. They were going to China."

"China?" Nick and Sabrina said at the same time.

"Yeah." Dingo considered everything. "What if he's a double agent working for two groups?"

"If he is, he's not playing for *our* team."

Dingo agreed with Sabrina. "Doesn't look that way."

She said, "Gage would know if Rikker was still with the CIA."

Silence struck like a stray lightning bolt and Nick started stepping back. "I'll go see what else I can find out."

Dingo asked Sabrina, "You really trust Gage?"

"It's no longer an issue. I told Gage I had to put a stop to us. It's too confusing with so much on the line."

"I haven't helped. I'm sorry."

"It's not your fault, Dingo, and it's not Josh's fault. I've let Gage ease back into my world and I have to either be all in or not at all." She shook her head as if brushing away a thought and stood up.

"Any idea how Rikker got away? I'm sick over that."

She put her hand on his arm. "I don't really care as long as you're alive. I wanted him so badly, then I saw how close you came to dying again, because we weren't there to back you up." She shook her head. "It hit me that I can't live my life for Rikker and that's what I've been doing. We'll still hunt him, but we aren't putting me, you or Josh in the jaws of death to catch him. To answer your question, he's got nine lives. The best we can tell, he made it down the side of the building with some jury-rigged rope."

"Shit. I left that rope there."

"We'll get him, Dingo." She stood up. "I need to go talk to some more people and make some calls. If they do lock you up, I'll have to squeeze heavy hitters to get you out."

"Just like old times when we were kids."

She put a smile on her face, but her eyes were too sad to sell it. "Sure."

"Think you can pull a string and get Valene sent over here?"

"See what I can do."

Sabrina went back to the SAC and waited while he went over to where Valene had been left sitting alone. The SAC said something to Valene that must have had a time limit because she jumped up and followed him over to where Dingo waited.

When she sat down, Dingo wanted to put his arm around her, but that would be tricky while he was wearing cuffs, so he just leaned over and kissed her cheek, whispering, "I'm sorry I had you give him the real scroll."

"It's okay. If I still had the scroll, these agencies would confiscate it from me. I'm just as glad not to have it if I can't give it back to the pope. I wouldn't trust anyone else to return the scroll to the Vatican. It might just turn up missing."

He let it go. "There'll be an investigation. I convinced my people that you really thought Smith was a client, but now we have to convince the world."

She looked guilty as hell, which was going to make his job of convincing everyone that she was innocent in all this even tougher. Sure, she'd been working with the bad guys, but she hadn't known it.

After chewing on her lip for a moment, she started to say something to Dingo when the SAC walked up to her. "Ms. Eklund, I need you to come with me."

Valene asked, "Why?"

"I don't have to answer that."

Dingo asked, "Where are you taking her?"

The FBI agent said, "I don't have to answer any of your questions."

Valene got up. "No problem. Just point me in the right direction." She looked at Dingo. "I'm okay."

Then she walked across the fifty feet separating him from where the Feds had set up their area. Nick walked up holding her purse. Valene reached for it, but the SAC snagged it, then Nick walked off.

The SAC said something to one of his men who stepped up with handcuffs.

Valene stood through all that with an open-mouthed look. Then she held her hands out and they clamped handcuffs on her.

Dingo fought his way to his knees and shouted, "What the fuck?"

Three LAPD officers stepped in front of him.

"Get out of my fucking way."

Valene called out, "I'll be okay. Don't leave me."

His heart was ripping to shreds. "Where are they taking her?"

"Dingo, please wait for me." Then she was gone.

He'd wait for the rest of his life if she went to prison, but he was not letting anyone lock her away.

Chapter 47

RIKKER RODE IN a limo the Orion Hunters had delivered close enough to Navarro's building for Rikker to reach by limping as fast as he could. Blood ran down both sides of his face. His head felt as if it had been split in half. He had cuts and a cracked rib, even with the Kevlar vest under his clothes.

Fucking Paddock had popped him with three rounds. It hurt to breathe.

Damn Sabrina Slye and her bastards had been a nuisance too long.

He lifted the mangled scroll in his hands. He was not returning to China empty-handed.

The General had been calling constantly, demanding to know why the assassinations ended up as a clusterfuck and why Perdido and Navarro had been left alive in FBI custody.

Rikker deleted those messages.

The General was no longer his problem. He'd have to cover his ass on his own from now on.

Wayan was another story. Rikker would rather face a cobra, naked and with his hands tied, than go back to Wayan without something.

Someone had to pay for what Rikker had lost. He needed answers and he needed them soon.

Sabrina Slye was the best place to get those answers and she wouldn't be surrounded by her guard dogs forever.

Chapter 48

VALENE FOLLOWED THE FBI agent leading her through the hall of a plush hotel in downtown LA. Two more agents stood outside the door and gave her agent a nod of acknowledgement.

They took one look at her handcuffs and ignored her.

When the door opened, she followed the leader into a spacious suite. She counted six people.

One was the pope.

The. Pope.

It might seem crazy, but the room felt powerful as if the pope just exuded energy that radiated all around him. He gazed at her and with the lift of his hand he waved over a middle-aged man who had neatly trimmed hair and was wearing a suit. Must be his assistant.

Once the pope finished speaking, the assistant came to Valene's FBI agent and spoke in low, quick bursts.

The next thing Valene knew, her handcuffs were gone and she was seated in a comfortable chair next to the pope.

Pope Lando had the kind of face that made you want to tell him your troubles. He reminded her of her dad in a way. That's who she'd always poured her heart out to, but she couldn't now, because her dad was so sick.

With one word from His Holiness, everyone departed the room, leaving her and the pope alone with tea.

She was pretty sure the FBI and the pope's staff were still close by, but he'd shocked her by sending the others away.

She was having tea with the pope, when Catholics around the world would love that opportunity. Talk about feeling guilty for bailing on her religion.

He said in perfect English, though with an Italian accent, "I understand that you have something important to tell me about a scroll that should have been in the Vatican."

She tried to talk but lost her breath.

Giving her a gentle smile, he said, "Take your time, child. You have nothing to fear from me."

She needed that little encouragement. "I was approached by a man who I thought represented the Vatican."

"The FBI offered some background as to what has happened."

Breathing was good. She kept drawing it in, hoping one of those deep breaths would settle her down. "I really thought I was retrieving it for you, but to be perfectly honest we had an arrangement that he would pay me really well to locate the scroll and to keep all this confidential. I understood that you wouldn't want it in the news so if anyone said anything to the press, it wasn't me."

"Why would you think I would fear this being public knowledge?"

She thought on that. "Everything he said made sense."

"Such as?"

"I know you're shaking up everyone who has dirty hands in the banking groups, and you're holding priests and others responsible for their service to the church."

"I'm holding all accountable to God and our people, then the church."

"Right, that was sort of what I meant."

"What was the reason I would keep this secret?"

"Because it would look bad for you to lose an artifact this rare and important from the Vatican. The media would turn it into you being careless with the Vatican treasures."

He tapped his chin. "That would be in conflict with my goal to clean up the secretive dealings within our organization, wouldn't it?"

When he put it that way, he had a point. "I suppose so."

"Was the money the only reason you agreed to find the scroll?"

"I'm not going to lie to you. The money was very important at first, but the deeper I got into this, the more I realized that everything I'd ever hunted for had held meaning for me. There was a time when I only searched for something that I felt *had* to be found."

"But you needed the money this time?" the pope said, bringing her back to what got her into this mess.

"I did and still do, but while trying to get my hands on the scroll, I almost destroyed people who mean more to me than all the artifacts in the world. I'll figure another way to deal with my problems and still protect the people around me."

It was so calm sitting in his presence. He glanced around and asked, "What happened to the scroll?"

She said, "If you'll ask the FBI agent who brought me here to return my purse, I'll answer that. He had it with him in the car."

Once the purse had been delivered and they were alone again, Valene tugged on the false bottom, revealing the extra space. She pulled out a silver cylinder that she handed to the Pope. "I truly thought I was returning it to you, but when I realized the man I'd been dealing with was a liar, I didn't know who to trust. So I had a duplicate made to use as bait to catch the man paying me, but that one burned up in the helicopter fire. I hid this one until I was positive it would end up in your hands, and this is the best chance I'll ever have for that."

A man named Nick had convinced her that he and Dingo were teammates and that he was the one in the hospital in LA when she'd helped Dingo's team find the doctor in Chinatown. Once he'd convinced her that he was a friend of Dingo's and wanted to know if she had any information that would help Dingo, like finding the scroll, she told him what she was going to do.

She thought he'd call her out, but he'd grinned and managed to not only find the scroll where she'd hidden it, and sneak it into her purse, he also got word to the pope that she'd requested a meeting with him.

The pope held the tube gently, staring at it with sad eyes, then he opened it and carefully reviewed the first part of the scroll before putting the parchment back in the cylinder. "You took a great risk in telling the FBI agent that I was expecting you and if he did not allow you to talk to me that he would regret it."

More of Nick's machinations, no doubt, but Valene just smiled rather than admit or deny anything of the sort. Then she said,

"Didn't seem like much of a gamble at the time, until he cuffed me."

"The FBI had received a bomb scare from someone who said if they didn't get to speak to me personally they were going to blow up this building."

Chill bumps lifted on her arms. The FBI could have locked her away forever until they decided she was not a part of that.

"However, my assistant keeps his ear to the ground in all situations and brought your request to my attention. We have a mutual friend who spoke to my assistant."

Did that mean Nick knew the pope?

She didn't care, because both Nick and Pope Lando had saved her bacon. "Thank you."

"Thank you for returning this scroll."

"It belongs to you ... or that would be the Vatican and the Catholic people," she quickly amended, taking his sense of duty to God and the church into account. "Will you allow anyone to study it?"

"Eventually, once the danger has passed."

"The scroll is bad news?" she said, her insatiable curiosity racing to the forefront.

"The scroll is tangible evidence of Galileo's writings while he was unfortunately under house arrest. He claimed these were visions, and I am not in a position to dispute that, but the people searching for this are not interested in Galileo's musings. They want to alter the course of our future by manipulating one man's writings. I have always heard that this script would dictate a horrible war between major powers in our world."

"That's what I heard, too, but you don't believe that this scroll can really predict that?"

When he just stared at her as one would a slow child, she nodded. "Right. Lots of prophesies in the scriptures. What exactly is the meaning of this scroll?"

"I believe the writings are a warning more than a prophecy."

"Have you read the scroll?"

"I have not."

"Do you intend to allow anyone to read it?" Yes, that sounded eager, but she'd like to read it.

"Yes, once the danger trying to rise up has passed." He sat quietly for a moment, pondering something, and it was so peaceful in his presence.

When he spoke, his voice was strong. "Thank you for returning something you could have claimed was lost or stolen, then sold. It shows how strong your heart is."

"I appreciate your wonderful words, but I don't deserve praise. I'm failing everyone who depends on me."

"Everyone is a large number, my child."

Valene sighed. "I'm failing my father, who needs to get into an experimental treatment program for a rare lung cancer, which was why I took this contract for the scroll. I'm failing my friend Henri who needed the money from this contract to move to a new location and save his relationship. And ... I let down the man I'm in love with, but that relationship was lost before I had a chance to have it. And ... " She'd been trying to come to terms with this and now seemed as good a time as any to admit something she'd been in denial about for too long. Her voice was raspy with unshed tears. "As long as I'm confessing, I'm fighting to keep my father here with me and he might be ready to go ..." She swallowed. "But I won't let him. I'm a bad person."

His Holiness put his hand on hers where it rested on the chair arm, and the tears she'd held back came rushing out. He let her cry, patting her hand and offering her tissues.

When she finally quieted, he started to speak and his assistant stepped into view. "I'm sorry to interrupt your Holiness, but you have a meeting with the Vice President in forty minutes. He arrived an hour ago."

The pope said, "I have something more important to do at the moment. Call and make my apologies for the delay and reschedule for this evening."

"Yes, your Holiness." The man left as silently as he'd entered.

Valene said, "I'm sorry to impose on your time. You're clearly busy and I should go."

"Not yet."

"I thought you had something to do." And it had to be major to include the Vice President of the US.

"I do. I must pray for a soul." Then he proceeded to tell her to bow her head, which she did, and he prayed for her father, that God might see fit to watch over him. He prayed for her friend that Henri would realize material goods would not save a relationship, and he prayed for Valene that she would follow her heart and allow it to lead her to love."

It might have been her crying, but she felt a huge burden lift just by being with the pope.

When she stood, she took his hand. "Thank you for being who you are."

"Just remember you have an angel watching over you. We all do."

She'd like to believe that, but any angel who took a look at Valene's life would put in for hazardous duty pay.

Chapter 49

TWELVE DAYS LATER, Valene walked out of the hospital with her father's doctor who was saying, "I'm surprised at Ronaldo's improvement. I'd like to say it's the new treatment we have him on, but I have to tell you this is hard to explain."

"Thank you for going to bat for my dad."

"After you called me on the mat in my own office, I had to face myself the next morning in the mirror. I asked myself the questions you asked me and decided to start looking for more options. I got excited when I found out about this new program, but I didn't want to contact you until I knew for sure the money wouldn't be an issue."

"It's not. I've got some new clients. I can handle this." She might even write a book about how to stay trim living on ramen noodles.

Doctor Bowen stopped her. "Didn't you get my email?"

"No." She'd stopped looking at her personal email account once her dad went into the program and wasn't online. Dingo hadn't been in touch. Henri wasn't speaking to her.

"The entire treatment plan is paid for."

"What? How can that be? I just made arrangements for the payments four days ago." Had Dingo sent the money? How would he have known?

"The money was received yesterday."

"Who paid it?"

Doctor Bowen gave her a fatherly smile. "The message I got said to tell you your angel was watching out for you."

She got chills. That was what the pope had told her. Tears blossomed in her eyes, but she didn't have the capacity to feel embarrassed this time.

"I'd say your angel has had a hand in your dad's care, too. I don't want to give you false hopes, but he's responding much better than I'd have ever imagined. The other doctors on his team are excited."

She grinned. "Someone said a very special prayer for my father and I'm pretty sure it went right up the line to the top of the chain."

"Your father is a very lucky man to have such a loyal daughter. Every man needs a woman like you in his life."

Every man except Dingo.

She thanked the doctor and stepped out into the balmy afternoon air. She turned to walk along the sidewalk to the parking lot and almost ran into someone she couldn't believe was waiting there.

"Hello, Valene."

"Hi, Henri. What are you doing here?"

"I stopped by to see your father at the assisted living and heard he was in the hospital. I was worried about you."

She'd been through so much that she thought she'd gotten over losing Henri as her friend, but she hadn't. "Thank you."

He stepped up to her and took her hands, ignoring the people passing them. "I almost lost Geoffrey."

"I know and I'm so sorry. That was not my intention."

"I realize that now. I got scared and fear made me angry so I lashed out at you. I was angry later with Geoffrey. I was angry in general. You and I never fought the way Geoffrey and I fight."

"I'm sure this will pass, Henri."

"I hope not." He laughed.

She smiled at seeing him happy. "I don't understand."

"You and I never fought because we were close but we always gave each other a lot of room to do what we needed. Even when I packed up to leave, you were angry but that's your normal operating level. We didn't speak for a long time because you were hurt and I felt guilty over the whole thing. But Geoffrey and I fight because there is so much passion."

The light bulb went off. "I know what you're saying. I fight with someone else like that. Or I did."

"The brooding Neanderthal you brought to my shop who found Geoffrey?"

"Yes." If she called Dingo brooding he'd get pissed off.

If she got the chance again, she'd do it just for the makeup sex.

"He was the one you were with back before your dad got sick the first time, wasn't he?"

"Yep. That was him." See? It didn't suffocate her to talk about it. In another ten years, she'd be downright casual when it came to discussing Dingo.

"You were so happy then. You should be with him."

"It's not always my choice, Henri."

He frowned. "I'm sorry."

"It's okay. Was that enough money for you to make the move?"

"That's another thing. Coming so close to losing Geoffrey made me think. When he returned from his harrowing mall experience, we both took a look at life and put it back into perspective. We're selling our high-rise apartment and buying a location where we can have our business and our home in the same spot. We won't be in a chic part of LA or Pasadena, but we are consultants at heart, and brokers. With our combined expertise, all we need to offer clients is a comfortable place to meet."

"That sounds like a wonderful idea, Henri." And she meant it. He was clearly happy. No, he was more than happy. He was content and at peace. "As long as you feel like it will be okay."

"It will be more than okay. We won't have a building as a yoke around our necks. Geoffrey would like to travel for consulting. We realized we could do just as much business, maybe even more, by streamlining, and in doing so, we would finally have time together, which was number one on our list of priorities."

Henri looked up and his eyes brightened.

She knew before she turned around that only one person could do that to Henri.

Geoffrey's gaze went from Henri down to where he held Valene's hand, then he seemed to brush it off with a long sigh and walked over to them.

Henri asked, "Did you get lost?"

Geoffrey scowled. "No. I was looking at a map print hanging in the hall."

"Oh?" Henri said.

Geoffrey waved it off. "Nothing of value."

Valene withdrew her hand from Henri's and stuck it out to Geoffrey. "Thank you for all that you did to help on the scroll contract, and congratulations on what you two have planned. It sounds really terrific." She swallowed how much she envied them, but in a good way.

Geoffrey nodded and went to withdraw his hand, but she held tight, causing panic to flair in his face.

She stifled the urge to chuckle and added, "Henri will always be my friend. I love him *as* a friend, but I will never be a threat simply because you make him very happy, and I want Henri to be happy. When you're both settled again, I'd like to meet for dinner so that I can get to know you, too, Geoffrey. I've learned that one can never have enough friends."

Geoffrey's gaze registered shock then his eyes watered and he showed his backbone. "Thank you. We'll send you an invitation to our housewarming."

She smiled and her heart no longer hurt when she looked at Henri. He'd been right. She'd loved him for so long as a friend, she'd confused that with being in love.

Now her heart only hurt when she looked at Dingo, which shouldn't be an issue since he was gone forever.

Chapter 50

VALENE PACKED HER T-bird trunk with a blanket, food, iPod and candles. The FBI had helped her get her car out of impoundment after she'd spent days giving them everything they asked for, right down to working with an artist on a rendering of Rikker's face. She'd also agreed to be a witness for the trials of Navarro and Perdido.

Charlie had been found dead in his apartment.

A bullet in each eye.

She drove to El Matador beach and hiked down to the sand, loaded down with all she needed. Staying alone in her apartment had been difficult. She couldn't sleep if it was noisy or if it was quiet. Nothing worked.

But she'd been sleeping soundly in their cove.

Her cove.

No one had told her a word about Dingo. The FBI said it was confidential information. No one would give her a number for Nick, the Italian guy who was Dingo's friend. The one who'd helped her get the scroll from its hiding place and into her purse.

That guy had asked a lot of questions before he got the scroll for her, but he'd given her no information.

Every door she tried to open slammed shut.

Her snooping too far had almost gotten Dingo killed in the past. Lesson learned. She would not even type his name into her laptop.

It was time to let it go. Navarro and his people were going away for a long time, as was Perdido.

She put out her spread and had some cheese and wine, but didn't listen to the music this time. The ocean put her to sleep.

Until something–an out-of-place sound–brought her awake so fast she jerked upright.

A dark figure stood down the beach, silhouetted by the early morning glow across the water. No sunshine yet.

This was usually her favorite time, but she was too shocked to appreciate the setting.

He stepped forward slowly and kept coming until he knelt and kissed her.

It wasn't a dream. Dingo was here.

She hugged him to her and trembled. "I thought–"

"I know," he said. "That you'd never see me again."

Words took too much effort, so she let him hold her and kiss her until he was sitting and she was in his lap. They stayed that way for long quiet moments. She nuzzled his neck, kissing him everywhere she could reach without moving out of his arms.

Catching her chin with his fingers, he drew her face away just enough for them to see each other. He said, "I'm sorry I was so distant before and left without telling you."

She started, "It's okay–"

"No, it's not. If you had done that to me, I'd have lost my mind. I had some time to think while I was gone."

"Where'd you go?"

"I spent some of it locked up."

"You're kidding. They aren't hanging that killing on you. I told the FBI–"

"I know, love. I heard about it."

Her skin tingled. He called her love.

Being stupid again, Valene?

Dingo was stroking her hair, studying her as if he needed to memorize her before he left again.

That took care of the stupids. She asked, "What happened?"

"The people I work for are my best friends and–"

"That woman you were talking to?"

"Yes. Sabrina."

Her skin tingled more. Dingo had just shared the name of someone Valene doubted he would have normally told her. She was afraid to ask about it, so she said, "Uh huh."

"Sabrina spent a lot of time getting into people's faces and putting pressure in the right areas. She got me out yesterday."

Valene smiled. "And you came to see me today. That's so sweet."

"Actually, I would have been here yesterday but I owed Sabrina a proper debriefing." He raised one eyebrow. "Speaking of debriefings, you owe me one too. Nick said you returned the scroll to the pope. Why'd you let me think you gave Rikker the real one?"

Crap. Did he think she'd held back on him again? "There were so many people around, I didn't know who I could trust. By that time, I was afraid the wrong person would overhear if I said I'd hidden the real one. To be honest, when Nick got me the meeting with the Pope, I'd gone there thinking I would offer him a trade if he could pull some strings to get you released." She shook her head hard. "But when I sat down in front of him, I knew I couldn't ask him to trade for something that was not mine to barter with, so ... I'm sorry, Dingo. Maybe you would have gotten out sooner and I swear I wasn't trying to hide anything from you. It wasn't that I didn't trust you—"

"Hey, stop. I don't think that." He stroked her face. "I didn't care about the scroll really, but I knew you did. I'd just been worried about making sure you would not be accused of any wrongdoing, so you'd be free to take care of your dad. Which brings me back to the other reason I had to see Sabrina yesterday. I had to tell her I'm taking the time off she's been harping at me to take."

Valene fought to find the right words and finally gave up. Better to speak her mind. "What are you going to do with those days?"

"That depends."

She would not allow him to back away from her again with the excuse that he put her at risk. "Argh! You have got to stop taking responsibility for everyone. I'm the reason I was in danger, not you."

"Not true."

She needed to convince him that he could be with her even if only on occasion. She'd suffer through the alone time if she knew he was coming back. "Okay, yes, your job is dangerous, but I've learned my lesson about being careful when I research and listening to my instincts when they try to tell me my client is not who he seems to be. I've also learned not to dig where I shouldn't. I haven't even typed your name into a computer. Honest. Please don't let the past dictate the future."

"You're not the only who has to learn from the past. I made mistakes and–"

She shook her head. "This sounds like we're back to maybe, possibly, don't know, can't tell you–"

He kissed her, tenderly at first, but then it turned hot with the promise of sex. When he pulled back, he said, "Give me a chance to explain. I'd planned to spend my time off here with you. And I'd like to meet your dad if he's able to have visitors."

"Really?" Could she sound any more like a pitiful little kid?

"As I said, all that *depends* on whether you really meant it when you said–"

"What? When I said what?" she demanded.

"You wanted to keep me."

She hugged him. "I might not know you, but you should know *me* by now and that if I say I'm keeping you, I mean it. You're mine, Dingo Paddock, forever. Do you hear me?" She unfolded herself from his lap and held his face so that she could let her forehead touch his. "Tell me you really mean this."

He cupped her face. "I've never said this to any woman, but I love you, Valene. I love you so much it scares me, but if you'll hold my hand I'm yours."

"Good. Just don't ever leave me without saying goodbye again."

"Never. I'd rather cut off an arm than hurt you, and I'm sorry I did before. I just ... still have a hard time worrying about the danger I might bring to your door."

"I'm in danger any time I walk outside that door, regardless. You know I'm trained, but you can teach me more about how to watch for threats, and you can teach me about the dangers inherent in my research. I'll add security cameras and I'll never blow you off again when you tell me there's a problem. I'll be *safer* with you in my life."

"I'll do everything I can to make sure you're safe. And I'll do my best to make you happy, but you should know up front, I have no idea how to be in a long-term relationship."

She whispered, "I never realized what you went through as a kid."

Dingo shrugged. "That's life."

That riled her up. She grabbed his cheeks. "That is *not* life. Not the way we're going to live it. I will never let you go. So get used to belonging to me because I'm a possessive bitch who does not share. You'd better think twice about pissing me off if you expect to live in any kind of peace." She stopped. "What are you smiling about?"

He started laughing and hugged her to him. "I don't want to live in peace. I like how you destroyed my calm. The way you took my world and turned it upside down. And I love when you get pissed at me."

"Are you crazy?"

"Absolutely. Crazy about you. The best part of pissing you off is makeup sex. You make love with as much passion as you fight."

She smiled again. "I'll make you pay."

"I sure as hell hope so." Then he kissed her and she felt his heart touch hers.

She couldn't believe he was here with her. But she needed him to know he wasn't going to be trapped. She said, "I know your work is in Atlanta, but just please call me sometimes while you're gone so that I'll know you're okay."

"Babe, you don't understand. I'm moving in with you and it's not going to be in that crummy apartment. I've never had a home, but we'll make one and I'll call you every day or you'll know why I can't. And you're going to meet the people on my team, my best friends. I want you to go to a wedding with me in Miami next week."

"Whose?"

"My friends Josh and Trish." He kissed her cheeks and her lips. "That will be good practice."

"For traveling together?" She smiled.

"For a wedding." He stared at her with a hint of fear, but he added, "How much do you want to keep me?"

"If that's a question, you're going to have to do a better job."

That threw him off for a moment, but Dingo had that look in his eye. The one she saw when he came for her when Rikker had her. He said, "Will you marry me?"

Telling her he loved her was enough. She didn't need him to ask her to marry him. But now she understood that he needed to hear her answer. To know that he would always be loved and wanted.

"Yes, Dingo Paddock, I will marry you and love you forever."

"I love you, babe."

"I love you more."

"Not possible."

She started laughing. "We'll see. I'm going to plan a wedding that'll make you crazy."

He sighed. "I was worried about that."

She nipped his lips. "But look at all the makeup sex we'll have while planning it."

Flipping her onto her back, he said, "You should start paying now."

⚬⚬⚬

I hope you enjoyed these two. You'll see them again in the next story – FATAL PROMISE – which is Sabrina and Gage's story.

Thank you so much for reading my books and making my life brighter with the wonderful notes you send and the reviews you post.

If you enjoyed this story, please help other readers find this book by posting a review.

To find out about new releases, sign up for Dianna's private newsletter list (emails are NEVER shared) at

AuthorDiannaLove.com

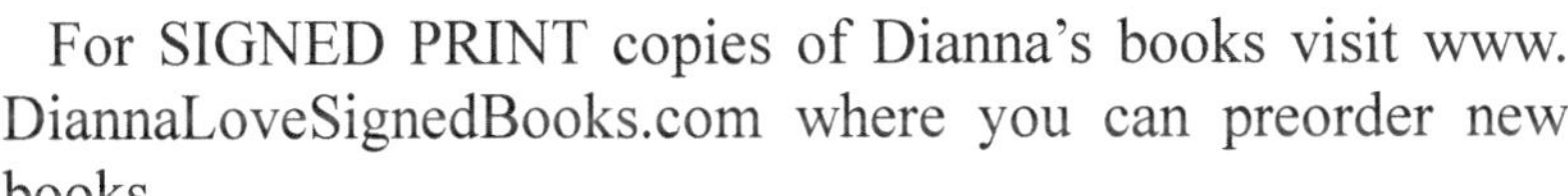

For SIGNED PRINT copies of Dianna's books visit www.DiannaLoveSignedBooks.com where you can preorder new books.

E-book and international fans:
You can also order a set of signed bookplates for your print books and/or signed cover cards just for the cost of postage at *www.DiannaLoveSignedBooks.com* (click MORE)

FATAL PROMISE is the last book in the
Slye Team Black Ops series,
which is Sabrina and Gage's story.

***The Slye Team Black Ops
romantic thriller series is 'completed'
(great for binging!)***

Prequel: Last Chance To Run
Book 1: Nowhere Safe
Book 2: Honeymoon To Die For
Book 3: Kiss The Enemy
Book 4: Deceptive Treasures
Book 5: Stolen Vengeance
Book 6: Fatal Promise

"It seems with each book, this series gets better…(Love) has an uncanny ability of always creating wonderful characters that you care about… one of the best I have read this year."
~~Barb, The Reading Cafe

Please enjoy the following sneak peek from
FATAL PROMISE

FATAL PROMISE

DIANNA LOVE

Chapter 1

NIGHTHAWK 1911 9MM, cocked and locked. *Check.*
PPSS bulletproof vest. *Check.*
Last will and testament updated. *Check*
Over accessorized for dinner? Maybe.
Sabrina Slye kept her eyes on everyone she passed along Baker Street near the Centennial Park area in downtown Atlanta. Sweat drizzled its way down her back, soaking her thin black T-shirt and sliding under the shoulder holster she'd hidden beneath a black windbreaker. A slight breeze swirled across her damp neck, offering some relief from the heat at twilight.

Welcome to the dog days of summer in Georgia.

July fourth had just passed in its usual dazzling glory.

She kept her stride easy and smooth, when she wanted to run to the restaurant where she'd make a trade for intel on the number one, most wanted man.

Maybe not for the FBI, but former CIA agent Len Rikker topped her must-die list. He had to pay for his part in selling out her team over three years ago in the UK, and for all the deaths he'd piled up since then.

She had the money for the trade tucked into a small shoulder bag, but that wicked sixth sense of hers warned she might not be spending a penny.

This could be a trap.

Okay, to be honest, in her line of work, any time she met someone covertly it could be a trap.

That's why rule number one was *Always Be Prepared.*

Whatever it took, she was not passing up a chance to finally end this hunt, especially if Rikker really was holed up somewhere healing.

Ziggie, a dependable snitch from her early days as a CIA contractor, had rubber stamped the contact wanting to meet with Sabrina. *Ziggie doesn't say a word for eight months, then calls ninety-eight minutes ago with news that he has a female willing to spill her guts?*

Yeah, like that didn't sound suspicious?

But... this information had a short shelf life.

Rikker had been hurt during a shootout with one of her Slye agents in California twelve days ago. She'd have thought he'd be out of the country by now. Evidently, the person he worked for had left him high and dry when, thanks to her people, he'd failed to get his hands on an ancient scroll from the Vatican.

What goes around comes around, you sorry dog.

He'd orchestrated the deaths of two people—*this* time. She'd need a calculator for a true count. He'd almost taken out the pope in California. As in *the* pope. Rikker was harder to kill than a cockroach strung out on crack. Anyone else would have died crashing in an out-of-control helo on a rooftop two weeks back, but Rikker managed to escape. She'd been concerned that the miserable excuse for a human might have bled out somewhere with no way for her to confirm his death.

The small fortune she'd spent hunting him over the past three years was finally paying off. She hoped.

If tonight's meeting turned out to be a bona fide lead, it would be worth every penny invested. Her team had barely survived a failed op in the UK a little over three years ago when they'd gone in to rescue Rikker. A terrorist group had captured him on foreign soil. The US government couldn't claim him, but Uncle Sam had wanted the CIA asset back, so they sent in Sabrina and her people.

Correction, Gage Laughton, her CIA handler at the time, had issued the contract for Rikker's extraction.

Going after the captured spook had seemed no different than any other high-risk contract she'd taken from the agency, but someone who knew the details had burned her team, trading all five of their lives for Rikker's that night.

She had mixed feelings about Gage, but Rikker?

Dead man walking.

Once she got her hands on him, she'd find out who pulled his strings. Who'd traded his ass for her team.

At the door to the restaurant she waited for a trio of happy women to enter ahead of her, then stepped inside, allowing her eyes to adjust. She searched for two empty seats at the very end of the bar.

Friday night packed house, but look at that. Two empty seats at the bar.

That did not happen by accident.

She'd like to hang back and force the contact to sit first, just to have a look at this unknown person, but that wasn't how these things went down. Nodding at the hostess that she was headed for the bar, Sabrina took her time strolling over so she could casually scope out everyone already inside.

The aroma of sizzling steak toyed with her senses.

She circled the end of the lacquered bar. It curved so the two vacant seats allowed an unobstructed view of the entire room, with a wall at her back. Mirrored.

Someone had done her homework, if Sabrina's contact really was a female.

Snagging the last spot, the best choice of the two seats, she left the one on her right empty. Once she met her contact and got what she needed, Sabrina would hook the thin strap of her purse on the chair back so the contact could slide it off without anyone noticing they'd made an exchange.

She angled her body in a way that allowed her to observe every waiter and waitress who swept past her to reach the cubbyhole used for the barback area.

Voices blended and turned into one indecipherable sound surrounding her. Pleasant, though. Wait staff hurried back and forth, smiling and nodding at appropriate times as they interacted with patrons.

She ordered a club soda and lime, which the bartender delivered with polished efficiency.

She'd just taken a sip when her skin tingled.

Someone watched her.

Slowly, she floated her gaze around covertly, observing everything in the restaurant again.

No one stood out.

The hostess led a group of five from the entrance. As she passed Sabrina's end of the bar, the last person following the group peeled off and took the empty seat next to her.

They had a brief stare down until she unlocked her jaws and asked, "What the hell are you doing here?"

Chapter 2

SABRINA SHOOK WITH the need to strangle Gage Laughton. He rested his elbow on the bar and turned toward her as if she'd agreed to meet him for drinks.

Had he really tapped her snitch just to arrange a clandestine meeting with her? Of course he had. He knew she'd jump at a chance to take down Rikker.

Still, the fact that he'd sink this low carved her up inside.

Gage started in, "We have to talk. I—"

She cut him off. "*You* might have to talk, but I've got nothing to say. I said it all this morning." That hadn't been a fun phone call. She'd left California two weeks ago with her insides twisted up. Everyone had a weakness.

Hers was staring at her hard enough to shove her off the stool.

Damn him for making her suffer more than she already did for being the strong one and cutting ties while they were still civil to each other.

It hadn't been easy.

And damn him twice over for tricking her into thinking she had a lead on Rikker tonight. Pulling this prank just so he could talk to her in person was classic CIA agent Gage Laughton.

He ordered a scotch on the rocks and sat quietly, allowing those whiskey-brown eyes to search her face for any tell. He could look all he wanted for something he could use to spin this conversation in his favor, but she'd locked down her emotions.

Okay, yes, her libido was doing a tango at the rush of having him so close. She missed running her fingers through his hair. Now maybe an inch long, it had grown out enough for red highlights to show in the rich brown. He had a harsh cut to his jaw. He was all man. Not a smooth edge on him when he showed his fierce side.

She missed touching the sculpted muscles hidden beneath the sport coat and T-shirt he wore with jeans. He pulled off that look like no other man.

What she *really* missed was the way this man took his time. When he focused on a woman, she was the only thing in his universe.

Gage never rushed into anything, well, except on the occasions that she'd taunted him sexually, determined to push that rigid control to snap. When it broke free, he'd rip her clothes off, then he'd pay her back with smoking sex.

Good times.

All in the past now.

She had to get her head out of yesterday and worry about today. Time to end this once and for all to keep Gage out of her way. Her heart seized at the idea of never seeing him again, but that organ didn't have a say.

It had a bad track record when it came to this man.

Flicking a look around the restaurant to check her surroundings out of habit, she parked her gaze on him. "What part of *we can't do this anymore* confused you? Tell me and I'll put it in shorter words this time."

Nothing showed in his face.

Not a hint of emotion. He had his game face on, which meant he'd come here with a plan in mind. Fine. She'd allow him to lay it out, then make him pack up and be on his way.

"I listened to you," he said just loud enough for her ears. "That doesn't mean I believe what you said."

"Believe it." She'd snapped that out sharper than she'd intended. "I allowed you, no not *you*, but us, to come between me, Josh and Dingo. I've never allowed that to happen in the past. I'm not going to deny that I enjoyed the time we had together before ... the UK mission. But all things come to an end, especially in our line of work."

Almost losing Dingo had brought that home with crystal clarity.

She caught Gage's flinch of pain at her reducing what they'd had to nothing more than sex, but dressing it up any other way would mean leaving a hint of possibility in her voice. The longer she allowed this to be dragged out between them, the more pain it would cause them both.

Gage had never wanted more than an easy-terms affair when they first hooked up, and she'd been fine with it at the time. She could admit to herself that he was special to her.

Even though they'd never have the bond she shared with Dingo and Josh ... she didn't want to watch Gage leave again with no idea when he'd return.

She was not adding one more person to worry about losing.

Undercover work had many faults and she didn't like her world much these days, but it was all she knew. One thing was for sure. She intended to find Rikkcr and stop him from ever threatening the people in her world again.

Once that happened, she'd have to figure out how to keep Josh and Dingo out of dangerous missions.

First, she had to finish ripping off this Band-Aid so her soul could start healing. Her heart never would. "There is no future for us, Gage. Not as long as we're in this business. Are you planning on leaving the agency?"

"No, but—"

"But nothing. This worked between us when I contracted with the agency and we partnered on missions. It worked because neither of us expected anything more than what we had, but ... that's changed for me. I'm not cut out for any life except the one I have and I now realize this life doesn't allow for a relationship, not a true one."

Pain filtered through his gaze.

Damn, she hated hurting him, but she was being honest.

Gage said, "Not true. You're cut out for anything you want to do ... if you want it bad enough."

She'd spent two long days alone once she got home, trying to make her decision, and kept coming back to one simple truth.

She and Gage had no common ground anymore. What they did have had created a rift with Dingo that she'd managed to repair.

Before she met Josh and Dingo, everyone who'd claimed to

care about her had always chosen something, or someone, else instead of her when things got real.

Gage had put the agency first in the past.

He still did and always would. She wouldn't hold that against him, but neither could she go back to living that way again. Even after what she'd gone through in the UK, Gage shielded the names of those in the agency who had been involved. In fact, he *still* blocked her from digging around to find the person who'd burned her team when they inserted to rescue that bastard, Rikker.

When the deal went bad, a local contact died and Sabrina almost lost Josh, one of two people in the world she considered family.

She'd trusted Gage beyond belief at one time.

But he'd interrogated Dingo in California, and in the process he tried to make Sabrina mistrust the man she considered a brother. Worse, Dingo had walked away. She wasn't losing Josh and Dingo. Not for anything. Especially not for a relationship that would never amount to any more than great sex.

Not true, whispered through her heart.

Stupid heart.

She drew herself up inside and put on her own battle face. "Okay, Gage. That was my nice attempt at ending this. You know why this is never going to work for us. I don't trust you and you don't trust me."

"I trust you."

If she'd trusted him, she wouldn't have spent two years out of touch after the UK mission.

And if he trusted her, he would have shared those names.

Leaning an elbow on the bar and propping her chin, she waited him out.

He shook his head and made a sound of disgust. "The fucking agency names. Why won't you let that bone go? That doesn't mean I don't trust you." He leaned in. "I told you in California that I've checked out everyone who knew about your UK mission and none of them sold you out. If I give you those names, either you're going to poke around and get killed by the person I haven't found yet or you're going to kill someone you'll regret later when you realize I've been telling you the truth. It's none of the obvious people."

She was done arguing about this. Trust was trust.

You couldn't talk it right.

She summed it up for him. "Oh, I see. I'm capable of putting my life and my team's lives at risk for the agency, but I'm not capable of protecting myself or controlling some unexpected urge to commit cold-blooded murder. Do I have that right?"

Gage cupped his forehead and washed the hand down over his face. "What possessed me to fall for a stubborn woman like you?"

Fall for her? Gage was a genius at strategy, but he had no idea that uttering three words would end this conversation faster than anything else he could say.

She'd learned better than to accept a man's claim of love after surviving childhood with a father who'd beaten her mother to death while proclaiming his love to both of *his girls*. Speaking of love, what had her mother done?

Chosen her monster of a father over protecting her daughter when Sabrina was too small to defend herself against a brutal beast.

She didn't place Gage—or any other man she allowed in her life now—in that category, but neither did she want meaningless words from him.

Sabrina forced herself to maintain a calm front and ignore Gage's persistence as he tried to put a chink in her emotional armor. She should be worried. He'd done it before.

His eyes lifted to hers.

The world saw little when looking at him because he was a master at concealing his real thoughts and feelings. But she knew him better than most, and she saw pain inch into that unyielding gaze.

Gage had not been the person who betrayed her, but someone in the CIA had and he protected them, which meant he was not a hundred percent on her side.

Just like others who had sworn they cared for her.

Words were the face of deceit.

He relaxed, acting as if he'd shaken off his irritation, but it continued to simmer just beneath the surface. "I'm sorry about what happened in California with Dingo. I stepped over a line with him. I promise you it won't happen again."

She appreciated the apology and heard his sincerity, but that wasn't going to fix this. She didn't hate him. She couldn't. In truth, she wasn't even angry anymore, just ... sad to give up what they had.

But it was either here and now, or a week from now, or a month later. It would happen no matter what.

She had to say something so she went with, "Thank you."

He waited and when she said nothing more, he said. "Thank you, as in, thank you, but no dice?"

She nodded.

"What's it going to take for me to convince you we can stay together?"

In that moment, she heard a longing so deep it twisted her heart. A man like Gage never exposed a vulnerability, but his was showing now and she had to clamp her lips shut to keep from giving in. She'd played that possibility out in her mind a hundred times.

It never ended well.

Taking a deep breath and sticking to her plan, she said, "You can't convince me to change my mind and you know me well enough to believe that, so please stop trying. Please don't make me keep repeating myself. I can't go back to the way it was before with us and I'm ... ready to move on. I mean it. I wouldn't jerk you around so stop punishing me by forcing me to say it over and over, and by showing up when I don't expect you."

He lifted his chin and looked away, but not before she saw how deeply she'd cut him.

Now she wanted to punch herself in the head for hurting the one man who had once brought warmth into her cold world. But that was back when she'd believed he was unlike any other man.

Back when she thought he would put her first.

Swallowing hard, he said, "Fine. If that's what you want, I'll ... honor it." He wiped his mouth, a tiny sign of his switching gears to business mode. "I had a second reason for finding you. You have to get off the radar."

"What?" She sat up straighter.

"Remember I told you that I have two people in the agency that I trust?"

"Yes. I bet *they* have the list of names you're keeping from me," she added tartly.

Ignoring that, his tone turned a shade dire. "Your name is surfacing in the wrong places. Someone is coming for you and it might be from inside our government. I can't protect you out here in the open. I need you to go to a safe house with me."

Was he serious? "Dream on," she muttered.

His eyebrows drew together in confusion. "I'm not joking, Sabrina."

"Good. Maybe the person looking for me is the one who sold out my team for some POS rogue agent, but why now?"

"I have no idea why now," he snapped, clearly unhappy she wasn't climbing aboard the do-it-my-way train. "It's intel, and you know that doesn't come with footnotes for clarity. If it is someone in the government, I don't think he or she is with the agency."

"So you say."

He muttered something dark, shook it off and said, "I don't know how much time you have before someone grabs you or what that person wants with you, so let's talk about what needs to be done to keep you safe."

"No."

His flint-hard eyes could stop a bullet, but it couldn't knock down her determination. He argued, "Yes."

"No. I can do this all night."

"Fuck. I knew you'd be this way."

"Oh, this way?" She pointed at herself. "You mean unwilling to go slinking away to some unknown location you pick? I'm not hiding from anyone. I'll hunt him or her, and when I get my hands on them—"

"What're you going to do?" he snarled with the force of a Rottweiler on attack, but not loud enough to draw attention.

His hand gripped the edge of the bar top. "This could be anyone." His voice dropped even lower. "Hell, we could be dealing with those fanatical Orion Hunters who've infiltrated the government."

"Exactly, Gage." She leaned in, tapping her index finger on the bar as she said, "That group is behind most of the terrorist operations my teams have shut down this year. That alone puts *all* of my people on their radar. Len ..." She caught herself before she said Rikker's last name, then continued. "*That* person is neck deep in all of this and he was the reason we almost died in the UK. I'm not about to hide somewhere and leave my team exposed."

Hope jump into his face. "Not a problem. I'll find places for them, too."

She chuffed out a sarcastic laugh. "News flash. They don't trust you and that's just another reason you and I have no business trying to be together."

He sat back, defeat clear in his face. "You're a walking target and I don't know who the enemy is, but you think it's me."

Why did he have to say crap like that? "I don't think you're my enemy, Gage," she countered softly.

"Yes you do, Sabrina. You've spent your entire life operating with one set of criteria. Someone is either on your team or not. I'm clearly not, as far you're concerned."

It didn't help that he was right. Her insides had turned into a battlefield where her heart waged war against her mind and her other organs were quickly becoming unavoidable casualties.

She'd be sleeping with a sleeve of Tums tonight.

Gage cared for her.

She knew it logically and heard the sincerity in his voice, but those were just words. Dingo and Josh had grown up on the streets with her. They'd stepped into any fight and shared everything they'd had with her even if it was one slice of bread to feed the three of them.

Even all these years later, they'd never used the L word with each other because love was *only* a word. What they had was stronger than anything you could put into words.

Gage had never understood their bond and never would.

This was why she had to be the strong one right now. If not, Gage would follow her home. If he did and she opened her door, they'd hole up without their clothes until the phone rang with a call to duty.

Then this vicious cycle would start all over again.

She'd watch Gage vanish or *she'd* vanish for days, weeks or months. One day, one of them would not come home.

She didn't want to be the one left behind, not by this man, and she couldn't continue half in and half out of a relationship any longer.

He reached over and grasped her hand. All her convictions wobbled on their unsteady foundation, but the truth pushed its way forward.

All they had were stolen moments here and there.

That wasn't a relationship. At least, not the kind she could live with now.

Standing up, she pulled out of his grip and slipped the purse strap over her shoulder, which reminded her why she'd come here to begin with—a phony snitch meeting that he'd set up.

All her unsteadiness fled. She put steel in her voice and said, "I'm through talking. Stay out of my way and don't *ever* screw with one of my snitches again."

He gave her a confused look. "What snitch?"

"Ziggie."

Gage shook his head. "Not following you."

Blood rushed through her so quickly the sound roared in her ears, blocking the noise of the restaurant. She took in the place with one sweeping scan then turned to him. "How did you know I was here?"

"Why?"

She dropped her head down and her voice came out in a low growl of warning. "Just *fucking* answer me for once."

He blinked at her rare curse. "I tailed your car from the airport. Picked you up leaving your office."

Her face chilled with a clammy feeling. "You didn't set this up with someone for me to meet you here?"

"No." He was stone-cold serious now. "What's up, Sabrina. Talk to me."

She wanted to swipe the glasses off the bar and knock him off that stool. He'd screwed up her meeting with the contact. Her anger rose with the power of a tidal wave, threatening to kill everything in its path.

Sucking in a deep breath, she said, "Don't call me. Don't come near me and don't you dare *ever* walk up to me uninvited again."

"Who were you expecting to meet here?" Gage was looking around, now up to speed on what he'd cost her.

"None of your damn business." She strode away, leaving him in a wake of her fury. He'd better stay the hell away before another word could be spoken.

If not, she'd say something she'd live to regret.

Outside, the street life had picked up with the approach of prime-time dinner hour.

Sabrina wove in and out of groups, then scooted through traffic against a *Don't Walk* sign. She picked up speed going downhill toward Peachtree Street, swinging into the parking deck before she got to the next intersection.

When she made it to the third floor, a middle-aged couple stepped onto the elevator as she hurried off and turned to the right. Her car was eight spaces down.

The lights on that end of the parking deck were out.

She'd arrived before they came on, so she had no idea if that was normal or not.

Drawing her 9 mm, she crossed her arms to keep it shielded as she walked toward her car. She watched and listened for any hint of threat, keeping to the middle of the lane between the lines of parked cars.

A raspy voice called out in a sharp whisper, *"Over here!"*

Damn. Sometimes she hated to be right.

She turned to find a hunched-over figure emerging from shadows where nothing had been a second ago. The plump, elderly woman in a gray blouse and stretch pants shuffled forward. She favored her left arm, holding it tucked against her body as though it were injured. Sabrina believed that *how much*?

Not one bit.

The woman kept her voice down and moved forward two more steps, asking, "Who was that man? You were supposed to meet me."

Ziggie's contact.

Sabrina held her position where she'd stopped two spaces from her car. The hinky feeling that had crept along her neck from the moment she'd stepped into the parking deck cranked up a notch.

She got right down to business. "I understand you have a location for me."

"Yes. I ... need the money. He'll kill me if he finds out." The woman kept moving slowly, limping actually, with her back to the light, which kept her face silhouetted. Had this woman been with Rikker? Had he abused her?

Sabrina said, "Stop."

The woman complied, pausing ten feet away. She picked her head up and Sabrina could make out a plain face with dark-rimmed glasses.

When silence stretched too long in Sabrina's mind, she said, "I have the money. Give me the location."

Nodding slowly, the woman pulled her right hand away from where it had been hooked around her left arm, and lifted her head as she straightened her posture. She held a Walther PPK. Her voice was soft, but urgent. "Come with me quietly and nothing will happen to you."

And yet again, she'd like to not be right.

Who had set this trap? Sabrina hadn't been asked to hand over her weapon yet, so maybe this woman didn't realize she was armed.

Had Rikker sent her?

Sabrina wanted to find out more before she might be pushed to use her weapon. She said, "I hate to disappoint you, but you're leaving without me *or* the money. You can tell Ziggie he owes me for this."

The woman dropped her voice to a whisper as if she thought someone was close enough to hear her low conversation. "Listen to me. You're in dan—"

An explosion blasted.

The shock wave hit Sabrina in the back.

She flew across the parking deck and smacked into the windshield of a car. Glass cracked. She slumped down the hood.

She couldn't feel anything. Bad sign. Her world faded to black.

Read FATAL PROMISE now!
Order your signed and personalized copy at
www.DiannaLoveSignedBooks.com

—•~•—

The Slye Team Black Ops
romantic thriller series is 'completed' (great for binging!)

Prequel: Last Chance To Run
Book 1: Nowhere Safe
Book 2: Honeymoon To Die For
Book 3: Kiss The Enemy
Book 4: Deceptive Treasures
Book 5: Stolen Vengeance
Book 6: Fatal Promise

Want more romance with suspense?
You might like Dianna's new shifter romance series:

The League of Gallize Shifters books are stand-alone paranormal romances written in an larger urban fantasy style world.

Book 1: Gray Wolf Mate
Book 2: Mating A Grizzly
Book 3: Stalking His Mate
Book 4: Scent of A Mate
Book 5: Wild Wolf Mate

Dianna Love and Mary Buckham created the sci-fi/fantasy, time travel Red Moon Trilogy, stories appropriate for Hunger Games readers.

(You can order signed/personalized print copies at
www.MicahCaidaSignedBooks.com)

Book 1: Time Trap
Book 2: Time Return
Book 3: Time Lock

Author's Bio

New York Times **Bestseller Dianna Love** once dangled over a hundred feet in the air to create unusual marketing projects for Fortune 500 companies. She now writes high-octane romantic thrillers, young adult and urban fantasy. Fans of the bestselling Belador urban fantasy series will be thrilled to know more books are coming after soon with the new Treoir Dragon Chronicles. Dianna's Slye Team Black Ops sexy romantic thriller series wrapped up with Gage and Sabrina's book–Fatal Promise–perfect for bingers! She has new League of Gallize Shifters paranormal romance series. Look for her books in print, e-book and audio. On the rare occasions Dianna is out of her writing cave, she tours the country on her BMW motorcycle searching for new story locations. Dianna lives in the Atlanta, GA area with her husband, who is a motorcycle instructor, and with a tank full of unruly saltwater critters.

Visit her website at *www.AuthorDiannaLove.com*
or *www.DiannaLoveSignedBooks.com*

Acknowledgements

Deep appreciation goes to my wonderful husband, Karl, who is my greatest fan, as I am his. In addition to teaching people how to be safe riding motorcycles and three-wheel vehicles, he handles everything imaginable around our home so that I can spend many hours in the cave writing. My world revolves around him.

Cassondra Murray is often my intrepid traveling companion, but she's invaluable as my first reader. She's been with me for so long I can't imagine releasing a book without her input. She sees each story all the way to the end and does an outstanding job helping me keep continuity threads connected and corrected. I'm doubly blessed to have her husband, Steve Doyle, a former Special Forces soldier, who advises me on technical things from weapons selection to brainstorming operational parts of Slye Team books, and catches important details when he reads the stories.

A special thanks to my long time friend, *USA Today* bestselling author Mary Buckham, who I meet with twice a year to brainstorm our books. When not plotting with me to destroy – and save – the world, Mary is hard at work on one of her new *Invisible Recruit* stories.

I would be nowhere without my terrific beta readers who give generously of their time to put fresh eyes on each story. One of my long time friends who became an early reader is Joyce Ann McLaughlin. She sees the books during their "not quite polished" stage and shares her valuable feedback. Her notes are detailed and she's just as quick to tell me what she loves, which is as important as critiques. Thank fully, Manuella Robinson and Sharon Livingston Griffiths are also familiar with the entire Slye Teamseries and step up to read whenever I need it.

Judy Carney is yet one more beta reader when she performs the first of two copy-edit reads, catching things that are hard for me to see after going through the book so many times. She's made working together a real joy.

I'm always hearing how beautiful my covers are, and I have Kim Killion to thank for designing those, plus creating a wonderful brand! Once I turn the story file over to Jennifer Jakes, she drives out all the gremlins and hands me back my book professionally formatted.

Any mistakes made or adjustments for fiction are my own, because every one who helped me went above and beyond the call to give me the best information.

Thanks also to Leiha Mann, Su Walker and the RBLs for supporting all authors! Love and appreciation goes to my amazing Dianna Love Reader Community group on Facebook who support me all through the year.